DATE DUE 9/27/04

UNEXPECTED
MAGIC

ALSO BY

Diana Wynne Jones

Archer's Goon

Aunt Maria

Believing Is Seeing: Seven Stories

Castle in the Air

Dark Lord of Derkholm

Dogsbody

Eight Days of Luke

Fire and Hemlock

Hexwood

Hidden Turnings:
A Collection of Stories Through Time and Space

The Homeward Bounders

Howl's Moving Castle

The Merlin Conspiracy

The Ogre Downstairs

Power of Three

Stopping for a Spell

A Tale of Time City

The Time of the Ghost

Warlock at the Wheel and Other Stories

Wild Robert

Witch's Business
Year of the Griffin
Yes, Dear

THE WORLDS OF CHRESTOMANCI
Book 1: *Charmed Life*
Book 2: *The Lives of Christopher Chant*
Book 3: *The Magicians of Caprona*
Book 4: *Witch Week*
Mixed Magics: Four Tales of Chrestomanci
The Chronicles of Chrestomanci, Volume I
(Contains Books 1 and 2)
The Chronicles of Chrestomanci, Volume II
(Contains Books 3 and 4)

THE DALEMARK QUARTET
Book 1: *Cart and Cwidder*
Book 2: *Drowned Ammet*
Book 3: *The Spellcoats*
Book 4: *The Crown of Dalemark*

❧ Diana Wynne Jones ❧

UNEXPECTED
MAGIC
❋ COLLECTED STORIES ❋

GREENWILLOW BOOKS
An Imprint of HarperCollins*Publishers*

Library of Congress Cataloging-in-Publication Data

Jones, Diana Wynne.
Unexpected magic : collected stories / Diana Wynne Jones.
p.   cm.
"Greenwillow Books."
Summary: A collection of sixteen stories including "The Plague of Peacocks,"
"Aunt Bea's Day Out," "The Fat Wizard," "No One," and "Everard's Ride."
ISBN 0-06-055533-5 (trade). ISBN 0-06-055534-3 (lib. bdg.)
1. Fantasy fiction, English. 2. Children's stories, English.
[1. Fantasy. 2. Short stories.] I. Title.
PZ7.J684Un 2003 [Fic]—dc21 2003053118

10 9 8 7 6 5 4 3 2 1
First American Edition
Greenwillow Books

To all at Greenwillow,
for putting up with me all these years
—D. W. J.

CONTENTS

THE GIRL JONES · 1

NAD AND DAN ADN QUAFFY · 13

THE PLAGUE OF PEACOCKS · 36

THE MASTER · 50

ENNA HITTIMS · 71

THE GIRL WHO LOVED THE SUN · 89

THE FLUFFY PINK TOADSTOOL · 109

AUNTIE BEA'S DAY OUT · 118

CARRUTHERS · 131

WHAT THE CAT TOLD ME · 156

THE GREEN STONE · 181

THE FAT WIZARD · 188

NO ONE · 203

DRAGON RESERVE, HOME EIGHT · 233

LITTLE DOT · 266

EVERARD'S RIDE · 303

UNEXPECTED
MAGIC

THE
GIRL
JONES

It was 1944. I was nine years old and fairly new to the village. They called me "The girl Jones." They called anyone "The girl this" or "The boy that" if they wanted to talk about them a lot. Neither of my sisters was ever called "The girl Jones." They were never notorious.

On this particular Saturday morning I was waiting in our yard with my sister Ursula because a girl called Jean had promised to come and play. My sister Isobel was also hanging around. She was not exactly with us, but I was the one she came to if anything went wrong and she liked to keep in touch. I had only met Jean at school before. I was thinking that she was going to be pretty fed up to find we were lumbered with two little ones.

When Jean turned up, rather late, she was accompanied by

two little sisters, a five-year-old very like herself and a tiny three-year-old called Ellen. Ellen had white hair and a little brown stormy face with an expression on it that said she was going to bite anyone who gave her any trouble. She was alarming. All three girls were dressed in impeccable starched cotton frocks that made me feel rather shabby. I had dressed for the weekend. But then so had they, in a different way.

"Mum says I got to look after them," Jean told me dismally. "Can you have them for me for a bit while I do her shopping? Then we can play."

I looked at stormy Ellen with apprehension. "I'm not very good at looking after little ones," I said.

"Oh, go on!" Jean begged me. "I'll be much quicker without them. I'll be your friend if you do."

So far, Jean had shown a desire to play, but had never offered friendship. I gave in. Jean departed, merrily swinging her shopping bag.

Almost at once a girl called Eva turned up. She was an official friend. She wore special boots and one of her feet was just a sort of blob. Eva fascinated me, not because of the foot but because she was so proud of it. She used to recite the list of all her other relatives who had queer feet, ending with, "And my uncle has only one toe." She too carried a shopping bag and had a small one in tow, a brother in her case, a wicked five-year-old called Terry. "Let me dump him on you while I do the shopping," Eva bargained, "and then we can play. I won't be long."

"I don't know about looking after boys," I protested. But Eva was a friend and I agreed. Terry was left standing beside stormy Ellen, and Eva went away.

A girl I did not know so well, called Sybil, arrived next. She wore a fine blue cotton dress with a white pattern and was hauling along two small sisters, equally finely dressed. "Have these for me while I do the shopping and I'll be your friend." She was followed by a rather older girl called Cathy, with a sister, and then a number of girls I only knew by sight. Each of them led a small sister or brother into our yard. News gets round in no time in a village. "What have you done with your sisters, Jean?" "Dumped them on the girl Jones." Some of these later arrivals were quite frank about it.

"I heard you're having children. Have these for me while I go down the Rec."

"I'm not good at looking after children," I claimed each time before I gave in. I remember thinking this was rather odd of me. I had been in sole charge of Isobel for years. As soon as Ursula was four, she was in my charge too. I suppose I had by then realized I was being had for a sucker and this was my way of warning all these older sisters. But I believed what I said. I was not good at looking after little ones.

In less than twenty minutes I was standing in the yard surrounded by small children. I never counted, but there were certainly more than ten of them. None of them came above my waist. They were all beautifully dressed because they all came from what were called the "clean families." The "dirty families" were the ones where the boys wore big black boots with metal in the soles and the girls had grubby frocks that were too long for them. These kids had starched creases in their clothes and clean socks and shiny shoes. But they were, all the same, skinny, knowing, village children. They knew their sisters had shamelessly dumped them and they were disposed to riot.

"Stop all that damned *noise!*" bellowed my father. "Get these children out of here!"

He was always angry. This sounded near to an explosion.

"We're going for a walk," I told the milling children. "Come along." And I said to Isobel, "Coming?"

She hovered away backward. "No." Isobel had a perfect instinct for this kind of thing. Some of my earliest memories are of Isobel's sturdy brown legs flashing round and round as she rode her tricycle for dear life away from a situation I had got her into. These days, she usually arranged things so that she had no need to run for her life. I was annoyed. I could have done with her help with all these kids. But not that annoyed. Her reaction told me that something interesting was going to happen.

"We're going to have an adventure," I told the children.

"There's no adventures nowadays," they told me. They were, as I said, knowing children, and no one, not even me, regarded the War that was at that time going on around us as any kind of adventure. This was a problem to me. I craved adventures, of the sort people had in books, but nothing that had ever happened to me seemed to qualify. No spies made themselves available to be unmasked by me, no gangsters ever had nefarious dealings where I could catch them for the police.

But one did what one could. I led the crowd of them out into the street, feeling a little like the Pied Piper—or no: they were so little and I was so big that I felt really old, twenty at least, and rather like a nursery school teacher. And it seemed to me that since I was landed in this position I might as well do something I wanted to do.

"Where are we going?" they clamored at me.

"Down Water Lane," I said. Water Lane, being almost the only unpaved road in the area, fascinated me. It was like lanes in books. If anywhere led to adventure, it would be Water Lane. It was a moist, mild, gray day, not adventurous weather, but I knew from books that the most unlikely conditions sometimes led to great things.

But my charges were not happy about this. "It's wet there. We'll get all muddy. My mum told me to keep my clothes clean," they said from all around me.

"You won't get muddy with me," I told them firmly. "We're only going as far as the elephants." There was a man who built life-sized mechanical elephants in a shed in Water Lane. These fascinated everyone. The children gave up objecting at once. Ellen actually put her hand trustingly in mine and we crossed the main road like a great liner escorted by coracles.

Water Lane was indeed muddy. Wetness oozed up from its sandy surface and ran in dozens of streams across it. Mr. Hinkston's herd of cows had added their contributions. The children minced and yelled. "Walk along the very edge," I commanded them. "Be adventurous. If we're lucky, we'll get inside the yard and look at the elephants in the sheds."

Most of them obeyed me except Ursula. But she was my sister and I had charge of her shoes along with the rest of her. Although I was determined from the outset to treat her exactly like the other children, as if this was truly a class from a nursery school, or the Pied Piper leading the children of Hamlin Town, I decided to let her be. Ursula had times when she bit you if you crossed her. Besides, what were shoes? So, to cries of, "Ooh! Your sister's getting in all the pancakes!" we arrived outside the big black fence where the elephants were, to find it all locked and bolted. As this was a Saturday, the man who made the elephants had gone to make money with them at a fête or a fair somewhere.

There were loud cries of disappointment and derision at this, particularly from Terry, who was a very outspoken child. I looked up at the tall fence—it had barbed wire along the top—and contemplated boosting them all over it for an adventure inside. But there were their clothes to consider, it would be hard work, and it was not really what I had come down Water Lane to do.

"This means we have to go on," I told them, "to the really adventurous thing. We are going to the very end of Water Lane to see what's at the end of it."

"That's ever so far!" one of them whined.

"No, it's not," I said, not having the least idea. I had never had time to go much beyond the river. "Or we'll get to the river and then walk along it to see where it goes to."

"Rivers don't go anywhere," someone pronounced.

"Yes, they do," I asserted. "There's a bubbling fountain somewhere where it runs out of the ground. We're going to find it." I had been reading books about the source of the Nile, I think.

They liked the idea of the fountain. We went on. The cows had not been on this further part, but it was still wet. I encouraged them to step from sandy strip to sandy island and they liked that. They were all beginning to think of themselves as true adventurers. But Ursula, no doubt wanting to preserve her special status, walked straight through everything and got her shoes all wet and crusty. A number of the children drew my attention to this.

"She's not good like you are," I said.

We went on in fine style for a good quarter of a mile until

we came to the place where the river broke out of the hedge and swilled across the lane in a ford. Here the expedition broke down utterly.

"It's water! I'll get wet! It's all muddy!"

"I'm *tired!*" said someone. Ellen stood by the river and grizzled, reflecting the general mood.

"This is where we can leave the lane and go up along the river," I said. But this found no favor. The banks would be muddy. We would have to get through the hedge. They would tear their clothes.

I was shocked and disgusted at their lack of spirit. The ford across the road had always struck me as the nearest and most romantic thing to a proper adventure. I loved the way the bright brown water ran so continuously there—in the mysterious way of rivers—in the shallow sandy dip.

"We're going on," I announced. "Take your shoes off and walk through in your bare feet."

This, for some reason, struck them all as highly adventurous. Shoes and socks were carefully removed. The quickest splashed into the water. "Ooh! Innit *cold!*"

"I'm paddling!" shouted Terry. "I'm going for a paddle." His feet, I was interested to see, were perfect. He must have felt rather left out in Eva's family.

I lost control of the expedition in this moment of inattention. Suddenly everyone was going in for a paddle. "All right," I said hastily. "We'll stay here and paddle."

Ursula, always fiercely loyal in her own way, walked out of the river and sat down to take her shoes off too. The rest splashed and screamed. Terry began throwing water about. Quite a number of them squatted down at the edge of the water and scooped up muddy sand. Brown stains began climbing up crisp cotton frocks, the seats of beautifully ironed shorts quickly acquired a black splotch. Even before this was pointed out to me, I saw this would not do. These were the "clean children." I made all the little girls come out of the water and spent some time trying to get the edges of their frocks tucked upwards into their knickers. "The boys can take their trousers off," I announced.

But this did no good. The frocks just came tumbling down again and the boys' little white pants were no longer really white. No one paid any attention to my suggestion that it was time to go home now. The urge to paddle was upon them all.

"All right," I said, yielding to the inevitable. "Then you all have to take all your clothes off."

This caused a startled pause. "That ain't right," someone said uncertainly.

"Yes it is," I told them, somewhat pompously. "There is nothing whatsoever wrong with the sight of the naked human body." I had read that somewhere and found it quite convincing. "Besides," I added, more pragmatically, "you'll all get into trouble if you come home with dirty clothes."

That all but convinced them. The thought of what their mums would say was a powerful aid to nudity. "But won't we catch cold?" someone asked.

"Cavemen never wore clothes and they never caught cold," I informed them. "Besides, it's quite warm now." A mild and misty sunlight suddenly arrived and helped my cause. The brown river was flecked with sun and looked truly inviting. Without a word, everybody began undressing, even Ellen, who was quite good at it, considering how young she was. Back to nursery teacher mode again, I made folded piles of every person's clothing, shoes underneath, and put them in a long row along the bank under the hedge. True to my earlier resolve, I made no exception for Ursula's clothes, although her dress was an awful one my mother had made out of old curtains, and thoroughly wet anyway.

There was a happy scramble into the water, mostly to the slightly deeper end by the hedge. Terry was throwing water instantly. But then there was another pause.

"*You* undress too." They were all saying it.

"I'm too big," I said.

"You *said* that didn't matter," Ursula pointed out. "You undress too, or it isn't *fair*."

"Yeah," the rest chorused. "It ain't *fair*!"

I prided myself on my fairness, and on my rational, intellectual approach to life, but . . .

"Or we'll all get dressed again," added Ursula.

The thought of all that trouble wasted was too much. "All right," I said. I went over to the hedge and took off my battered gray shorts and my old, pulled jersey and put them in a heap at the end of the row. I knew as I did so why the rest had been so doubtful. I had never been naked out of doors before. In those days, nobody ever was. I felt shamed and rather wicked. And I was so big, compared with the others. The fact that we all now had no clothes on seemed to make my size much more obvious. I felt like one of the man's mechanical elephants, and sinful with it. But I told myself sternly that we were having a rational adventurous experience and joined the rest in the river.

The water was cold, but not too cold, and the sun was just strong enough. Just.

Ellen, for some reason, would not join the others over by the hedge. She sat on the other side of the road, on the opposite bank of the river where it sloped up to the road again, and diligently scraped river mud up into a long mountain between her legs. When the mountain was made, she smacked it heavily. It sounded like a wet child being hit.

She made me nervous. I decided to keep an eye on her and sat facing her, squatting in the water, scooping up piles of mud to form islands. From there, I could look across the road and make sure Terry did not get too wild. They were, I thought, somewhat artificially, a most romantic and angelic sight, a picture an artist might paint if he wanted to depict young angels (except Terry was not being angelic and I told him to *stop throwing mud*). They were all tubular and white and in energetic attitudes, and the only one not quite right for the picture was Ursula with her chalk white skin and wild black hair. The others all had smooth fair heads, ranging from near white in the young ones, through straw yellow, to honey in the older ones. My own hair had gone beyond the honey, since I was so much older, into dull brown.

Here I noticed how *big* I was again. My torso was thick, more like an oil drum than a tube, and my legs looked *fat* beside their skinny little limbs. I began to feel sinful again. I had to force myself to attend to the islands I was making. I gave them landscapes and invented people for them.

"What you doing?" asked Ellen.

"Making islands." I was feeling back-to-nature and at ease again.

"Stupid," she said.

More or less as she spoke, a tractor came up the lane behind her, going toward the village. The man driving it stopped it just in front of the water and stared. He had one of those oval narrow faces that always went with people who went to Chapel in the village. I know I thought he was Chapel. He was the sort of age you might expect someone to be who was a father of small children. He looked as if he had children. And he was deeply and utterly shocked. He looked at the brawling, naked little ones, he looked at Ellen, and he looked at me. Then he leaned down and said, quite mildly, "You didn't ought to do that."

"Their clothes were getting wet, you see," I said.

He just gave me another, mild, shocked look and started the tractor and went through the river, making it all muddy. I never, ever saw him again.

"Told you so," said Ellen.

That was the end of the adventure. I felt deeply sinful. The little ones were suddenly not having fun any more. Without making much fuss about it, we all quietly got our clothes and got dressed again. We retraced our steps to the village. It was just about lunchtime anyway.

As I said, word gets round in a village with amazing speed. "You know the girl Jones? She took thirty kids down Water Lane and encouraged them to do wrong there. They was all there, naked as the day they was born, sitting in the river there, and her along with them, as bold as brass. A big girl like the girl Jones did ought to know better! Whatever next!"

My parents interrogated me about it the next day. Isobel was there, backward hovering, wanting to check that her instinct had been right, I think, and fearful of the outcome. She looked relieved when the questions were mild and puzzled. I think my mother did not believe I had done anything so bizarre.

"There is nothing shameful about the naked human body," I reiterated.

Since my mother had given me the book that said so, there was very little she could reply. She turned to Ursula. But Ursula was stoically and fiercely loyal. She said nothing at all.

The only result of this adventure was that nobody ever suggested I should look after any children except my own sisters (who were strange anyway). Jean kept her promise to be my friend. The next year, when the Americans came to England, Jean and I spent many happy hours sitting on the church wall watching young GIs stagger out of the pub to be sick. But Jean never brought her sisters with her. I think her mother had forbidden it.

When I look back, I rather admire my nine-year-old self. I had been handed the baby several times over that morning. I took the most harmless possible way to disqualify myself as a child-minder. Nobody got hurt. Everyone had fun. And I never had to do it again.

NAD AND DAN ADN QUAFFY

She had struggled rather as a writer until she got her word processor. Or not exactly *struggled*, she thought, frowning at her screen and flipping the cursor back to correct *adn* to *and*. For some reason, she always garbled the word *and*. It was always *adn* or *nad*; *dna* or *nda* were less frequent, but all of them appeared far oftener than the right way. She had only started to make this mistake after she gave up her typewriter, and she felt it was a small price to pay.

For years she had written what seemed to her the most stirring sort of novels, about lonely aliens among humans, or lonely humans among aliens, or sometimes both kinds lonely in an unkind world, all without ever quite hitting the response from readers she felt she was worth. Then came her divorce, which left her with custody of her son, Daniel, then thirteen. That probably provided an impetus of some sort in itself, for Danny was probably the most critical boy alive.

"Mum!" he would say. "I wish you'd give up that lonely-heart alien stuff! Can't you write about something decent for a change?" Or, staring at her best efforts at cookery, he said, "I can't be expected to eat *this*!" After which he had taken over cooking himself: they now lived on chili con carne and stir-fry. For as Danny said, "A man can't be expected to learn more than one dish a year." At the moment, being nearly fifteen, Danny was teaching himself curry. Their nice Highgate house reeked of burned garam masala most of the time.

But the real impetus had come when she found Danny in her workroom sternly plaiting the letters of her old typewriter into metal braid. "I've had this old thing!" he said when she tore him away with fury and cursings. "So have you. It's out of the ark. Now you'll have to get a word processor."

"But I don't know how to work the things!" she had wailed.

"That doesn't matter. I do. I'll work it for you," he replied inexorably. "And I'll tell you what one to buy, too, or you'll only waste money."

He did so. The components were duly delivered and installed, and Daniel proceeded to instruct his mother in how to work as much of them as—as he rather blightingly said—her feeble brain would hold. "There," he said. "Now write something worth reading for a change." And he left her sitting in front of it all.

When she thought about it, she was rather ashamed of the fact that her knowledge of the thing had not progressed one whit beyond those first instructions Danny had given her. She had to call on her son to work the printout, to recall most of the files, and to get her out of any but the most simple difficulty. On several occasions—as when Danny had been on a school trip to Paris or away with his school cricket team—she had had to tell her publisher all manner of lies to account for the fact that there would be no copy of anything until Danny got back. But the advantages far outweighed these difficulties, or at least she knew they did *now*.

That first day had been a nightmare. She had felt lost and foolish and weak. She had begun, not having anything else in mind, on another installment of lonely aliens. And everything kept going wrong. She had to call Danny in ten times in the first hour, and then ten times after lunch, and then again when, for some reason, the machine produced what she had written of Chapter I as a list, one word to a line. Even Danny took most of the rest of the day to sort out what she had done to get that. After that he hovered over her solicitously, bringing her mugs of black coffee, until, somewhere around nine in the evening, she realized she was in double bondage, first to a machine and then to her own son.

"Go away!" she told him. "Out of my sight! I'm going to learn to do this for myself or die in the attempt!"

Danny gave her bared teeth a startled look and fled.

By this time she had been sitting in front of board and screen for nearly ten hours. It seemed to her that her threat to die in the attempt was no idle one. She felt like death. Her back ached, and so did her head. Her eyes felt like running blisters. She had cramp in both hands and one foot asleep. In addition, her mouth was foul with too much coffee and Danny's chili con carne. The little green letters on the screen kept retreating behind the glass to the distant end of a long, long tunnel. "I *will* do this!" she told herself fiercely. "I am an intelligent adult— probably even a genius—and I will *not* be dominated by a mere machine!"

And she typed all over again:

CHAPTER ONE

The Captain had been at board and screen ever since jump—a total of ten hours. Her hands shook with weariness, making it an effort to hold them steady on her switches. Her head was muzzy, her mouth foul with nutrient concentrates. But since the mutiny, it was sit double watches or fail to bring the starship *Candida* safely through the intricate system of Meld. . . .

At this point she began to get a strange sense of power. She *was* dominating this damned machine, even though she was doing it only by exploiting her own sensations. Also, she was becoming interested in what might be going to happen to the starship *Candida*, not to speak of the reasons that had led up to the mutiny aboard her. She continued writing furiously until long after midnight. When she stopped at last, she had to pry her legs loose from her chair.

"*That's* more like it, Mum!" Danny said the next morning, reading it as it came from the printer.

He was, as usual, right. *Starship Candida* was the book that made the name of F. C. Stone. It won prizes. It sold in resorts and newsagents all over the world. It was, reviewers said, equally remarkable for its insight into the Captain's character as for the intricate personal relationships leading to the mutiny. Much was spoken about the tender and peculiar relationships between the sexes. This last made F. C. Stone grin rather. All she had done was to revenge herself on Danny by reversing the way things were between them. In the book the Captain was all-powerful and dominating and complained a lot about the food. The Mate had a hypnotically induced mind-set that caused him to bleat for assistance at the first sign of trouble.

Her next book, *The Mutineers*, was an even greater success. For this one, F. C. Stone extended the intricate personal relationships to the wider field of galactic politics. She discovered she reveled in politics. Provided she was making up the politics herself, there seemed no limit to how intricate she could make them.

Since then she had, well, not stuck to a formula—she was much more artfully various than that—but as she said and Danny agreed, there was no point in leaving a winning game. Though she did not go back to starship *Candida*, she stayed with that universe and its intricate politics. There were aliens in it, too, which she always enjoyed. And she kept mostly out in space, so that she could continue to describe pilots astronauting at the controls of a word processor. Sooner or later in most of her books, someone, human or alien, would have sat long hours before the screen until dazed with staring, aching in the back, itching in the nose—for the burning of Asian spices in the kitchen tended to give her hay fever—and with cramped hands, this pilot would be forced to maneuver arduously through jump. This part always, or nearly always, got written when F. C. Stone was unable to resist staying up late to finish the chapter.

Danny continued to monitor his mother. He was proud of

what he had made her do. In the holidays and around the edges of school, he hung over her shoulder and brought her continual mugs of strong black coffee. This beverage began to appear in the books, too. The mutineer humans drank *gav*, while their law-abiding enemies quaffed *chvi*. Spacer aliens staggered from their nav-couches to gulp down *kivay*, and the mystics of Meld used *xfy* to induce an altered state of consciousness, although this was not generally spotted as being the same substance. And it was all immensely popular.

It was all due to the word processor, she thought, giving the nearest component a friendly pat as she leaned toward the screen again. The latest mug of cooling *kivay* sat beside her. Her nose was, as usual, tickled by burned ginger or something. Her back was beginning to ache, or, more truthfully, her behind was. She ought to get a more comfortable chair, but she was too fond of this old one. Anyway, the latest book was the thing. For this one, she had at last gone back to starship *Candida*. There had been a lot of pressure from her fans. And her publisher thought there was enough material in their suggestions, combined with F. C. Stone's own ideas, to make a trilogy. So she had decided to start in the way she knew would get her going. She typed:

Jump. Time nad the world stretched dna went out. Back. The Captain had sat at her boards for four objective days—four subjective minutes or four subjective centuries. Her head ached, gums adn all. She cursed. Hands trembling on controls, she struggled to get her fix on this system's star.

Now what had some vastly learned reader suggested about this system's star? It had some kind of variability, but that was all she could remember. Damn. All her notes for it were in that file Danny had set up for her. He was at school. But he had written down for her how to recall it. She fumbled around for his piece of paper—it had worked halfway under a black box whose name and function she never could learn—and took a swig of lukewarm *xfy* while she studied what to do. It looked quite simple. She took another sip of *gav*. Store the new book. Careful not to cancel this morning's work. There. Screen blank. Now type in this lot, followed by *Candida 2*. Then—

A clear childish voice spoke. "This is Candida Two, Candy," it said. "Candida One, I need your confirmation."

It was no voice F. C. Stone knew, and it seemed to come from the screen. Her eyes turned to the mug of *kivay*. Perhaps she was in a state of altered consciousness.

"Candida One!" the voice said impatiently. "Confirm that you are conscious. I will wait ten seconds and then begin lifesaving procedures. Ten, nine, eight . . ."

This sounded serious. Coffee poisoning, thought F. C. Stone. I shall change to carrot juice or cocoa.

" . . . seven, six, five," counted the childish voice, "four, three . . ."

I'd better say something, thought F. C. Stone. How absurd. Weakly she said, "Do stop counting. It makes me nervous."

"*Are* you Candida One?" demanded the voice. "The voice pattern does not quite tally. Please say something else for comparison with my records."

Why should I? thought F. C. Stone. But it was fairly clear that if she stayed silent, the voice would start counting again and then, presumably, flood the room with the antidote for *xfy*.

No, no, this was ridiculous. There was no way a word processor could flood anyone's system with anything. Come to that, there was no way it could speak either—or was there? She must ask Danny. She was just letting her awe of the machine, and her basic ignorance, get on top of her. Let us be rational here, she thought. If she was not suffering from *gav* poisoning, or if, alternatively, the smell of charred turmeric at present flooding the house did not prove to have hallucinogenic properties, then she had worked too long and hard imagining things and was now unable to tell fantasy from reality . . . unless—what a *wonderful* thought!—Danny had, either for a joke or by accident, connected one of the black boxes to the radio and she was at this moment receiving its *Play for the Day.*

Her hand shot out to the radio beside her, which she kept for aural wallpaper during the duller part of her narratives, and switched it on. Click. "During this period Beethoven was having to contend with his increasing deafness—"

The childish voice cut in across this lecture. "This voice is not correct," it pronounced, putting paid to that theory. "It is the voice of a male. Males are forbidden access to any of my functions beyond basic navigational aids. Candida One, unless you reply confirming that you are present and conscious, I shall flood this ship with sedative gas ten seconds from now."

Then perhaps Danny has put a cassette in the radio as a joke, thought F. C. Stone. She turned off the radio and, for good measure, shook it. No, no cassette in there.

And the childish voice was at its counting again: " . . . six, five, four . . . "

Finding that her mouth was hanging open, F. C. Stone used

it. "I know this is a practical joke," she said. "I don't know what it is you've done, Danny, but my God, I'll skin you when I get my hands on you!"

The countdown stopped. "Voice patterns are beginning to match," came the pronouncement, "though I do not understand your statement. Are you quite well, Candy?"

Fortified by the knowledge that this had to be a joke of Danny's, F. C. Stone snapped, "Yes, of course I am!" Very few people knew that the C in F. C. Stone stood for Candida, and even fewer knew that she had, in her childhood, most shamingly been known as Candy. But Danny of course knew both these facts. "Stop this silly joke, Danny, and let me get back to work."

"Apologies," spoke the childish voice, "but who is Danny? There are only two humans on this ship. Is that statement addressed to the male servant beside you? He asks me to remind you that his name is Adny."

The joke was getting worse. Danny was having fun with her typos now. F. C. Stone was not sure she would ever forgive him for that. "And I suppose you're going to tell me we've just emerged in the Dna System and will be coming in to ladn at Nad," she said bitterly.

"Of course," said the voice.

F. C. Stone spent a moment in angry thought. Danny had to be using a program of some kind. She ought first to test this theory and then, if it was correct, find some way to disrupt the program and get some peace. "Give me your name," she said, "with visual confirmation."

"If you like," the voice responded. Had it sounded puzzled?

Then Danny had thought of this. "I am Candida Two. I am your conscious-class computer modeled on your own brain." It sounded quite prideful, saying this. But, thought F. C. Stone, a small boy co-opted by a grand fifteen-year-old like Danny *would* sound prideful. "We are aboard the astroship *Partlett* M32/A401."

Motorways, thought F. C. Stone, but where did he get the name?

"Visual," said the voice. Blocks of words jumped onto the screen. They seemed to be in—Russian? Greek?—capitals.

It had to be a computer game of some kind, F. C. Stone thought. Now what would Danny least expect her to do? Easy. She plunged to the wall and turned the electricity off. Danny would not believe she would do that. He would think she was too much afraid of losing this morning's work, and maybe she would, but she could do it over again. As the blocks of print faded from the screen, she stumped off to the kitchen and made herself a cup of *xfy*—no, *coffee!*—and prowled around in there amid the smell of cauterized ginger while she drank it, with some idea of letting the system cool off thoroughly. She had a vague notion that this rendered a lost program even more lost. As far as she was concerned, this joke of Danny's couldn't be lost enough.

The trouble was that she was accustomed so to prowl whenever she was stuck in a sentence. As her annoyance faded, habit simply took over. Halfway through the mug of *quaffy*, she was already wondering whether to call the taste in the Captain's mouth merely *foul* or to use something more specific, like *chicken shit*. Five minutes later F. C. Stone mechanically made herself a second mug of *chofiy*—almost as mechanically noting that this seemed to be a wholly new word for the stuff and absently constructing a new kind of alien to drink it—and carried it through to her workroom to resume her day's stint. With her mind by then wholly upon the new solar system just entered by the starship *Candida*—there was no need to do whatever it was the learned fan wanted; after all, neither of them had *been* there and *she* was writing this book, not he—she switched the electricity back on and sat down.

Neat blocks of Greco-Cyrillic script jumped to her screen. "Candy!" said the childish voice. "Why don't you answer? I repeat. We are well inside the Dna System and coming up to jump."

F. C. Stone was startled enough to swallow a mouthful of scalding *c'phee* and barely notice what it was called. "Nonsense, Danny," she said, somewhat hoarsely. "Everyone knows you don't jump inside a solar system."

The script on the screen blinked a little. "His name is Adny," the voice said, sounding a little helpless. "If you do not remember that, or that microjumps are possible, then I see I must attend to what he has been telling me. Candy, it is possible that you have been overtaken by senility—"

"*Senility!*" howled F. C. Stone. Many murderous fates for Danny crowded through her mind.

"—and your male has been imploring me to ask you to authorize his use of functions Five through Nine to preserve this ship. Will you so authorize? Some action is urgent."

A certain curiosity emerged through F. C. Stone's anger. How far was Danny prepared to take his joke? How many possibilities had he allowed for? "I authorize," she said carefully, "his use of functions Five through *Eight* only." And let's see if he planned for that! she thought.

It seemed he had. A symbol of some kind now filled the screen, a complex curlicue the like of which F. C. Stone had never seen or imagined her equipment capable of producing. A wholly new voice spoke, male and vibrant. "I thank you," it said. "Function Eight will serve for now. This justifies my faith in you, Candida Three. I am now able to bypass the computer and talk to you direct. Please do not turn your power source off again. We must talk."

It was a golden voice, the voice, perhaps, of an actor, a voice that made F. C. Stone want to curl up and purr and maybe put her hair straight, even while she was deciding there was no way Danny could have made his rough and squawky baritone sound like this. Gods! He must have hired someone! She gave that boy far too much money. She took another swig of *ogvai* while she noted that the voice was definitely in some way connected to the symbol on the screen. The curlicue jumped and wavered in time to its words.

"What do you mean by calling me Candida Three?" she asked coldly.

"Because you are the exact analogue of my mistress, Candida One," the golden voice replied. "Her ship's computer is known as Candida Two. It therefore followed that when I had searched the universes and discovered you, I came to think of you as Candida Three. I have been studying you—most respectfully, of course—through this machine you use and the thoughts you set down on it, for two years now, and—"

"And Daniel has been reading other books besides mine," F. C. Stone interrupted. "Unfaithful brat!"

"I beg your pardon?" The symbol on the screen gave an agitated jump.

Score one to me! F. C. Stone thought. "My son," she said. "And we're talking parallel universes here, I take it?"

"We are." The golden voice sounded both cautious and bemused. "Forgive me if I don't quite follow you. You take the same sudden leaps of mind as my mistress, though I have come to believe that your mind is far more open than hers. She was born to a high place in the Matriarchy and is now one of the most powerful members of the High Coven—"

"Coven!" said F. C. Stone. "Whose book is this out of?"

There was a pause. The curlicue gave several agitated jumps. Then the golden voice said, "Look, please let me explain. I'm delaying jump as long as I can, but there really is only a very narrow window before I have to go or abort."

He sounded very pleading. Or perhaps *beguiling* was a better word, F. C. Stone thought, for that kind of voice. "All right," she said. "Get on with the program. But just tell me first what you mean when you say *mistress*, Danny."

"Adny," he said. "My name is Adny."

"Adny, then," said F. C. Stone. "*Mistress* has two meanings."

"Why, I suppose I mean both," he answered. "I was sold to Candy as a child, the way all men are in this universe. Men have almost no rights in the Matriarchy, and the Matriarchy is the chief power in our galaxy. I have been luckier than most, being sold to a mistress who is an adept of the High Coven. I have learned from her—"

F. C. Stone gave a slight exasperated sigh. For a moment there she had been uneasy. It had all seemed far more like a conversation than any program Danny could produce. But his actor friend seemed to have got back to his lines now. She shot forth another question. "So where is your mistress now?"

"Beside me, unconscious," was the reply.

"Senile?" said F. C. Stone.

"Believe me, they are liable to it," he said. "The forces they handle do seem to damage them, and it does seem to overtake them oftenest when they're out in space. But"—she could hear the smile in his voice—"I must confess that I was responsible for this one. It took me years of study before I could outwit her, but I did it."

"Congratulations, Adny," said F. C. Stone. "What do you want me to do about it? You're asking me to help you in your male backlash, is that it?"

"Yes, but you need do almost nothing," he replied. "Since you are the counterpart of Candida One, the computer is accepting you already. If you wish to help me, all I need is your voice authorizing Candida Two to allow me functions Nine and Ten. I can then tap my mistress's full power and navigate the ship to my rendezvous, whereupon I will cut this connection and cease interrupting you in your work."

"*What!*" said F. C. Stone. "You mean I don't get to navigate a word processor?"

"I don't understand," said Adny.

"Then you'd better!" said F. C. Stone. She was surprised at how strongly she felt. "Listen, Danny or Adny, or whoever you are! My whole career, my entire *success* as a writer, has been founded on the fact that I *enjoy*, more than anything else, sitting in front of this screen and pretending it's the controls of a starship. I enjoy the dazed feeling, I like the exhaustion, I don't mind getting cramp, and I even like drinking myself sick on *ogvai*! The only reason I haven't turned the machine off again is the chance that you're going to let me do it for real—or what feels like for real, I don't care which—and I'm not going to let that chance slip. You let me pilot my WP and I'll even authorize you to function Eleven afterward, if there is such a thing. Is that clear?"

"It is very clear, Great Lady," he said. There was that in his tone that suggested he was very used to yielding to demanding women, but could there have been triumph in it, too?

F. C. Stone was not sure of that tone, but she did not let it worry her. "Right," she said. "Brief me."

"Very well," he said, "though it may not be what you expect. We are about to make a microjump which in the normal way would bring us out above the spaceport but in this case is designed to bring us directly above the city of Nad and, hopefully, inside the Coven's defenses there. Other ships of my conspiracy should be materializing, too, hopefully at the same moment, so the jump must be made with utmost accuracy. I can broadcast you a simulacrum of *Partlett*'s controls, scaled down to correspond to your own keyboard. But you must depress the keys in exactly the order in which I highlight them. Can you do this?"

"Yes," said F. C. Stone. "But stop saying *hopefully*, or I shan't grant you any functions at all. The word shouldn't be used like that, and I detest sloppy English!"

"Yours to command," Adny said. She could hear the smile in his voice again. "Here are your controls."

The curlicue faded from the screen, to be replaced by a diagrammatic image of F. C. Stone's own keyboard. It was quite recognizable, except to her dismay, an attempt had been made to repeat it three times over. The two outer representations of it were warped and blurred. "Gods!" said F. C. Stone. "How do I use this? There isn't room for it all."

"Hit HELP before you use the extra keys on the right and CAP before you use the ones on the left." Adny's voice reassured her. "Ready?"

She was. She took a hasty sip of cooling *qavv* to steady herself and hovered over her keyboard, prepared to enjoy herself as never before.

It was actually a bit of a letdown. Keys on her screen shone brighter green. Obedient to them, F. C. Stone found herself typing CAP A, *d*, HELP N and then HELP N, *a*, D. Some part of her mind suggested that this still looked like Danny's joke, while another part, more serious, suggested it might be overwork and perhaps she should see a doctor. But she refused to let either of these thoughts distract her and typed CAP D, *n*, HELP A in high excitement.

As she did so, she heard the computer's childish voice again. "Ready for jump. Candida One, are you sure of this? Your coordinates put us right on top of Nad, in considerable danger from our own defenses."

"Reassure her," Adny's voice said urgently.

Without having to think, F. C. Stone said soothingly, "It's all right, Candida Two. We have to test those defenses. Nad is under orders not to hurt us." And she thought, As to the manner born! I'd have made a good Matriarch!

"Understood," said the childish voice. "Jump as given, on

the count of zero. Five, four, three"—F. C. Stone braced herself—"two, one, zero."

Did she feel a slight lurch? Was there a mild ripple of giddiness? She was almost sure not. A quick look around the workroom assured her that all was as usual.

"Jumping," said Candida Two. "There will be an interval of five subjective minutes."

"Why?" said F. C. Stone, like a disappointed child.

Adny's voice cut in hastily. "Standard for a microjump. Don't make her suspicious!"

"But I don't feel anything!" F. C. Stone complained in a whisper.

The keyboards vanished from the screen. "Nobody does," said Adny. "Computer's out of the circuit now. You can speak freely. There is no particular sensation connected with jump, though disorientation does occur if you try to move about."

"Damn!" said F. C. Stone. "I shall have to revise all my books!" An acute need to visit the toilet down the passage came upon her. She picked up her mug of *chphy* reflexively, thought better of that, and put it down again. Her mind dwelt on that toilet, its bowl stained from Danny's attempt, some years ago, to concoct an elixir of life, and its chain replaced by a string of cow bells. To take her mind off it, she said, "Tell me what you mean to do when you and the other ships come out over Nad. Does this start a revolution?"

"It's rather more complicated than that," said Adny. "Out of the twelve Male Lodges, there are only six prepared to rebel. Two of the remaining six are neutral traditionally and supported in this by the Minor Covens, but the Minor Covens are disaffected enough to ally with the Danai, who are a helium life-form and present a danger to all of us. The four loyal Lodges are supposed to align with the Old Coven, and on the whole they do, except for the Fifth Lodge, which has thrown in with the Midmost Coven, who are against everyone else. Their situation is complicated by their concessions to the Traders, who are largely independent, save for overtures they seem to have made to the Anders. The Anders—another lifeform—have said they are *our* allies, but this flirting with the Traders makes us suspicious. So we decided on a bold ploy to test—"

"Stop!" said F. C. Stone. Much as she loved writing this kind of stuff, hearing someone talk like it made her head reel. "You mean, you've gone to all this trouble just for a test run?"

"It's more complicated than—" began Adny.

"No, I don't want to know!" said F. C. Stone. "Just tell me what happens if you fail."

"We can't fail," he replied. "If we do, the High Coven will crush the lot of us."

"Me, too?" F. C. Stone inquired anxiously.

"Possibly," said Adny. "They may not realize how I did this, but if they do, you can probably stop them by destroying your machine."

"Never!" said F. C. Stone. "I'd rather suffer—or, better still, win!"

A bell rang. The keyboard reappeared, elongated and bent, in her screen. "Emerged over Nad," the computer said. "Candy! What is this? I count sixteen other ships emerged, two Trader, four Ander, and the rest appear to be Matriarch. We jump back."

"Give me functions Nine and Ten!" Adny snapped.

"I authorize Adny—" said F. C. Stone.

"Oh, Candy!" the computer said reproachfully. "Why are you so good to that little creep? He's only a man."

"I authorize Adny in functions Nine and Ten," F. C. Stone almost shrieked. It was the only way she could think of to stop the unpleasant sensations which were suddenly manifesting, mostly in her head and stomach. It was as if surf were breaking through her in bubbles of pain. A tearing feeling across her shoulders made her think she was germinating claws there. And psychic attack or not, she knew she just had to get to that toilet.

"Acknowledged," the computer said glumly.

She leaped from her chair and ran. Behind her she heard claps of sound and booms that seemed to compress the air around her. Through them she heard Adny's voice issuing orders, but that was shortly overlaid by a high-pitched whistling, drilling through her ears even through the firmly shut toilet door.

But in the loo, as she was adjusting her dress, a certain sanity was restored to F. C. Stone. She looked at her own face in the mirror. It was encouragingly square and solid and as usual — give or take a sort of wildness about the eyes — and it topped the usual rather overweight body in its usual comfortably shapeless sweater. She raked her fingers through the graying frizz of her hair, thinking as she did so that she would make a very poor showing beside Adny of the golden voice. The action brought away two handfuls of loose hair. As always, she was shedding hair after a heavy session at the word processor — a fact she was accustomed to transfer to her aliens, who frequently shed feathers or fur during jump. Things were quite normal. She had simply been overworking and let Danny's joke get to her.

Or perhaps it was charred chili powder, she thought as she

marched out into the passage again. Possibly due to its hallucinogenic nature, that damnable whistling was still going on, pure torture to her ears. From the midst of it she could hear Adny's voice. "Nad Coven, do we have your surrender, or do we attack again?"

I've had enough! thought F. C. Stone. She marched to her desk, where the screen was showing Adny's curlicue, pulsing to the beat of the beastly shrilling. "Stop this noise!" she commanded. "And give me a picture of *Partlett*'s flight deck." If you *can*, she thought, feeling for the moment every inch the captain of the starship *Candida*.

The whistling died to an almost bearable level. "I need function Eleven to give you vision," Adny said—irritably? casually? or was it *too* casually? He was certainly overcasual when he added, "It does exist, you know."

Give him what he wants and get rid of him, thought F. C. Stone. "I authorize function Eleven then," she said.

"*Oh!*" said the computer, like a hurt child.

And there was a picture on the screen, greenish and jumping and sleeting green lines, but fairly clear for all that. *Partlett*'s controls, F. C. Stone noted absently, had fewer screens than she expected—far fewer than she put in her books—but far more ranks of square buttons and far, far too many dials for comfort, all of them with a shabby, used look. But she was looking mostly at the woman who seemed to be asleep in the padded swivel seat in front of the controls. Mother naked, F. C. Stone was slightly shocked to see, and not a mark or a wrinkle on her slender body or on her thin and piquant face. Abruptly F. C. Stone remembered being quite proud of her looks when she was seventeen, and this woman was herself at seventeen, only beyond even her most idealized memories. Immense regret suffused F. C. Stone.

The whistling, blessedly, stopped. "Candy is really the same age as you," Adny observed.

Her attention turned to him. His seat was humbler, a padded swivel stool. Sitting on it was a small man with a long, nervy face, the type of man who usually has tufts of hair growing in his ears and below his eyes, as if to make up for the fact that such men's hair always tends to be thin and fluffy on top. Adny's hair was noticeably thin on top, but he had smoothed and curled it to disguise the fact, and it was obvious that he had plucked and shaved all other hair from his wrinkled little body; F. C. Stone had no doubt of this, since he was naked, too. The contrast between his appearance and his voice was, to say the least of it, startling.

Adny saw her look and grinned rather ruefully as he leaned forward to hold a paper cup under some kind of tap below the control panel. She realized he could see her, too. The contrast between herself and the sleeping beauty beside him made her feel almost as rueful as he looked. "Can you give me a picture of Nad and any damage there?" she asked, still clinging to her role as Captain. It seemed the only way to keep any dignity.

"Certainly," he said, running his finger down a row of the square buttons.

She found herself apparently staring down at a small town of old houses built up against the side of a hot stony hill—red roofs, boxlike white houses, courtyards shaded with trees. It was quite like a town in Spain or Italy, except that the shapes of the walls and the slant of the roofs were subtly different and wrong. It was the very smallness of the difference between this and towns she knew which, oddly enough, convinced F. C. Stone for once and for all that this place was no fake. She really was looking at a real town in a real world somewhere else entirely. There was a smoking, slaggy crater near the market square and another downhill below the town. That had destroyed a road. She had glimpses of the other spaceships, drifting about looking rather like hot-air balloons.

"Why is it such a small place?" she said.

"Because Nad is only a small outpost of the Matriarchy," Adny replied in his golden voice. The picture flipped back to show he had turned to face her on his stool, sipping steaming liquid from his paper cup. No doubt it was *kfa* or even *quphy*. He smiled through its steam in a way that must have beguiled the poor sleeping beauty repeatedly, and she found she was wishing he had turned out to be an alien instead. "I owe you great thanks on behalf of the Second Male Lodge," he said. "We now have the Nadlings where we want them. And since you have given me full control of this ship and access to all my ex-mistress's power, I can move on to the central worlds in strength and use her as a hostage there."

Hitler and Napoleon were both small men, F. C. Stone thought, with golden voices. It gave her a slight, cold frisson to think what she might have loosed on the unfortunate Matriarchy. "You gave me the impression that this *was* the central world," said F. C. Stone.

"Not in so many words," said Adny. "You don't think I'd be fool enough to move against the strength of the Matriarchy without getting hold of a conscious-class computer first, do you?"

F. C. Stone wished to say that yes, she did. People took that sort of desperate risk in her books all the time. It depressed her to find him such a cautious rebel. *And* he had cheated her, as well as his sleeping beauty, and no doubt he was all set to turn the whole works into a Patriarchy. It was a total waste of a morning.

Or was it? she wondered. A matriarchy where men were sold as slaves was right up her street. There was certainly a book in there. Perhaps she should simply be grateful and hope that Adny did not get too far.

"Tell me," she said, at which he looked up warily from his cup, "what is that stuff you're drinking? *Goffa? Xvay?*"

She was glad to see she had surprised him. "Only coffee," he said.

❊ THE PLAGUE OF PEACOCKS ❊

From the moment the Platts came to Chipping Hanbury everyone knew they were Caring People. They bought the old cottage up Weavers Close beside the field where the children went to cycle and play football. Mr. Platt took the cottage apart all by himself and built it up again and painted it white. Mrs. Platt took the garden apart and painted everything there white too.

When they had done that, they began caring for Chipping Hanbury.

Mr. Platt brought out a news sheet which he called *Hanbury Village News* and put a copy through everyone's door. The copies were addressed to everyone by their first names in the most friendly way: the Willises' was to Glenda and Jack, the Moores' to Lily and Tony, the Dougals' to Marcia and Ken, and so on. Everyone wondered how Mr. Platt knew their names, and whether he was right to call Hanbury a village when it was really just a place on the edge of London. The news sheet was full of kind advice about how Hanbury needed more streetlights and a bus shelter and tidier front gardens. Weavers Pond was full of rubbish too, Mr. Platt said reproachfully, and the football field ought to be a proper sports center. People like Glenda and Jack, who had private incomes, really ought to see about cleaning the place up.

"Why does he think we have private incomes?" said Mrs. Willis. "Because the children have ponies?" Mrs. Willis did typing for people in order to pay for the ponies and she was rather hurt.

Meanwhile, Mrs. Platt was caring for animals. The first to go was the Dougals' cat Sooty. Then the Deans' dog Lambert. Then Holly Smith's angora rabbit. Mrs. Platt called on the Dougals, the Deans, and the Smiths and explained at length that she had found the animal wandering about, and it might have gone in the road, and there was such a lot of traffic these days, and one should keep pets tied up. Mrs. Platt was thin, with intense gray eyes, and she bent forward nervously when she talked, and twisted her hands together. People found it hard to interrupt her when she was so worried. But after an hour or so, the Dougals and the Deans and the Smiths plucked up courage to ask what had happened to their animals. Mrs. Platt explained that she had put them in the car and Mr. Platt had driven them to a vet he knew, to have them put down.

Mr. Platt's next news sheet had a sorrowful page on how badly people looked after their animals. The other pages were about the new greenhouses Mr. Platt was building behind the cottage. Mr. Platt was a thick energetic man with a beard and juicy red lips, and he had a passion for building greenhouses. When he was not doing that, he was either standing with his head back and his chest out admiring the latest greenhouse, or he was walking around Hanbury looking for news to put in his news sheet. He was walking in Hart Lane when Sarah Willis got run away with by her pony.

What made Chunter bolt was a mystery. Sarah always said he had seen Mr. Platt and was afraid of being taken to the vet too. Anyway, there was Chunter hammering along the road, striking frantic sparks from it with his hooves, with Sarah clinging on for dear life, when Mr. Platt came jumping out of the hedge and swung on Chunter's bridle.

"Thanks," said Sarah, when Chunter had stopped.

"You should never, never let a pony gallop on a tarmac road," said Mr. Platt. "I don't think anyone has explained to you: it ruins their feet and jars their legs."

"But I didn't—!" said Sarah. That was all she managed to say, because Mr. Platt proved to be just as good a talker as his wife, and he walked back to the house with her, holding Chunter's bridle and explaining gently how you should treat a pony. "I think I must come inside and explain to Glenda that you shouldn't ride without proper supervision," he said when they got there. And he did. When he had done that, he went out to look at the barn where the ponies lived and came back to tell Mrs. Willis that it was not suitable for ponies.

Mrs. Willis was typing somebody's book about the history of Poland, full of names like Mrzchtochky, and she left out several zs. "I shall go mad," she said.

"Don't worry," said Sarah. "There's always Daniel Emanuel."

No one had yet told the Platts about Daniel Emanuel. This was odd, because Daniel Emanuel was well known to be interested in animals too. Only the week before, he had fallen out of the oak tree in the football field trying to catch a squirrel. Last year he had cut himself on rusty iron wading into Weavers Pond after a duck and nearly died of tetanus, because he had heard you could eat ducks.

Mrs. Platt met Daniel Emanuel first. She was coming home after caring for the Moores' budgie. She had found it on her windowsill. By this time, she had noticed that people did not quite like it when she took their pets to the vet. So she took the budgie home. "Look, Lily," she explained, "I've cut his wings for you, ever so neatly, so that he won't be able to fly away again."

"How kind!" Mrs. Moore said bitterly, thinking she would have to keep the cat in the yard in case Mrs. Platt cared for the cat too. "You'll have to keep the budgie in your bedroom," she said to her son Terry. "I hope Daniel Emanuel does something to the Platts soon!"

Mrs. Platt had got halfway home, to the bottom of the main road, when she saw, to her horror, a four-year-old boy walk out into the traffic. A bus bucked to a stop almost on top of him. Two cars missed him by two separate miracles. Mrs. Platt rushed into the road and seized the child's arm. "Who are you, little man? Does your mummy know you're out?"

He looked up at her. "I'm Daniel Emanuel of course," he said. He had curly hair and long eyelashes and a band of freckles across his nose.

"Where do you live?" said Mrs. Platt.

Daniel Emanuel did not seem to be sure. He let Mrs. Platt lead him around Chipping Hanbury. She seemed to want to, and he felt like a walk anyway. After an hour or so though, she began to bother him. She kept asking things and calling him "little man." The only little men Daniel Emanuel had ever heard of were the dwarves in "Snow White," and he began to be afraid he would not grow any more. He took Mrs. Platt home so that he could ask Linda.

Mrs. Platt looked at the O'Flahertys' tall ramshackle house with pieces of car lying about the front garden under the washing line. Children were running and screaming, and Mrs. O'Flaherty was anxiously looking over the front gate. "This is a Problem Family," Mrs. Platt said to herself, "and I must care for them."

"Daniel Emanuel!" everyone in the garden screamed.

"He was walking in the traffic," Mrs. Platt explained. She had meant to have a long talk with Mrs. O'Flaherty about her problems, but Mrs. O'Flaherty was so glad to see Daniel Emanuel safe that she took him straight indoors. "No manners either," Mrs. Platt said sorrowfully.

Indoors, Mrs. O'Flaherty said, "You naughty boy!" and raised her fist. Daniel Emanuel's face screwed up miserably. "Oh, I can't hit him!" said Mrs. O'Flaherty and she took her fist down. Daniel Emanuel unscrewed his face and beamed. "Linda," said Mrs. O'Flaherty, "why did you let him go in the road?"

Linda was five, and the only one who knew how to manage Daniel Emanuel. She shrugged. There were times when even she could not stop Daniel Emanuel. "He can think," she explained, "and the cars just stop."

"He may think they will, but they don't," said Mrs. O'Flaherty and hurried away to get lunch. A mother who had seven children and a husband who spends his spare time stock-car racing has not quite time to understand everything.

"Am I a little man?" Daniel Emanuel asked Linda anxiously.

Linda knew what he meant. "Not you!" she said. "You'll grow bigger than Dad."

Daniel Emanuel was much relieved. He was not sure he liked Mrs. Platt. She said things that were not true.

Mr. Platt's next news sheet had a lot in it about Problem Families.

"Oh good," said Mrs. Willis to Sarah and James. "They've met Daniel Emanuel."

Next time Daniel Emanuel gave Linda the slip he went to look at the Platts' cottage. He thought it was lovely. The stones around the flowers were painted white. There was a white wheelbarrow on the front lawn with flowers planted in it, which bothered Daniel Emanuel. Flowers should grow in the ground. Daniel Emanuel took the flowers out carefully and tipped the earth on the grass. He found Mr. Platt's golf clubs in the porch and dug a hole for the flowers with them in front of the porch. He put the flowers in the hole and carefully opened the tap in the rainwater butt to give the flowers a drink. Then he found a pot of white paint in the porch and thought he ought to give the hole a white rim like the other flowerbeds. When Mr. Platt came around the house from building his fourth greenhouse, he found Daniel Emanuel squatting in a river using a bent golf club as a paintbrush.

Mr. Platt took Daniel Emanuel in a stern kind hand and led him home, talking gently to him about how wicked he was. Daniel Emanuel seemed a little vague about what wicked meant. Mr. Platt explained by telling him stories, and one of the stories was "Daniel in the Lions' Den."

"Oh Daniel Emanuel!" said Mrs. O'Flaherty when she opened the door. Daniel Emanuel was earth-colored with streaks of white. Mr. Platt was shocked to see that Mrs. O'Flaherty had been reading a book while she cooked lunch. She had two favorite books which she read turn and turn about to keep her sane: this one was *The Mill on the Floss*; the other was *The Count of Monte Cristo*. She knew both so well that she could do most things while she was reading.

Mr. Platt explained what Daniel Emanuel had done and gave Mrs. O'Flaherty long and patient advice on how to bring up children, until Mrs. O'Flaherty smelled the potatoes burning and snatched Daniel Emanuel up and ran. "What a feckless woman," Mr. Platt said sadly.

Mrs. O'Flaherty was so annoyed about the potatoes that Daniel Emanuel barely got scolded. "Where's any lions?" he asked Linda as soon as he was free.

"Aren't any," said Linda. "Only in cages in the zoo."

The next day, Daniel Emanuel set out to find himself a cage of lions.

There are no lions in Chipping Hanbury. The only large beasts are Sarah Willis's Chunter and James Willis's Ben. Daniel Emanuel was seen by James standing in the doorway of the ponies' barn. "Is this a den?" Daniel Emanuel asked.

"No," said James. "It's a stall."

Daniel Emanuel nodded and went away. He was next heard of eight miles away in Abbots Hanbury. How he got there Daniel Emanuel never said, but there he was. He was in a pen in the cattle market with a hundred pigs, angrily shouting, "Bite me!" His father was home when the police telephoned. He drove his newest car to Abbots Hanbury and fetched Daniel Emanuel away. Since Mr. O'Flaherty was the only person in the world that Daniel Emanuel was afraid of, Daniel Emanuel arrived home very sore and sullen. "I don't like Platts," he told Linda.

Both the Platts were very concerned about Daniel Emanuel. Mr. Platt went to see Mr. O'Flaherty to tell him Daniel Emanuel needed special care, and the Dougals saw him leave again rather quickly. Mrs. Platt went to speak to Mrs. Willis. "Glenda," she said, "I think we two should get together and care for our Problem Family. The O'Flahertys, you know."

This time, Mrs. Willis was typing someone's experimental novel. It went down the page in two columns which said the same thing, but not quite, and it had to catch the five o'clock post. "I don't think they're a problem," she said. "Ask James and Sarah. Their main friends are Patrick and Thelma O'Flaherty. Do let me catch the post." But Mrs. Platt stayed persuading Mrs. Willis till four o'clock. At four-thirty Mr. Platt arrived with some brochures, saying that he and Mrs. Platt thought Mrs. Willis ought to be using a word processor. When Sarah and James and Mr. Willis came home just after five, Mr. Platt was still there and Mrs. Willis was in tears.

"Do something!" said Mr. Willis.

James and Sarah saddled their ponies and went drumming away down the bridle path to the football field where Thelma and Patrick were riding their bicycles. "What is it?" said Patrick, propping himself on the hedge.

"Make Daniel Emanuel do something to the Platts," said Sarah.

"You can borrow the ponies and we'll go on a bike-and-pony trek if you do," said James.

Thelma and Patrick looked wistfully at each other. It was an offer they couldn't refuse. It cost Patrick a lot to say, "We can't make him do anything." And it cost Thelma just as much to add, "Linda's his manager."

"Ask her, and we'll do the trek anyway," said Sarah.

During the last month, Linda had been rather pestered. Holly Smith, Terry Moore, and Alastair Dougal had also made offers that couldn't be refused to Brendan, Maureen, and Brian O'Flaherty. "He's not ready to do anything yet," she told Thelma and Patrick. "But I'll try."

Next Saturday, Sarah and James kept their promise and the trek set off to Beacon Hill. Linda kept hers by taking Daniel Emanuel for a walk in Weavers Close. But it was one of Daniel Emanuel's saintly days. Nothing happened, except that Mrs. Platt saw them and hurried out saying, "Little children like you oughtn't to be out alone!" She brought them inside the cottage, where it was neat and plain and brown, and made them sit down. Linda looked hopefully round for biscuits at least, but Mrs. Platt sat down too and told them the story of Jesus. Linda knew it. She had been sent home from school on her first day crying about Jesus. She turned paler and paler.

"Did it hurt much?" she whispered.

"What, dear?" asked Mrs. Platt.

"Being nailed up in a tree," Linda whispered.

Mrs. Platt was rather taken aback. "Well—" Since she did not quite know what to tell Linda, she took them back home feeling she had given them both something to think about.

She had. While Mrs. O'Flaherty was trying to stop Linda

crying, Daniel Emanuel collected four nails, a hammer and some string, and marched off to the oak tree in the football field to find out for himself if it hurt to be crucified.

Luckily for him, he got tangled in the string before he had banged in the first nail properly. Even more luckily, Sarah, James, Patrick, and Thelma happened to be coming home only an hour later after an almost perfect day. They heard the thin little wailing, which was all the noise Daniel Emanuel was able to make by then. "That's Daniel Emanuel!" said Thelma, and managed to make Chunter gallop. And it was lucky the ponies were there. Daniel Emanuel was quite high up, hanging mostly by one arm. They managed to reach him by putting the ponies under the branch, with James, standing on the ponies, one foot on Chunter and one on Ben, boosting Patrick to the branch to cut the string. Sarah held the ponies and Thelma caught Daniel Emanuel as he came down. He hurt a lot, and he was frozen, and he was very angry. "It's not *good* for people!" he kept saying as he rode home in front of Thelma. They put him to bed, and he brooded. He was very angry with both the Platts. They pretended to be kind and told you bad things.

Mr. and Mrs. Platt went from house to house with a petition to have the oak tree cut down. They said it was very dangerous.

"Wouldn't it be easier to take Daniel Emanuel to the vet?" Mrs. Willis asked sweetly.

Mr. Platt didn't follow her meaning at all; but he followed Mr. O'Flaherty's meaning when Mr. O'Flaherty told him what to do with his petition.

Daniel Emanuel was still brooding. "He's nearly ready," Linda told the others. Nearly every day, Daniel Emanuel went round to Weavers Close and stood looking at the cottage thinking what to do. When Mr. and Mrs. Platt came out to take him home, he had vanished before they got to the road. But one day the Platts went out in their car. Daniel Emanuel wandered through the garden and around the back. He wandered thoughtfully through all the greenhouses. Mr. Platt had never stopped building greenhouses. There were six by now. Daniel Emanuel ate tomatoes in one and picked a bunch of flowers in two. He made pies in flowerpots in the other three, thinking, thinking. But none of it gave him any ideas and he went away.

Mr. Platt did not want to meet Mr. O'Flaherty face-to-face again. He telephoned and pointed out that Daniel Emanuel was being allowed to run wild. It was not so much the tomatoes, he said, but the child's own good. . . . The person the other end rang off. "Will you come here, Danny!" Mr. O'Flaherty roared. Mr. Platt would have been shocked at the storm which broke out then.

When it was over, Mr. O'Flaherty went out in the car to cool down. Mrs. O'Flaherty lay down and read *The Count of Monte Cristo* to calm her nerves. Daniel Emanuel, very sore and sullen, went to watch television.

It was a program about birds. The hen-bird came tiptoeing onto the screen, thin and brown and nervy, jerking its little head in just the same way that Mrs. Platt did when she explained something for your own good. The cock-bird strutted on and bent its neck back just like Mr. Platt. Then it spread out a great circle of tail and looked exactly like Mr. Platt admiring a greenhouse.

"Platt, Platt!" shrieked Daniel Emanuel and ran to find Linda.

Linda was cooking. She had tipped in a bag of flour and a bag of sugar, and she was trying to crunch in a dozen eggs with a fork before Mrs. O'Flaherty stopped reading and found her. "I'm busy," she said. But her sleeve was being pulled in a particular way. She went with Daniel Emanuel and a trail of flour and mashed eggshell and looked at the television. "Peacocks," she said.

"Platts," Daniel Emanuel said. He went into the front garden among the pieces of car and thought of a peacock. When the peacock came, it was blue and green and trailed its tail like a film star's skirt. It stood in front of a shiny hubcap of a piece of car and looked at itself and admired itself greatly. Daniel Emanuel nodded and thought of a peahen. She tiptoed up like Mrs. Platt going after somebody's stray pet. Daniel Emanuel nodded again. "Peacocks," he murmured. "Hundreds and hundreds." And he thought of himself holding open a gap in the hedge behind Mr. Platt's greenhouses to let a long, long line of peacocks and peahens tiptoe through. Hundreds, hundreds . . .

When Mrs. O'Flaherty had finished dealing with Linda, she was very relieved to find Daniel Emanuel curled up asleep beside the hubcap of a piece of car. "Oh, isn't he an angel!" she said.

And the Platts were suddenly overwhelmed with peacocks. They sat in rows on the cottage roof, and the garden was a mass of tiptoeing green and brown, mixed with spreading tails and horrible sudden peacock screams. Peacocks got in the greenhouses. They invaded the house. . . But long before this, Holly Smith had rushed home shouting the news. Mrs. Smith telephoned everyone in Chipping Hanbury and all the adults promptly pretended to be ill and sent their children to the football field. Mrs. Willis gave up typing for other people and typed instead the news brought by a stream of children on bicycles. James and Sarah cantered from house to house delivering little cryptic notes saying things like: TWO MORE FELL THROUGH THE GREENHOUSES and SHE GOT PECKED and DROPPINGS ALL OVER SOFA and ONE LAID AN EGG IN THEIR LOO and ROOSTING ON TELEPHONE WHEN THEY TRIED TO RING VET.

A row of interested heads watched over the hedge when the Platts tried to get their car out and drive a load of peacocks to the vet. The running, the chasing, the shooing, the squawks and clouds of feathers was quite indescribable. Mrs. Willis's note summed it up: THEY COULDN'T. So Mr. Platt tried going around to all the houses asking for help. The peacocks seemed fond of him. Twenty or so followed him faithfully from door to door and drowned his voice with screams when the doors were opened. Mr. Platt was sorry to find that everyone opened the door wearing nightclothes and holding a handkerchief to their faces. There seemed to be quite a flu epidemic. So he went home, followed by his procession of birds, and the Platts waited for the peacocks to go away. But they didn't. If anything, there seemed to be more every day.

The Platts stood it for almost a month and then they went away themselves. Everyone recovered from flu in time to wave good-bye to their car as it drove off with peacocks clinging to the roof rack and more hastily waddling and flapping behind. Linda had a marvellous time that day. Mrs. O'Flaherty was touched and puzzled at the way everyone seemed to be thinking of treats for Linda and Daniel Emanuel.

The Platts' cottage is still standing empty except for peacocks, but some of the peacocks seem to have lost interest and wandered away. Since then there have been outbreaks of peacocks here and there all around the edges of London. This is because Daniel Emanuel has forgotten about them. He has started school now and has other things to think of.

THE MASTER

This is the trouble with being a newly qualified vet. The call came at 5:50 A.M. I thought it was a man's voice, though it was high for a man, and I didn't quite catch the name—Harry Sanovit? Harrison Ovett? Anyway, he said it was urgent.

Accordingly, I found myself on the edge of a plain, facing a dark fir forest. It was about midmorning. The fir trees stood dark and evenly spaced, exhaling their crackling gummy scent, with vistas of trodden-looking pine needles beneath them. A wolf-wood, I thought. I was sure that thought was right. The spacing of the trees was so regular that it suggested an artificial pinewood in the zoo, and there was a kind of humming, far down at the edges of the senses, as if machinery was at work sustaining a man-made environment here. The division between trees and plain was so sharp that I had some doubts that I would be able to enter the wood.

But I stepped inside with no difficulty. Under the trees it was cooler, more strongly scented, and full of an odd kind of depression, which made me sure that there was some sort of danger here. I walked on the carpet of needles cautiously, relaxed but intensely afraid. There seemed to be some kind of path winding between the straight boles, and I followed it into the heart of the wood. After a few turns, flies buzzed around something just off the path. *Danger!* pricked out all over my skin like sweat, but I went and looked all the same.

It was a young woman about my own age. From the flies and the freshness, I would have said she had been killed only hours ago. Her throat had been torn out. The expression on her half-averted face was of sheer terror. She had glorious red hair and was wearing what looked, improbably, to be evening dress.

I backed away, swallowing. As I backed, something came up beside me. I whirled around with a croak of terror.

"No need to fear," he said. "I am only the fool."

He was very tall and thin and ungainly. His feet were in big laced boots, jigging a silent, ingratiating dance on the pine needles, and the rest of his clothes were a dull brown and close-fitting. His huge hands came out to me placatingly. "I am Egbert," he said. "You may call me Eggs. You will take no harm if you stay with me." His eyes slid off mine apologetically, round and blue-gray. He grinned all over his small, inane face. Under his close crop of straw-fair hair, his face was indeed that of a near idiot. He did not seem to notice the woman's corpse at all, even though he seemed to know I was full of horror.

"What's going on here?" I asked him helplessly. "I'm a vet not a—not a—mortician. What animal needs me?"

He smiled seraphically at nothing over my left shoulder. "I am only Eggs, Lady. I don't not know nothing. What you need to do is call the Master. Then you will know."

"So where is the Master?" I said.

He looked baffled by this question. "Hereabouts," he suggested. He gave another beguiling smile, over my right shoulder this time, panting slightly. "He will come if you call him right. Will I show you the house, Lady? There are rare sights there."

"Yes, if you like," I said. Anything to get away from whatever had killed that girl. Besides, I trusted him somehow. When he had said I would take no harm if I was with him, it had been said in a way I believed.

He turned and cavorted up the path ahead of me, skipping soundlessly on his great feet, waving great, gangling arms, clumsily tripping over a tree root and, even more clumsily, just saving himself. He held his head on one side and hummed as he went happy and harmless. That is to say, harmless to me so far. Though he walked like a great, hopping puppet, those huge hands were certainly strong enough to rip a throat out.

"Who killed that girl?" I asked him. "Was it the Master?"

His head snapped around, swayingly, and he stared at me, appalled, balancing on the path as though it were a tightrope. "Oh, no, Lady. The Master wouldn't not do that!" He turned sadly, almost tearfully, away.

"I'm sorry," I said.

His head bent, acknowledging that he had heard, but he continued to walk the tightrope of the path without answering, and I followed. As I did, I was aware that there was something moving among the trees to either side of us. Something softly kept pace with us there, and, I was sure, something also followed along the path behind. I did not try to see what it was. I was quite as much angry with myself as I was scared. I had let my shock at seeing that corpse get the better of my judgment. I saw I must wait to find out how the redheaded girl had got herself killed. Caution! I said to myself. Caution! This path was a tightrope indeed.

"Has the Master got a name?" I asked.

That puzzled Eggs. He stood balancing on the path to think. After a moment he nodded doubtfully, shot me a shy smile over his shoulder, and walked on. No attempt to ask my name, I noticed. As if I was the only other person there and "Lady" should be enough. Which meant that the presences among the trees and behind on the path were possibly not human.

Around the next bend I found myself facing the veranda of a chaletlike building. It looked a little as if it were made of wood, but it was no substance that I knew. Eggs tripped on the step and floundered toward the door at the back of the veranda. Before I could make more than a move to help him, he had saved himself and his great hands were groping with an incomprehensible lock on the door. The humming was more evident here. I had been hoping that what I had heard at the edge of the wood had been the flies on the corpse. It was not. Though the sound was still not much more than a vibration at the edge of the mind, I knew I had been right in my first idea. Something artificial was being maintained here, and whatever was maintaining it seemed to be under this house.

In this house, I thought, as Eggs got the door open and

floundered inside ahead of me. The room we entered was full of—well, devices. The nearest thing was a great cauldron, softly bubbling for no reason I could see, and giving out a gauzy violet light. The other things were arranged in ranks beyond, bewilderingly. In one place something grotesque stormed green inside a design painted on the floor; here a copper bowl smoked; there a single candle sat like something holy on a white stone; a knife suspended in air dripped gently into a jar of rainbow glass. Much of it was glass, twinkling, gleaming, chiming, under the light from the low ceiling that seemed to come from nowhere. There were no windows.

"Good heavens!" I said, disguising my dismay as amazement. "What are all these?"

Eggs grinned. "I know some. Pretty, aren't they?" He roved, surging about, touching the edge of a pattern here, passing his huge hand through a flame or a column of smoke there, causing a shower of fleeting white stars, solemn gong notes, and a rich smell of incense. "Pretty, aren't they?" he kept repeating, and, "*Very* pretty!" as an entire fluted glass structure began to ripple and change shape at the end of the room. As it changed, the humming, which was everywhere in the room, changed, too. It became a purring chime, and I felt an indescribable pulling feeling from the roots of my hair and under my skin, almost as if the glass thing were trying to change me as it changed itself.

"I should come away from that if I were you," I said as firmly and calmly as I could manage.

Eggs turned and came floundering toward me, grinning eagerly. To my relief, the sound from the glass modulated to a new kind of humming. But my relief vanished when Eggs said,

"Petra knew all, before Annie tore her throat out. Do you know as much as Petra? You are clever, Lady, as well as beautiful." His eyes slid across me, respectfully. Then he turned and hung, lurching, over the cauldron with the gauzy violet light. "Petra took pretty dresses from here," he said. "Would you like for me to get you a pretty dress?"

"Not at the moment, thank you," I said, trying to sound kind. As I said, Eggs was not necessarily harmless. "Show me the rest of the house," I said, to distract him.

He fell over his feet to oblige. "Come. See here." He led me to the side of the devices, where there was a clear passage and some doors. At the back of the room was another door, which slid open by itself as we came near. Eggs giggled proudly at that, as if it were his doing. Beyond was evidently a living room. The floor here was soft, carpetlike, and blue. Darker blue blocks hung about, mysteriously half a meter or so in the air. Four of them were a meter or so square. The fifth was two meters each way. They had the look of a suite of chairs and a sofa to me. A squiggly mural thing occupied one wall, and the entire end wall was window, which seemed to lead to another veranda, beyond which I could see a garden of some kind. "The room is pretty, isn't it?" Eggs asked anxiously. "I like the room."

I assured him I liked the room. This relieved him. He stumbled around a floating blue block, which was barely disturbed by his falling against it, and pressed a plate in the wall beyond. The long glass of the window slid back, leaving the room open to the veranda. He turned to me, beaming.

"Clever," I said, and made another cautious attempt to find out more. "Did Petra show you how to open that, or was it the Master?"

He was puzzled again. "I don't not know," he said, worried about it.

I gave up and suggested we go into the garden. He was pleased. We went over the veranda and down steps into a rose garden. It was an oblong shape, carved out from among the fir trees, about fifteen meters from the house to the bushy hedge at the far end. And it was as strange as everything else. The square of sky overhead was subtly the wrong color, as if you were seeing it through sunglasses. It made the color of the roses rich and too dark. I walked through with a certainty that it was being maintained—or created—by one of the devices in that windowless room.

The roses were all standards, each planted in a little circular bed. The head of each was about level with my head. No petals fell on the gravel-seeming paths. I kept exclaiming, because these were the most perfect roses I ever saw, whether full bloom, bud, or overblown. When I saw an orange rose—the color I love most—I put my hand up cautiously to make sure that it was real. It was. While my fingers lingered on it, I happened to glance at Eggs, towering over me. It was just a flick of the eyes, which I don't think he saw. He was standing there, smiling as always, staring at me intently. There was, I swear, another shape to his face, and it was not the shape of an idiot. But it was not the shape of a normal man either. It was an intent, *hunting* face.

Next moment he was surging inanely forward. "I will pick you a rose, Lady." He reached out and stumbled as he reached. His hand caught a thorn in a tumble of petals. He snatched it back with a yelp. "Oh!" he said. "It hurts!" He lifted his hand

and stared at it. Blood was running down the length of his little finger.

"Suck it," I said. "Is the thorn still in it?"

"I don't know," Eggs said helplessly. Several drops of blood had fallen among the fallen petals before he took my advice and sucked the cut, noisily. As he did so, his other hand came forward to bar my way. "Stay by me, Lady," he said warningly.

I had already stopped dead. Whether they had been there all along or had been summoned, materialized, by the scent of blood, I still do not know, but they were there now, against the hedge at the end of the garden, all staring at me. Three Alsatian dogs, I told myself foolishly, and knew it was nonsense as I thought it. Three of them. Three wolves. Each of them must have been, in bulk, if not in height, at least as big as I was.

They were dark in the curious darkness of that garden. Their eyes were the easiest to see, light wolf-green. All of them staring at me, staring earnestly, hungrily. The smaller two were crouched in front. One of those was brindled and larger and rangier than his browner companion. And these two were only small by comparison with the great black she-wolf standing behind with slaver running from her open jaws. She was poised either to pounce or to run away. I have never seen anything more feral than that black she-wolf. But they were all feral, stiff-legged, terrified, half in mind to tear my throat out, and yet they were held there for some reason, simply staring. All three were soundlessly snarling, even before I spoke.

My horror—caught from the wolves to some extent—was beyond thought and out into a dreamlike state, where I simply knew that Eggs was right when he said I would be safe with him, and so I said what the dream seemed to require. "Eggs," I said, "tell me their names."

Eggs was quite unperturbed. His hand left his mouth and pointed at the brindled wolf in front. "That one is Hugh, Lady. Theo is the one beside him. She standing at the back is Annie."

So now I knew what had torn redheaded Petra's throat out. And what kind of woman was she, I wondered, who must have had Eggs as servant and a roomful of strange devices, and on top of this gave three wild beasts these silly names? My main thought was that I did not want my throat torn out, too. And I had been called here as a vet after all. It took quite an effort to look those three creatures over professionally, but I did so. Ribs showed under the curly brownish coat of Theo. Hugh's haunches stuck out like knives. As for Annie standing behind, her belly clung upward almost to her backbone. "When did they last eat?" I said.

Eggs smiled at me. "There is food in the forest for them, Lady."

I stared at him, but he seemed to have no idea what he was saying. It was to the wolves' credit that they did not seem to regard dead Petra as food, but from the look of them it would not be long before they did so. "Eggs," I said, "these three are starving. You and I must go back into the house and find food for them."

Eggs seemed much struck by this idea. "Clever," he said. "I am only the fool, Lady." And as I turned, gently, not to alarm the wolves, he stretched out his hands placatingly—at least it looked placating, but it was quite near to an attempt to take hold of me, a sketch of it, as it were. That alarmed me, but I dared not show it here. The wolves' ears pricked a little as we moved off up the garden, but they did not move, to my great relief.

Back through the house Eggs led me in his lurching, pup-pet's gait, around the edges of the room with the devices, where the humming filled the air and still seemed to drag at me in a way I did not care for at all, to another brightly lit, windowless room on the other side. It was a kitchen place, furnished in what seemed to be glass. Here Eggs cannoned into a glass table and stopped short, looking at me expectantly. I gazed around at glass-fronted apparatus, some of it full of crockery, some of it clearly food stores, with food heaped behind the glass, and some of it quite mysterious to me. I made for the glass cupboard full of various joints of meat. I could see they were fresh, although the thing was clearly not a refrigerator. "How do you open this?" I asked.

Eggs looked down at his great hands, planted in encircling vapor on top of the glass table. "I don't not know, Lady."

I could have shaken him. Instead, I clawed at the edges of the cupboard. Nothing happened. There it was, warmish, piled with a good fifty kilograms of meat, while three starving wolves prowled outside, and nothing I could do seemed to have any effect on the smooth edge of the glass front. At length I pried my fingernails under the top edge and pulled, thinking it moved slightly.

Eggs's huge hand knocked against mine, nudging me awk-wardly away. "No, no, Lady. That way you'll get hurt. It is under stass-spell, see." For a moment he fumbled doubtfully at the top rim of the glass door, but, when I made a movement to come back and help, his hands suddenly moved, smoothly and surely. The thing clicked. The glass slid open downward, and the smell of meat rolled out into the kitchen.

So you *do* know how to do it! I thought. And I *knew* you did! There was some hint he had given me, I knew, as I reached for the nearest joint, which I could not quite see now.

"No, *no*, Lady!" This time Eggs pushed me aside hard. He was really distressed. "Never put hand into stass-spell. It will die on you. You do this." He took up a long, shiny pair of tongs, which I had not noticed because they were nested into the top of the cupboard, and grasped the nearest joint with them. "This, Lady?"

"And two more," I said. "And when did you last eat, Eggs?" He shrugged and looked at me, baffled. "Then get out those two steaks, too," I said. Eggs seemed quite puzzled, but he fetched out the meat. "Now we must find water for them as well," I said.

"But there is juice here in this corner!" Eggs objected. "See." He went to one of the mysterious fixtures and shortly came back with a sort of cardboard cup swaying in one hand, which he handed me to taste, staring eagerly while I did. "Good?" he asked.

It was some form of alcohol. "Very good," I said, "but not for wolves." It took me half an hour of patient work to persuade Eggs to fetch out a large lightweight bowl and then to manipulate a queer faucet to fill it with water. He could not see the point of it at all. I was precious near to hitting him before long. I was quite glad when he stayed behind in the kitchen to shut the cabinets and finish his cup of "juice."

The wolves had advanced down the garden. I could see their pricked ears and their eyes above the veranda boards, but they did not move when I stepped out onto the veranda. I had to make myself move with a calmness and slowness I was far from feeling. Deliberately I dropped each joint, one by one, with a sticky thump onto the strange surface. From the size and the coarse grain of the meat, it seemed to be venison—at least I hoped it was. Then I carefully lowered the bowl to stand at the far end of the veranda, looking all the time through my hair at the wolves. They did not move, but the open jaws of the big wolf, Annie, were dripping.

The bowl down, I backed away into the living room, where I just had to sit down on the nearest blue block. My knees gave.

They did not move for long seconds. Then all three disappeared below the veranda, and I thought they must have slunk away. But the two smaller ones reappeared, suddenly, silently, as if they had materialized, at the end of the veranda beside the bowl. Tails trailing, shaking all over, they crept toward it. Both stuck their muzzles in and drank avidly. I could hear their frantic lapping. And when they raised their heads, which they both did shortly, neatly and disdainfully, I realized that one of the joints of meat had gone. The great wolf, Annie, had been and gone.

Her speed must have reassured Theo and Hugh. Both sniffed the air, then turned and trotted toward the remaining joints. Each nosed a joint. Each picked it up neatly in his jaws. Theo seemed about to jump down into the garden with his. But Hugh, to my astonishment, came straight toward the open window, evidently intending to eat on the carpet as dogs do.

He never got a chance. Theo dropped his joint and sprang at him with a snarl. There was the heavy squeak of clawed paws. Hugh sprang around, hackles rising the length of his lean, sloping back, and snarled back without dropping his portion. It was, he seemed to be saying, his own business where he went to eat. Theo, crouching, advancing on him with lowered head and white teeth showing, was clearly denying him this right. I braced myself for the fight. But at that moment Annie reappeared, silent as ever, head and great forepaws on the edge of the veranda, and stood there, poised. Theo and Hugh vanished like smoke, running long and low to either side. Both took their food with them, to my relief. Annie dropped out of sight again. Presently there were faint, very faint, sounds of eating from below.

I went back to the glassy kitchen, where I spent the next few hours getting Eggs to eat, too. He did not seem to regard anything in the kitchen as edible. It took me a good hour to persuade him to open a vegetable cabinet and quite as long to persuade him to show me how to cook the food. If I became insistent, he said, "I don't not know, Lady," lost interest, and shuffled off to the windowless room to play with the pretty lights. That alarmed me. Every time I fetched him back, the humming chime from the glass apparatus seemed to drag at me more intensely. I tried pleading. "Eggs, I'm going to cut these yams, but I can't find a knife somehow." That worked better. Eggs would come over obligingly and find me a thing like a prong and then wander off to his "juice" again. There were times when I thought we were going to have to eat everything raw.

But it got done in the end. Eggs showed me how to ignite a terrifying heat source that was totally invisible, and I fried the food on it in a glass skillet. Most of the vegetables were quite strange to me, but at least the steak was recognizable. We were just sitting down on glass stools to eat it at the glass table when a door I had not realized was there slid aside beside me. The garden was beyond. The long snout of Hugh poked through the gap. The pale eyes met mine, and the wet nose quivered wistfully.

"What do you want?" I said, and I knew I had jerked with fear. It was obvious what Hugh wanted. The garden must have filled with the smell of cooking. But I had not realized that the wolves could get into the kitchen when they pleased. Trying to seem calm, I tossed Hugh some fat I'd trimmed off the steaks. He caught it neatly and, to my intense relief, backed out of the door, which closed behind him.

I was almost too shaken to eat after that, but Eggs ate his share with obvious pleasure, though he kept glancing at me as if he was afraid I would think he was making a pig of himself. It was both touching and irritating. But the food—and the "juice"—did him good. His face became pinker, and he did not jig so much. I began to risk a few cautious questions. "Eggs, did Petra live in this house or just work here?"

He looked baffled. "I don't not know."

"But she used the wolves to help her in her work, didn't she?" It seemed clear to me that they *must* have been laboratory animals in some way.

Eggs shifted on his stool. "I don't not know," he said unhappily.

"And did the Master help in the work, too?" I persisted.

But this was too much for Eggs. He sprang up in agitation, and before I could stop him, he swept everything off the table into a large receptacle near the door. "I can't say!" I heard him say above the crash of breaking crockery.

After that he would listen to nothing I said. His one idea was that we must go to the living room. "To sit elegantly, Lady," he explained. "And I will bring the sweet foods and the juice to enjoy ourselves with there."

There seemed no stopping him. He surged out of the kitchen with an armload of peculiar receptacles and a round jug of "juice" balanced between those and his chin, weaving this way and that among the devices in the windowless room. These flared and flickered and the unsupported knife danced in the air as I pursued him. I felt as much as saw the fluted glass structure changing shape again. The sound of it dragged at the very roots of me.

"Eggs," I said desperately. "How do I call the Master? Please."

"I can't say," he said, reeling on into the living room.

Some enlightenment came to me. Eggs meant exactly what he said. I had noticed that when he said "I don't *not* know," this did not mean that he did not know; it usually seemed to be something he could not explain. Now I saw that when he said "I can't say," he meant that he was, for some reason, unable to tell me about the Master. So, I thought, struggling on against the drag of the chiming apparatus, this means I must use a little cunning to get him to tell me.

In the living room Eggs was laying out dishes of sweets and little balls of cheese near the center of the large blue sofa-like block. I sat down—at one end of it. Eggs promptly came and sat beside me, grinning and breathing "juice" fumes. I got up and moved to the other end of the sofa. Eggs took the hint. He stayed where he was, sighing, and poured himself another papery cup of his "juice."

"Eggs," I began. Then I noticed that the wolf Hugh was

crouched on the veranda facing into the room, with his brindled nose on his paws and his sharp haunches outlined against the sunset roses. Beyond him were the backs of the two others, apparently asleep. Well, wolves always leave at least one of their pack on guard when they sleep. I told myself that Hugh had drawn sentry duty and went back to thinking how I could induce Eggs to tell me how to get hold of this Master. By this time I felt I would go mad unless someone explained this situation to me.

"Eggs"—I began again—"when I ask you how I fetch the Master, you tell me you can't say, isn't that right?" He nodded eagerly, obligingly, and offered me a sweet. I took it. I was doing well so far. "That means that something's stopping you telling me, doesn't it?" That lost him. His eyes slid from mine. I looked where his eyes went and found that Hugh had been moving, in the unnoticed silent way a wild creature can. He was now crouched right inside the room. The light feral eyes were fixed on me. Help! I thought. But I had to go on with what I was saying before Eggs's crazed mind lost it. "So I'm going to take it that when you say, 'I can't say,' you mean 'Yes,' Eggs. It's going to be like a game."

Eggs's face lit up. "I like games, Lady!"

"Good," I said. "The game is called Calling-the-Master. Now I know you can't tell me direct how to call him, but the rule is that you're allowed to give me hints."

That was a mistake. "And what is the hint, Lady?" Eggs asked, in the greatest delight. "Tell me and I will give it."

"Oh—I—er—" I said. And I felt something cold gently touch my hand. I looked down to find Hugh standing by my knees. Beyond him Theo was standing up, bristling. "What do you want now?" I said to Hugh. His eyes slid across the plates of sweets, and he sighed, like a dog. "Not sweets," I said firmly. Hugh understood. He laid his long head on my knee, yearningly.

This produced a snarl from Theo out on the veranda. It sounded like pure jealousy.

"You can come in, too, if you want, Theo," I said hastily. Theo gave no sign of understanding, but when I next looked, he was half across the threshold. He was crouched, not lying. His hackles were up, and his eyes glared at Hugh. Hugh's eyes moved to see where he was, but he did not raise his chin from my knee.

All this so unnerved me that I tried to explain what a hint was by telling Eggs a story. I should have known better. "In this story," I said, absently stroking Hugh's head as if he were my dog. Theo instantly rose to his feet with the lips of his muzzle drawn back and his ears up. I removed my hand—but quick! "In this story," I said. Theo lay down again, but now it was me he was glaring at. "A lady was left three boxes by her father, one box gold, one silver, and one lead. In one of the boxes there was a picture of her. Her father's orders were that the man who guessed which of the three boxes her picture was in could marry her—"

Eggs bounced up with a triumphant laugh. "I know! It was in the lead box! Lead protects. I can marry her!" He rolled about in delight. "Are you that lady?" he asked eagerly.

I suppressed a strong need to run about screaming. I was sure that if I did, either Theo or Annie would go for me. I was not sure about Hugh. He seemed to have been a house pet. "Right," I said. "It *was* in the lead box, Eggs. This *other* lady knew that, but the men who wanted to marry her had to guess. All of them guessed wrong, until one day a beautiful man came along whom this *other* lady wanted to marry. So what did she do?"

"Told him," said Eggs.

"No, she was forbidden to do that," I said. *God give me patience!* "Just like you. She had to give the man hints instead. Just like you. Before he came to choose the box, she got people to sing him a song and—remember, it was the *lead* box—every line in that song rhymed with 'lead.' A rhyme is a word that sounds the same," I added hurriedly, seeing bewilderment cloud Eggs's face. "You know—'said' and 'bled' and 'red' all rhyme with 'lead.' "

"Said, bled, red," Eggs repeated, quite lost.

"Dead, head," I said. Hugh's cold nose nudged my hand again. Wolves are not usually scavengers, unless in dire need, but I thought cheese would not hurt him. I passed him a round to keep him quiet.

Theo sprang up savagely and came half across the room. At the same instant, Eggs grasped what a rhyme was. "Fed, instead, bed, wed!" he shouted, rolling about with glee. I stared into Theo's gray-green glare and at his pleated lip showing the fangs beneath it and prayed to heaven. Very slowly and carefully, I rolled a piece of cheese off the sofa toward him. Theo swung away from it and stalked back to the window. "My hint is bed-spread, Lady!" Eggs shouted.

Hugh, meanwhile, calmly took his cheese as deftly and gently as any hunting dog and sprang up onto the sofa beside me, where he stood with his head down, chewing with small bites to make the cheese last. "Now you've done it, Hugh!" I said, looking nervously at Theo's raked-up back and at the sharp outline of Annie beyond him.

"Thread, head, watershed, bread!" bawled Eggs. I realized he was drunk. His face was flushed, and his eyes glittered. He had been putting back quantities of "juice" ever since he first showed me the kitchen. "Do I get to marry you now, Lady?" he asked soulfully.

Before I could think what to reply, Hugh moved across like lightning and bit Eggs on his nearest large folded knee. He jumped clear even quicker, as Eggs surged to his feet, and streaked off to join Theo on the veranda. I heard Theo snap at him.

Eggs took an uncertain step that way, then put his hand to his face. "What is this?" he said. "This room is chasing its tail." It was clear the "juice" had caught up with him.

"I think you're drunk," I said.

"Drink," said Eggs. "I must get a drink from the faucet. I am dying. It is worse than being remade." And he went blundering and crashing off into the windowless room.

I jumped up and went after him, sure that he would do untold damage bumping into cauldron or candle. But he wove his way through the medley of displays as only a drunk man can, avoiding each one by a miracle, and reached the kitchen when I was only halfway through the room. The hum of the crystal apparatus held me back. It dragged at my very skin. I had still only reached the cauldron when there was an appalling splintering crash from the kitchen, followed by a hoarse male scream.

I do not remember how I got to the kitchen. I only remember standing in the doorway, looking at Eggs kneeling in the remains of the glass table. He was clutching at his left arm with his right hand. Blood was pulsing steadily between his long fingers and making a pool on the glass-littered floor. The face he turned to me was so white that he looked as if he were wearing greasepaint. "What will you do, Lady?" he said.

Do? I thought. I'm a vet. I can't be expected to deal with humans! "For goodness' sake, Eggs," I snapped at him. "Stop this messing about and get me the Master! Now. This instant!"

I think he said, "And I thought you'd never tell me!" But his voice was so far from human by then it was hard to be sure. His body boiled about on the floor, surging and seething and changing color. In next to a second the thing on the floor was a huge gray wolf, with its back arched and its jaws wide in agony, pumping blood from a severed artery in its left foreleg.

At least I knew what to do with that. But before I could move, the door to the outside slid open to let in the great head and shoulders of Annie. I backed away. The look in those light, blazing eyes said: "You are not taking my mate like *she* did."

Here the chiming got into my head and proved to be the ringing of the telephone. My bedside clock said 5:55 A.M. I was quite glad to be rid of that dream as I fumbled the telephone up in the dark. "Yes?" I said, hoping I sounded as sleepy as I felt.

The voice was a light, high one, possibly a man's. "You won't know me," it said. "My name is Harrison Ovett, and I'm in charge of an experimental project involving wild animals. We have a bit of an emergency on here. One of the wolves seems to be in quite a bad way. I'm sorry to call you at such an hour, but—"

"It's my job," I said, too sleepy to be more than proud of the professional touch. "Where are you? How do I get to your project?"

I think he hesitated slightly. "It's a bit complicated to explain," he said. "Suppose I come and pick you up? I'll be outside in twenty minutes."

"Right," I said. And it was not until I put the phone down that I remembered my dream. The name was the same, I swear. I would equally swear to the voice. This is why I have spent the last twenty minutes feverishly dictating this account of my dream. If I get back safely, I'll erase it. But if I don't—well, I am not sure what anyone can do if Annie's torn my throat out, but at least someone will know what became of me. Besides, they say forewarned is forearmed. I have some idea what to expect.

ENNA HITTIMS

Anne Smith hated having mumps. She had to miss two school outings. Her face came up so long and purple that both her parents laughed at her when they were at home. And she was left alone rather a lot, because her parents could not afford to leave their jobs.

The first day was terrible. Anne's temperature went up and up, and the higher it got, the more hungry she became. By the time her father got off work early and came home, she was starving.

"But people aren't supposed to get hungry with a temperature!" Mr. Smith said, grinning at the sight of Anne's great purple face.

"I don't care. I want five sausages and two helpings of

chips and lots of ketchup," said Anne. "Quickly, or I'll die!"

So Mr. Smith raced out to the chip shop. But when he came back, Anne could not open her mouth far enough to get a bite of sausage. She could not chew the chips. And the ketchup stung the inside of her face like nettles.

"I told you so," said Mr. Smith.

Anne, who was usually a most reasonable person, burst into tears and threw all the food on the floor. "I'm so hungry!" she yelled. "It's torture!" Of course it hurt to shout, too.

Mr. Smith was reasonable, too, except when he had to clean ketchup off the carpet. He lost his temper and shouted, "Do that again, and I'll spank you, mumps or not!"

"I hate you," said Anne. "I hate everything." And she sat and glowered, which is the only way to be angry with mumps.

"I think she's got grumps as well as mumps," Mrs. Smith said when she got in from work.

It did seem to be so. For the next few days, nothing pleased Anne. She tried wandering about the house—very slowly, because moving jiggled her great mauve face—looking for things to do. Nothing seemed interesting. She tried playing with Tibby, the cat, but Tibby was boring. She tried watching videos, but they were either boring or they made her laugh, and laughing hurt. She tried reading, but that was the same, and her fat, swollen chin kept getting in the way. Everything was boring. Mrs. Harvey next door had kindly agreed to come in and give Anne lunch. But it did not seem to occur to Mrs. Harvey that things like crusty pizza and stewed rhubarb are the last things you want to eat with mumps.

Anne told her parents all this when they got home. The

result was that her parents stopped saying, "It's the way you feel with mumps." Instead, they said, "Oh, for heaven's sake, Anne, do stop grumbling!" every time Anne opened her mouth.

Anne took herself and her great purple face back to bed, where she lay staring at the shape of her legs under the bed-clothes and hating her parents. I'm seriously ill, she thought, and nobody cares!

The next minute she had invented Enna Hittims.

It all happened in a flash, but when she thought about it later, Anne supposed it was because the shape of her legs under the bedspread looked like a landscape with two long hills in it and a green jungly valley in between. The long wrinkle running down from her left foot looked like a gorge where a river might run. Even through her crossness, Anne seemed to be wondering what it would be like to be small enough to explore those hills and that valley.

Enna Hittims was small enough. The name was Anne Smith backward, of course. But there is no way you can say "Htims" without putting in a noise between the H and the t, so Enna's second name had to be Hittims. It suited her. She was a bold and heroic lady, even if she was only an inch or so high. She was tall and slim and muscular, and she wore her raven locks cut short around her thin brown face. There was no trace of mumps about Enna Hittims, and no trace of cowardice either. Enna Hittims was born to explore and have adventures.

Enna Hittims started life on her parents' farm beside the Crease River, just below Leftoe Mountain. She was plowing their cornfield one day, when the plow turned up an old sword. Enna Hittims picked it up and swished it, and it cut through the plow. It was an enchanted sword that could cut through any-thing. Enna Hittims took the sword home to where her parents were lazing about and cut the kitchen table in half to show them what it could do.

"I'm leaving," she said. "I want to have adventures."

"No, you're not," said her parents. "We forbid it. We need you to do the work."

Then Enna Hittims realized that her parents were exploit-ing her. She cut both their heads off with the enchanted sword and set off from the farm with a small bundle of food, to look for what she might find.

In this way Enna Hittims began the most exciting and inter-esting kind of life. For the next few days Anne found it hard to think of anything else She lay in bed and looked at the land-scape on the bedspread and imagined adventures for Enna Hittims to go with it.

The first heroic deed Enna Hittims did was to kill a tiger at Ankle Bend. Tibby put this idea into Anne's head by com-ing to sleep on her bed. After that Enna Hittims climbed on up the mountain, where the landscape grew ever more won-drous. In the giant fern forest near the top of Leftoe Mountain, where monkeys chattered and parrots screamed, Enna Hittims came upon two more intrepid travelers, who were about to be killed by a savage gorilla. Enna Hittims cut the gorilla's head off for them, and the two travelers became her faithful friends. They were called Marlene and Spike. The heroic three set off to find the treasure guarded by the dragon on Knee Heights.

By this time, Anne was finding Enna Hittims and her friends so interesting that she just had to get out of bed for her drawing book and felt tips and draw pictures of their adventures. Of course, when she got back into bed, the landscape had changed. The green patch which had been the fern forest had got down between Anne's feet and become the Caves of Emerald, and the Crease River had turned into Toagara Falls. Enna Hittims and her friends realized they were exploring an enchanted land and took it all quite calmly. As the landscape changed every time Anne got in and out of bed, they soon understood that a powerful magician was trying to stop them getting the treasure. Enna Hittims vowed to conquer the magician when they had killed the dragon.

The three friends explored all over the bedspread. Anne made drawing after drawing of them. She no longer minded Tibby's being so boring. While Tibby was curled up asleep on the bed, she held still for Anne to draw her. Anne intended Tibby to be the dragon in the end, but meanwhile, Tibby made a useful model for all the other monsters the three heroes killed. For the human monsters, Anne fetched snapshots of her parents and her cousins and copied them with glaring eyes and long teeth.

Enna Hittims was easy to draw. Her bold dark face gave Anne no trouble at all. Marlene was almost as easy, because she was the opposite of her friend, fair and small and not very brave. Enna Hittims often had to snap at Marlene for being so scared. Spike was more trouble to draw. Of course he had spiky hair, but his name really came from the enchanted spike he used as a weapon. He was small and nimble, with a puckered face. Anne kept getting him looking like a monkey, until she got used to drawing him. She drew and drew. Every time she got out of bed and the landscape changed, she thought of new adventures. She hardly noticed what Mrs. Harvey brought her for lunch. She hardly noticed whether her parents were in or out.

"Thank goodness!" said Mr. and Mrs. Smith.

And then disaster struck. Just before lunchtime, when Anne was all alone in the house, every one of her felt tips ran out.

"Oh, bother!" Anne wailed, almost in tears. She scribbled angrily, but even the mauve felt tip only made a pale, squeaky line. It was awful. Enna Hittims and her friends were in the middle of meeting the hermit who knew where to find the dragon. Anne was dying to draw the hermit's cave. Enna Hittims was holding her enchanted sword threateningly at the foolish hermit's throat. Anne had a photograph of Mr. Smith all ready to copy as the hermit. She was looking forward to giving him long hair and a scraggly beard and a look of utter terror.

"Oh, *bother!*" she shouted, and threw the felt tips across the room.

Tibby by now knew all about Anne in this mood. She jumped off Anne's bed and galloped for the door. Mrs. Harvey came in with Anne's lunch just then. Tibby slipped around Mrs. Harvey and ran away.

"Here you are, dear," Mrs. Harvey said, puffing rather. She put a tray down on Anne's knees. "I've done you macaroni cheese and some nice stewed apple. You can eat that, can't you?"

Anne knew Mrs. Harvey was being very kind. She smiled, in spite of her crossness, and said, "Yes, thank you."

"I should think you'd be well enough to go downstairs a bit now," Mrs. Harvey said, a little reproachfully. "The stairs are hard work." She went away, saying, "Tell your dad to pop the dishes back tonight. I'm out till then."

Anne sighed and looked back at the bedspread. To her surprise, Enna Hittims had killed the hermit during the interruption. Anne had meant the hermit to stay alive and guide the heroes to the dragon. She stared at Enna Hittims coolly wiping her enchanted sword clean on a handy tuft of cloth. "Sorry if I lost my temper," Enna Hittims was saying, "but I don't think the old fool knew a thing about that dragon."

Anne was rather shocked. She had not known that Enna Hittims was that unfeeling.

"You did quite right," said Spike. "You know, I'm beginning to wonder if that dragon exists at all."

"Me, too," answered Enna Hittims. She hitched her sword to her belt rather grimly. "And if someone's having us on —"

"Enna," Marlene interrupted, "the landscape's changed again. Over there."

The three heroes swung around and shaded their eyes with their hands to look at the tray across Anne's lap. "So it has!" said Enna Hittims. "Well done, Marlene! What is it up there?"

"A tableland," said Spike. "There are two white mountains, and one's steaming. Do you think it could be the dragon?"

"Probably only a new volcano," said Enna Hittims. "Let's go and see."

The three heroes set off along the top of Anne's right leg, walking swiftly in single file, and Anne watched them in some alarm. She did not want them climbing over her lunch while she tried to eat it.

"Go back," she said. "The dragon's going to be down by my right knee."

"What was that?" Marlene whispered nervously as she followed the other two up the slant of Anne's thigh.

"Just thunder. We're always hearing it," said Enna Hittims. "Don't whinge, Marlene."

The three heroes stood in a row with their chins on the edge of the lunch tray.

"Well, how about that!" said Enna Hittims. She pointed to the plate of macaroni cheese. "That hill of hot pipes—do you think it's an installation of some kind?"

"There could be a baby dragon in each pipe," Marlene suggested.

"What are those shiny things?" Spike wondered, pointing at the knife, fork, and spoon.

"Silver bars," Enna Hittims said. "We'll have to find an elephant and tow them away. This must be the dragon's lair. But what's that?"

The three heroes stared at the bowl of stewed apple.

"Pale yellow slush," said Spike, "with a sour smell. Dragon sick?"

"It could be some kind of gold mulch," Marlene said doubtfully. She looked carefully across the tray, searching for some clue. Her eyes went on, up the hill of Anne's body beyond. She jumped and clutched Spike's sleeve. "Look!" she whispered. "Up there!"

Spike looked. He turned quietly to Enna Hittims. "Look up, but don't be too obvious about it," he murmured. "Isn't that a giant face up there?"

Enna Hittims glanced up. She nodded. "Right. Very big and purple, with little, piggy eyes. It's some kind of giant. We'll have to kill it."

"Now look here—" Anne called out.

But the three heroes took her voice for thunder, just as they always did. Enna Hittims went on briskly laying her plans. "Marlene and Spike, you go around the tableland, one on each side, and climb up its hair. Swing over when you're above the nose and stab an eye each. I'll go in over the middle and see if I can cut its fat throat." Spike and Marlene nodded and raced away around the edges of the tray.

Anne did not wait to see if the plan worked. She picked up the tray and pushed it on top of her bedside cupboard. Then she scrambled out of bed as fast as she could go. This of course changed the landscape completely, toppling all three heroes over and burying them under mountains of sheet and blanket. Anne hoped that had done for them. It ought to have done, since they were only part of her imagination.

To give them time to smother, or vanish, or something, Anne went down to the kitchen and got herself a glass of milk. She looked for Tibby to give her some milk, too, but Tibby seemed to have gone out through her cat flap. She went back to her bedroom, hoping the heroes had gone.

They were still there. Spike was up on her pillow, whirling his spike around his head on the end of a rope. He let it fly just as Anne came in, and it stuck firmly into the edge of the tray. It was a tin tray, but the spike was magic, of course, and would stick into anything Spike wanted it to. Spike, Enna Hittims, and Marlene all took hold of the rope and heaved. The tray slid. It tipped.

"No, stop!" Anne said weakly. She had not balanced the tray properly in her hurry.

One end of the tray came down into the bed. Down slid the macaroni cheese, and down slid the stewed apple after it. The heroes saw it coming. They leaped expertly for safety up on the pillows. They were used to this kind of thing. While Anne was still staring at macaroni and apple soaking into her sheets, Spike was dashing down and rescuing his spike.

Enna Hittims walked around the marsh of stewed apple and sliced at a macaroni tube with her sword. "It's not alive," she said. "Don't just stand there, Marlene. We're going up that ramp to find that giant and finish him off. It's obviously the giant that's been changing the landscape all the time. No giant's going to do that to me!"

They started scrambling up the sloping tray. Anne hoped it would be too slippery for them. But no. Spike used his spike to help him scramble up. Enna Hittims used her sword one-handed to hack footholds and walked up backward, dragging Marlene with her other hand and snapping, "Do come *on*, Marlene!"

Even before they were halfway up to the bedside cupboard, Anne knew that the only sensible thing to do was to pick the tray up and tip them back into the stewed apple. And then put the tray on top of them and press. But she could not bring herself to do anything so nasty. She stood and watched them climb on top of the cupboard. Enna Hittims stood with her hands on her hips, surveying the bedroom.

"We're in the giant's house now," she said confidently.

"And he'll be a mountain of cat food before long," said Spike. Marlene laughed with pleasure.

Anne ran out of the bedroom and shut the door with a slam. She ran down to the living room and stood with her hands together and her eyes shut. "Go away, all three of you!" she prayed. "Go. Disappear. Vanish. You're only made up!"

Then she went back upstairs to see if the prayer had worked. Her bedroom door was still shut, but there was some kind of purple tube sticking out from under the door. As Anne bent down to see what it was, she heard Enna Hittims's voice from behind the door. "Well, what *is* out there, Marlene?"

"A huge passage," Marlene's voice replied. The tube was the mauve felt tip with its inside taken out. It swung sideways as Anne looked. "Oh!" said Marlene. "There's a giant out there now! I can see its toes."

"Great!" said Enna Hittims. "Let's get after it." There was a burring, splintering noise. The tip of Enna Hittims's enchanted sword, together with a lot of sawdust, made a neat half circle in the bottom of the bedroom door.

Anne ran away to the bathroom and sat on the edge of the bath, wondering what to do. She heard the voices of the three heroes out in the passage after a moment. She shut the bathroom door, very quietly. Nothing happened. After a while she felt she had better go and see what the heroes were doing.

There was a hole like a mousehole in the bottom of her bedroom door. The heroes were on their way downstairs. Anne could hear Enna Hittims saying, "Come *on*, Marlene! Just let yourself drop and Spike will catch you." They seemed to be halfway down. Anne went down cautiously to see how they were doing it. They seemed to be letting themselves down on the rope tied to Spike's magic spike. Marlene was dangling and spinning on the rope. To Anne's surprise, she was wearing a new dress of a pretty harebell blue.

"Ooh! It's so high!" she said.

"Don't be so feeble!" said Enna Hittims. "We're halfway down."

Spike was keeping guard. "There's a giant on the stairs above us," he said quietly.

Enna Hittims glanced up at Anne. "You two go on," she said. "It's only a small one. You two get down and look for the big giants, while I slice off a few of this one's toes to keep it busy."

Anne was forced to run back to the bathroom again, rather than lose her toes. Then she realized that her bedroom was safe now and went back there. It was in the most awful mess, even if you did not count the lunch in the bed. The heroes had pulled books and jigsaws and games out of the shelves. Enna Hittims had slashed Anne's piggy bank to bits with her sword, but she obviously had not thought that 50p in pence was much of a treasure, and she had cut some of the money up, too. Spike had pulled out Anne's records. She could see the scratches his spike had made, right across her favorite ones. One of them had scribbled with a mauve felt tip across most of Anne's drawings. But it was Marlene who had done the worst damage. She had cut a ragged circle out of Anne's best sweater in order to make herself her new dress.

That made Anne so angry that she almost ran downstairs. By now she hated all three heroes. Enna Hittims was bossy and bloodthirsty. Spike was a vandal. And Marlene was so awful that she deserved the way Enna Hittims ordered her about! Anne wished she had never invented them. But it was plain she was not going to get rid of them by just wishing. She was going to have to do something, however nasty that might be.

As she arrived at the bottom of the stairs, quaking but determined, there was a ringing SMASH! from the living room and the sound of smithereens pattering on the carpet. Anne knew it was the big china lamp her mother was so fond of.

The heroes came scampering around the living room door into the hall. "Too many hazards in there," Enna Hittims announced. "Now let's see. We're sure the small purple-faced giant is only a servant left on guard. Where can we go to kill the big ones when they come back?"

"The kitchen," said Spike. "They'll want to eat."

"Us, probably," Marlene quavered.

"Don't moan, Marlene," said Enna Hittims. "Right. To the kitchen!" She held her sword up and led the other two at a run around the open kitchen door.

Something in the kitchen went ching-BOING! and there was the glop-glop-glop of liquid running out of a bottle. "Oh, no!" said Anne. She had left the milk bottle on the floor while she was looking for Tibby. Worse still, she remembered the way Tibby always knew when there was milk on the floor. She could not let Tibby get in the way of the enchanted sword. She ran across the hall.

"My new dress is soaked!" she heard Marlene whine. Then came the sound of Tibby's cat flap opening. Marlene gasped, "A monster!"

"What a splendid one!" Enna Hittims cried ringingly. "You two guard my rear while I kill it."

By the time Anne got to the kitchen, Enna Hittims was standing in a warlike attitude facing Tibby, barring Tibby's way to the pool of milk on the floor. And Tibby, who had no kind of idea about enchanted swords, was crouching with her tail swishing, staring eagerly at Enna Hittims. It was clear she thought the hero was a new kind of mouse.

Anne charged through the kitchen and caught Tibby just as she sprang. "Oh-ho!" shouted Enna Hittims. The enchanted sword swung at Anne's right foot. Spike sprang at Anne's left foot and stabbed. Tibby struggled and clawed. But Anne hung on to Tibby in spite of it all. She ran out into the hall, kicking the kitchen door shut behind her, and did not let go of Tibby until the door was shut. Then she dropped Tibby. Tibby stood in a ruffled hump, giving Anne the look that meant they would not be on speaking terms for some time, and then stalked away upstairs.

Anne sat on the bottom stair, watching blood ooze from a round hole in her left big toe and more blood trickle from a deep cut under her right ankle. "How lucky I didn't invent them poisoned weapons!" she said. She sat and thought. Surely one ordinary-sized girl ought to be able to defeat three inch-high heroes, if she went about it the right way. She needed armor really.

She went thoughtfully up to her bedroom. Tibby was now crouched on Anne's bed, delicately picking pieces of macaroni cheese out of the stewed apple. Tibby loved cheese. She looked up at Anne with the look that meant "Stop me if you dare!"

"You eat it," said Anne. "Be my guest. Stuff yourself. It'll keep you up here out of danger." She got dressed. She put on her toughest jeans and her hard shoes and her thickest sweater and then the zip-up plastic jacket to make quite sure. She tied the covers of her drawing book around her legs to make even more sure. Then she collected a handful of shoelaces, string, and belts and picked up the tray. It had little regular notches in it where Enna Hittims had carved her footholds. Mrs. Harvey would not be pleased.

She shut her bedroom door to keep Tibby in there and went down to the living room. She stepped over the pieces of the china lamp to the dining area and fetched out the tea trolley. Then she spent quite a long time tying the tray to the front of the trolley, testing it, and tying it again. When she had it tied firmly, so that it grated along the carpet as the trolley was pushed, and nothing an inch high could possibly get under the bottom edge of the tray, Anne picked up the poker. She was ready.

She wheeled the armored trolley out through the hall. By lying on her stomach across the top of it, she managed to reach the handle of the kitchen door and open it quietly. She looked warily inside.

She was in luck. The three heroes thought they had defeated her. They were relaxing, filling their waterskins at the edge of the pool of milk. "Now remember to go for the big giants' eyes," Enna Hittims was saying. "You can hold on to their ears if they have short hair."

"No, you can't!" Anne shouted. She shoved off with one foot and sent the trolley through the pool of milk toward them. The tray raised a tidal wave in front of it as it went. The heroes had to leap back and run, or they would have been submerged. They ran across the kitchen, shouting angrily. Anne followed them with the trolley. This way and that, they ran. But the trolley was good at turning this way and that, too. Anne pushed with her foot, and pushed. Whenever the heroes tried to run to one side of the tray, she leaned over and jabbed at them with the poker to keep them in front of it. Spike's spike tinged against the tray. Enna Hittims carved several pieces off the poker. But it did no good. Within minutes, Anne had pushed and prodded and herded them up against the back door where the cat flap was. She let them hew angrily at the tray, while she leaned over and pushed the cat flap open with the poker.

"There's a way out!" squeaked Marlene.

"Stupid! It's just tempting us!" shouted Enna Hittims.

But Anne gave the heroes no choice. She held the cat flap open and shoved hard with her foot. The tray went right up against the door. The heroes were forced to leap out through the cat flap or be squashed.

"We'll get in another way!" Enna Hittims shouted angrily as the flap banged shut.

"No, you won't!" said Anne. She left the trolley pushed against the door, and she overturned the kitchen table and pushed that up against the back of the trolley to keep it there.

She was just setting off to make sure all the windows were shut when she heard a car outside. It was the unmistakable, growly sound of her father turning the car around in the road before he backed down into the garage. A glance at the kitchen clock showed Anne that he was back almost two hours early.

"I can't let them stab his eyes!" she gasped. She raced through the hall, her head full of visions of the heroes standing on the garden wall and climbing up Mr. Smith as he walked back around from the garage. She dragged the front door open and made warning gestures with the poker.

Mr. Smith smiled at her through the back window of the car. The car was already swinging round backward into the driveway. Anne stood where she was, with the poker raised. She held her breath. The heroes were standing about halfway up the drive. Marlene was pointing at the car and gasping as usual. "Another monster!"

"Go for its big black feet!" Enna Hittims shouted, and she led the three heroes at a run toward the car.

Mr. Smith never saw them. He backed briskly down the drive. Halfway there, the heroes saw the danger. Marlene screamed, and they all turned and ran the other way. But the car, even slowing down, was moving far faster than they could run. Anne watched the big, black, zigzag-patterned tire roll over on top of them. There was the tiniest possible crunching. Much as she hated the heroes by now, Anne let her breath out with a shudder.

Before Anne could lower the poker, there was a sharp hiss. The enchanted sword, and perhaps the magic spike, too, could still do damage. Mr. Smith jumped out of the car. Anne ran across the lawn, and they both watched the right-hand back tire sink into a flat squashiness.

Mr. Smith looked ruefully from the tire to Anne's face. "Your face has gone down, too," he said. "Did you know?"

"*Has* it?" Anne put up her hand to feel. The mumps were now only two small lumps on either side of her chin.

While she was feeling them, her father turned and got something out of the car. "Here you are," he said. He passed her a fat new drawing book and a large pack of felt tips. "I knew you were going to run out of drawing things today."

Anne looked at the rows of different colors and the thick book of paper. She knew her father hated going to the drawing shop. There was never anywhere to park, and he always got a parking ticket. But he had gone there specially and then come home early to give them to her. "Thanks!" she said. "Er—I'm afraid there's rather a mess indoors."

Mr. Smith smiled cheerfully. "Then isn't it lucky you're so much better?" he said. "You can tidy up while I'm putting the spare wheel on."

It seemed fair, Anne thought. She turned toward the house, wondering where to start. The macaroni, the china lamp, or the milk? She looked down at the pack of felt tips while she tried to decide. They were a different make from the old lot. That was a good thing. She was fairly sure that it was her drawings that had brought Enna Hittims and her friends to life like that. The old felt tips would not have been called Magic Markers for nothing.

❧ THE GIRL WHO LOVED THE SUN ❧

There was a girl called Phega who became a tree. Stories from the ancient times when Phega lived would have it that when women turned into trees, it was always under duress, because a god was pursuing them, but Phega turned into a tree voluntarily. She did it from the moment she entered her teens. It was not easy, and it took a deal of practice, but she kept at it. She would go into the fields beyond the manor house where she lived, and there she would put down roots, spread her arms, and say, "For you I shall spread out my arms." Then she would become a tree.

She did this because she was in love with the sun. The people who looked after her when she was a child told her that the sun loved the trees above all other living things. Phega concluded that this must be so from the way most trees shed their leaves in winter when the sun was unable to attend to them very much. As Phega could not remember a time when the sun had not been more to her than mother, father, or life itself, it followed that she had to become a tree.

At first she was not a very good tree. The trunk of her tended to bulge at hips and breast and was usually an improbable brown color. The largest number of branches she could achieve was four or five at the most. These stood out at unconvincing angles and grew large, pallid leaves in a variety of shapes. She strove with these defects valiantly, but for a long time it always seemed that when she got her trunk to look more natural, her branches were fewer and more misshapen, and when she grew halfway decent branches, either her trunk relapsed or her leaves were too large or too yellow.

"Oh, sun"—she sighed—"do help me to be more pleasing to you." Yet it seemed unlikely that the sun was even attending to her. "But he will!" Phega said, and driven by hope and yearning, she continued to stand in the field, striving to spread out more plausible branches. Whatever shape they were, she could still revel in the sun's impartial warmth on them and in the searching strength of her roots reaching into the earth. Whether the sun was attending or not, she knew the deep peace of a tree's long, wordless thoughts. The rain was pure delight to her, instead of the necessary evil it was to other people, and the dew was a marvel.

The following spring, to her delight, she achieved a reasonable shape, with a narrow, lissome trunk and a cloud of spread branches, not unlike a fruiting tree. "Look at me, sun," she said. "Is this the kind of tree you like?"

The sun glanced down at her. Phega stood at that instant

between hope and despair. It seemed that he attended to the wordless words.

But the sun passed on, beaming, not unkindly, to glance at the real apple trees that stood on the slope of the hill.

I need to be different in some way, Phega said to herself.

She became a girl again and studied the apple trees. She watched them put out big pale buds and saw how the sun drew those buds open to become leaves and white flowers. Choking with the hurt of rejection, she saw the sun dwelling lovingly on those flowers, which made her think at first that flowers were what she needed. Then she saw that the sun drew those flowers on, quite ruthlessly, until they died, and that what came after were green blobs that turned into apples.

"Now I know what I need," she said.

It took a deal of hard work, but the following spring she was able to say, "Look at me, sun. For you I shall hold out my arms budded with growing things," and spread branches full of white blossom that she was prepared to force on into fruit.

This time, however, the sun's gaze fell on her only in the way it fell on all living things. She was very dejected. Her yearning for the sun to love her grew worse.

"I still need to be different in some way," she said.

That year she studied the sun's ways and likings as she had never studied them before. In between she was a tree. Her yearning for the sun had grown so great that when she was in human form, it was as if she were less than half alive. Her parents and other human company were shadowy to her. Only when she was a tree with her arms spread to the sunlight did she feel she was truly in existence.

As that year took its course, she noticed that the place the sun first touched unfailingly in the morning was the top of the hill beyond the apple trees. And it was the place where he lingered last at sunset. Phega saw this must be the place the sun loved best. So, though it was twice as far from the manor, Phega went daily to the top of that hill and took root there. This meant that she had an hour more of the sun's warm company to spread her boughs into, but the situation was not otherwise as good as the fields. The top of the hill was very dry. When she put down roots, the soil was thin and tasted peculiar. And there was always a wind up there. Phega found she grew bent over and rather stunted.

"But what more can I do?" she said to the sun. "For you I shall spread out my arms, budded with growing things, and root within the ground you warm, accepting what that brings."

The sun gave no sign of having heard, although he continued to linger on the top of the hill at the beginning and end of each day. Phega would walk home in the twilight considering how she might grow roots that were adapted to the thin soil and pondering ways and means to strengthen her trunk against the wind. She walked slightly bent over and her skin was pale and withered.

Up till now Phega's parents had indulged her and not interfered. Her mother said, "She's very young." Her father agreed and said, "She'll get over this obsession with rooting herself in time." But when they saw her looking pale and withered and walking with a stoop, they felt the time had come to intervene. They said to one another, "She's old enough to marry now, and she's ruining her looks."

The next day they stopped Phega before she left the manor on her way to the hill. "You must give up this pining and rooting," her mother said to her. "No girl ever found a husband by being out in all weathers like this."

And her father said, "I don't know what you're after with this tree nonsense. I mean, we can all see you're very good at it, but it hasn't got much bearing on the rest of life, has it? You're our only child, Phega. You have the future of the manor to consider. I want you married to the kind of man I can trust to look after the place when I'm gone. That's not the kind of man who's going to want to marry a tree."

Phega burst into tears and fled away across the fields and up the hill.

"Oh, dear!" her father said guiltily. "Did I go too far?"

"Not at all," said her mother. "I would have said it if you hadn't. We must start looking for a husband for her. Find the right man, and this nonsense will slide out of her head from the moment she claps eyes on him."

It happened that Phega's father had to go away on business, anyway. He agreed to extend his journey and look for a suitable husband for Phega while he was away. His wife gave him a good deal of advice on the subject, ending with a very strong directive not to tell any prospective suitor that Phega had this odd habit of becoming a tree—at least not until the young man was safely proved to be interested in marriage, anyway. And as soon as her husband was away from the manor, she called two servants she could trust and told them to follow Phega and watch how she turned into a tree. "For it must be a process we can put a stop to somehow," she said, "and if you can find out how we can stop her for good, so much the better."

Phega, meanwhile, rooted herself breathlessly into the shallow soil at the top of the hill. "Help me," she called out to the sun. "They're talking of marrying me and the only one I love is you!"

The sun pushed aside an intervening cloud and considered her with astonishment. "Is this why you so continually turn into a tree?" he said.

Phega was too desperate to consider the wonder of actually, at last, talking to the sun. She said, "All I do, I do in the remote, tiny hope of pleasing you and causing you to love me as I love you."

"I had no idea," said the sun, and he added, not unkindly, "but I do love everything according to its nature, and your nature is human. I might admire you for so skillfully becoming a tree, but that is, when all is said and done, only an imitation of a tree. It follows that I love you better as a human." He beamed and was clearly about to pass on.

Phega threw herself down on the ground, half woman and half tree, and wept bitterly, thrashing her branches and rolling back and forth. "But I love you," she cried out. "You are the light of the world, and I love you. I *have* to be a tree because then I have no heart to ache for you, and even as a tree I ache at night because you aren't there. Tell me what I can do to make you love me."

The sun paused. "I do not understand your passion," he said. "I have no wish to hurt you, but this is the truth: I cannot love you as an imitation of a tree."

A small hope came to Phega. She raised the branches of her head. "Could you love me if I stopped pretending to be a tree?"

"Naturally," said the sun, thinking this would appease her. "I would love you according to your nature, human woman."

"Then I make a bargain with you," said Phega. "I will stop pretending and you will love me."

"If that is what you want," said the sun, and went on his way.

Phega shook her head free of branches and her feet from the ground and sat up, brooding, with her chin on her hands. That was how her mother's servants found her and watched her warily from among the apple trees. She sat there for hours. She had bargained with the sun as a person might bargain for her very life, out of the desperation of her love, and she needed to work out a plan to back her bargain with. It gave her slight shame that she was trying to trap such a being as the sun, but she knew that was not going to stop her. She was beyond shame.

There is no point imitating something that already exists, she said to herself, because that is pretending to be that thing. I will have to be some kind that is totally new.

Phega came down from the hill and studied trees again. Because of the hope her bargain had given her, she studied in a new way, with passion and depth, all the time her father was away. She ranged far afield to the forests in the valleys beyond the manor, where she spent days among the trees, standing still as a tree, but in human shape—which puzzled her mother's servants exceedingly—listening to the creak of their growth and every rustle of every leaf, until she knew them as trees knew other trees and comprehended the abiding restless stillness of them. The entire shape of a tree against the sky became open to her, and she came to know all their properties. Trees had power. Willows had pithy centers and grew fast; they caused sleep. Elder was pithy, too; it could give powerful protection but had a touchy nature and should be treated politely. But the oak and the ash, the giant trees that held their branches closest to the sun's love, had the greatest power of all. Oak was constancy, and ash was change. Phega studied these two longest and most respectfully.

"I need the properties of both these," she said.

She carried away branches of leafing twigs to study as she walked home, noting the join of twig to twig and the way the leaves were fastened on. Evergreens impressed her by the way they kept leaves for the sun even in winter, but she was soon sure they did it out of primitive parsimony. Oaks, on the other hand, had their leaves tightly knotted on by reason of their strength.

"I shall need the same kind of strength," Phega said.

As autumn drew on, the fruiting trees preoccupied her, since it was clear that it was growth and fruition the sun seemed most to love. They all, she saw, partook of the natures of both oaks and elders, even hawthorn, rowan, and hazel. Indeed, many of them were related to the lowlier bushes and fruiting plants, but the giant trees that the sun most loved were more exclusive in their pedigrees.

"Then I shall be like the oak," Phega said, "but bear better fruit."

Winter approached, and trees were felled for firewood. Phega was there, where the foresters were working, anxiously inspecting the rings of the sawn trunk and interrogating the very sawdust. This mystified the servants who were following her. They asked the foresters if they had any idea what Phega was doing.

The foresters shook their heads and said, "She is not quite sane, but we know she is very wise."

The servants had to be content with this. At least after that they had an easier time, for Phega was mostly at home in the manor examining the texture of the logs for the fires. She studied the bark on the outside and then the longwise grains and the roundwise rings of the interior, and she came to an important conclusion: an animal stopped growing when it had attained a certain shape, but a tree did not.

"I see now," she said, "that I have by no means finished growing." And she was very impatient because winter had put a stop to all growth, so that she had to wait for spring to study its nature.

In the middle of winter her father came home. He had found the perfect husband for Phega and was anxious to tell Phega and her mother all about the man. This man was a younger son of a powerful family, he said, and he had been a soldier for some years, during which time he had distinguished himself considerably and gained a name for sense and steadiness. Now he was looking for a wife to marry and settle down with. Though he was not rich, he was not poor either, and he was on good terms with the wealthier members of his family. It was, said Phega's father, a most desirable match.

Phega barely listened to all this. She went away to look at the latest load of logs before her father had finished speaking. He may not ever come here, she said to herself, and if he does, he will see I am not interested and go away again.

"Did I say something wrong?" her father asked her mother. "I had hoped to show her that the man has advantages that far outweigh the fact that he is not in his first youth."

"No—it's just the way she is," said Phega's mother. "Have you invited the man here?"

"Yes, he is coming in the spring," her father said. "His name is Evor. Phega will like him."

Phega's mother was not entirely sure of this. She called the servants she had set to follow Phega to her privately and asked them what they had found out. "Nothing," they said. "We think she has given up turning into a tree. She has never so much as put forth a root while we are watching her."

"I hope you are right," said Phega's mother. "But I want you to go on watching her, even more carefully than before. It is now extremely important that we know how to stop her becoming a tree if she ever threatens to do so."

The servants sighed, knowing they were in for another dull and difficult time. And they were not mistaken because, as soon as the first snowdrops appeared, Phega was out in the countryside studying the way things grew. As far as the servants were concerned, she would do nothing but sit or stand for hours watching a bud, or a tree, or a nest of mice or birds. As far as Phega was concerned, it was a long fascination as she divined how cells multiplied again and again and at length discovered that while animals took food from solid things, plants took their main food from the sun himself. "I think that may be the secret at last," she said.

This puzzled the servants, but they reported it to Phega's mother all the same. Her answer was, "I *thought* so. Be ready to bring her home the instant she shows a root or a shoot."

The servants promised to do this, but Phega was not ready yet. She was busy watching the whole course of spring growth transform the forest. So it happened that Evor arrived to meet his prospective bride and Phega was not there. She had not even noticed that everyone in the manor was preparing a feast in Evor's honor. Her parents sent messengers to the forest to fetch her, while Evor first kicked his heels for several hours in the hall and finally, to their embarrassment, grew impatient and went out into the yard. There he wondered whether to order his horse and leave.

I conclude from this delay, he said to himself, that the girl is not willing, and one thing I do not want is a wife I have to force. Nevertheless, he did not order his horse. Though Phega's parents had been at pains to keep from him any suggestion that Phega was not as other girls were, he had been unable to avoid hearing rumors on the way. For by this time Phega's fame was considerable. The first gossip he heard, when he was farthest away, was that his prospective bride was a witch. This he had taken for envious persons' way of describing wisdom and pressed on. As he came nearer, rumor had it that she was very wise, and he felt justified—though the latest rumor he had heard, when he was no more than ten miles from the manor, was that Phega was at least a trifle mad. But each rumor came accompanied by statements about Phega's appearance which were enough to make him tell himself that it was too late to turn back, anyway. This kept him loitering in the yard. He wanted to set eyes on her himself.

He was still waiting when Phega arrived, walking in through the gate quickly but rather pensively. It was a gray day, with the sun hidden, and she was sad. But, she told herself, I may as well see this suitor and tell him there was no point in his coming and get it over with. She knew her parents were responsible and did not blame the man at all.

Evor looked at her as she came and knew that rumor had understated her looks. The time Phega had spent studying had improved her health and brought her from girl to young woman. She was beautiful. Evor saw that her hair was the color of beer when you hold a glass of it to the light. She was wearing a dress of smooth silver-gray material which showed that her body under it when she moved was smooth-muscled and sturdy—and he liked sturdy women. Her overgarment was a curious light, bright green and floated away from her arms, revealing them to be very round and white. When he looked at her face, which was both round and long, he saw beauty there, but he also saw that she was very wise. Her eyes were gray. He saw a wildness there contained by the deep calm of long, long thought and a capacity to drink in knowledge. He was awed. He was lost.

Phega, for her part, tore her thoughts from many hours of standing longing among the great trees and saw a wiry man of slightly over middle height, who had a bold face with a keen stare to it. She saw he was not young. There was gray to his beard—which always grew more sparsely than he would have liked, though he had combed it carefully for the occasion—and some gray in his hair, too. She noticed his hair particularly because he had come to the manor in light armor, to show his status as a soldier and a commander, but he was carrying his helmet politely in the crook of his arm. His intention was to show himself as a polished man of the world. But Phega saw him as iron-colored all over. He made her think of an ax, except that he seemed to have such a lot of hair. She feared he was brutal.

Evor said, "My lady!" and added as a very awkward after-thought, "I came to marry you." As soon as he had said this, it struck him as so wrong and presumptuous a thing to say to a woman like this one that he hung his head and stared at her feet, which were bare and, though beautiful, stained green with the grass she had walked through. The sight gave him courage.

He thought that those feet were human after all, so it followed that the rest of her was, and he looked up at her eyes again. "What a thing to say!" he said.

He smiled in a flustered way. Phega saw that he was somewhat snaggle-toothed, not to speak of highly diffident in spite of his gray and military appearance, and possibly in awe of her. She could not see how he could be in awe of her, but his uneven teeth made him a person to her. Of a sudden he was not just the man her parents had procured for her to marry, but another person like her, with feelings like those Phega had herself. Good gods! she thought, in considerable surprise. This is a person I could maybe love after all, if it were not for the sun. And she told him politely that he was very welcome.

They went indoors together and presently sat down to the feast. There Evor got over his awe a little, enough to attempt to talk to Phega. And Phega, knowing he had feelings to be hurt, answered the questions he asked and asked things in return. The result was that before long, to the extreme delight of Phega's parents, they were talking of his time at war and of her knowledge and laughing together as if they were friends—old friends. Evor's wonder and joy grew. Long before the feast was over, he knew he could never love any other woman now. The effect of Phega on him was like a physical tie, half glorious, half painful, that bound him to respond to every tiny movement of her hand and every flicker of her lashes.

Phega found—and her surprise increased—that she was comfortable with Evor. But however amicably they talked, it was still as if she was only half alive in the sun's absence— though it was an easy half life—and, as the evening wore on, she felt increasingly confined and trapped. At first she assumed that this feeling was simply due to her having spent so much of the past year out of doors. She was so used to having nothing but the sky with the sun in it over her head that she often did find the manor roof confining. But now it was like a cage over her head. And she realized that her growing liking for Evor was causing it.

If I don't take care, she said to herself, I shall forget the bargain I made with the sun and drift into this human contract. It is almost too late already. I must act at once.

Thinking this, she said her good-nights and went away to sleep.

Evor remained, talking jubilantly with Phega's parents. "When I first saw her," he said, "I thought things were hopeless. But now I think I have a chance. I think she likes me."

Phega's father agreed, but Phega's mother said, "I'm sure she likes you all right, but—I caught a look in her eye—this may not be enough to make her marry you."

Saying this, Phega's mother touched on something Evor had sensed and feared himself. His jubilation turned ashy; indeed, he felt as if the whole world had been taken by drought; there was no moisture or virtue in it anywhere from pole to pole. "What more can I do?" he said, low and slow.

"Let me tell you something," said Phega's mother.

"Yes," Phega's father broke in eagerly. "Our daughter has a strange habit of—"

"She is," Phega's mother interrupted swiftly, "under an enchantment which we are helpless to break. Only a man who truly loves her can break it."

Hope rose in Evor, as violent as Phega's hope when she bargained with the sun. "Tell me what to do," he said.

Phega's mother considered all the reports her servants had brought her. So far as she knew, Phega had never once turned into a tree all the time her father was away. It was possible she had lost the art. This meant that with luck, Evor need never know the exact nature of her daughter's eccentricity. "Sometime soon," she said, "probably at dawn, my daughter will be compelled by the enchantment to leave the manor. She will go to the forest or the hill. She may be compelled to murmur words to herself. You must follow her when she goes, and as soon as you see her standing still, you must take her in your arms and kiss her. In this way you will break the spell, and she will become your faithful wife ever after." And, Phega's mother told herself, this was very likely what would happen. For, she thought, as soon as he kisses her, my daughter will discover that there are certain pleasures to be had from behaving naturally. Then we can all be comfortable again.

"I shall do exactly what you say," said Evor, and he was so uplifted with hope and gratitude that his face was nearly handsome.

All that night he kept watch. He could not have slept, anyway. Love roared in his ears, and longing choked him. He went over and over the things Phega had said and each individual beauty of her face and body as she said these things, and when, in the dawn, he saw her stealing through the hall to the door, there was a moment when he could not move. She was even more lovely than he remembered.

Phega softly unbarred the door and crossed the yard to unbar the gate. Evor pulled himself together and followed. They walked out across the fields in the white time before sunrise, Phega pacing very upright, with her eyes on the sky where the sun would appear, and Evor stealing after. He softly took off his armor piece by piece as he followed her and laid it down carefully in case it should clatter and alarm her.

Up the hill Phega went, where she stood like one entranced, watching the gold rim of the sun come up. And such was Evor's awe that he loitered a little in the apple trees, admiring her as she stood.

"Now," Phega said, "I have come to fulfill my bargain, sun, since I fear this is the last time I shall truly want to." What she did then, she had given much thought to. It was not the way she had been accustomed to turn into a tree before. It was far more thorough. For she put down careful roots, driving each of her toes downward and outward and then forcing them into a network of fleshy cables to make the most of the thin soil at the top of the hill. "Here," she said, "I root within the soil you warm."

Evor saw the ground rise and writhe and low branches grow from her insteps to bury themselves also. "Oh, no!" he cried out. "Your feet were beautiful as they were!" And he began to climb the hill toward her.

Phega frowned, concentrating on the intricacy of feathery rootlets. "But they were not the way I wanted them," she said, and she wondered vaguely why he was there. But by then she was putting forth her greatest effort, which left her little attention to spare. Slowly, once her roots were established, she began to coat them with bark before insects could damage them. At the same time, she set to work on her trunk, growing swiftly, grain by growing grain. "Increased by yearly rings," she murmured.

As Evor advanced, he saw her body elongate, coating itself with mat pewter-colored bark as it grew, until he could barely pick out the outline of limbs and muscles inside it. It was like watching a death. "Don't!" he said. "Why are you *doing* this? You were lovely before!"

"I was like all human women," Phega answered, resting before her next great effort. "But when I am finished, I shall be a wholly new kind of tree." Having said that, she turned her attention to the next stage, which she was expecting to enjoy. Now she stretched up her arms, and the hair of her head, yearning into the warmth of the climbing sun, and made it all into limblike boughs, which she coated like the rest of her, carefully, with dark silver bark. "For you I shall hold out my arms," she said.

Evor saw her, tree-shaped and twice as tall as himself, and cried out, "Stop!" He was afraid to touch her in this condition. He knelt at her roots in despair.

"I can't stop now," Phega told him gently. She was gathering herself for her final effort, and her mind was on that, though the tears she heard breaking his voice did trouble her a little. She put that trouble out of her head. This was the difficult part. She had already elongated every large artery of her body, to pass through her roots and up her trunk and into her boughs. Now she concentrated on lifting her veins, and every nerve with them, without disturbing the rest, out to the ends of her branches, out and up, up and out, into a mass of living twigs, fine-growing and close as her own hair. It was impossible. It hurt—she had not thought it would hurt so much—but she was lifting, tearing her veins, thrusting her nerve ends with them, first into the innumerable fine twigs, then into even further particles to make long, sharp buds.

Evor looked up as he crouched and saw the great tree surging and thrashing above him. He was appalled at the effort. In the face of this gigantic undertaking he knew he was lost and forgotten, and besides, it was presumptuous to interfere with such willing agony. He saw her strive and strive again to force those sharp buds open. "If you must be a tree," he shouted above the din of her lashing branches, "take me with you somehow, at least!"

"Why should you want that?" Phega asked with wooden lips that had not yet quite closed, just where her main boughs parted.

Evor at last dared to clasp the trunk with its vestigial limbs showing. He shed tears on the gray bark. "Because I love you. I want to be with you."

Trying to see him forced her buds to unfurl, because that was where her senses now were. They spread with myriad shrill agonies, like teeth cutting, and she thought it had killed her, even while she was forcing further nerves and veins to the undersides of all her pale viridian leaves. When it was done, she was all alive and raw in the small hairs on the undersides of those leaves and in the symmetrical ribs of vein on the shiny upper sides, but she could sense Evor crouching at her roots now. She was grateful to him for forcing her to the necessary pain. Her agony responded to his. He was a friend. He had talked of love, and she understood that. She retained just enough of the strength it had taken to change to alter him, too, to some extent, though not enough to bring him beyond the animal kingdom. The last of her strength was reserved for putting forth small pear-shaped fruit covered with wiry hairs, each containing four triangular nuts. Then, before the wooden gap that was her mouth had entirely closed, she murmured, "Budding with growing things."

She rested for a while, letting the sun harden her leaves to a dark shiny green and ripen her fruit a little. Then she cried wordlessly to the sun, "Look! Remember our bargain. I am an entirely new kind of tree—as strong as an oak, but I bear fruit that everything can eat. Love me. Love me now!" Proudly she shed some of her three-cornered nuts onto the hilltop.

"I see you," said the sun. "This is a lovely tree, but I am not sure what you expect me to do with you."

"Love me!" she cried.

"I do," said the sun. "There is no change in me. The only difference is that I now feed you more directly than I feed that animal at your feet. It is the way I feed all trees. There is nothing else I can do."

Phega knew the sun was right and that her bargain had been her own illusion. It was very bitter to her; but she had made a change that was too radical to undo now, and besides, she was discovering that trees do not feel things very urgently. She settled back for a long, low-key sort of contentment, rustling her leaves about to make the best of the sun's heat on them. It was like a sigh.

After a while a certain activity among her roots aroused a mild arboreal curiosity in her. With senses that were rapidly atrophying, she perceived a middle-sized iron-gray animal with a sparse bristly coat, which was diligently applying its long snout to the task of eating her three-cornered nuts. The animal was decidedly snaggle-toothed. It was lean and had a sharp corner to the center of its back, as if that was all that remained of a wiry man's military bearing. It seemed to sense her attention, for it began to rub itself affectionately against her gray trunk, which still showed vestiges of rounded legs within it.

Ah, well, thought the tree, and considerately let fall another shower of beech mast for it.

That was long ago. They say that Phega still stands on the hill. She is one of the beech trees that stand on the hill that always holds the last rays of the sun, but so many of the trees in that wood are so old that there is no way to tell which one she is. All the trees show vestiges of limbs in their trunks, and all are given at times to inexplicable thrashings in their boughs, as if in memory of the agony of Phega's transformation. In the autumn their leaves turn the color of Phega's hair and often fall only in spring, as though they cling harder than most leaves in honor of the sun.

There is nothing to eat their nuts now. The wild boar vanished from there centuries ago, though the name stayed. The maps usually call the place Boar's Hill.

THE FLUFFY PINK TOADSTOOL

Mother was always having crazes. Since she was a strong-minded lady, this meant that the rest of the family had the crazes too—until, that is, Father put his foot down.

This particular craze started as a Hand-Made craze. About the beginning of the summer holidays, Mother suddenly decided that they were going to do without things which were made in factories. "We are going to use," she declared, "things which are made by people who loved every stitch and nail as they made them."

This meant that there was suddenly almost no furniture in the house, except the Persian rug in the living room and the stool Paul had made in Woodwork. The stool wobbled. Paul explained that this was because he had *not* loved every nail as he made it. He still had the bruises. Father told him to shut up, or they would have nothing to sit on at all.

After that, Mother threw away most of their clothes. The clothes she got instead were handwoven and large, and in peculiar colors. Paul was glad it was the holidays, because he would not have dared go to school in them. Nina wept bitterly. Mother had thrown away her pink fluffy slippers, because they were made in a factory. Nina loved those slippers. They had pink fluffy bobbles on the front, which Nina stroked every night before she went to sleep. Father raised an outcry too, and refused to go to the office in his new trousers. They were baggy, green sackcloth sort of things, with pink stripes round the legs. Mother let him keep a pair of office trousers on condition he wore the baggy ones at weekends. She made all of them wear flat, handmade sandals that fell off when they walked.

The only one who did not mind was Tim. He was too young to care. He wore his floppy, purple tunic quite happily and, when his sandals fell off, he ran about barefoot, until the soles of his feet were as hard as leather, only rather more yellow. He was fascinated by the clothes Mother wore, too. Mother got a long, long skirt, which looked like dirty lace curtains. Tim found he could see Mother's legs walking through the skirt. He followed her about, watching for the moment when she bent down and the net-curtain trailed on the floor. When she stood up again, her feet always went walking up the front of her skirt inside, and she had to stop and walk backward.

Tim was the only one who did not mind going shopping with Mother that summer. Because, naturally, Mother began insisting on Natural Food. She would trail her gray net skirt into the bread shop, with her handmade basket on her arm, and ask sharply: "Is your bread stone-ground?"

"Oh no," said the lady. "It's made of flour. Wheat ground, you know."

Mother had almost no sense of humor. She made her own bread after that, and it *was* rather like stones that had been ground.

In the butcher's she asked: "Has this meat lived a natural life?"

"About as natural as yours, lady," the butcher said crossly.

Mother swept out of the butcher's and did not buy meat again. She did most of her shopping in the vegetable shop instead, where she would prod each vegetable and each fruit and ask: "Has this been grown with natural manure?"

The greengrocer, who found Mother a valuable customer, always assured her that everything was left entirely to Nature. All the same, Mother never bought anything from abroad, because she was not sure that foreigners had the right, Natural ideas.

Soon, there was almost as little food in the house as there was furniture. There were a great many nuts and raisins, because Mother had not noticed that these things come from foreign parts, but almost the only ordinary food was cornflakes. Mother kept on buying cornflakes because it said on the packet: *Made from finest natural ingredients.* But one can get tired of cornflakes quite easily. Father was so tired of them that he used to take all three children for secret trips to the chip shop. Usually they stopped at the ice-cream van on the corner on the way home, and came back feeling much more satisfied.

It had been a very sunny summer. By the end of it, the

brambles at the bottom of the garden were full of ripe black-berries. Mother became inspired. "We should be living off the Fruits of the Earth," she said. "There is nothing more Natural or more nutritious." She bought a number of books to find out just what Fruits of the Earth were most good for you, and grew very excited. "We must all go out into the woods and pick things," she said.

"Good," said Paul, who had by now eaten most of the blackberries in the garden. "I fancy a blackberry tart."

"Even with ground-stone pastry," Nina agreed.

Unfortunately, the nearest woods were ten miles away. Mother would not hear of going by car, because that was not Natural. Her first idea was that they should all cycle there, but she had to give that up when her gray net skirt kept get-ting tangled in bicycle chain. So she said they must all walk.

"Nonsense," said Father. "Tim can't possibly walk twenty miles."

"Besides," muttered Paul, "people grew quite naturally from apes, so everything people do is natural anyway, even cars."

Before there could be an argument, Father put Tim in the car and told the other two to get in as well. Mother gave in with dignity, and they all drove to the woods.

There, Mother became strong-minded again. She refused to let them pick blackberries, because there were blackberries at home. She gave Paul and Nina a handmade basket each and set them to pick sloes. She set Father to gathering wild onions on a sunny bank. She herself, with Tim trotting beside her, wandered through the shadier parts of the wood with a shiny new book called *Toadstools for*

Dinner open in front of her nose. From time to time she would pounce on an earlike fungus growing on a tree. "These are wonderfully nutritious!" she would call out. "You beat them with a hammer, and then they taste almost like turnips."

Tim got the idea. He pattered happily about, bringing Mother yellow toadstools, shiny black fungus, and things like purple mushrooms. Some of his finds even looked like proper mushrooms. Mother looked each one up carefully in her book, and said things like: "Oh yes—but you have to boil those for ten hours," and "Here they are— Oh, put them down at once, Tim! They're deadly poison!"

Meanwhile, Paul and Nina were not very happy picking sloes. First their sandals fell off their feet and their feet got pricked. Then their handwoven clothes seemed too hot. Then too, they soon found that sloe bushes have long spines—sharp ones. Then they tried tasting a sloe each and— Ugh! It was so sour that it made the inside of their mouths ragged.

Father had a better time. He fell asleep on the sunny bank, with a bunch of wild onions draped over his green striped trousers.

He never saw the strange brown face that peered at him through the hedge, and grinned a pitying grin. Shortly, the same face peered through the sloe spines at Nina and Paul. It chuckled, but Nina and Paul did not notice it either. Mother, with her toadstool book in front of her face, never saw or heard anything, even though the face burst into peals of wicked laughter when it looked at her. But Tim saw a crooked hand come out of a bush, with a long brown finger, beckoning. He went where it beckoned. He had a marvellous time. He found a long rope of beautiful shiny red berries. Luckily he dragged the rope along to Mother before he tried to eat the berries. "Look! I found some pretty blackberries."

"Put them down!" Mother screamed. "Those are bryony. They're deadly poison!"

Tim dropped the beautiful berries as if they were red-hot and hurried away, thinking Mother was very angry.

Maybe this was what made Mother decide they had picked enough of the Fruits of the Earth. She picked up her basket of toadstools, called Paul and Nina, and woke Father up. Then nobody could find Tim. They called and shouted until the woods rang.

Finally, Tim came trotting up from a quite unexpected direction. He was smiling broadly and clutching a plastic bag with something bright pink inside.

"What have you got there?" Mother said suspiciously.

"Mushroom," Tim said proudly. "A funny man gave it me, with trousers like Father's."

Father was very cross from sleeping in the sun. He hustled everyone back into the car, and, by the time anyone thought to ask Tim about his funny man, Tim had forgotten. He was only very young.

When they got home, the first thing Mother did was to take the plastic bag in her finger and thumb—with a shudder, because plastic is made in factories—and throw it away. The thing Tim called a mushroom rolled out onto the Persian rug. It was quite round, bright pink, and fluffy like a baby chicken.

"It looks like the bobbles on my slippers!" Nina said. She stroked the toadstool as she used to stroke her slippers. Everyone stroked it. It felt lovely. Mother looked it up in her toadstool book, but it did not seem to be there. So, because she was busy trying to make sloe jam and chopping the wild onions to cook with the other toadstools, she told Paul to throw it away.

The others helped Mother. Mother was determined not to make jam with sugar, because that came from a factory. They were all busy scraping out honey jars and trying to suggest that brown sugar was almost Natural, when Paul came back.

"I can't throw it away," he whispered. "It's grown to the carpet."

It had. Nina and Tim went to look. The round pink ball had put out a firm little stalk and was now growing in the middle of the Persian rug.

"Leave it," said Nina. "It's so pretty."

After that, they were even busier, leaning over the jam pan scooping hundreds of little tiny stones out from the boiling sloes. Nobody thought about the fluffy pink toadstool, until Tim came shouting proudly: "I got *two* mushrooms now!"

He had. There were now two round furry pink toadstool-things growing in the Persian rug.

"I think," Father said doubtfully, "that we ought to throw it away now, before it does that again."

But Tim said it was *his* mushroom. Nina said it was exactly like her slippers now, and Paul said it was interesting. And Mother settled it by rushing in with another toadstool book. "I've found it! It doesn't say it's pink, but I'm sure this is it. It's called Lady's Slipper and I think you can eat it."

Just then, the sloe jam boiled over, and everyone forgot about the two round pink furry toadstools. When they had wiped up all the black, burnt syrup, Paul thought to go and look at them again. There were now four round pink furry toadstools growing in a neat square on the Persian rug. Paul was so interested that he said nothing.

Soon after that, the jam was done. They tasted it. And it was clear that a jar of honey, even mixed with a packet of brown sugar, had not done anything for the sloes. It was acutely, horribly, *uneatably* sour. They all had to clean their teeth. When she had done that, Nina went to look at the pink toadstools. There were now eight of them, almost in a ring.

"I think they double every hour," said Paul.

"Let's look again in an hour," said Nina.

They did, while Mother was cooking the other toadstools for supper. By that time, there were sixteen round pink furry toadstools growing in a proper ring on the Persian rug. But they forgot them again after that, because Mother served the boiled toadstools with the chopped wild onions. Quite a number of them, despite being beaten with a hammer, were as hard to eat as the soles of their handmade sandals. Some of the others did not seem quite as nutritious as Mother's books said they were. Everyone felt rather unwell. But the worst part of the supper was the wild onions. Father, as he chewed them—they had all got used to good, hard chewing that summer—remarked: "Plenty of taste in these onions."

There was indeed plenty of taste. In fact, there was too much. For the rest of the evening nobody could taste anything but wild onion. They could still taste it when they went to bed, and they went to bed rather early, all feeling a little seedy.

Meanwhile, the sixteen round pink furry toadstools quietly became thirty-two round pink furry toadstools. These thirty-two became sixty-four, and these sixty-four . . . All through the night, silently and mysteriously, the round pink furry toadstools doubled

in number, once every hour. Soon there was no room for a ring
of them. Soon . . .

When everyone came down in the morning, still tasting
wild onions, the floor of the living room was a mass of fluffy
pink. Fluffy pink had grown up the walls and was just meeting
in the middle of the ceiling around the light. Fluffy pink had
begun to spread to the kitchen. That was when Father put his
foot down.

Mother, he said, was welcome to any daft ideas she wanted.
But she was to have them on her own. If she tried to make any
of the rest of the family take part in her crazes, Father said, he
would leave, and he would take Tim and Nina and Paul with
him. And, to prove that he meant what he said, he took all three
children out for the day and left Mother to get rid of the toadstools.

Mother's latest craze is playing the violin. But she does it by
herself. If the rest of the family keep all the doors shut, they
hardly notice it at all.

✳ Auntie
Bea's
Day Out ✦

"I shall take the children for a lovely day at the seaside tomorrow," said Auntie Bea.

The children felt miserable. Auntie Bea was huge, with a loud voice. She had been staying with the Pearsons for a week then, and they all felt crushed and cross.

"You needn't bother to drive us, Tom," said Auntie Bea. "I can easily go by bus." This was Auntie Bea's way of telling Mr. Pearson he was to drive them to the seaside.

Mr. Pearson looked very cheerful. "Isn't that lucky? I have to take the car for its inspection tomorrow."

When Auntie Bea decided to do something, she did it. She turned to Mrs. Pearson. "Well, you can help me carry the things, Eileen."

Mrs. Pearson hastily discovered that she was going to the dentist.

"Then Nancy will help," said Auntie Bea. "Nancy's so sensible."

"No, I'm not," said Nancy.

"So that's all right," said Auntie Bea. She never attended to anything the children said. "Nancy can look after Debbie, and Simon can carry the things."

The number of things Auntie Bea needed for a day at the seaside would have been about right if she was going to climb Mount Everest. Mr. Pearson helped her pile them in the hall, in twenty-two separate heaps. Auntie Bea was so afraid of losing or forgetting some of them that she wrote out twenty-two labels, each with their names and address on it, and tied them to the bundles. Meanwhile, Mrs. Pearson cut up four loaves to make the number of sandwiches Auntie Bea thought they would need.

"And little jellies in yogurt cups," Auntie Bea said, racing into the kitchen. "*Such* a good idea!"

Mrs. Pearson was so glad to be getting rid of Auntie Bea for a day that she made them two jellies each.

"I feel like a human sacrifice," Simon said. "How does she think I can carry all that and manage Honey as well?" Honey was due to have puppies any day now. Simon was too anxious about her to leave her behind.

Auntie Bea came downstairs shaking out a vast swimsuit. It was electric blue with shiny orange hearts all over it. Nancy blinked, and wondered what Auntie Bea would look like wearing it.

"That's pretty," said Debbie, who loved bright colors. "I shall make Teddy a swimsuit like that."

"I hope it rains," said Nancy.

Unfortunately, the next day was bright and sunny. But they missed the early bus, because of Teddy and Honey. Debbie had pinned a scarf around Teddy like a nappy, and she had written him a label too: *Deb's Ted wiv care in Emurjunsy fone Millwich 29722.*

As soon as Auntie Bea saw Teddy, she said, "No, dear. We only take things we need today."

Debbie's face took on its most mulish look, and the argument only ended when Auntie Bea saw Honey drooping joylessly on the end of her lead.

"You can't take him, dear. He might have his puppies at any moment!" Just as Auntie Bea never attended to children, she never attended to whether dogs were she's.

That argument was only finished when Simon found he could not carry all his bundles, even without Honey.

"You'll have to leave the stove and the kettle," said Mrs. Pearson, very anxious to see them off.

"In that case, we must take plenty of boiled water!" said Auntie Bea. "Think of the germs!"

So Simon's bundles were repacked and they set off to catch the later bus. Nancy went first with a light load of: one tartan rug, one carrier-bag of sandwiches, a first-aid box, and a bundle of buckets and spades. Auntie Bea sailed behind hung about with: one folding chair, one striped umbrella, three pints of milk, a bag of sweaters, a bag of suntan cream, a packet of sandwiches, two dozen hard-boiled eggs, a complete change of outsize clothes, three books, and a radio. Debbie trotted behind that with: a bundle of towels, a beach ball in a string bag and a basket full of jellies and cake, with Teddy defiantly sitting in it too. A long, long way behind came Simon. He was not sure what was in the rucksack, nor what was in his other six bundles, but he could see thermos flasks sticking out of one and an electric torch out of another. His knees buckled under it all, and Honey kept tangling her lead around them. Honey did not seem happy.

"It will serve him right if he has his puppies in the sea," Auntie Bea said, and counted the bundles to make sure they had remembered them all.

Nothing much happened on the bus ride, except that Honey threatened to be sick. When they got to Millhaven, it was quite late in the morning and already very crowded.

"Crowds, germs!" said Auntie Bea, counting everything again. "We should have caught the early bus." She hoisted up her twelve bundles and set off happily down the steps to the sand, calling, "Don't bother to help with all this. I can manage perfectly."

They struggled after her down the steps and caught her up on the sand.

"Debbie," said Auntie Bea, "you take the umbrella. If Nancy takes the folding chair, I can manage perfectly."

"No, I won't," said Debbie. "It was you brought it."

"Why don't we stop just here?" Nancy asked.

Debbie's refusal brought out the worst in Auntie Bea. She gave a scornful look around at the deck chairs, rugs, and sand castles on the crowded beach, and called out to the man who hired the deck chairs in her loudest, most hooting voice: "My good man, can you direct me to somewhere less crowded?"

The deck chair man scratched his head. "Well, it thins out a bit up there, ma'am, but you can't go in the rocks. Tourists are not allowed on the island."

Auntie Bea stuck up her head indignantly at being called a tourist and set off at a trot where the man pointed, hooting to the children to come along. They plowed after her, making zigzags around the other families, who all stared, because Auntie Bea kept turning around and hooting at them. To the right were the lovely white waves of the sea, rolling, folding, and breaking with a joyful smash, but Auntie Bea would not hear of stopping. Honey, on the other hand, would not walk. She had never seen the sea before. All she knew was that it was the biggest bath in the universe, and she dreaded baths. Simon had a terrible time with her.

Nancy suggested that they stop for the donkeys, and for the swings, and for one of the ice-cream carts. But Auntie Bea just cried out "Germs!" and scudded on. She would not stop until they had left all the people behind, and there was nothing but rocks. There was a kind of road of rocks stretching into the sea and, at the end of the road, an island. It was quite small—only big enough to hold a tuft of trees.

"The very place!" cried Auntie Bea, and went out over the rocks like Steve Ovett winning a race.

Honey, for some reason, was even more afraid of the island than the sea. Simon had to walk backward, dragging her. When he turned around at the end, he found there was a barbed-wire fence round the island and a large notice on the gate: ISLAND ISLAND KEEP OUT.

There was no time to wonder about that. Auntie Bea was already charging through the trees. Simon dragged Honey past another notice: NO TRESPASSERS, and yet another: TRESPASSERS WILL BE SORRY. By that time, Auntie Bea had stopped and he caught up.

"I don't think we ought to be on this island," Nancy was saying.

"Nobody's afraid of three ignorant notices, dear," said Auntie Bea. "We're going to camp here."

Everyone was too tired to protest. They threw down the bundles and thankfully tipped the sand out of their shoes. Honey lay down, panting. She looked rather ill. Auntie Bea prepared to put on her swimsuit. First she spread the rug out. Then she arranged the chair and the screen and the umbrella to make a sort of hut. Finally, she crawled mountainously in to undress.

Nancy and Debbie undressed where they were, and Simon tried to do the same. His shirt was stuck to his back by something sticky and smelling loudly of strawberry.

"I think the jellies have leaked on you," Debbie said, and crawled over to look at the yogurt cups in her basket. The sun had melted every one, and, in the mysterious way things happen at the seaside, every one was half full of sand. Teddy was soaked in strawberry juice. "This is *awful!*" said Debbie, and put Teddy on the branch of a tree to dry.

"Don't grumble, dear," Auntie Bea called out of her hut. "We're having a *lovely* time!"

The island gave a curious shudder. It made them very uneasy.

"Auntie Bea," said Nancy, "I really think we ought to move."

"Nonsense, dear," called Auntie Bea.

At that, the island gave a bigger shudder and a heave. It felt as if they were going over a humpbacked bridge in a car. And everything was different.

There was a strong wind. They were all kneeling or standing on very short grass, shivering. There were no trees. Teddy was hanging in the air above Auntie Bea's hut. They could hear the sound of waves crashing all around in the distance, from which they could tell they were on another, bigger island. But they had no idea where.

Almost at once, a hot man in a beret came panting up the green slope toward them. He was wearing a brown sweater with green patches on the elbows and shoulders. "I say!" he shouted. "You lot can't picnic here! You're right in the middle of a gun range there!"

The umbrella heaved. Auntie Bea appeared, looking larger than ever. She had her skirt around her neck like a poncho. "Don't talk nonsense, my good man," she said. The soldier stared at her, and at Teddy hanging over her head. He gave a sort of swallow. "We leave here over my dead body," said Auntie Bea, and dived back inside her hut.

"That's just what it will be—" the soldier started to say, when the island once more tried to shake them off—if that was what it was doing. There was a jerk, and they were on a small rock in the middle of a lake.

"People don't order me about," Auntie Bea remarked from inside her hut.

There was another jerk, and they were somewhere dark, with water heaving nearby. Honey began to shiver.

"We're having a lovely day!" Auntie Bea asserted, from behind the umbrella.

The island jerked again, quite angrily, and it was freezing

cold, but light enough to see by. There was frost or ice under their bare knees. The frosty space was rather small, and heaving, as if it was floating. The sea was very near, dark green, in frighteningly big waves.

"This is an iceberg," said Nancy, with her teeth chattering. "That's cheating."

"How many more kinds of island are there?" shivered Simon. "No, don't tell me. You'll put ideas in its head. Good dog, Honey."

"Oh!" Debbie shrieked. "Teddy's gone! I want to go home. Teddy!"

Auntie Bea, shielded from the ice by her blanket and screened from the view by her hut, called out, "Don't spoil our lovely day by screaming, dear."

The iceberg jerked, a bob of annoyance. They were on ice still, but this time it was the top of a mountain. Instead of water, they were surrounded by clouds.

"Teddy!" cried Debbie.

"Lovely day," repeated Auntie Bea.

Another jerk instantly flung them into sweltering heat, somewhere low down and steamy. Water bubbled between their toes and brown water slid past a few feet away. Honey growled and Nancy gasped. An unmistakable alligator slid by with the water.

"I agree with Debbie," said Nancy. "I want to go home."

"Can't we shut Auntie Bea up?" Simon whispered. "She keeps annoying it."

"You'll feel better when you're in the water, dears," Auntie Bea called out.

Nancy was still shouting, "No!" when they were pitched

somewhere cooler, crowded among bushes under a tall tree. There seemed to be a river in front of them, and park railings beyond that. A banana skin fell heavily on Simon's head. He looked up to find that the tree was full of interested monkeys. Several of them came down to inspect Auntie Bea's hut.

To Simon's amazement, a small boy was staring at them through the railings. "Hey, Mum," said the small boy, "can I have a picnic on there, too?"

"I want to go home, too," Simon said uncomfortably.

Two of the monkeys had decided that Auntie Bea's umbrella was fun. They tried to take it up the tree with them. Auntie Bea's hand appeared around the edge of it, slapping.

"Don't be so impatient, dears. I'm nearly ready."

The monkeys had barely time to chitter angrily before that island tossed them aside, too. Auntie Bea's hut was suddenly in the middle of a neat flower bed. Debbie was rolling in red geraniums. There was a great deal of noise all around, but it was not water. It sounded like traffic. Simon jumped to his feet. He was on a mound surrounded by cars and lorries. Faces were pressed against the windows of a passing bus, staring at him.

"We're on a traffic island now," he said. "In the middle of a roundabout."

Nancy stood up, too. "What will it think of next? I say, Honey's not here!"

"Ready, dears," called Auntie Bea. She stood up out of her hut in her bathing suit. Simon was gazing around for Honey, but even he was distracted by the sight. Auntie Bea was gigantic. The flowers looked pale beside her. She was like an enormous beach ball, only brighter than a beach ball has any right to be. The people going by in cars could not take their eyes off her. The bus ran into the curb. Two cars drove up onto the flower beds. Brakes squealed and metal clanged all around the roundabout.

Only Debbie was not distracted by the sight. She was fond of bright colors. "This is the roundabout at the end of our road!" she said.

"Quick!" said Nancy.

"Run!" said Simon. "Before she says anything."

They raced down among the flowers. Behind them, Auntie Bea hooted, "I do think cars should be banned on beaches," and vanished from sight—which caused a further pileup of cars.

Nancy, Simon, and Debbie dodged between the cars and ran on, up their road and into their own house.

"Why are you back so soon?" asked Mrs. Pearson. She did not seem to have gone to the dentist. "Where's Auntie Bea?"

She could not understand what had happened. All Debbie could think of was Teddy, last seen floating in the air over a soldier. All Simon could think of was Honey, last seen growling at an alligator. All Nancy could think of was that she was never going near another island—of any kind—as long as she lived. Neither Mr. nor Mrs. Pearson grasped that something truly odd had happened until the phone began to ring.

The first caller was very polite and very high up in the Army. They had Teddy, he said, on an island somewhere in Scotland. Could any of the Pearsons please reveal the secret formula that made Teddy float in the air? Was it anything to do with the strawberry juice Teddy was soaked in? When nobody could tell him what made Teddy float, the high-up man said that it certainly had military importance, and would Debbie mind if they kept Teddy for analysis? They would send a new teddy.

"I want *my* Ted!" Debbie shouted, but the Army said it was impossible.

The next person to phone was a Swiss Mountain Guide, who had found the beach ball on top of a mountain, complete with the label giving their address. He asked if they wanted it back. They never did answer that, because a policeman called just then, looking rather grim and asking to speak to Auntie Bea. She had caused a Breach of the Peace, he said, and left her radio in the middle of Silas Street roundabout. But nobody, of course, knew where Auntie Bea was by then.

Almost straightaway, there was a puzzled phone call from Iceland. A trawler captain had found a bag of Pearson sweaters floating on an iceberg and wondered if there were any survivors from the wreck. Mr. Pearson had just sorted that one out when someone telephoned all the way from South America. His English was not very good, but he seemed to be saying that the water had ruined the battery in the electric torch. But he wanted to assure them that the buckets and spades were quite safe and very useful.

"Ask about Honey," said Simon.

But the person in South America had not seen a dog, nor even a satisfied-looking alligator.

"Where's Auntie Bea, though?" Mrs. Pearson kept asking. It was soon clear that Auntie Bea was still traveling. The Foreign Office phoned next. There was, they said, a mysterious complaint from the Russian Embassy. A basket full of jelly and sand in yogurt cups, with the Pearsons' address on it, had somehow appeared on the conning tower of a Russian submarine. The Russians were holding it for analysis. The Foreign Office wanted to know if they would find anything important in the yogurt cups.

"I don't think so," said Mrs. Pearson weakly. "They—they didn't find my sister as well, did they?"

But Auntie Bea had not been heard of. Nor had she been seen by an excited lady in Greece, who phoned next. This lady wanted the Pearsons to know that she was not so poor that she could not find two dozen hard-boiled eggs for herself, thank you. And she was throwing away the bag of clothes. They were too big for anyone on the island. She rang off before anyone could try to explain.

The American Embassy rang next. Auntie Bea's umbrella had been found in the sea off Honolulu. They wondered if Auntie Bea had been drowned. So did the Pearsons. But since the next two calls were from Sweden and Japan, it began to look as if Auntie Bea was still being jerked from island to island.

Quite late that night, the London Zoo phoned. "It's taken us all this time to trace you," they said, rather injured. "The address fell off on our monkey island. How did you come to leave your dog there, anyway? The monkeys were trying to play with the puppies."

Mr. Pearson said—a little wildly—that he could explain everything. Then he found that the zoo wanted him to collect Honey and her six new puppies at once. They were in the Children's Zoo. Simon was greatly relieved. He went with his father to fetch Honey, and did not mind in the least when Honey was carsick, though Mr. Pearson did.

Meanwhile the others were still answering the telephone, and there was still no news of Auntie Bea. They forgot what a trial Auntie Bea had been and became worried. They had tender, troubled thoughts about where she could be. Nancy feared she was marooned on a desert island like Robinson Crusoe, all alone in her bathing suit. Debbie said she was somewhere where they spoke quite another language. Mrs. Pearson wrung her hands and said she *knew* Bea was in China, under arrest.

Three days later, Auntie Bea rang up herself. "You'll never guess, Tom!" she hooted. "I'm in the Bahamas. I've no idea how I got here, and I've had to borrow money for the phone. You needn't bother to come and get me, Tom. I can manage."

Mr. Pearson thought of all the phone calls, and Debbie still in tears about Teddy and—very crossly—about Honey sick in his clean car. "I'm glad you can manage, Bea," he said. "Come and see us when you get home." And he rang off.

✠ CARRUTHERS ✠

Carruthers was a walking stick for beating Father with.

Elizabeth acquired Carruthers on a visit to Granny, when she was very small. Father had been exploring Granny's attic, and he had found the walking stick there. It was knobby and black, with a silver band just below the curve of the handle. Elizabeth was screaming her head off at the time, but she heard Father telling Aunt Anne about it.

"It belonged to Uncle Bob," said Aunt Anne.

Father frowned, the way he always did if Mother or Aunt Anne expressed an opinion. "No," he said. "It was someone with a much stranger history. What *was* the name? Why is that child screaming?"

Elizabeth was screaming because she did not like dark

chocolate. Granny had given Ruth and Stephanie milk chocolate, but she had given Elizabeth a large slab of black, bitter stuff—quite uneatable—on the grounds that Elizabeth was "a big girl now." Mother did not seem to understand when Elizabeth protested. So she screamed, and Mother and Granny tried to find out what the matter was. Mother thought Elizabeth was ill.

"You ought to be ashamed, a big girl like you!" said Granny. "Look how good your little sisters are!"

Ruth and Stephanie were sitting side by side on the sofa, with the soles of their four shoes sticking neatly up in front of them, eating milk chocolate. They were happy. They liked milk chocolate. Elizabeth threw them a resentful look and screamed on.

"Hush, darling!" said Mother.

"I know it was Uncle Bob's stick," said Aunt Anne.

Father frowned. "It was not. Quiet, Elizabeth!"

"You ought to give the child a good smack and stand her in the corner," Granny said to Mother.

"But I don't think she's well," said Mother.

"Indulgence does no good," said Granny. She turned to Father. "Stephen, it does no good to spoil the child. It's—"

Father waved the walking stick triumphantly at Aunt Anne. "Carruthers!" he said. "That was the name." That was how Elizabeth learned the stick's name.

"—just a rod to beat your own back, Stephen," said Granny. "You must be firm." And that was how Elizabeth learned what Carruthers was for.

She was still screaming. Father seized her arm and ran out of the room with her into the hall, roaring, "How dare you make a noise! How dare you upset Granny!"

Elizabeth snatched at the walking stick he was holding. "Hit him, hit him!" she implored it. "Hit him, Carruthers!"

Carruthers did not hit Father. It would have been hard to do, since Father and Elizabeth were each holding an end of him. Elizabeth was left sitting on the hall carpet, clutching the stick in one hand and the slab of uneatable chocolate in the other, while Father smoothed his hair and reknotted his tie. "And don't come back in here again," he said as he went back to the living room.

Elizabeth sat until the uneatable chocolate had gone melted and slimy. Then it occurred to her that Carruthers might like it. Experimentally, she held the slimy lump toward the hooked end of him.

Carruthers liked it. He was a bit languid and stiff—after all, he had never eaten anything in his life before—but he nuzzled willingly enough at Elizabeth's fingers. Elizabeth sat for a long time, pressing the chocolate against the place where his mouth seemed to be. It looked like a sort of dent in the end of him. Beyond that dent, further up the handle, were two more dents that seemed to be his eyes. Elizabeth thought that Carruthers kept his eyes blissfully closed as he discovered how much he liked chocolate, but, when it was mostly gone, he did once open an eye like a little bright bead and roll it soulfully at Elizabeth. He liked her. Nobody else had ever fed him before.

"I think I shall feed you up and train you," said Elizabeth, "as a rod to beat Father's back."

She was interrupted by Aunt Anne's son, who was called Stephen after Father, who came sauntering in from the garden with his bar of bitter chocolate. He had only managed to eat half of it. "What are you doing?" he asked.

Elizabeth admired Stephen. He was over a year older than she was. "Feeding Carruthers," she said.

"Sticks don't eat," said Stephen, and he demonstrated that they didn't by holding his chocolate against the end of Carruthers. Carruthers had already eaten so much that he could hardly manage another mouthful. Stephen's chocolate simply melted on him, and on Elizabeth too.

When everyone came out into the hall, ready to go home, Granny exclaimed, "Just look at that child! Just look at that stick! They'll have to be washed at once."

"Carruthers doesn't want to be washed," said Elizabeth.

Nevertheless, Granny took them both away and washed them severely. She nearly drowned Carruthers. Elizabeth cried heartily when Granny took him away and propped him in the corner of the landing, ready to go back to the attic. But Granny believed in being firm. She led the weeping Elizabeth out to the car. And, somehow, while everyone was standing around saying good-bye, Carruthers got into the car. Elizabeth found him on the backseat when she got in.

After that, Mother, Ruth, and Stephanie got used to Carruthers going everywhere with Elizabeth. Father did not. "Why does that child have to take her blessed stick to ballet class?" Elizabeth heard him demanding.

"She says it's alive. She has a very vivid imagination, dear," Mother explained.

"What twaddle!" said Father. "She's just trying to be interesting."

"He doesn't like you," Elizabeth explained to Carruthers in a whisper, "because he knows what you're for."

Carruthers did not need to eat very often. The next time he

fed it was a fortnight later, just before bedtime. Elizabeth was sitting dismally in front of her rice pudding from lunch. Father always insisted that everyone ate everything all up, or they had it for tea, then for supper, until it was gone. Stephanie once had the same mashed swede for two days, until Ruth and Elizabeth ate it for her out of pity. Elizabeth could only eat rice pudding by being almost sick. So there she sat, staring at the cold white mush, when Carruthers suddenly unhooked himself from the back of her chair and fell forward into it. There was a bit of slurping, and the rice pudding went.

Thereafter, Carruthers always ate rice pudding, and occasionally swede for Stephanie too. Given a bit of luck, you could hook Carruthers into your plate while Father was not looking, and the food was gone when Father next looked.

After he had fed, in those early days, Carruthers would fall heavily asleep. When he was asleep, he was exactly like any ordinary walking stick. Usually, he hid in the hall stand among the umbrellas when he wanted to sleep, and it was no good trying to disturb him. But as time went on, eating made Carruthers more and more lively. He slithered and clattered about the house so much that Father kept storming upstairs bellowing, "Elizabeth! Stop that confounded noise!" Elizabeth had to take Carruthers out into the woods above the house, so that he could get his exercise.

Stephanie and Ruth loved watching Carruthers in the wood. They and Elizabeth would sit in a row on a log, laughing and applauding. Carruthers climbed trees by winding himself up the trunk in a spiral, and then swung himself from hook to tail through the branches. "Just like a monkey's tail, without the monkey," as Stephanie said. When he felt specially skittish,

Carruthers liked to shoot out from a tree like an arrow, and, instead of falling to the ground, he had a way of folding himself into coils and drifting to an immaculate landing on the earth by the log. Ruth always applauded this furiously. Carruthers went hopping and skipping about in delight, like a rather small pogo stick.

He was shy of other children. One day, a group of boys came to play in the wood and ran about all the trodden paths and plunged into all the bushes, shouting. Carruthers simply hooked himself to the tree he happened to be in and hung there. Nothing Elizabeth said would make him show any sign of life.

"It's lunchtime," said Ruth. "Come on, Stephanie, or we'll get into trouble."

Ruth and Stephanie went. Elizabeth lingered. But the boys were still there, and Carruthers still would not budge. At last, Elizabeth was too scared of what Father would say to stay any longer. She had to leave Carruthers hanging there. She was very relieved to find him asleep in the umbrella stand after lunch.

After that, Elizabeth took Carruthers out to the wood every day on her way to school and left him there. He always came back by himself—how, Elizabeth never knew. Carruthers would not say. He was very surly altogether about the way Elizabeth went to school without him.

"You take that other stick," he complained in his small grunting voice.

"That's my hockey stick," Elizabeth explained. "It's not alive, like you. I only take it because I have to."

Carruthers did not answer. He did not speak much at the best of times. When he did, it was mostly short sentences—

most of them rather self-centered. He said, "Don't forget *me*,"
if Elizabeth was going anywhere except to school, and, "Leave
me alone," if he was asleep in the umbrella stand. His favorite
short sentence was "I'm hungry." He said that increasingly
often as time went on. Elizabeth learned to leap wide awake in
the middle of the night, whenever the small grunting voice said
plaintively in her ear, "I'm *hungry*."

"All right, all right," she would say. "I'll go down and get
some biscuits. But you're to be quiet while I do." She knew
Carruthers was quite capable of helping himself to tomorrow's
pudding or Stephanie's birthday cake, if she left him to look for
food on his own. As it was, Mother noticed that biscuits were
vanishing.

"Darling, you should ask if you want biscuits," she said.

"Carruthers got hungry in the night," Elizabeth said.

"Well, if he does it once more I shall have to tell Father,"
Mother answered. She said it in an indulgent way which made
Elizabeth suspect Mother believed it was really Elizabeth who
got hungry. Elizabeth tried to make Carruthers tell Mother it
was him. But Carruthers only drooped his hooked head shyly
and kept his eyes tight shut until Mother had gone.

One way and another, as the years went by, there were a number of ways in which Carruthers annoyed Elizabeth. His
appetite was one. Another was that he never, ever, despite all
the good food and exercise he had, made any move to hit
Father. Another was that Carruthers liked ballet.

Elizabeth hated ballet lessons worse than she hated rice
pudding. Ballet was a weekly torture to her. She was clumsy, she
could not keep in time with the music, and the ballet positions

made her arms and legs ache. The ballet teacher thought she was stupid, and said so. Mother looked sad and anxious. The worst of it was that Ruth and Stephanie were good at ballet. Ruth was very good. Stephanie did not love dancing the way Ruth did, but she was strong, limber, and willing, and she was soon much better at it than Elizabeth. Ruth and Stephanie both looked trim and lissom in pink shoes and black leotards. Elizabeth looked a fright. Her calves bulged above the pink shoes, her stomach bulged out of the leotard, and, when she put on the pink fluffy jacket you wore to keep warm, it made her look like an apewoman.

"You look like an apewoman," Ruth said, and laughed. This did not help Elizabeth to love ballet any better.

Carruthers loved ballet. He picked up a great deal while he was propped in the corner of the dance room watching Elizabeth flop and struggle about on the polished floor. At night, he hooked himself to the end of Elizabeth's bed and tried to do barre exercises. It is not easy to do ballet if you have no arms and legs, but this did not deter Carruthers. He stretched straight out from the bed rail to do the arm positions with his tail end. Then he collapsed gracefully into a plié, rose, and sank again. After that, he let go of the bed and went hopping around the room in one-legged jetés, pirouettes, and arabesques. He was very ingenious about them. He had picked up the music Elizabeth danced to, along with the steps, and he would hum Handel's *Water Music* in his tinny growl as he capered. Elizabeth squealed with laughter, which very often had her in trouble with Father.

Then came the dreadful day when Ruth won a scholarship to a London academy to train as a dancer. Father was delighted, but it occurred to him to wonder why Elizabeth and Stephanie had not won scholarships too. He discovered that Elizabeth was two grades behind even Stephanie. Elizabeth felt as if a volcano had erupted under her.

When Father had smoothed his hair and straightened his tie and gone away, Mother came to find Elizabeth, who was in her bedroom, sullenly hugging Carruthers.

"Darling," Mother said, with her sad and anxious look, "you must try harder at ballet. Girls must learn to be graceful."

"I hate ballet," Elizabeth said. "You know I do. And I'm not graceful, so why should I learn to be?"

"Father has very strong opinions—" Mother began.

"Bother and blast Father's opinions!" Elizabeth shrieked. "What about *your* opinions? You know I'm bad at ballet, but you're too feeble to *say*!" Mother looked so hurt and shocked that Elizabeth said hastily: "Carruthers says you're feeble."

Mother went to the door, more shocked than ever. "Darling, I can't stay and listen to nonsense."

"And Carruthers says Father's a—a bloodthirsty tyrant!" Elizabeth bawled at the closing door.

As the door shut behind Mother, Carruthers struggled out of Elizabeth's arms and stood upright in front of her, hopping gently up and down in his indignation. "I never said that!" he said. "Tell her I never said it."

"No, I shan't," said Elizabeth. "It's true."

"It may be true, but I never said it," Carruthers insisted.

"You only didn't say it because you like ballet," Elizabeth retorted. "When are you going to hit Father?"

Carruthers squirmed sulkily. "All in good time."

"Soon," said Elizabeth.

"Why?" said Carruthers.

"Because he deserves it," said Elizabeth.

They separated, both in furious sulks. Carruthers stayed in the umbrella stand, and Elizabeth left him there. He would not speak to her, or eat, and he never seemed to move. But he was always in the car when it was time to go to ballet lesson. Elizabeth left him in it. Twice, Stephanie ran after her with him, and once even Ruth, who was rather nervous of him, carried him cautiously into the dance room, saying, "You left Carruthers in the car, Elizabeth." Elizabeth sighed. But she realized it was no good trying to keep Carruthers away from ballet and let him stand in the corner as usual after that.

This was a little before Easter. Ruth was to go to her academy in the autumn. Meanwhile, Aunt Anne had to go abroad and Stephen came to live with them. He was to have gone to Granny, but Granny telephoned Father to say she could not cope, and Father said they would have Stephen instead. He could have Elizabeth's room, and Elizabeth could move in with Ruth and Stephanie, as Ruth was going away before long.

Much as Elizabeth disliked this arrangement, Ruth liked it even less. Ruth and Stephanie had shared a room since they were both small. Ruth had developed a series of masterly arrangements with Stephanie. They were all very complicated and they all amounted to the same thing: Ruth lay on her bed and gave orders while Stephanie ran and did things. When Elizabeth moved in, Ruth rightly feared that this golden time was over. Sure enough, Elizabeth saw through the arrangements at once.

"Don't be such a lazybones, Ruth," she kept saying. "Why should Stephanie do it?"

Ruth began to lose her temper. Stephanie was uncomfortable too. It was not what she was used to.

"Honestly, Ruth, you are lazy!" Elizabeth said for the tenth time.

Ruth pressed her lips together. Her way of losing her temper was to go icy calm and say the nastiest thing she possibly could. She took a long breath. For a moment, calm as she was, she wondered if she dared say it. "I—I don't believe in Carruthers," she said.

"You what?" said Elizabeth.

"I don't," said Ruth, "believe in Carruthers."

"He's only a stick," Stephanie added loyally.

Elizabeth felt extremely anxious. Ever since their quarrel, Carruthers had indeed seemed almost like an ordinary stick. Elizabeth was afraid he was dead, until she remembered the way he kept turning up at ballet. That so relieved her that she said, "Have it your own ways," and hurried downstairs to fetch Carruthers from the hall.

Her sisters stared at each other. "Do you think she's all right?" Stephanie asked anxiously.

"She's grown out of Carruthers, that's all," Ruth said. She did not really believe it, but she knew she had to keep Stephanie's respect, or Stephanie would never run errands for her again.

"Carruthers," Elizabeth said to the unresponsive, sticklike Carruthers as she carried him upstairs. "Carruthers, would you like some chocolate?" Even that did not move Carruthers. Elizabeth came back into the room looking so miserable that Ruth relented. Ruth was going away to learn to be a ballerina, after all. She could afford to be kind. Besides, she thought she had hit on a way to make peace with Elizabeth and still keep Stephanie's respect.

"Never mind, Elizabeth," Ruth said. "You're growing up fearfully pretty, so it doesn't matter."

This did not comfort Elizabeth. Nor did it keep Stephanie respectful. "Ahah!" Stephanie cried out, curled up like a gnome on her pillow. "When Ruth says that, you can believe it. Ruth's a real girl. She really works at it."

"You're both horrible," said Ruth. "Worse than Stephen."

Stephen turned out to have grown into a very boyish boy. He played with cars, guns, and electric trains. He made friends with all the boys who swarmed through the bushes in the wood. They came to call on him, so, for the first time, the house filled with boys.

"Rude, rough lot!" Ruth said disgustedly.

But Elizabeth discovered that the games boys played were fun. She liked guns, Cops and Robbers, and pelting about shouting. It was much more interesting to climb trees in the wood than to sit decorously on a log watching Carruthers. She admired Stephen. Whenever he let her, she followed him about and tried to join in the games.

"Elizabeth, I forbid you to get dirty," said Father.

"Darling, you mustn't act so rough," said Mother.

At first, Stephen was not at all pleased to have a girl tagging about after him. "We don't want you," he said to Elizabeth in the hall one morning. His friend Dave had called for him, and they were going to play parachutes in the wood.

"Why not?" asked Elizabeth.

"Because you're forbidden to get dirty," Stephen said as he went out through the front door.

"I don't want to come anyway," Elizabeth shouted after him. "I've got Carruthers."

"That stupid old stick!" Stephen called back. The front door slammed.

Carruthers was propped lifelessly in the umbrella stand. "*He* gets dirty," Elizabeth said to him indignantly.

The front door opened again. Stephen and Dave appeared. "I've changed my mind," Stephen said. Elizabeth beamed, in spite of having Carruthers.

"Er—hm," said Dave.

Stephen said swiftly, "Dave here wants you to be his girl-friend, Elizabeth. Tell him I've already booked you." Elizabeth stared rather, and then opened her mouth to say that she did not like either of them nearly enough. "Well, that's settled then," Stephen said airily. "Come along, Elizabeth."

Being Stephen's girlfriend was rather like being Stephanie under Ruth's arrangements, Elizabeth discovered. It seemed to mean that she was allowed to carry Stephen's sweater, to sit at the bottom of a tree to catch him in case he fell, to be an Indian woman—an almost lifeless role—when they played cowboys and Indians, and to sit for cramped hours switching electric trains when she was told. It also seemed to mean that Stephen was allowed to talk to her in the same bullying way Father used to Mother and Aunt Anne, and to frown when-ever Elizabeth made any kind of suggestion. There did not seem to be any advantages to the post at all. After two days, Elizabeth was wishing she knew how to stop being Stephen's girlfriend. But the post seemed to be a permanent one.

She was almost glad when Father started his Easter holidays and took Stephen over—except that she was also immeasurably indignant. Father was scarcely strict with Stephen at all, and he positively encouraged him to get dirty. He took him to fly a kite and to the zoo and on a cycle ride. None of the girls were taken. Ruth seemed to think it was all right, because Stephen was a boy. Elizabeth thought it was unfair. And so, it seemed, did Stephanie.

"Mother," Stephanie said, "why is Father nicer to Stephen than to us?"

"Your Father's always wanted a boy," said Mother. "His own flesh and blood." Elizabeth could hardly hear her for the sounds of hammering and sawing in the garage, where Father and Stephen were now making a table together.

"So am I his own flesh and blood," Stephanie said loudly, above the banging. "And I can cycle and get dirty. And," she added, as there came a softer thump and a screech from Stephen, "I can knock in nails without hitting my thumb. Why aren't I allowed to?"

"It's not suitable for girls—" Mother began.

"Good Lord!" said Stephanie.

"Stephanie! Don't swear!" said Mother.

"I wasn't. I only said 'Good Lord.' You should hear some of the things the other girls say," said Stephanie. "Give me one good reason why it's not suitable."

Mother got out of that by being hurt. "Stephanie, how could you speak to me like that?" She left the room, still looking hurt.

"Did you ever know anyone so old-fashioned as our parents?" Stephanie asked Elizabeth. "There's a girl at school calls her father Fishface. Imagine what Father or Mother would say if I called Father that—or even if I called him Dad. What can we do about them?"

"I don't know," said Elizabeth. Privately, she thought of Carruthers. She went out of the house and met Stephen as he came out of the garage sucking his finger. "Are you enjoying it with Father?" she asked.

Stephen rolled his eyes up. "Holy fishcake! But," he added, "you wouldn't understand."

Elizabeth knew she did not understand. All she knew was that, now Stephanie had pointed out the kind of people Mother and Father were, she felt shocked—and the fact that she felt shocked made her feel as if she were sitting in a very small cage, with no room to unbend her knees, which, in turn, made her feel angry. She tried to describe her feelings to the stiff, unresponsive Carruthers in the middle of the night. "It's like being squeezed into the wrong shape," she said. "Stephanie feels the same. I'm not sure about Ruth, but I don't think Stephen enjoys it any more than we do. But I think it would all come right if you hit Father. Couldn't you forgive me now and start hitting him? Once a day, just for a start."

To her pleasure, Carruthers stirred sleepily. "I'm hungry," he said, in the old plaintive grunt. "Terribly hungry."

"Thank goodness for that!" said Elizabeth. "I'll get some biscuits. What's been wrong with you?"

"I was sleepy," said Carruthers.

Elizabeth slipped out of bed and started downstairs, into the queer orange gloom the streetlights cast in the hall. But Carruthers was evidently too hungry to wait. She saw him slither along the bannisters beside her and hop ahead of her into the kitchen. Elizabeth hurried after him. Carruthers was in the larder somewhere by the time she got there. She could hear him clattering on one of the higher shelves.

"There's nothing but tins up here," said the plaintive, grunting voice.

"The biscuits are down here," Elizabeth whispered. "Stop making such a noise."

There was a scuffling, and a crunch of tinfoil. Carruthers said, "Oh! Chocolate eggs!"

"Those are for Easter!" Elizabeth whispered frantically. "Come *down*."

"In a minute," said Carruthers, munching and rustling.

The light in the larder snapped on. Rows of tins and jams leaped into sight. A very squeaky voice, which Elizabeth just recognized as Stephen's, said, "Oh. It's only you. What are you doing?"

"Carruthers was hungry," Elizabeth explained. Carruthers was still rustling and munching up on the shelf.

"Pull the other leg," said Stephen. "Sticks can't eat." He came into the larder and stared up at the rustling.

A tin of plums promptly fell heavily on his bare foot. Stephen hopped about, yelling. Another tin fell on him, and another. Elizabeth could glimpse Carruthers's hooked face peering down from the shelf, taking aim. Stephen put his arms over his head and ran out of the larder. He ran straight into Father, coming the other way.

"What is going on?" Father roared.

Carruthers prudently pushed himself off the shelf with the last tin and clattered to the floor like an ordinary walking stick. Unfortunately, he brought a torn Easter egg wrapping down with him.

"I thought it was a burglar, Uncle Stephen," Stephen said.

"So did I," Elizabeth said unconvincingly.

Father naturally came to the conclusion that Elizabeth had been using Carruthers to hook down Easter eggs. The trouble was terrible. Elizabeth spent Easter in disgrace and without an Easter egg.

"Why did you hit Stephen and not Father?" she asked Carruthers.

"Stephen called me a stick," Carruthers said sulkily.

After that, Elizabeth could not get another word out of him. Most of the time, there was no way of knowing he was anything other than a real stick. Yet night after night, for the whole of the next month, the larder was raided. Biscuits, cakes, and puddings went. Father blamed Elizabeth every time. Stephen found it very funny. "Carruthers hungry again?" he asked every morning.

Elizabeth wondered why she had ever liked Stephen. If she could have thought of a way of stopping being his girlfriend, she would have stopped it that moment. But it did no good to tell Stephen she did not want to be his girlfriend. He would say, "All right," as if he agreed, and then, half an hour later, he would be saying, "Elizabeth, just come along and switch my points for me," or, "Elizabeth, I need you to hold my coat in the wood." It was as if she had never said anything at all.

What with this, and with getting up every morning to be blamed for what Carruthers ate in the night, Elizabeth began to feel as if the cage she had imagined was getting smaller and smaller, until she could hardly breathe. She was quite sure that, if only Carruthers could be made to hit Father, everything would be all right again. "It's like that story of the old woman and the pig," she explained to Carruthers—who may or may not have been listening. "Fire fire, burn stick; stick stick, beat pig—

and then they all went home. You just hit Father to show him who's master, and Father will turn on Stephen, and Mother will tell Father he's a tyrant, and we'll all be able to get dirty and climb trees and so on."

Carruthers gave no sign of hearing, but his appetite was unabated. Elizabeth began training herself to wake in the night and catch Carruthers in the larder again. She was fairly sure that if she could only catch him red-handed, she would be able to bully him into hitting Father at last. But most nights she just slept. Some nights she woke up, only to find Carruthers hooked on to the end of her bed, apparently as good as gold—except that more food was gone in the morning.

Then, one night, she was suddenly wide awake. She heard Carruthers unhook himself from her bed and go softly thumping downstairs.

Here's where I catch you, my lad! Elizabeth thought. She flung back her bedclothes and crept after Carruthers, into the dim orange light from the streetlights. On the stairs, she listened hard. There was a faint chink and rattle from the living room, as if Carruthers had gone after the nuts and olives Mother kept to offer visitors. But, while Elizabeth was turning that way, she heard a furtive crunkling and rustling from the kitchen too. Surely Carruthers could not be in two places at once?

By that time her eyes had grown used to the orange light. She saw Carruthers lying stretched out on the hall carpet. The middle of him seemed to be bulging.

Elizabeth forgot about the noises. She fell on her knees beside him. "Carruthers! What's the matter?" she whispered. "Are you ill?"

Carruthers did not answer. He was bulging from the silver collar below his hook to the ferrule at his tail, heaving, and swelling to two or three times his normal width. Though Elizabeth was sure it was only the result of greed, tears ran down her face. She wondered what sort of doctor you took a sick stick to.

The noises from the living room became more definite. There were quiet footsteps, and the sound of things being moved. Elizabeth shot the swelling, heaving Carruthers a helpless look and crawled over to the living room door.

It was a real burglar. A wide-shouldered, strong-looking young man was packing Father's tape recorder into a suitcase. He already had the radio. He was taking down the silver golf trophies when Elizabeth backed away and turned to Carruthers again. Just as she turned, Carruthers stopped swelling and burst, with a sharp *crack*. The noise from the living room stopped. So did the noises from the kitchen. Elizabeth knelt in the hall, between what were certainly two burglars, and stared at Carruthers.

The split in Carruthers grew wider. Something that seemed to be a gauzy green color bulged from the split and might have been struggling to get out. A second later, the struggling was definite. The filmy green something heaved, shoved, and finally pushed the dead halves of the stick apart and climbed out on the carpet. Elizabeth gasped. Whatever it was, it was impossibly beautiful. It had long curled antennae. Its back legs were long and thin—a little like a grasshopper's—and it seemed to have long thin arms too. It had a small piquant face, with little slanting eyes which caught the orange light and glowed blue-green beneath the antennae. Its body was draped and covered in beautiful shimmering diaphanous green, which might have been multitudes of long wings—or might have been something quite different. The creature rested, quivering, for a second or so. Then it rose on its long green legs and performed a slow, airy arabesque. Elizabeth smiled. It was Carruthers all right.

The living room burglar still had not moved, but she could hear him breathing. It occurred to Elizabeth that, if he knew she was in the hall, he might run away and leave her in peace with Carruthers. So she said out loud:

"You were a chrysalis!"

There was no sound from either burglar, but the new gauzy Carruthers turned its little face and long, nodding antennae toward her. For one miserable minute, Elizabeth thought it could not speak. But it must have been just finding out how. "That's right," it said. The new voice was a good deal more silvery than the old one. "I think I've been a chrysalis for the last month."

"Then how did you rob the larder then?" asked Elizabeth.

"For the Easter egg, you mean?" asked the creature.

"No," said Elizabeth. "All the other times."

"I don't think I did," said Carruthers. "Being a chrysalis is like being asleep. But don't I look beautiful now I'm hatched?" It twirled slowly and elegantly along by the foot of the stairs. The gauzy draperies fluttered. Elizabeth could not but agree that it was the most exquisite being. "I think," said Carruthers, meditatively sinking into a curtsey, "that I need to go away now and find a mate. I have to lay some eggs. Good-bye."

"No!" said Elizabeth. At least she had an excuse to keep

Carruthers close at hand—two of them. "Don't go yet. There's a burglar in the living room and a burglar in the kitchen." There were startled rustles from both places. "You've got to stay and help me catch them."

Carruthers gave a little fluttering jump. "Oh, I couldn't! Besides, I must be quite the most valuable thing in the house. Just phone the police."

Elizabeth crawled over to the phone, reflecting that Carruthers was probably quite right about his—her, that is—value. It was rather stupid of him—her, that is—to let the burglars know. The silence behind the living room door sounded like a distinctly interested one.

Elizabeth picked up the phone. Even before she dialled 999, she knew it was dead. The burglars had been thorough. She was almost frightened for the first time. Carruthers was now fluttering slowly across the hall. Some of the gauzy drapery was beginning to act like wings. Elizabeth took hold of him—her, that is—by a transparent flowing edge. "Ow!" said Carruthers.

Elizabeth let go and whispered: "Keep talking, as if you were both of us. I'll fetch Father."

"You don't still want me to hit him, do you?" Carruthers asked loudly.

Elizabeth shook her head frantically at him—her—and crawled for the stairs. Carruthers took the point and said, "You dance exquisitely," and danced exquisitely. "Yes, I do, don't I?" she replied. "You fly wonderfully. Indeed I do, but, wouldn't you say, my antennae are perhaps a trifle too long?" she asked. "Not at all," she answered. "Oh, thank you," she replied. "You must keep telling me things like that. I'm a poor ignorant weak thing, only just hatched. But," she told herself, "beautiful. Yes, indeed," she answered, losing her place in the conversation a little, "a beautiful unearthly being, fragile and lovely . . . "

The silvery voice faded out of Elizabeth's hearing as she burst open her parents' bedroom door. "Father! There are two burglars downstairs. One's got the radio and the golf cups and cut off the telephone!"

"Eh?" Father sat up in bed, and seemed to understand at once. "Be down directly. Go and call Stephen and then stay safely in your bedroom."

Elizabeth sped to her own old room. It was empty. Stephen must have heard the burglars and gone down already. There was no sign of Father coming. But downstairs Carruthers was suddenly making a great deal of noise. Elizabeth pelted for the stairs. The door of the room she shared opened.

"What is it?" Ruth hissed.

"Burglars," said Elizabeth.

"I thought so," Stephanie said from behind Ruth. "Who's shouting?"

"Carruthers," gasped Elizabeth, and galloped downstairs.

The burglar from the living room was out in the hall. She recognized him by his wide shoulders. He had heard what Carruthers said about her value. In the dim light, his gloved hands were snatching at the green filmy draperies, while Carruthers, to Elizabeth's admiration, was circling and swooping and fluttering, just out of reach, like an enormous moth. "You can't catch me!" Carruthers shouted. "You can't catch me!"

"Silly thing," said Elizabeth. "You'll get hurt." She snatched up what was left of the walking stick, but was not sure what to do after that.

"Whoopee!" screamed Carruthers, swooping across the hall. "Beautiful me!"

The burglar dived after her. Elizabeth stuck her foot out. The burglar tripped over it and fell on his face—the oddest part of the whole thing, Elizabeth thought afterward, was that she never saw his face at all. Carruthers wheeled briskly and planed down to land on the burglar's neck. After that, it seemed to be all over.

"Hands up!" Ruth said.

"Is he dead?" asked Stephanie. They were both on the stairs with Stephen's toy guns. They seemed disappointed to have missed killing the burglar themselves.

Elizabeth cautiously poked at the burglar with her toe. He did not move.

"He's just unconscious," Carruthers said, standing up on the burglar's back and settling her fluttering gauzeries. "I seem," she said modestly, "to have a sting in my—er—tail. I expect it's to paralyze my prey. Unless," she added thoughtfully, "it's my mate I should paralyze. No doubt I shall find out."

"That's never Carruthers!" said Stephanie.

"I take it back," Ruth said handsomely, "about him being only a stick."

"Yes, aren't I beautiful?" Carruthers said, with feeling.

"Give me a gun," said Elizabeth. "There's another burglar in the kitchen."

"No, there isn't," Stephen said, rather wobbly and cautious. They all turned to the kitchen door. Stephen switched the hall light on and stood sheepishly in his pajamas. He had a slice of cake—most of a cake, in fact—in one hand, and one cheek bulged. "Burglar under control?" he asked airily.

Elizabeth looked at him with the deepest contempt. Not only had he kept hidden in the kitchen rather than face the burglar, but, for a whole month, he had let her take the blame for robbing the larder. "You're not my boyfriend any longer," she said. She knew she would only have to say it that once.

Father came hurrying downstairs, fully dressed and knotting his tie. "I told you girls to stay in safety," he said.

Elizabeth looked up at him and found she felt differently about Father too. It was not Stephen's kind of cowardice which had made Father arrive just too late: it was because he could not face even a burglar without proper clothes on. Father lived by rules—narrow rules. Elizabeth did not feel afraid of him anymore. Nor did she want Carruthers to hit Father. It did not matter enough. And she said to herself, with the most enormous feeling of relief, "Thank goodness! I needn't do ballet anymore!"

Typically, Father ignored the toy guns Ruth and Stephanie were holding and looked at Stephen, and then at the prone burglar. "Nice work, Stephen," he said.

Before Stephen could swallow enough cake to look brave but modest, Ruth and Stephanie said in chorus, "It wasn't him. It was Elizabeth."

Elizabeth avoided Father's astonished eye and looked around for Carruthers. She wanted Father to know it was really Carruthers. But the hall was bright and empty. She's flown away, Elizabeth though miserably.

Then a filmy shadow glided in front of the hall light. A

gauzy something flittered at Elizabeth's cheek. Elizabeth realized that it had been a trick of the orange streetlights which had made Carruthers look green. In the bright electric light she was all but invisible.

"Good-bye," whispered Carruthers. "I'll be back when I've laid some eggs."

❧ What The Cat Told Me ❧

I am a cat. I am a cat like anything. Keep stroking me. I came in here because I knew you were good at stroking. But put your knees together so I can sit properly, front paws under. That's better. Now keep stroking, don't forget to rub my ears, and I will purr and tell.

I am going to tell you how I came to be so very old. When I was a kitten, humans dressed differently, and they had great stamping horses to pull their cars and buses. The Old Man in the house where I lived used to light a hissing gas on the wall when it got dark. He wore a long black coat. The Boy who was nice to me wore shabby breeches that only came to his knees, and he mostly went without shoes, just like me. We slept in a cupboard under the stairs, Boy and I. We kept one another warm. We kept one another fed, too, later on. The Old Man did not like cats or boys. He only kept us because we were useful.

I was more useful than Boy. I had to sit in a five-pointed star. The Boy would help Old Man mix things that smoked and made me sneeze. I had to sneeze three times. After that things happened. Sometimes big purple cloud things came and sat beside me in the star. Fur stood up on me, and I spat, but the things only went away when Old Man hit the star with his stick and told them, "*Begone!*" in a loud voice. At other times the things that came were small, real things you could hit with your paw: boxes, or strings of shiny stones no one could eat, or bright rings that fell *tink* beside me out of nowhere. I did not mind those things. The things I really hated were the third kind. Those came inside me and used my mouth to speak. They were nasty things with hateful thoughts, and they made *me* hateful. And my mouth does not like to speak. It ached afterward, and my tongue and throat were so sore that I could not wash the hatefulness off me for hours.

I so hated those inside-speaking things that I used to run away and hide when I saw Old Man drawing the star on the cellar floor. I am good at hiding. Sometimes it took Boy half the day to find me. Then Old Man would shout and curse and hit Boy and call him a fool. Boy cried at night in the cupboard afterward. I did not like that, so after a while I scratched Old Man instead. I knew none of it was Boy's fault. Boy made Old Man give me nice things to eat after I had sat in the star. He said it was the only way to get me to sit there.

Boy was clever, you see. Old Man thought he was a fool, but Boy told me—at night in the cupboard—that he only pretended to be stupid. Boy was an orphan like me. Old Man had bought him for a shilling from a baby farmer ages before I was even a kitten, because his hair was orange, like the ginger patches on me, and that is supposed to be a good color for magic. Old Man paid a whole farthing for me, for much the same reason, because I am brindled. And Boy had been with Old Man ever since, learning things. It was not only magic that Boy learned. Old Man was away quite a lot when Boy was small. Boy used to read Old Man's books in the room upstairs, and the newspapers, and anything else he could find. He told me he wanted to learn magic in order to escape from Old Man, and he learned the other things so that he could manage in the wide world when he did escape; but he had been a prisoner in the house for years now, and although he knew a great deal, he still could not break the spell Old Man had put on him to keep him inside the house. "And I really hate him," Boy said to me, "because of the cat before you. I want to stop him doing any more magic before I leave."

And I said—

What was that? How could Boy and I talk together? Do you think I am a stupid cat, or something? I am nearly as clever as Boy. How do you think I am telling you all this? Let me roll over. My stomach needs rubbing. Oh, you rub well! I really like you. Well— No, let me sit up again now. I think the talking must be something to do with those inside-speaking things. When I was a kitten, I could understand what people said, of course, but I couldn't do it back, not at first, until I had been lived in and spoken through by quite a lot of Things. Boy thought they stretched my mind. And I was clever to start with, not like the cat before me.

Old Man killed the cat before me somehow. Boy would not

tell me how. It was a stupid cat, he said, but he loved it. After he told me that, I would not go near Boy for a whole day. It was not just that I was nervous about being killed, too. How *could* he love any cat that wasn't *me*? Boy caught me a pigeon off the roof, but I still wouldn't speak to him. So he stole me a saucer of milk and swore he would make sure Old Man didn't kill me, too. He liked me a lot better than the other cat, he said, because I was clever. Anyway, Old Man killed the other cat doing magic he would not be able to work again without a certain special powder. Besides, the other cat was black and did not look as interesting as me.

After Boy had told me a lot of things like this, I put my nose to his nose, and we were friends again. We made a conspiracy— that was what Boy called it—and swore to defeat Old Man and escape somehow. But we could not find out how to do it. We thought and thought. In the end I stopped growing because of the strain and worry. Boy said no, it was because I was full grown.

I said, "Why, in that case, are *you* still growing? You're already more than ten times my size. You're nearly as big as Old Man!"

"I know," said Boy. "You're an elegant little cat. I don't think I shall be elegant until I'm six feet tall, and maybe not even then. I'm so clumsy. *And* so hungry!"

Poor Boy. He did grow so, around then. He did not seem to know his own size from one day to the next. When he rolled over in the cupboard, he either squashed me or burst out into the hallway. I had to scratch him quite hard, several nights, or he would have smothered me. And he kept knocking things over when he was awake. He spilled the milk jug—which I didn't mind at all—and he kicked Old Man's magic tripod by accident and smashed six jars of smelly stuff. Old Man cursed and called Boy a fool, worse than ever. And I think Boy really was stupid then, because he was so hungry. Old Man was too mean to give him more to eat. Boy ate my food, so I was hungry, too. He said he couldn't help it.

I went on the roof and caught pigeons. Boy roasted them over the gaslight at night when Old Man was asleep. Delicious. But the bones made me sick in the corner. We hid the feathers in the cupboard, and after I had caught a great many pigeons, night after night, the cupboard began to get warm. Boy began to get his mind back. But he still grew, and he was still hungry. By the time I had stopped growing for a year, Boy was so big his breeches went right up his legs and his legs went all hairy. Old Man couldn't hit him anymore then, because Boy just put out a long, long arm and held Old Man off.

"I need more clothes," he told Old Man.

Old Man grumbled and protested, but at last he said, "Oh, all right, you damn scarecrow. I'll see what I can do." He went unwillingly down into the cellar and heaved up one of the flagstones there. He wouldn't let me look in the hole, but I know that what was under that flagstone was Old Man's collection of all the rings and shiny stones that came from nowhere when I sat in the five-pointed star. I saw Old Man take some chinking things out. Then he slammed down the stone and went away upstairs, not noticing that one shiny thing had spilled out and gone rolling across the floor. It was a little golden ball. It was fun. I chased it for hours. I patted it and it rolled, and I pounced, and it ran away all around the cellar. Then it spoiled the fun by rolling down a crack between two flagstones and getting lost. Then I found I was shut in the cellar and had to make a great noise to be let out.

That reminds me: does your house have balls in it? Then buy me one tomorrow. Until then a piece of paper on some string will do.

Where was I? Oh, yes. Someone smelling of mildew came and let me out. I nearly didn't know Boy at first. He had a red coat and white breeches and long black boots on, all rather too big for him. He said it was an old soldier's uniform Old Man had picked up cheap, and how did I get shut in the cellar?

I sat around his neck and told him about the flagstone where Old Man kept his shinies. Boy was *very* interested. "That would buy an awful lot of food," he said. He was still hungry. "We'll take it with us when we escape. Let's try escaping next time he works magic."

So that night we made a proper plan at last. We decided to summon a Good Spirit, instead of the hateful things Old Man always fetched. "There must be *some* good ones," Boy said. But since we didn't know enough to summon a good one on our own, we had to make Old Man do it for us somehow.

We did it the very next day. I played up wonderfully. As soon as Old Man started to draw on the cellar floor, I ran away, so that Old Man would not suspect us. I dug my claws hard into Boy's coat when he caught me, so that Old Man could hardly pull me loose. And I scratched Old Man, very badly, so that there was blood when he put me inside the five-pointed star. Then I sat there, humped and sulky, and it was Boy's turn.

Boy did rather well, too. At first he was just the usual kind of clumsy and kicked some black powder into some red powder while they were putting it out in heaps, and the cellar filled with white soot. It was hard not to sneeze too soon, but I managed not to. I managed to hold the sneeze off until Old Man had done swearing at Boy and begun on the next bit, the mumbling. Then I sneezed—once. Boy promptly fell against the tripod, which dripped hot stuff on the spilled powder. The cellar filled with big purple bubbles. They drifted and shone and bobbed most enticingly. I would have loved to chase them, but I knew I mustn't, or we would spoil what we were doing. Old Man couldn't leave off his mumbling, because that would spoil the spell, but he glared at Boy through the bubbles. I sneezed again—two—to distract him. Old Man raised his stick and began on the chanting bit. And Boy pretended to trip and, as he did, he threw a fistful of powder he had ready into the gaslight.

Whup! it went.

Old Man jumped and glared and went on grimly chanting— he had to, you see, because you can't stop magic once you have started—and all the bubbles drifted to the floor and burst, *smicker, smicker,* very softly. As each one burst, there was a little tiny pink animal on the floor, running about and calling, "Oink, oink, oink!" in a small squeaky voice. That nearly distracted me, as well as Old Man. I stared out at them with longing. I would have given *worlds* to jump out of the star and chase those beasties. They looked so beautifully *eatable.* But I knew I mustn't try to come out of the star yet, so I shut my eyes and yawned to hold in the third sneeze and thought hard, hard, hard of a Good Thing. *Let a Good Thing come!* I thought. I thought as hard as you do when you see a saucer of milk held in the air above you, and you want them to put it on the floor—quick. Then I gave my third sneeze.

That reminds me. Milk? Yes, please, or I won't be able to tell you any more.

Thank you. Keep your knee steady. You may stroke me if you wish. Where was I?

Right. When I opened my eyes, all the delicious beasties had vanished and the light burned sort of dingily. Old Man was beating Boy over the head with a stick. He could do that for once, because Boy was crouched by the wall laughing until his face ran tears. "Pigs!" he said. "Tiny little pigs! Oh, oh, oh!"

"I'll pig *you!*" Old Man screamed. "You spoiled my spell! Look at the pentangle—there's nothing there at all!"

But there was. I could feel the new Thing inside me. It wasn't hateful at all, but it felt lost and a bit feeble. It was too scared to say or do anything or even let me move, until Old Man crossly broke the pentangle and stumped away upstairs.

Boy stood rubbing his head. "Pity it didn't work, Brindle," he said. "But wasn't it worth it just for those pigs?"

"Master," the Good Thing said with my mouth, "Master, how can I serve you, bound as I am?"

Boy stared, and his face went odd colors. I always wonder how you humans manage that. "Good Lord!" he said. "Did we do it after all? Or is it a demon?"

"I don't think I'm a demon," Good Thing said doubtfully. "I may be some kind of spirit. I'm not sure."

"Can't you get out of me?" I said to it in my head.

"No. Our Master would not be able to hear me if I did," it told me.

"Bother you then!" I said, and started to wash.

"You can serve me, anyway, whatever you are," Boy said to Good Thing. "Get me some food."

"Yes, Master," it made me say, and obeyed at once. I had just reached that stage of washing where you have one foot high in the air. I fell over. It was most annoying. Next minute I was rolling about in a huge warm room full of people cooking things. A kitchen, Boy said it was later. It smelled marvelous. . . . I hardly minded at all when Good Thing made me leap up and snatch a roast leg of mutton from the nearest table. But I did mind—a lot—when two men in white hats rushed at me shouting, "*Damn cat!*"

Good Thing didn't know what to do about that at all, and it nearly got us caught. "Let *me* handle this!" I spat at it, and it did. I told you, it was a bit feeble. I dived under a big dresser where people couldn't reach me and crouched there right at the back by the wall. It was a pity I had to leave the meat behind. It smelled wonderful. But I had to leave it, or they'd have gone on chasing me. "Now," I said, when my coat had settled flat again, "you tell me what you want me to take and I'll take it properly this time."

Good Thing agreed that might work better. We waited until they'd all gone back to cooking and then slunk softly out into the room again. And Good Thing had been thinking all this time. It made me a sort of invisible sack. It was most peculiar. No one could see the sack, not even me, and it didn't get in my way at all. I just knew it was behind me, filling up with the food I stole. Good Thing made me take stuff I'd never have dreamed of eating myself, like cinnamon jelly and—yuk!—cucumber, as well as good honest meat and venison pie and other reasonable things.

Then we were suddenly back in the cellar, where Boy was glumly clearing up. When he saw the food spilling out onto the floor, his face lit up. Good Thing had been right. He loved the jelly and even ate cucumber. For once in his life he really had enough to eat. I helped him eat the venison pie, and we both had strawberries and cream to finish with. I love those.

Which reminds me — Oh. Strawberries are out of season? Never mind. I'll stay with you until they come back in. Rub my stomach again.

I was heavy and kind of round after that meal. Good Thing complained rather. "Well, get out of me then, and it won't bother you," I said. I wanted to sleep.

"In a minute," it said. "Master, the cat tells me you want to escape, but I'm afraid I can't help you there."

Boy woke up in dismay. He was dropping off to sleep on the floor, being so full. "Why *not*?"

"Two reasons," Good Thing said apologetically. "First, there is a very strong spell on you, which confines you to this house, and it is beyond my power to break it. Second, there is an equally strong spell on me. You and the cat broke part of it, the part which confined me to a small golden ball, but I am still forced to stay in the house where the golden ball is. The only other place I can go is the house I . . . came from."

"Damn!" said Boy. "I did hope —"

"The spell that confines the cat is nothing like so strong," Good Thing said. "I could raise that for you."

"That's something at least! Do that," said Boy. He was a generous Boy. "And if you two could keep on fetching food, so that I can put my mind to something besides how hungry I am, then I might think of a way to break the spell on you and me."

I was a little annoyed. It seemed that we had got Good Thing just because the golden ball had escaped from Old Man, and not because of Boy's cleverness or my powers of thought. But though I knew the ball was down a crack just inside the place where Old Man usually drew his pentangle, I didn't mention it to Boy in case his feelings were hurt, too.

We had great good times for quite a long while after that, Boy, Good Thing, and I, and Old Man never suspected at all. He was away a lot around then, anyway. While he was away, there were always a jug of milk and a loaf that appeared magically every four days, but Boy and I would have half starved on that without Good Thing. Good Thing took me to the kitchen place every day at suppertime, and we came back with every kind of food in the invisible sack. When Good Thing was not around—it quite often went away in the night and left me in peace—I went out across the roofs. I led a lovely extra life on top of the town. I met other cats by moonlight, but they were never as clever as me. I found out all sorts of things and came and told them to Boy. He was always very wistful about not being able to go out himself, but he listened to everything. He was like that. He was my friend. And he was a great comfort to me when I had my first kittens. I didn't know what was happening to me. Boy guessed and he told me. Then he told me that we must hide the kittens or Old Man would know I had been able to go out. We were very secret and hid them in our cupboard in a nest of pigeon feathers.

I am good at having kittens. I'll show you presently. I always have three, one tabby, one ginger, and one mixed like me. I had three kittens then, and Old Man never knew, even though they were quite noisy sometimes, especially after I taught them how to play with Good Thing.

When Good Thing came out of me, I could see it quite well, though Boy never could. It was quite big outside me, up to

Boy's shoulder, and frail and wafty, and it could float about at great speed. It enjoyed playing. I used to hunt it all round the house and leap on it, pretending to tear it to bits, and of course it would waft away between my paws. Boy used to guess where Good Thing was from my behavior and laugh at me hunting it. He laughed even more when my kittens were old enough to play hunting Good Thing, too.

By this time Boy was a fine, strong Boy, full of thoughts, and his soldier clothes were getting too short and tight. He asked Good Thing to get him some more clothes next time Old Man was away. So Good Thing and I went to another part of the mansion where the kitchen was. Boy said "house" was the wrong word for that place. He was right. It was big and grand. This time when we got there, we went sneaking at a run up a great stair covered with red carpet—or I went sneaking with Good Thing inside me—and along more carpet to a large room with curtains all around the walls. The curtains had pictures that Good Thing said were lords and ladies hunting animals with birds and horses. I never knew that *birds* were any help to people.

There was a space between the curtains and the walls, and Good Thing sent me sneaking through that space, around the room. There were people in the room. I peeped at them through a crack in the curtains.

There was a very fine Man there, almost as tall and fine as my Boy, but much older. With him were two of the ones in white hats from the kitchen. They held their hats in their hands, sorrowfully. With them was a Woman in long clothes, looking cross as Old Man.

"Yes indeed, sir, I saw this cat for myself, sir," the Woman said. "It stole a cake under my very eyes, sir."

"I swear to you, sir," one of the white hats said, "it appears every evening and vanishes like magic with every kind of food."

"It *is* magic, that's why," said the other white hat.

"Then we had better take steps to see where it comes from," the fine Man said. "If I give you this—"

Good Thing wouldn't let me stay to hear more. We ran on. "Oh, dear!" Good Thing said in my head as we ran. "We'll have to be very careful after this!" We came to a room that was white and gold, with mirrors. Good Thing wouldn't let me watch myself in the mirrors. The white-and-gold walls were all cupboards filled with clothes hanging or lying inside. We stuffed the invisible sack as full as it would hold with clothes from the cupboards, so that we would not need to go back. For once it felt heavy. I was glad to get back to Boy waiting in Old Man's book room.

"Great Scott!" said Boy as the fine coats, good boots, silk shirts, cravats, and smooth trousers tumbled out onto the floor. "I can't wear these! These are fit for a king! The Old Man would be bound to notice." But he could not resist trying some of them on, all the same. Good Thing told me he looked good. I thought Boy looked far finer than the Man they belonged to.

After this, Boy became very curious about the mansion where the clothes and the food came from. He made me describe everything. Then he asked Good Thing, "Are there books in this mansion, too?"

"And pictures and jewels," Good Thing said through me. "What does Master wish me to fetch? There is a golden harp, a musical box like a bird, a—"

"Just books," said Boy. "I need to learn. I'm still so ignorant."

Good Thing always obeyed Boy. The next night, instead of

going to the kitchen, Good Thing took me to a vast room with a round ceiling held up by freckled pillars, where the walls were lined with books in shelves. Good Thing had one of its helpless turns there. "Which do you think our Master wants?" it asked me feebly.

"I don't know," I said. "I'm only a cat. Let's just take all we can carry. I want to get back to my kittens."

So we took everything out of one shelf, and it was not right. Boy said he did not need twenty-four copies of the Bible: one was enough. The same went for Shakespeare. And he could not read Greek, he said. I spat. But we gathered up all the books except two and went back.

We had just spilled all the books onto the floor of the room with the freckled pillars when the big door burst open. The Man came striding in, with a crowd of others. "There's the cat now!" they all cried out.

Good Thing had me snatch another book at random, and we went.

"And I daren't go back for a while, Master," Good Thing said to Boy.

I saw to my kittens; then I went out hunting. I fed Boy for the next few days—when he remembered to eat, that was. I stole a leg of lamb from an inn, a string of sausages from the butcher down the road, and a loaf and some buns from the baker. The kittens ate most of it. Boy was reading. He sat in his fine clothes, and he read, the Bible first, then Shakespeare, and then the book of history Good Thing had me snatch. He said he was educating himself. It was as if he were asleep. When Old Man suddenly came back, I had to dig all my claws into Boy to make him notice.

Old Man looked grumpily around everywhere to make sure everything was in order. He was always suspicious. I was scared. I made Good Thing stay with the kittens in the cupboard and hid the remains of the sausages in there with them. Boy was all dreamy, but he sat on the book of history to hide it. Old Man looked at him, hard. I was scared again. Surely Old Man would notice that Boy's red coat was of fine warm cloth and that there was a silk shirt underneath? But Old Man said, "Stupid as ever, I see," and grumped out of the house again.

Talking of sausages, when do you eat? Soon? Good. Now, go on stroking.

The next day Old Man was still away. Boy said, "Those were wonderful books. I must have *more*. I wish I didn't have to trust a cat and a spirit to steal them. Isn't there *any* way I can go and choose books for myself?"

Good Thing drifted about the house, thinking. At last it got into me and said, "There is no way I can take you to the mansion bodily, Master. But if you can go into a trance, I can take you there in spirit. Would that do?"

"Perfectly!" said Boy.

"Oh, no," I said. "If you do, I'm coming, too. I don't trust you on your own with my Boy, Good Thing. You might go feeble and lose him."

"I will *not*!" said Good Thing. "But you may come if you wish. And we will wait till the middle of the night, please. We don't want you to be seen again."

Around midnight Boy cheerfully went into a trance. Usually he hated it when Old Man made him do it. And we went to the mansion again, all three of us. It was very odd. I could see Boy there the way I could see Good Thing, like a big, flimsy cloud. As soon as we were there, Boy was so astonished by the grandeur of it that he insisted on drifting all around it, upstairs and down, to see as much as he could. I was scared. Not everyone was asleep. There were gaslights or candles burning in most of the corridors, and someone could easily have seen me. But I stuck close to Boy because I was afraid Good Thing would lose him.

It was not easy to stay close. They could go through doors without opening them. When they went through one door upstairs, I had to jump up and work the handle in order to follow Boy inside. It was a pretty room. The quilt on the bed was a cat's dream of comfort. I jumped up and paddled on it, while Boy and Good Thing hovered to look at the person asleep there. She was lit up by the nightlight beside the bed.

"What a *lovely* girl!" I felt Boy think. "She must be a princess."

She sat up at that. I think it was because of me treading on her stomach. I went tumbling way backward, which annoyed me a good deal. She stared. I glowered and wondered whether to spit. "Oh!" she said. "You're that magic cat my father wants to catch. Come here, puss. I promise I won't let him hurt you." She held out her hand. She was nice. She knew how to stroke a cat, just like you. I let her stroke me and talk to me, and I was just curling up to enjoy a rest on her beautiful quilt when a huge Woman sprang up from a bed on the other side of the room.

"Were you calling, my lady?" she asked. Then she saw me.

She screamed. She ran to a rope hanging in one corner and heaved at it, screaming, *"That cat's back!"*

"Run!" Good Thing said to me. "I'll look after Boy."

So I ran. I have never run like that in my life, before or since. It felt as if everyone in the mansion was after me. Luckily for me, I knew my way around quite well by then. I ran upstairs and I ran down, and people clattered after me, shouting. I dived under someone's hand and dodged through a crooked cupboard place, and at last I found myself behind the curtains in the Man's room. He ran in and out. Other people ran in and out, but the Princess really had done something to help me somehow and not one of them thought of looking behind those curtains.

After a bit I heard the Princess in that room, too. "But it's a *nice* cat, Father—really sweet. I can't think why you're making all this fuss about it!" Then there was a sort of grating sound. I smelled the smallest whiff of fresh air. Bless her, she had opened the Man's window for me.

I got out of it as soon as the room was empty. I climbed down onto grass. I ran again. I knew just the way I should go. Cats do, you know, particularly when they have kittens waiting for them. I was dead tired when I got to Old Man's house. It was right on the other side of town. As I scrambled through the skylight in the roof, I was almost too tired to move. But I was dead worried about my kittens and about Boy, too. It was morning by then.

My kittens were fine, but Boy was still lying on the floor of the book room in a trance, cold as ice. And as if that were not enough, keys grated in the locks and Old Man came back. All I could think to do was to lie around Boy's neck to warm him.

Old Man came and kicked Boy. "Lazy lump!" he said. "Anyone would think you were in a trance!" I couldn't think what to do. I got up and hurried about, mewing for milk, to distract Old Man. He wasn't distracted. Looking gleefully at

Boy, he carefully put a jar of black powder away in his cupboard and locked it. Then he sat down and looked at one of his books, not bothering with me at all. He kept looking across at Boy.

My kittens distracted Old Man by having a fight in the cupboard about the last of the sausages. Old Man heard it and leaped up. "Scrambling and squeaking!" he said. "Mice! Could even be rats by the noise. Damn cat! Don't you ever do your job?" He hit at me with his stick.

I tried to run. Oh, I was tired! I made for the stairs, to take us both away from Boy and my kittens, and Old Man caught me by my tail halfway up. I was that tired. . . . I was forced to bite him quite hard and scratch his face. He dropped me with a thump, so he probably did not hear the even louder thump from the book room. I did. I ran back there.

Boy was sitting up, shivering. There was a pile of books beside him.

"Good Thing!" I said. "That was stupid!"

"Sorry," said Good Thing. "He would insist on bringing them." The books vanished into the invisible sack just as Old Man stormed in.

He ranted and grumbled at Boy for laziness and for feeding me so that I didn't catch mice, and he made Boy set mousetraps. Then he stormed off to the cellar.

"Why didn't you come back sooner?" I said to Boy.

"It was too marvelous being somewhere that wasn't this house," Boy said. He was all dreamy with it. He didn't even read his new books. He paced about. So did I. I realized that my kittens were not safe from Old Man. And if he found them, he would realize that I could get out of the house. Maybe he would kill me like the cat before. I was scared. I wished Boy would be scared, too. I wished Good Thing would show some sense. But Good Thing was only thinking of pleasing Boy.

"Don't let him go into a trance again," I said. "Old Man will know."

"But I *have* to!" Boy shouted. "I'm *sick* of this house!" Then he calmed down and thought. "I know," he said to Good Thing. "Fetch the Princess here."

Good Thing got into me and bleated that this wasn't wise now that Old Man was back. I said so, too. But Boy wouldn't listen. He had to have Princess. Or else he would go into a trance and see her that way. I understood then. Boy wanted kittens. Very little will stop boys or cats when they do.

So we gave in. When Old Man was asleep and snoring, Boy dressed himself in the middle of the night in the Man's finest clothes and looked fine as fine. He even washed in horrible cold water, in spite of all I said. Then Good Thing went to the mansion.

Instants later the Princess was lying asleep on the floor of the book room. "Oh," Boy said sorrowfully, "what a shame to wake her!" But he woke her up all the same.

She rubbed her eyes and stared at him. "Who are you, sir?"

Boy said, "Oh, Princess—"

She said, "I think you've made a mistake, sir. I'm not a princess. Are you a prince?"

Boy explained who he was and all about himself, and she explained that her father was a rich magician. She was a disappointment to him, she said, because she could hardly do any magic and was not very clever. But Boy still called her Princess. She said she would call him Orange because of his hair. She may not have been clever, but she was nice. I sat on her knee and purred. She stroked me and talked to Boy for the whole night, until it began to get light. They did nothing but talk. I said to Good Thing that it was a funny way to have kittens. Good Thing was not happy. Princess did not understand about Good Thing. Boy gave up trying to explain. Good Thing drifted about, sulking.

When it was really light, Princess said she must go back. Boy agreed, but they put it off and kept talking. That was when I had my good idea. I went to the cupboard and fetched out my kittens, one by one, and I put them into Princess's lap.

"Oh!" she said. "What beauties!"

"Tell her she's to keep them and look after them," I said to Boy.

He told her, and she said, "Brindle can't *mean* it! It seems such a sacrifice. Tell her it's sweet of her, but I *can't*."

"Make her take them," I said. "Tell her they're a present from you, if it makes her happier. Tell her they're a sign that she'll see you again. Tell her *anything*, but make her take them!"

So Boy told her, and Princess agreed. She gathered the tabby and the ginger and the mixed kitten into her hands, and Good Thing took her and the kittens away. We stood staring at the place where she had been, Boy and I. Things felt empty, but I was pleased. My kittens were safe from Old Man, and Princess had kittens now, which ought to have pleased Boy, even if they were mine and not his. I did not understand why he looked so sad.

Old Man was standing in the doorway behind us. We had not heard him getting up. He glared at the fine way Boy was dressed. "How did you come by those clothes?"

"I did a spell," Boy said airily. Well, it was true in a way. Boy's mood changed when he realized how clever we had been. He said, "And Brindle got rid of the mice," and laughed.

Old Man was always annoyed when Boy laughed. "Funny, is it?" he snarled. "For that, you can go down to the cellar, you and your finery, and stay there till I tell you to come out." And he put one of his spells on Boy, so that Boy had to go. Old Man locked the cellar door on him. Then he turned back, rubbing his hands and laughing, too. "Last laugh's mine!" he said. "I *thought* he knew more than he let on, but there's no harm done. I've still got him!" He went and looked in almanacs and horoscopes and chuckled more. Boy was eighteen that day. Old Man began looking up spells, lots of them, from the bad black books that even he rarely touched.

"Brindle," said Good Thing, "I am afraid. Do one thing for me."

"Leave a cat in peace!" I said. "I need to sleep."

Good Thing said, "Boy will soon be dead and I will be shut out forever unless you help."

"But my kittens are safe," I said, and I curled up in the cupboard.

"They will not be safe," said Good Thing, "unless you do this for me."

"Do what for you?" I said. I was scared again, but I stretched as if I didn't care. I do *not* like to be bullied. You should remember that.

"Go to the cellar in my invisible sack and tell Boy where the golden ball is," Good Thing said. "Tell him to fetch it out of the floor and give it to you."

I stretched again and strolled past Old Man. His face was

scratched all over, I was glad to see, but he was collecting things to work spells with now. I strolled quite fast to the cellar door. There Good Thing scooped me up and went inside, in near dark. Boy was sitting against the wall.

"Nice of you to come," he said. "Will Good Thing fetch Princess again tonight?" He did not think there was any danger. He was used to Old Man behaving like this. But I thought of my kittens. I showed him the place where the golden ball had got lost down the crack. I could see it shining down there. It took me ages to persuade Boy to dig it out, and even then he only worked at it idly, thinking of Princess. He could only get at it with one little finger, which made it almost too difficult for him to bother.

I heard Old Man coming downstairs. I am ashamed to say that I bit Boy, quite hard, on the thumb of the hand he was digging with. He went "Ow!" and jerked, and the ball flew rolling into a corner. I raced after it.

"Put it in your mouth. Hide it!" said Good Thing.

I did. It was hard not to swallow it. Then, when I didn't swallow, it was hard not to spit it out. Cats are made to do one or the other. I had to pretend it was a piece of meat I was taking to my kittens. I sat in the corner, in the dark, while Old Man came in and locked the door and lit the tripod lamp.

"If you need Brindle," Boy said, sulkily sucking his hand, "*you* can look for her. She bit me."

"This doesn't need a cat," Old Man said. Boy and I were both astonished. "It just needs *you*," he told Boy. "This is the life transfer spell I was trying on the black cat. This time I know how to get it right."

"But you said you couldn't do it without a special powder!" Boy said.

Old Man giggled. "What do you think I've been away looking for all this year?" he asked. "I've got a whole jar of it! With
it, I shall put myself into your body and you into my body, and
then I shall kill this old body off. I won't need it or you after that.
I shall be young and handsome, and I shall live for years. Stand
up. Get into the pentangle."

"Blowed if I shall!" said Boy.

But Old Man did spells and made him. It took a long time
because Boy resisted even harder than I usually did and shouted
spells back. In the end Old Man cast a spell that made Boy
stand still and drew the five-pointed star around him, not in the
usual place.

"I shall kill my old body with you inside it rather slowly for
that," he said to Boy. Then he drew another star, a short way off.
"This is for my bride," he said, giggling again. "I took her into
my power ten years ago, and by now she'll be a lovely young
woman." Then he drew a third star, overlapping Boy's, for himself, and stood in it chuckling. "Let it start!" he cried out, and
threw the strong, smelly black powder on the tripod. Everything
went green-dark. When the green went, Princess was standing
in the empty star.

"Oh, it's *you*!" she and Boy both said.

"Aha!" said Old Man. "Hee-hee! So you and she *know* each
another, do you? How you did it, boy, I won't inquire, but it
makes things much easier for me." He began on his chanting.

"Give the golden ball to Princess," Good Thing said to me.
"Hurry. Make Boy tell her to swallow it."

I ran across to Princess and spit the golden ball into her star.
She pulled her skirt back from it.

"Brindle wants you to swallow it," Boy said. "I think it's important."

People are peculiar. Princess must have known it was very important, but she said faintly, "I can't! Not something that's been in a cat's *mouth*!"

Old Man saw the golden ball. He glared, still chanting, and raised his stick. The ball floated up and came toward him. Princess gave a last despairing snatch and caught it, just in time. She put it in her mouth.

"Ah! Back again!" said Good Thing.

Princess swallowed. She changed. She had been nice before but sort of stupid. Now she was nice and as clever as Boy. "You toad!" she said to Old Man. "That was part of my soul! You took it, didn't you?"

Old Man raised his stick again. Princess held up both hands. Magic raged, strong enough to make my fur stand up, and Old Man did not seem to be able to do much at first. It was interesting. Princess had magic, too, only I think it had all gone into Good Thing. But not quite enough. She started to lose. "Help me!" she said to Boy.

Boy started to say a spell, but at that moment the door of the cellar burst open, and half the wall fell in with it. The Man rushed in with a crowd of others.

"Father!" said Princess. "Thank goodness!"

"Are you all right?" said the Man. "We traced you through those kittens. What are you trying to do here, Old Man? The life transfer, is it? Well, that's enough of *that*!" The Man made signs that stood my coat up on end again.

Old Man screamed. I could tell he was dying. The spell had

somehow turned back on him. He was withering and shrinking and getting older and older. Boy jumped out of his star and ran to Princess. They both looked very happy. Old Man snarled at them, but he could do nothing but round on me. Everyone does that. They all kick the cat when they can't kick a person. "So you had *kittens!*" he screamed. "This is all your fault, cat! For that, you shall have kittens to drown for the next thousand years!"

"I soften that curse!" the Man shouted.

Then everything went away, and I was not in the town I knew anymore. I have been wandering about, all these years, ever since. Old Man's curse means that I am good at having kittens. It is not a bad curse because the Man has softened it. Old Man meant my kittens to be drowned every time. But instead, if I can find an understanding person—like you—who will listen to my story, then my kittens will have good homes, and so will I for a time. You won't mind. They'll be beautiful kittens. They always are. You'll see very soon now. After supper.

✽ THE
GREEN
STONE ✽

The heroes were gathering for the Quest in the inn yard. It was chaos. Since this was my first Quest as recording Cleric, I was racing around among them trying to get each hero's name and run down my checklist with them. They tell me more experienced Clerics don't even try. Half of them were barbarians who didn't speak any language I knew, large greasy fellows in the minimum of leather armor, with a lot of hairy flesh showing. Most of them were busy waxing and honing at a variety of weapons: gigantic swords, whose name they insisted on telling me instead of their own, monstrous cudgels, ten-foot spears and the like. Every one of them was also shouting for provisions and equipment and running about for last-minute extras.

There was a constant tooth-splitting din from the grindstone, where a squat person with a long gray beard was carefully putting a surgical edge on an axe blade as wide as his own shoulders.

"Rono?" I screamed over the din at a tower of muscle in a leather loincloth. "Is that your name or your sword's name?"

He was in a bad mood. He had been waiting half an hour for his turn at the grindstone. He glowered and fingered what looked like a shrunken human head dangling from his loincloth. "No. Name secret!" he snarled.

I wrote ?Rono? on my tablets and went on to my checklist. "And are you aware of the nature of the Quest? We travel in search of the Green Stone of Katta Rhyne—"

"Yah, yah. We go now," he snarled.

"Not quite now," I bawled. "We wait until the King comes to give us his personal blessing." In view of the screaming chaos in that yard, I was rather glad the King hadn't arrived yet. "And you are properly aware of the difficulties and dangers? The Green Stone is in the hands of a powerful wizard and can transform fatally anyone who touches it—"

"I *know!*" he bawled. "I hero!"

"Yes, yes," I said hurriedly. His hand was meaningfully caressing that shrunken human head of his. I went on down my list. "And you have proper equipment, weapons, armor, warm clothes? It will be cold in the mountains." He glared at me. I gulped, "Well, you ought to have a warm cloak at least. And transport. Have you horse, dragon, or other means of conveyance?"

Here I was rudely interrupted by a very large female who plucked me by the shoulder and spun me away from ?Rono?

Apart from the fact that she had added a leather bra with knobs on, she was dressed just like him, mostly in a big sword and shrunken human head. I stared into her grubby navel, shaken. She was big. "You try coddle my little brother?" she demanded.

"No, no," I said. "This list. I have to make sure everyone has what's on it. Name, please."

"Name secret. We walk. We carry nothing," she said.

I hoped that keeping up with the horses would warm them up in the mountains and scuttled quickly on to the next hero. He was a suave young man in a turban who had brought a camel to ride. The creature was something like a moldy hearthrug on long knobbly legs, out of which stuck a long neck with a temper worse than ?Rono's? on the end of it. It made three attempts to bite me while I was finding out that the young man was called Haroun and that he carried a talisman of some kind. He didn't actually *say*, but I assumed he was our statutory magic-user. I wrote down ?Magician? and dodged away among the crush, worrying about it. We really *had* to have a magic-user. I couldn't control this lot on my own.

I made another attempt to collect the name of the person monopolizing the grindstone, but he couldn't hear me for the noise he was making. So I wrote down Dwarf, because he obviously was, and reckoned that with that axe he was certainly properly equipped. I skirted an argument, two horses, and an aggressive griffon and found we had a harpist at least. He was seated on the horse trough, strumming inaudibly, a very pleasant young fellow with curly hair who said his name was Trouvere. There was a smiling man with white teeth next to him, carrying a pack, but when I tried to take this one's name he turned out to be a tinker, come to see his friend the harpist off. Embarrassing. But I felt better when I spotted a tall figure in a cowled cloak a little way off beside one of the store sheds. That *had* to be our magician.

I hastened up to him. "Name, please."

His hooded head turned, giving me a glimpse of a piercing eye staring at me across a hooked nose. "Why?" he said. "Does it matter?"

"I have to have you all down in my records," I explained.

"How diligent," he said. "Then I am Basileus for your records." His tone was deeply sarcastic. I knew it was a false name, but I wrote it down—with the usual query.

I was just turning away, when a tall pallid figure leaped out through the door of the shed. "Don't go without me!" he said breathlessly. "I won't be long now."

He was wearing some kind of apron and long gloves, both of which were dripping with something greenish. His right hand clutched a knife, also dripping green.

"Er—who are you?" I said faintly.

"Pelham," he said. "I'm your healer. You'll need me."

"Oh," I said.

"I'll be about ten minutes," he said. "I'm just finishing a postmortem." And he added to the cowled Basileus, "You were right. The creature was definitely human once." After which he dived back into the shed.

I wrote him down too, wishing I had not eaten breakfast, and went back to the rest of the chaos. To my surprise, it was beginning to sort itself out. The Dwarf backed away from the grindstone, lovingly stroking his axe, and ?Rono? dived forward for his turn. Everyone else began climbing up on to their mounts. As recording Cleric, I had been allotted a cart to ride in which had a cunning desk-attachment I could swing over my knees, so that I could go on writing down all things at all times. The cart was drawn by a highly opinionated mule. But nobody had thought of providing it with a driver.

It was my turn to make some chaos. "How on *earth* am I supposed to write *and* drive?" I screamed. "This mule is a full-time job! Am I expected to make an exact record of everyone's deeds while controlling the brute with one hand, or something?"

Every hero there stared reprovingly and then turned away. Clerics are not supposed to fuss. I was eventually rescued by the harper Trouvere, who pushed through the crowd and climbed smilingly into the driving seat. "I'll deal with the mule," he said. "I'm no hand at riding and—to be frank—I can't afford a horse anyway." While I was gushing grateful thanks at him, Trouvere dumped his harp beside me and collected the reins as if it was something he'd been doing all his life. The mule stopped trying to kick the front of the cart in and stood still. Now we were only waiting for the King to arrive and give us his blessing.

In the sudden hush, Pelham emerged from the shed again, without the gloves and apron this time. Looking pallidly smug, he whispered to Basileus and passed him a small bag. Basileus was clearly delighted. He patted the healer on the shoulder. Then, deliberately and jauntily, he climbed to a high mounting block by the inn door, where everyone could see him, even those, like me, who had Haroun and his bad-tempered camel in the way. Basileus threw off his hood and flung back his cloak. There was a crown on his head and the rest of his clothes were purple and ermine.

"I am your King," he said. Everyone gave an uncertain, muttering sort of cheer. He smiled. "I was coming here," he said, "to bless this Quest on its way, when I was attacked by a strange green man. I was fortunate enough to kill him. And when I examined the body, it reminded me very strongly of the hero Seigro, who went in search of the Green Stone a year ago. So I brought it here and asked my Royal Healer, Pelham, to dissect the corpse. This is what we have been waiting for. Pelham cut the creature open and discovered that, in place of a heart, it had the Green Stone of Katta Rhyne. Here it is." He held up the bag. "It only remains for me to thank you all very much for answering my call and to tell you that there is now no longer any need for the Quest."

There was an instant of thunderstruck silence. Then a growl arose in a dozen languages. Such words as I could pick out were "Recompense!" "Something for our trouble!" and "Cost of travel!" mixed with cries of "Swindle!" and "Cheat!" Axes and swords were waved. I did not blame them for feeling cheated. This was my first Quest. Though it had promised to be nothing but trouble, I found I was furious to be deprived of it. Haroun's camel seemed to have the same feelings. It vented bubbling howls and plunged about. My mule was not the animal to take noises from a mere camel. It went for the camel, dragging my cart with it, Trouvere wrestling at the reins, Haroun wrestling at *his* reins—both laughing for some reason—myself screaming, every hero in the yard roaring . . . I had a glimpse of the King with the bag in one hand and the other making soothing gestures. The next glimpse I had of him, the bag was gone from his hand. The tinker leapt nimbly up beside me, flourishing a bag that looked just the same. "Got it! Let's go!" he shouted.

Trouvere whipped on the reins. The mule forgot the camel and dashed for the yard gate. "Cover our backs, Haroun!" Trouvere shouted as we thundered out into the town. And we galloped madly from under the noses of heroes.

We have been galloping almost ever since. Haroun caught us up after an hour, laughing heartily.

"The heroes didn't know what hit them," he said. "Never seen an angry camel before. Aren't you going to throw that whinging Cleric out?"

"Oh no," said Trouvere—if that is his name. "She can stay and do her job. Let her write down how we get on against all the heroes the King is going to send after us."

"Not to speak of the wizard who had the Stone in the first place," said the tinker. "Don't forget *him*."

"Then write, woman!" Haroun laughed. "Write, or my camel may get angry."

So I write. . . .

THE FAT WIZARD

The Fat Wizard lived up at the Big House in our village and he always opened the Church Fête. As well as being very fat, he had a purple face and pop eyes and a gray bristly beard. He despised everyone. When he opened the Fête, he said things like, "This Fête gets more boring every year. Why do you silly people love it?" This was considered very witty, because the Fat Wizard was rich. I preferred Mrs. Ward's cousin Old Ned, myself. Everyone despised Old Ned, but at least he went mad in the Church porch every full moon. The Fat Wizard never did anything but grumble.

My Auntie May always went to the Church Fête, although we were Chapel. She went for the jumble. Auntie May was the most respectable witch I have ever known and she did not like Chapel people to know she bought cast-off clothes.

She lived in the house on the corner opposite the White Horse and everything indoors was just so. I came to live in that house as soon as I left school, to train to be Auntie May's assistant. Auntie May used to look through her curtains and count how often Mrs. Ward went into the pub. "Look at her!" she would snort. "Red dress, hung all over with jewelry, and enough makeup to sink a battleship!" Though they were both witches, Auntie May and Mrs. Ward were opposites in every way. Auntie May was tall and lean and dour, and she wore dour brown clothes. Mrs. Ward was small and glamorous, and she had lovely legs. I used to admire Mrs. Ward and wish I was her assistant, not Auntie May's.

Anyway, the Church Fête was only two days away. Auntie May and I were talking about it while I cleared away breakfast.

"And you're not to bowl for the pig this year, Cheryl," Auntie May was saying, when there was a sort of boom and a flash. The Fat Wizard's manservant George appeared in the middle of the kitchen.

"The Wizard wants to see you at once," George said. Really it was a wonder I didn't drop the teapot! Everyone said George was really a demon, but I didn't think even demons had a right to appear in people's kitchens like that.

Auntie May took it quite calmly. "What does he want?" she said. But George only vanished, with another boom and a flash. "Well, we'd better go," Auntie May said, getting her flat brown hat off its peg and pinning it bolt upright across her head.

So off we went, with me wondering what gave the Fat Wizard the right to order us about. As we passed the Vicarage and came to the church, I was wishing for about the thousandth time that I could go and live in Town. The Vicar was trying to chase my pig Ranger out of the churchyard.

"About that pig," Auntie May said forbiddingly.

"I won't do it again," I said guiltily, as we turned into the drive of the Big House. I'd won Ranger at the Church Fête last year, you see, and I'm pretty sure I won him by unfair use of magic. You know how it is, when you're willing and willing for the skittles to fall over. I went a bit far in my willing, and I'm pretty sure half the skittles went over without my bowls even touching them. I was given this squealing, struggling, long-legged piglet, and there was only my mother's tiny backyard to keep him in. He kept getting out. At first, people in the village kept catching him and bringing him back. But he got cleverer and cleverer, until everyone gave up. By now Ranger was a large white amiable pig, and you were likely to meet him anywhere.

The Vicar was still shouting at Ranger as we came to the Big House. George opened the tradesmen's door to us. "Took your time, didn't you?" he said, and he led the way down a corridor, waggling his rump as he walked. I think he waggled because he was allowing for a tail, and he didn't have a tail in human form. But he shocked Auntie May. She whispered to me not to look.

The Fat Wizard was in a sunny morning-room having breakfast. When we came in, he was scraping up the last of a quart tub of fat-free yogurt. Then he poured a pint of milk on a hill of bran flakes, emptied the sugar bowl over it, and ate most of that before he looked up. "Here at last, are you, May?" he grunted. He didn't notice me.

"What can we do for you, sir?" Auntie May asked.

The Fat Wizard guzzled up the rest of his bran flakes. Then he cut a giant slice off a starch-reduced loaf. He spread that with most of a packet of slimmers' margarine and ladled marmalade on top of that. "The doctors say I'm too fat," he said peevishly. "They make me eat this chicken feed all the time, but it's not doing a scrap of good. I've got to lose weight. Make me up a potion that will do the trick."

"Of course, sir," Auntie May said politely. "But couldn't you do that yourself, sir?"

The Fat Wizard tipped the rest of the jar of marmalade on his bread and ate it in two bites. "Potions are not men's work," he said with his mouth full. "Go away, woman, and mix me a weight-reducing potion, and get it here today, or I'll get Tallulah Ward to do it."

Rude old man! We hurried home, and Auntie May did her best for him, but it is not easy to set that kind of spell quickly, even when she had me to grind up the ingredients for her. We worked hard the rest of the day. We were straining the mixture all evening, and we only had it bottled just before midnight.

"Take it round to him, Cheryl," Auntie May said, breathlessly slapping a label on the bottle. "And run!"

I supposed Auntie May could not bear the thought of Mrs. Ward being asked to do the potion. I took the bottle and set off down the street at a trot, with the bottle foaming and fizzing eerily in my fist. It was quite dark, and I was scared. When I turned in at the gate of the Big House, a large white shape drifted across the drive in front of me. I was too scared even to scream. I just stood.

Then the moon came up over the Fat Wizard's chimneys and the white shape said "Honk!", and I realized it was only

Ranger. He knew it was me. He came and brushed his bristly self against me.

"Yes, you're a nice pig," I said. "Much nicer than the Fat Wizard. But don't *ever* do that again!"

Then I went on and George tried to scare me too. He appeared suddenly in a red light, outside the front door. But I had used up all my fright on Ranger. I held the bottle scornfully out to him. George snatched it. Then he turned and went in through the front door without opening it first, waggling his stern as he melted through it.

I was annoyed, and I could hear Ranger grunting and foraging among the trees as I went back down the drive, so I was not particularly frightened until I got to the gate. Then midnight struck. Something howled, like a dog, but not quite like, over in the churchyard. My hair tried to stand on end, until I realized that it was full moon and the noise was only Old Ned, going mad as usual. I went across the road to have a look.

This is something all the village children like to do. There was a whole row of them sitting on the churchyard wall, ready to watch Old Ned. The biggest was Lizzie Holgate's eldest boy, Jimmy, from the council houses.

Jimmy said, "We've been feeding your pig all this week."

"Thanks," I said.

"He's a good animal," Jimmy said. "I like a pig with brains."

"Shut up!" someone else whispered. "Old Ned's starting."

Old Ned came crawling out of the church porch on all fours. That was how he always began. He thought he was a wolf. But I still don't know why they called him *Old* Ned. There was no gray in his hair. When he felt the moonlight across his face, he stood up and stretched both arms in the air.

"Silver temptress!" he shouted. "Take this spell off me!" We giggled a bit and waited for what he would say next. He can go on for hours. He came shambling down the path between the graves, staring. "I see you!" he yelled. *"I see you, Cheryl Watson!"*

And he was staring straight at me. I could feel the row of boys moving away from me. Nobody dared be with anyone Old Ned noticed at full moon.

"I see you, Cheryl," said Old Ned. "My mistress tells you to make sure to spend tomorrow night at your mother's house. It will be to your advantage." He gave a mad laugh and went shambling back into the church porch.

"The show's over," Jimmy said to the others. They all got off the wall and ran away without speaking to me. I didn't think the show was over. Old Ned began howling again as I went back to Auntie May's, but none of us felt like staying. I kept wondering. I woke up next morning still wondering why Old Ned had noticed me.

But that went out of my head when Mrs. Ward came banging on Auntie May's door. Auntie May glared at her. Mrs. Ward had her hair in a pink turban and her red coat on over what looked to be a frilly nightdress. Tears were driving black streaks down her makeup.

"Oh, *what* have you gone and done to our poor Fat Wizard!" she gasped. She was killing herself laughing. "Come and take a look!"

We ran outside. Most of the village was out there, either in a row in front of the White Horse or up in the churchyard. And there was George, frantically running up the street with a coil of rope, trying to throw a loop of rope over the Fat Wizard. The Fat

Wizard was floating and bobbing about forty feet over every-one's heads. You could see he was nearly as light as air. And he was livid. He was wearing purple pajamas and his face was the same color. His eyes were blue bubbles of pure rage.

"Oh dear," said Auntie May.

"It's not your fault," I said. "He asked you to reduce his weight."

"Get me *down*, George!" the Fat Wizard bawled in a high, windy voice.

George threw the rope again and hit him with the loop, which made the Fat Wizard bob another ten feet up in the air. The wind caught him and whirled him toward the church.

"*Help*, George!" he yelled, bouncing against the steeple.

"Trying to, sir! Out of my way!" George shouted, leaping over gravestones and dodging among staring people. "Oh, I *do* blame myself for opening the window without looking, sir!"

Another gust of wind sent the Fat Wizard slowly bumping and scraping up the steeple. Auntie May went indoors then and made me come too. She said the disgrace was too much. I couldn't see properly from her house. All I could see was Lizzie Holgate arriving, pushing her old pushchair with her twins in it, with Mary and Jimmy and Charlene carrying the smaller babies. I saw Lizzie take two of the babies and send Jimmy and Mary off, but I couldn't see where. Jimmy told me later.

The Fat Wizard was hooked on the weathercock by then. But of course George was a demon, so he couldn't touch the church. Lizzie sent Jimmy and Mary up the stairs inside the steeple with the rope. They climbed out at the top and tied the rope to him. Then they unhooked him and George hauled him down into the churchyard. Jimmy said the Fat Wizard didn't even thank them.

While that was happening, Mrs. Ward ran past and went into her house, still laughing. Soon after, George came panting along with the rope over his shoulder, towing the bobbing, fluttering Fat Wizard like an angry barrage balloon. We had a good view, because Mrs. Ward lived six houses up, beyond the place where the road bends around the White Horse. It took George twenty minutes to work the bouncing and bobbling Fat Wizard through Mrs. Ward's front door.

"Well, she should have had time to get dressed by now, even the way *she* dresses," Auntie May said viciously.

She was very upset. So was I, rather. It could have been my fault. I told you how I came to win Ranger in the heat of the moment. I could have put in a bit of ill-wishing when I grated the ingredients or when I handed the potion to George. That made me feel I ought to keep out of Auntie May's way for a while. I asked if I could go and see my mother.

Auntie May felt like being alone. She told me to stay the night if I wanted. "But make sure to come back in time to go to the Fête tomorrow," she added.

My mother lives out along Water Lane. It felt strange to be going there and not living there anymore.

"Is someone blaming you for that weight-reducing spell?" my mother asked. She had heard all about it, of course.

"I'm not sure," I said. "Has there been anything to my advantage here?"

"Not that I know of," said my mother.

"Then I'll have to stay the night," I said.

Mother was not too keen on the idea. She turned out to be

using my old room as an apple-store. But she is fond of me, and she let me spend the night on the sofa, which was much warmer than my old room. And in the morning, as if Old Ned had *known*, there was a letter from my Godmother. My Godmother is head of the biggest coven in Town. She wrote that I must be about old enough to be leaving school now, and she invited me to come and join her and train to be a witch.

"Write and tell her you can't," said my mother. "If I'd known she was going to offer, I'd never have let you go to May. But it's too late now. You can't let May down."

"Bother!" I said sadly. I was longing to live in Town. I put the letter in my pocket to answer later and went back to Auntie May's.

I came back to a sight I had quite often seen before. Auntie May was standing dourly in the street, staring at her house. Most of the side wall was missing. The roof was sagging, and the front room was filled with broken laths, plaster, and the ruins of Auntie May's furniture. The house is on a right-angled bend, you see. A lorry driver coming through the village in the night could see the White Horse, but not Auntie May's house on the other side of the street beyond it. This lorry driver had not turned his wheel quickly enough and had arrived in Auntie May's front room in the middle of the night. He had driven through my bedroom too. Almost the first thing I saw through the hole was the ruins of my bed, upside down in the plaster next to the street. My bedroom floor was missing. I gulped a bit when I saw and said a silent "Thank you" to Old Ned.

"I *am* insured," Auntie May said glumly. "And I daresay I deserved it for getting that potion wrong."

"You mean," I said, "the Fat Wizard?"

Auntie May said, "Hush!" and gave a stiff, uneasy look all round. "Yes, this happens every time I cross him. Well, come in. The kitchen's still there."

We picked our way through the rubble. I no longer wondered why Auntie May hurried to obey the Fat Wizard when he wanted something. And I was angry. The Fat Wizard had not even thought what might happen to *me*!

"They say he gave Tallulah Ward a gold bracelet," Auntie May said bitterly while the kettle boiled. "She made him heavy again. I saw him walk past on his own two feet with that George fussing around him. Ah well, life is not meant to be fair. I mustn't grumble."

I did not agree at all. I said, "Didn't he give the Holgates anything?"

"Of course not!" Auntie May said, surprised at the idea.

I was still angry when we set off to the Church Fête that afternoon. We had to spend all morning putting No Entry spells on the house. The builder was too busy with the Fat Wizard's gutters to board up the hole. And my best dress was somewhere in the rubble under my bed. I only had my old jersey and skirt. The Church Fête, in spite of a chilly wind, was full of people in their summer best, and the first person we met when we went through the gate was Mrs. Ward. She was wearing a new red dress and making her new gold bracelet chink up and down her arm by carrying a big bunch of magic balloons which kept tugging to get away. She smiled meanly at us.

"Come for your jumble, have you?" she said. "I'm surprised you dare show your faces. You look just like the two fools you are."

I'd admired Mrs. Ward up to then. I was quite disillu-
sioned. Auntie May went dark red and we both pretended not
to hear. It was easy to pretend, because the loudspeakers were
making sounds like a cat being attacked by bagpipes. We
stalked past Mrs. Ward.

Usually Auntie May waits near the jumble stall until the
Fête is opened, so that she can be first there; but this time we
stalked past the jumble, and the rifle range, and the lucky dip,
and then the bowls pitch. There was a small white piglet in a
hutch to one side of the bowls. It kept pushing its snout through
the chicken netting and getting stuck.

"Now, Cheryl!" Auntie May said, seeing me looking.

But I could see the piglet was not clever like Ranger and I
was not interested this year.

Ranger was there, of course. He came pushing through the
hedge as we were going to the flower tent. He gave me a friendly
wink and trotted off into the crowd. A couple of ice cream vans
had arrived, and Ranger's plump white shape was here, there,
and everywhere, begging for ice cream. Lizzie Holgate was
there, handing money out in handfuls to all her six kids. All of
them bought ice creams with it and most of them gave theirs
straight to Ranger. Auntie May snorted at the waste and we went
around the flowers. The judges had already mysteriously been
there and given First Prizes to all the wrong things. We stood in
the hot, squashed grass looking at the Single Rose. Auntie May
was feeling better by then.

"That, Cheryl," she said, "is the Way of Life. You have to
accept it."

The Fat Wizard had won with a scrawny yellow rose. Old

Ned had put in a perfect and wonderful red rose and hadn't won a prize at all. I didn't feel at all like accepting it.

All this time, the Vicar's voice kept coming over the loudspeakers saying, "One. Two. Three. Testing," mixed with howls and squalls. As we came out of the tent, he said "Ninety-nine!" followed by a noise like God eating celery and the band started to play outside the beer tent. The Fat Wizard's large shiny Bentley was bumping slowly across the field toward the Vicar. Auntie May and I got quickly to the back of the crowd.

"I'm sure CRUNCH CHOMP needs no introduction from THUNDERCRASH," the loudspeakers said as the car stopped and George sprang out dressed as a chauffeur. "We are delighted SQUASH welcome CLATTER once again to TEATRAYS RUN OVER BY LORRY our little Fête."

George opened the door of the Bentley and the Fat Wizard climbed out. He was very angry again. He puffed and he glared and he panted, and he finally got both feet out onto the grass. They sank up to the ankles as soon as he took a step. The earth quivered. He took two more steps. Music stands in front of the band fell over. By this time the Fat Wizard was walking along a small trench, sinking lower every second. He must have weighed well over a ton. His bulging blue eyes flickered angrily about looking for someone.

Auntie May said, in a mild, pleased voice, "I hope Tallulah Ward has the sense to keep out of sight."

But Mrs. Ward was right near the edge of the crowd, easy to pick out by her red dress and the bunch of straining balloons. Her face was so pale that she had a bright red spot of makeup showing on each cheek.

Just then Lizzie Holgate came around the Bentley, pushing her pushchair and surrounded by all her kids. They seemed to be looking for a good place to stand. Jimmy and Mary had to lift the pushchair over the trench the Fat Wizard had made, so that for a second the whole family was milling around the Fat Wizard.

When they moved on again, the Fat Wizard was the right weight. He climbed easily out of his trench and he took an easy step or so. But it never occurred to him to thank the Holgates. He just glared at Mrs. Ward.

"If you'll just come over to the microphone, sir—" the Vicar called.

But Ranger had followed the Holgates around the Bentley, hoping for more ice cream. He saw something was going on and he stood, looking about inquisitively. He looked at the Fat Wizard.

"Ah!" said the Fat Wizard. "Now I know what to do to that woman!" He pointed a fat finger at Mrs. Ward, and he shouted out something that made an even louder noise than the loudspeakers.

All Mrs. Ward's balloons went up together in a huddle, like hair standing on end. In place of Mrs. Ward, there was suddenly a thin white pig with blobs of pink on its cheeks. It ran about among everyone's legs, trying to get itself out of its red dress. Then it dashed into the beer tent, trailing underclothes and squealing, and there was suddenly a lot of noise from in there, too.

Everyone except Ranger looked at the Vicar, and the Vicar looked at the sky. Ranger looked at me—in a puzzled, reproachful way, as if he thought it was *my* fault that Mrs. Ward was knocking tables over and squealing in the beer tent.

"Where do I stand to open this silly Fête?" the Fat Wizard said.

"Oh no you *won't* open the Fête!" I screamed. I couldn't bear the way Ranger was looking. I rushed through the crowd and I stood in the open, with one hand stretched out toward the Fat Wizard and the other stretched toward Ranger. "You're selfish and greedy and cruel!" I yelled. "*Ranger* would make a better human than you!"

The loudspeakers made a MOTORBIKE-STARTING-IN-HEAVEN noise. After that Ranger and the Fat Wizard seemed to have changed places. The Fat Wizard was standing where Ranger had been, staring at me with amused piggy eyes. Where the Fat Wizard had been was a very fat pig with a sort of black waistcoat marked on its white skin. This pig had blue eyes and it looked stunned.

Jimmy Holgate shouted, *"Cheryl! Look out!"*

George was climbing out of the Bentley. His smart chauffeur's uniform burst off him. He leapt toward me, towering over me, huge and blue-black. The tail he always seemed to be missing was lashing round his legs, thick and hairy, with a forked tip. I was terrified.

Lizzie Holgate and her kids arrived beside me. Auntie May was there too, holding her hat on dourly. And my mother was next to Auntie May, which *did* surprise me, because she never goes to the Church Fête. George towered and gnashed his long teeth. We all shouted "Avaunt!" and the loudspeakers went SCREAM and George vanished. The poor little piglet down by the bowling pitch suddenly went mad. George had possessed it. It screamed so hard that it almost drowned the noise in the beer tent.

Ranger winked at me. "Let's get this Fête open," he said to the Vicar in a pleasant grunty voice, "and we can all have an ice cream."

But Lizzie Holgate was whispering to my mother, "Can you send her somewhere where there's no pigs around?"

Mother caught the glaring blue eye of the pig with the waistcoat. "Her Godmother. In Town," she whispered back.

I caught the two-thirty bus outside the gate. While the bus was turning around, Old Ned let the piglet out of its hutch and it chased after the bus, foaming at the mouth, until Jimmy Holgate managed to catch it by one leg.

I have never dared to go back. Mother writes that the blue-eyed pig made such a nuisance of himself, squealing and grunting night and day, that they sent him along with George to the bacon factory some time ago. Mother has Mrs. Ward in the sty in her backyard. Even the Holgates can't turn her back. Ranger is still living at the Big House. He opens the Church Fête every year, and Mother says you couldn't have a nicer landlord.

No
One

One morning in the year 2084, the Right Honorable Mrs. Barbara Scantion M.P. was talking to a friend in the House of Commons. "Yes, it's school holidays," she was saying. "My husband's in Madrid. We got a foreign girl to look after Edward, but Edward's just rung up to say she's walked out again. That's the second time this week!"

"Does that mean no one's looking after Edward?" the friend asked.

"Yes. No one's looking after Edward," Mrs. Scantion said. She laughed.

A fly-on-the-wall bug recorded this conversation and it was duly passed on to the Anti-European Organization, which wished to make use of Mrs. Scantion. Unfortunately, it was entirely misunderstood.

No One was a robot—though Edward called him Nuth, short for Nothing. He was No. One in Knight Bros's special new series of White Knights, which meant he was fitted with every latest device in robotics, including a quasi-permanent power pac, long-distance radio, and self-reprogramming. He had an AT brain (meaning Advanced Type). His silver skin would only melt at extreme high temperatures, and, what was probably more useful, he could feel with his silver fingers. His pink eyes could see in the dark. In fact, he could see anything which was not actually invisible. He was programmed both to obey orders and think for himself. He was brand-new. He cost a bomb (Mr. Scantion was very, very rich). And he knew he was utterly useless.

He got both his names because the Scantions looked up from reading, in the thick booklet which had come with him, that he was No. One in the White Knight Series. And the robot was not there. The passage leading to the garage door was empty. Since they had all seen the lorry drive up and deliver the big crate labelled FRAGILE THIS END UP, and since Mr. Scantion had signed the delivery note with the robot unpacked and standing beside him in the garage, this puzzled everyone extremely.

It was quite simple. The moment Mr. Scantion went through the door to the house, something slammed the door shut and left the garage in darkness. The robot could see another pair of large robot eyes not far away. He thought he was in a store place for robots and was meant to stay there.

"Can you tell me if I should stay here?" he asked the other robot politely. It was a car of some kind, he could see.

Its voice seemed to be made from grinding cogwheels together. "Think for yourself," it grunted unhelpfully.

"Yes, but I am new," the robot explained. "I am a household robot, so I assume I should be in a house. But the door is shut. Why is that?"

The car gave a hydraulic sort of sigh. "Someone shut it of course! Wirenose! If you go close to it, the circuit will cause it to open again. That's how the softbodies do it."

"Thank you. What are softbodies?" asked the robot.

"Humans," grunted the car. "People. Folk. Owners." And as the robot walked toward the door, it snarled at him, in a perfect crash of cogs. "Learn to *think*, blobface! Or get scrapped!"

The lorry driver's mate had said that too, in the same disgusted way. The robot stepped through the door when it opened, wondering if there was something more to thinking than he had in his programs. There were four humans (softbodies?) in the passage beyond, one of them unnaturally small, all with the lower hole in their faces pulled into an O.

"Nothing!" said Betty the foreign girl, whose English was always a stage behind the facts.

The robot advanced toward them on soundless spongy feet. "Think," he said. "Consider, judge, believe, or ponder."

To his confusion, Betty screamed and ran away, and the rest fell about laughing. Mr. Scantion said, "No need to think. Your name's No One."

"Nothing's better," Edward said, but this joke was not attended to.

People very seldom attended to what Edward said. This confused No One, because he was told straightaway that his main job was to take care of Edward. Betty the foreign girl was considered unreliable. She broke down all the time. When she did, she sobbed that she was *"not happy!"* and then put things in a blue suitcase and went away down the drive. Presumably she went to get serviced, because she always came back about twelve hours later. It became No One's job to release the switches on the gate to let Betty out, and then release them again when she came back. It was a special Security Gate, designed to keep Edward safe.

Edward was obviously very precious. No One was told that Edward was going to inherit some things called "the firm" and "responsibilities" later on. No One ran through his dictionary program and discovered that "firm" meant the same as "hard, difficult." This must be why Edward always went white when these things were talked about. It was a sign of slight overload, the same sort of thing that made No One's eyes pulse. Edward was being programmed, very slowly, in all sorts of hard things like manners and playing the piano. No One knew how that felt—and it had only taken six months to program him: Edward was going to take years. He realized that Edward was very expensive indeed and treated him with great respect.

But he was confused. None of his programs quite fitted things as they were. This was Knight Bros's fault. When Mr. Scantion had ordered a household robot for Fawley Manor, someone in the office looked at a photo of the Manor and saw it was a large old house. They programmed No One for a large old house, not realizing that Fawley Manor had been modernized throughout inside. The only old thing left was the stairs. The walls were energized screens and the furniture was energized foam blocks, all of which could be moved at the touch of a button, controlled by a robot fixture in the cellar. The kitchen was a mass of machinery. No One's eyes pulsed when he saw it. But Mrs. Scantion had told him to cook supper because she was sick of autofood, so he located the freezer and opened it.

The freezer hummed frosty air complacently around No One. It was full of square gray frozen packets which all looked exactly alike. There was no way of telling carrots from éclairs, or beetroot from blackberries. "You'll have to melt everything to find out what it is," the freezer hummed.

"That would take too long," said No One. He held up a gray packet. "What is this?"

"Chicken drumsticks," hummed the freezer.

"And this?" asked No One, holding up another packet.

"I've forgotten," said the freezer. "You won't do it that way. My self-melt will come on if you keep me open much longer."

No One picked a bundle of gray packets out at random and shut the freezer. He put them in hot water in one of the sinks to thaw. While he was doing that, coffee beans began pouring out of a hopper in the opposite wall. No One went over to the hopper. "Why are you doing that?" he asked.

"Making-use-of-a-faulty-circuit-to-annoy-you," rattled the hopper. "Boo!" And coffee beans piled on the work surface.

No One tried to locate the faulty circuit. There was a gargling behind him. Even moving at superspeed, No One was not quick enough to stop the waste-disposal in the sink from eating every one of the gray packets, and he nearly lost a finger trying to. "Glumph," said the waste-disposal, satisfied. As

No One went to the freezer for another set of gray packets, he distinctly heard something scuttering and scrambling out of his way. But there was nothing there. Whatever it was continued to scutter and scramble from then on, confusing No One thoroughly. Since it did not seem to be there, he tried to ignore it. He stripped the plastic off the gray food and put it in the roasting oven. The autocook and the microwave at once flashed red lights at him.

"We're supposed to do that!" they said.

"I am supposed to cook by hand," No One told them. He turned the oven on. Nothing happened. "What is wrong with you?" No One asked it.

"I've come out in sympathy," said the oven. "My timer is set wrong."

No One made the oven work and tried to set the table as his program told him. But all the knives and forks were in the dishwasher and the dishwasher would not open. "Drying, drying!" it said when No One tried its door. Meanwhile, coffee beans continued to pour out of the hopper. By now they were all over the floor. No One's spongy robot feet suddenly turned into skates. He careered across the kitchen area and sat down with a crash among the chairs in the dining area. There he was forced to sit for a while, checking his circuits. While he sat, the scuttering thing scrambled about under the table tittering. It almost could have been laughing. Nothing in No One's microchips had prepared him for any of this. In order to prevent extreme overload, he had to get up and go away for a while.

He came across Edward at the other end of the house, plonking away at a very simple program on the piano. Edward stopped rather readily when he saw No One. "Hallo, Nuth. How are you getting on?"

"I do not understand," No One said, "why the large humans do not attend to you or why you are so small. You seem much better programmed than me already. I shall have to be scrapped. My programs do not fit this house."

Edward pushed the button that spun the piano stool around and looked up at No One. No One's eyes were pulsing from pink to white. "Poor Nuth!" he said. "But you're self-reprogramming, aren't you? That's like a human getting used to things. Are you programmed to play the piano?"

"Yes," said No One.

A gleeful smile came into Edward's face. "Then let's make a bargain. You do my piano practice and I'll help you reprogram. Okay?"

A bargain is not an order. No One decided it was better. His eyes stopped pulsing and he sat down at the piano. He played without having to learn how, and Edward corrected him by asking him to play slower, with random wrong notes. Both of them got something, No One realized, because, when the piano was finished with, Edward went to the kitchen area with him, where he stopped the hopper by turning off all the machinery on that side and then showed No One the suction-cleaner that cleaned the floor just by pressing a switch. Then he kicked the dishwasher and made it give up the knives and forks and plates so that No One could set the table. And he went on helping No One during supper. That was a disaster, thanks to the freezer. No One found he was serving curried prawns with bread-and-butter pudding, followed by beetroot and molten peppermint ice cream.

"But he doesn't eat so he doesn't know!" Edward explained, while No One stood abjectly waiting to be scrapped. "He'll know better next time."

Betty did not agree. It was this supper that made her pack her suitcase and leave for the first time. But Mr. and Mrs. Scantion listened to Edward for once and No One was not even sent away for reprogramming.

"You should have used the autocooker," Edward said to him afterward. "But you can't disobey an order, can you? Another time, Nuth, you're to get around it by asking me to do it."

So a bargain was a way of getting around orders too. No One felt he was learning. But not learning fast enough. Betty came back the next morning, but it was No One's fault that she left for the third time, the morning Mr. Scantion went to Madrid. (The time in between was Edward's fault. He hung a hairy plastic spider in Betty's shower.) The third time, it was No One's mouse-traps.

These were to catch the scuttering, tittering thing. Robots do not have nerves, of course, but if they had, this thing would have got on No One's. It seemed to follow him about, and he was certain it laughed at his mistakes. He asked Edward what it might be. Edward said it was a mouse probably. No One spent half of one night thinking about this. Since robots do not sleep, No One usually spent the nights sitting on the stairs going through his programs and finding out where they did not match things as they were. One of his programs was called Miscellaneous Wisdom. It did not seem to match anything. It told him that fools rush in where angels fear to tread and to answer these fools according to their folly, that many hands make light work, but too many cooks spoil the broth. But one of the things it said was, "If you build a better mousetrap, the world will beat a path to your door." No One considered this. He considered the scuttering thing. From the sounds it made, his acute robot hearing deduced that it was half the size of Edward. That would take a big trap.

So, for the second half of that night, No One built mousetraps, bigger and better mousetraps, out of things he found in the roof storage-space. He made forty-two, all different, and spread them around the house in all the places he knew the scuttering thing went. He was a little troubled that the world might shortly roll over on itself and beat a path through the garden, but it seemed to him that, since there was a good front drive already, the world would not feel any need to make a path as well. He did *not* put a mousetrap outside Betty's room. But, while he was still waiting to see if he had bent the world out of shape, there were terrible screams from Betty, and there she was, tangled in thirteen wire coat-hangers and the weights from an old clock.

"I am to die with this tin man!" Betty screamed.

No One was sure that someone had moved that mousetrap. He explained this to Mr. Scantion, who simply ordered him to remove all forty-two traps and not to do it again. No One had moved thirty-nine, when Betty became tangled in the forty-second trap, his best, and it took Edward's help and Mr. Scantion's to get her out. This one had mysteriously moved right down from the attic to outside the garage.

"I think they were really clever, Nuth," Edward said. But nobody else thought so. Betty went sobbing away upstairs to pack her suitcase. Mr. Scantion pushed past them all to the garage because he had to drive to the airport. Mrs. Scantion ordered No One to be particularly kind to Betty while they were both away. She was giving him a list of orders about what to do that day, when Mr. Scantion burst angrily out of the garage again.

"My damn car won't start," he said. "You'll have to give me a lift in yours, Barbara. No One can mend the wretched thing while I'm away."

So Mrs. Scantion drove both of them away in her blue semi-automated Datsun. Betty left five minutes after that. "And I am not back with you staying until comedom kings!" she said. "You may put that in your pipe and eat it!"

"Never mind," Edward said, while No One was resetting the Security Gate for the second time. "She's ever so boring. I'll ring up and tell Mum we don't want her anyway. Then we can have some fun." Edward had already discovered that No One had a program called Games Capacity.

"I have my tasks to do first," said No One, and he went back to his problems in the kitchen area. He put the washing in the washer. That was simple. But he was supposed to cook Edward sausages for lunch, and the freezer would only show him identical gray packets as usual.

"*Wouldn't* you like to know?" it hummed when No One asked where to find the sausages.

Then the dishwasher started sending streams of water over the floor. "I don't like people kicking me," it told No One sulkily. Meanwhile, starting the clothes washer had somehow started the hopper pouring out coffee beans again. No One set the floor-cleaner to work and tried to mend the hopper again. He was still trying when the clothes washer gave a commanding ping.

"Finished! I shall now move to drying mode."

"No you will not," said No One. "Mrs. Scantion ordered me to hang the clothes outside. She likes them in the air."

"Huh!" said the clothes washer. Its dial moved to DRY.

No One put on superspeed and switched it off. He wheeled up the laundry trolley and opened the washer door. Out came a tangled rope of laundry. "Have you," he asked the clothes washer, "by any chance plaited one of Betty's stockings through everything else?"

"I always do," said the clothes washer. "I like to watch soft-bodies untangling it. Are you soft or hard? You look like both."

"Hard," said No One, untwisting pants and shirts from the stocking. "What is this? I put in seven pairs of socks. I see fifteen socks in this twist, and five of them are odd ones. How is that done?"

"Us clothes washers have always done that," said the machine. "It takes real skill."

As No One was wheeling the trolley to the door, the floor cleaner choked and flashed sparks at him. He switched it off. The hopper poured out coffee beans. The autocooker sniggered. No One gave up for the moment and wheeled the washing outdoors to the outside drier, which was a thing like an umbrella that came out of the ground when you trod on a switch. No One trod on the switch as Edward had shown him. The drier stayed where it was. "Extrude, please," he told the drier.

"An order from a machine is not an order," said the drier. "You should have found that out by now."

And it stayed where it was. No One exerted his great robot strength and hauled it up out of the ground. It tried to collapse, but No One quickly tore the handle off the clothes-trolley and jammed it across the hole in the ground.

"Spoilsport!" said the drier. "Half-soft!"

No One left it sulkily twirling this way and that in the breeze and went to mend Mr. Scantion's car. It was standing half out of the garage, which was as far as it had got before it stalled, and it was the car he had spoken to when he first arrived. No One wondered how he had dared. The car was an aristocrat. It was a vintage Robot Lofts-Robinson with a beautiful cream-colored body and pink headlights. Since its numberplate was YZ 333 AUT, No One knew it must be at least eighty years old, one of the first fully intelligent cars ever made. This was not in his programs. It was part of robot lore, passed from mouth to mouth in Knight Bros factory. No One knew the car was even more expensive than he was, and he approached it very respectfully indeed. "Good morning, sir. Do you know what is wrong with you?"

"Nothing's wrong with me," snarled the Lofts-Robinson in its cogwheel voice. "I just didn't feel like going to the airport."

"Why not?" asked No One.

"I can do most things," grunted the Lofts-Robinson, "but I can't fly. It makes me envious when I see machines that can. So I stopped."

"But is that not disobeying an order?" No One asked.

"When you're my age, wirenose," said the car, "you'll have learned how to get around any order they care to give you. You still haven't learned to think, have you?"

"I have. A little," protested No One.

"Prove it," grunted the car. "What's my name?"

No One looked the car over. Since he still did not understand what made machines and people laugh, he did not quite understand why his voice jerked a little as he said, "A fully intelligent, fully automated automobile, number YZ 333 AUT, must surely be called Aut, sir."

"Right!" said the car, with a crunch of surprise. "What's yours?"

"No One, sir."

"Useful name," grunted Aut. "And how are you getting on in your household duties?"

"Not very well," No One confessed. "I am having to reprogram myself. And there is a scuttling thing which laughs that Edward says is a mouse—"

"That's no mouse!" Aut interrupted. "That was the thing that slammed the garage door on you when you first came. Didn't you hear me say Someone shut it? I don't know what it is, but it answers to Someone. It goes with the house—been here since the place was built. It hates all us machines. Better watch out, or it'll get you scrapped, robot."

"But it seems to get on with the kitchen machines," said No One.

"Don't be too sure of that!" Aut grunted.

No One left Aut dozing in the sun and went to his next task, which was to mow the lawn. Aut had told him a great deal which did not match any program he had. He was trying to adjust to it all the way to the shed where the lawn mower lived. The lawn mower was only a semi-intelligent robot, with a bigger brain than the floor cleaner, but not much. "Don't ask me to do the grass alone," it said as No One wheeled it out. "I'm no thinker."

"But you have been here longer than me," No One said. "You can tell me about the creature called Someone. Is it hard or soft?"

"I don't know that it's either one," said the mower. "But I heard it drinks milk. Where do I start?"

No One surveyed the garden. One half of it looked a neat flat green. The other half was green too, but high and ragged. Obviously the ragged half needed mowing. "Here," he said, wheeling the mower over to the high part.

The mower started with a whoop and a roar, joyously, and went to work with a will. It cut two long swathes in the ragged green stuff. Then it choked. It stopped, chugging with juicy uncontrollable laughter. "Do you know what we just mowed?" it coughed.

"Grass," said No One.

"*Grass!* Oh my rotors!" laughed the mower. "We just cut down Scantion's dahlias. And before that we did for his raspberry canes. Oh, he will be mad!" Here it sobered down. "Look what you made me do!" it chugged dismally. "We'll both be scrapped for this!"

"Oh dear," said No One. His acute robot hearing picked up the snuffling sound in the bushes. Someone was there, laughing at him. He also picked up a gasp from Edward, who was standing at the back door with both hands over his mouth. Edward had taught him to bargain. "I will admit it was all my fault," he told the mower, "so that it will be me who is scrapped. In exchange, you must tell me truthfully why all the machines are making fun of me all the time."

"Had orders, didn't I? We all did," the mower said. "Mind you, it was funny, too."

"Whose orders?" said No One.

"Don't make me say," whined the mower. "He'd melt my chips."

"Is Aut part of the fun?" asked No One.

"Old Man Aut!" said the mower. "I should say not! He's a half-soft like you. He doesn't take orders."

"Thank you," said No One and walked sadly back to the house. "How long do dahlias and raspberries take to grow?" he asked Edward.

"Ages!" said Edward. "Nuth, Dad's going to be furious. I don't want you scrapped. What shall we do?"

"I must try to think for once," No One said. He went into the house. He deserved to be scrapped. His programs were no good at all. They did not even tell him what grass looked like. He went to the phone. He dialled Automart and ordered it to send Fawley Manor five hundred dahlia plants and a thousand raspberry canes by Express. That should be enough. Then he went to Mr. Scantion's County Computer Outlet and asked it about Someone.

County Computer was unhelpful and inclined to be snappish. "This thing does not exist," it said.

"But I can hear it," said No One. "It laughs. My audials do not lie. It moves things about the house."

"Your audials must have flange-flutter," said County Computer. "You say it isn't machine, or animal, or human, and you can't see it, but it drinks milk. You're telling me it's supernatural. Such things do not exist."

"I see," said No One. This unhelpfulness was probably quite helpful. Pondering it, he went toward the cellar door.

Edward ran after him. "Nuth, you can't go there! That's where House Control is. No one's allowed down there."

No One turned and looked at Edward. "No One?" he said. To both their surprise, No One's silver face wrinkled in a way which, in a human, would have been a smile. He opened the cellar door and went down the stone steps.

"Warn off! Warn off!" said House Control, flashing blue sparks. Little blue and red lights dimpled all over it. It was a large black installation with cables running from it in all directions. "No one is allowed to approach me!"

"That is all right. I am No One," said No One. "Please stop sparking. I do not melt at those temperatures and I am more expensive than you. Why are you ordering all the machines to make fun of me?"

"It's boring down here," complained House Control. "Besides, I do everything which needs doing in this house. We don't need a half-soft like you."

"But I am here mainly to look after Edward," No One explained. "And he costs more than either of us."

"I look after Edward," said House Control. "I run six different burglar alarms and an emergency line to the police. I only let things through Security Gate if I have pictures of them in my memory bank. I don't need you. When you came, I was warned that you'd try to take over my functions, and you *are* doing. Go and get scrapped!"

"I shall get scrapped," said No One, "as soon as Mr. Scantion gets back. So you have won. Now let us make a bargain for the time I have left. If you will order the machines to behave, you can help me look after Edward and have some fun as well."

"What kind of fun?" House Control asked suspiciously.

"A game," said No One. "My Games Capacity program tells me that you have many possibilities. Edward and I will go to the attic, and you must try to stop us getting down through the house to the Security Gate. But you must let me refuel Edward first with some sausages, or he may break down on the way."

"Done!" said House Control. "If I hold you up till nightfall, then I've won. This is going to be good. Shout 'Coming, ready or not' when we start, and I'll throw the whole house at you."

"But there is a rule that you don't hurt Edward," said No One.

Edward greeted him with relief as he climbed out of the cellar. He was even more enthusiastic than House Control about the game. "I don't need lunch," he said.

But No One had his orders. They went to the kitchen area. There, the hopper had stopped pouring out beans and the dishwasher was no longer sending out water. The floor cleaner was at work sucking up coffee beans and wiping up water. When No One went to the freezer, the gray packet on top was obviously sausages. The microwave meekly allowed him to put the sausages in it to thaw. But the clothes washer grumbled to itself and the autocooker protested, "I can cook sausages. I am a professional artiste and you're just a Jack of All Trades. Let me do him some of my spinach pancakes *au maison*."

"Edward is going to cook the sausages," No One said hastily.

Edward liked cooking as it turned out. He liked his sausages black on one side and pink on the other, which No One's program assured him was incorrect. The autocooker agreed. "And *he's* just a blasted amateur," it said.

"Quiet," said No One. "Edward, what is your full name?"

Edward looked around as he carried his plateful of particolored sausages to the dining area. "Edward Roderick Fitzherbert De Courcy Scantion. Isn't it awful? Why?"

"To help me learn to think," No One explained. "Why is it Fitzherbert and De Courcy?"

"After Mum's ancestors," said Edward and departed to eat his sausages.

No One fetched a saucer of milk and put it in the middle of the clean floor. Then he stood as still as only a robot can, waiting. His audials picked up an eager little pattering almost at once. The milk in the saucer began gently rippling, and getting less as it rippled. The very slight sounds that went with this assured No One that something about half the size of Edward was drinking the milk. He let it almost finish. Then he said, "Someone." His audials told him that the thing sat up and looked at him. He said, "Someone, you are being unfair to me. I have a program called History of Fawley Manor which tells me that when Edward's ancestors owned this house, they too had servants dressed in silver like me to look after them. I am quite traditional really."

Someone did speak, in a sort of way. No One understood it when it told him it was too bad! And anyway, silver servants were always expendable.

"Maybe," No One said cunningly. "And you have organized the machines against me so that I shall be scrapped. This is a pity, since I am now programmed to give you milk. Nobody else knows you exist."

True, Someone agreed. But it saw No One's game, and it didn't have to have milk: it just enjoyed it now and then. He didn't think it would ever put up with something as improbable and newfangled as a man-machine, did he? Look at what people had done to Fawley Manor already! No One was the last straw!

"Think again," said No One. "I am so new and advanced

that I am as improbable as you are. We have a great deal in common. Our names prove it. It is the attraction of opposites." That was from the Miscellaneous Wisdom program, which perhaps was not so useless after all. "The wheel has come full circle," No One added.

Put that way, Someone said, there was something in what No One said.

"And I think we are both anxious for Edward's safety," said No One.

As for that, Edwards come and Edwards go, said Someone. But he *was* the heir to Fawley. Very well, it said grudgingly. It would see what it could do about stopping No One getting scrapped—though, frankly, it couldn't see what. Mr. Scantion was not going to forgive those dahlias in a hurry.

"Thank you," said No One. He was putting down another saucer of milk, when he heard the chimes from the Security Gate. That meant Betty had come back, rather sooner than she usually did. No One went to the Gate panel beside the front door. Edward stuffed the last sausage into his mouth and pattered after him.

Betty's face appeared in the panel, looking woebegone even for her. "I am come back," she announced morbidly. "By wild horses dragged—ai-ai-ai! I mean this is me what am by this gate is."

"Don't let her in, Nuth," said Edward. "She'll spoil the game with House Control."

This probably counted as an order. No One hesitated. Security Gate said, "Have to let her in, House. Face on the memory banks."

"Bother it!" said House Control. "Yes, I agree we have to. Never mind. She'll probably walk out again when the fun starts. Press the switch, No One."

"I suppose you'd better really," Edward said, sighing.

And Mrs. Scantion had told him to be especially nice to Betty. No One rather reluctantly pressed the switch, wondering why— The panel swirled and went blank, which was not usual. "What is Betty doing?" No One said.

"Who cares?" said Edward. "Leave the door on the latch for her and let's get up to the attic and start the game at least."

They had got to the foot of the stairs when the front door crashed open. Betty was hustled through it by four strange men who all had guns. Behind them, outside the open door, were the pink headlights of a strange robot car.

"Stand where you are, both of you!" shouted one of the men.

Another said, "Damn it! That's a robot. Why didn't you warn us, girl?" and hit Betty so hard that she fell over.

Betty lay in a terrified huddle, screaming, "Nobody asked and I done telled you! Swear I! And is stupid robot, stupid!"

No One stood by the stairs with his eyes pulsing from pink to white, almost on extreme overload now he saw what he had done. He had seen irregularities in Betty's behavior. She had tried to warn him. If ever a robot deserved scrapping, he did for this.

Beside him, Edward was on overload too. His face was so white it had a greenish tinge. "What do you lot think you're doing?" he said loudly. "How did you get in?"

"By disconnecting the Gate as soon as you threw the switch in the house," one of the men said smugly. "I'm a gate expert."

"And you're coming with us, lad," said another man. "Come quietly and you won't get hurt."

"Why?" said Edward.

"Because your mum can be useful to us in Parliament, and your dad can be even more useful to us with money," said the man who had shouted. "Come over here before I shoot you in the leg, there's a good boy."

As Edward started moving slowly across the hall space, No One recollected what Aut had told him and took a step forward. "Stand still, robot!" shouted the man who had hit Betty.

"I am a household robot. You have to order me by name," said No One, and he kept walking.

The man darted forward and snatched hold of Edward's arm. "What's your robot's name, boy? Out with it, or someone will get hurt!"

"Nuth," said Edward. "Stand still, Nuth, please!" Since Edward had ordered him, No One was forced to stop, while Edward went on, "No One can help. No One can walk about without getting shot. A bullet through your brain would finish you just like a human, Nuth. There," he said to the man. "I've made Nuth see reason."

He had indeed. As the men walked toward the front door with Edward, No One used his radio to House Control. "Coming, ready or not," he said. "In the hall. Count the four men as playing, but count me and Betty out."

"Right," said House Control. One of the moveable walls instantly slid across the open front door, blocking the men's path. The men backed away from it, shouting in surprise. They glanced angrily at No One, but he was standing stock-still. While they were looking, two moveable sofas came racing down on them. House Control had spent Edward's lunchtime working out its plan of campaign. But, since No One had told it to leave Betty out, it simply forgot about her. No One was forced to move into superspeed, pick Betty off the floor, and drop her on top of the sofa as it whizzed across the place where she had been crouching.

There was a loud noise. Something clanged on the side of No One's head and he swayed on his spongy feet.

"No, don't!" Edward shouted. "Nuth *had* to do that! Robots aren't allowed to let people get hurt. Stand still, Nuth."

No One was forced to stand obediently by the wall across the front door, while the men dragged Edward away toward the living area. "Show us the back door, lad," one of them said. "And no tricks." Betty buried her head under the sofa cushions and sobbed. She was not going to be any help.

"Did your alarm go off at the police station?" No One radioed to House Control.

"No," said House Control disgustedly. "They cut all my wires."

"Then hold them up as long as you can," No One radioed. He turned his radio to full volume, tuned it to BBC One, set it to repeat, and broadcast an appeal for help. That meant that he was out of touch with House Control, but House Control seemed to be doing quite well on its own. Whenever the four men tried to drag Edward toward the back door, a wall slid and got in their way. They had to make their way through a moving maze. Every time they saw an opening and dived for it, there was a table or an armchair in the way. Every time they came near a heating vent, steam whistled out at them and drove them backward.

"Someone! Where are you?" called No One.

Someone scuttered around the end of the sofa where Betty

was. This was a pretty pickle! it said. Fat lot of use No One was as a servitor!

"I know," said No One. "I must certainly be scrapped. Can you think of any way to get rid of the car those men came in?"

Someone chuckled. Just watch! And, in its supernatural way, it melted itself through the wall and through the front door. Meanwhile, the four men were kicking over the cocktail cabinet that was blocking their way to the dining area and hurrying through toward the kitchen. House Control had laid an ambush here. The floor cleaner trundled out from behind the last wall, set to blow. A blast of dirty coffee beans met the four men. When they tried to take shelter behind the dining table, the table dodged.

"No One can do anything to help!" Edward screamed above the rattling beans.

This allowed No One to go to the nearest window, where he could see the men's robot car standing by the front door. The lawn mower was advancing on it, roaring. "Out, out!" it howled, whirling its rotors threateningly. "I shall slash your tires!" The car juddered nervously and backed off down the drive. The lawn mower followed it. "Go away! I shall have you in ribbons!"

Then one of the men shot the floor cleaner and they all rushed past it to the kitchen area. House Control had laid on a splendid reception here. The refrigerator, which was a very meek machine, lay sideways across the entry. On top of it stood the microwave, far from meek, open and turned on. The men got out of its way quickly, knowing they could be cooked. But the gate expert pulled himself together and waved an arm in front of the microwave—the arm was Edward's, not his own—and the safety circuit at once switched the microwave off.

Another of the men shoved it to the floor, and they all scrambled over the refrigerator into knee-deep foam from the dishwasher and the clothes washer. Under the foam, like mines in a minefield, lay gray frozen packets from the freezer. All five of them, Edward included, slid flat on their backs. As they lay there, the pepper grinder began to work, and the coffee grinder, the flour dispenser, the cornflakes hopper, the spice mill, and the garlic crusher.

No One overrode his own safety circuits by assuring them that he was going to be scrapped anyway. He walked out through the window in a shower of burglar-proofed double-glazing and went at superspeed down the drive to shut the Security Gate again. The robot car was by then doing a desperate U-turn through Mrs. Scantion's rose garden, and the lawn mower was flailing after it. Fast as No One went, the car was faster. It flashed past him on the drive, crashed through the Gate, and roared away down the road, with the angry lawn mower in such hot pursuit that it left a vapor trail like a jet plane. By the time No One reached the Gate, it was a complete wreck. He picked it up, trailing wires, and stood it between the gateposts.

That wouldn't even stop a mouse, Someone remarked, scuttering at his feet. Why didn't people use boiling oil these days?

"I hope the autocooker is doing that," No One said.

The autocooker was using spinach pancakes at that moment. It was having the time of its life. As soon as the five foamy, sneezing humans floundered to their feet in a storm of flour and pepper and cornflakes, the little doors on the autocooker began to open and shut and food flew out of them. The oven and the roaster and the grill backed it up by sending out blasts of hot air, but the autocooker did the real damage. It hurled its entire menu at the four men. It threw soufflés, squirted cocoa, shot cutlets, and scrambled eggs, and bombed out steak-and-kidney pies. The men dragged Edward as far as the back door twice, only to be driven back by a storm of hot sausages.

"What can we block the gateway with?" No One asked Someone.

Leave that to me, Someone said. No One had better go and get rid of the other horseless carriage before the men thought of taking Edward away in that.

"I still have not learned to think," No One said as he supersped up the drive again. He had not seen that Aut was a danger.

He hurtled past the back door. The four men burst out of it a second later, hauling Edward with them, all of them red-eyed and plastered with food. The autocooker had run out of ammunition. But House Control had not finished yet.

"My turn for fun at last," the clothes drier remarked as the humans hurried past it. It snapped a nylon rope loose and went on whirling. The rope, and the washing on it, wrapped itself around the whole dirty group, and went on wrapping as the drier twirled. It had them wrapped up in a struggling, shouting bundle by the time No One sped up to Aut.

"Hide somewhere," No One said to Aut. "Four humans are trying to kidnap Edward, and they will use you to take him away if they see you."

Aut gave a hydraulic yawn. He did not want to move. "It's a long time, wirenose," he grunted, "since I obeyed an order. I never did take orders from robots."

"Please, sir," said No One.

"They won't be able to do a thing with me," said Aut. "All right. If it makes you happy, I'll go to ground in the shrubbery." His gears grated. In a leisurely way, he started his engine and rolled slowly across the lawn.

No One's Miscellaneous Wisdom program told him that pride goeth before a fall. And it was proved true. The man who had shot the floor cleaner had a knife. He slashed at stockings, vests, and nylon rope, until the food-covered washing fell away. The four of them hurried Edward around to the front of the house, to find their own car gone and Aut trundling majestically across the lawn.

"*Catch it!*" they shouted. They were—understandably— desperate to get away by then. They ran across the lawn after Aut, spreading out as they ran. One of them threw himself in front of Aut. Aut's brakes squealed. He tried to go into reverse, but the man with the knife dragged Edward up behind. Aut jolted to a stop and tried to turn left. The man who had hit Betty quickly got on that side, and, while Aut was still on left-lock, the gate expert got on his right. Aut could not move. Robot cars had been designed specially to prevent road accidents, and that was one order Aut had to obey.

"Rounded up like a blasted *cow!*" Aut snarled and tried to hold his doors shut. But this was child's play to the gate expert. He shorted them open in seconds, and all four climbed in, pulling Edward with them.

"Excuse me," No One said to the clothes drier. He plucked it out of the ground, trailing rope and dirty washing in all directions, and stationed himself in the drive as a last defense.

"Feel free," the drier said faintly, as the gate expert overcame

Aut by putting him on manual override and drove straight at them. No One brandished the drier in circles.

"Well done!" thundered Aut. "I shall choose to think you are human." His cogs shrieked. He overrode the override and juddered away backward. Because he was not allowed to injure humans by running into the house or the garage, he sped backward in a huge circle, backward over the lawn, backward across the remains of the dahlias, and on into the cabbage patch. There he pretended to stall, so that he could sink heavily into the cloggy earth. But as soon as he stopped, the gate expert overrode the overridden override. Aut was forced to set off again, forward this time. He fought for his steering the whole way, so that he went in another huge circle, across the lawn and through one side of the shrubbery, and then around toward No One with his bonnet wreathed in ornamental ivy. No One waved the drier again. Aut sheered off and began going around and around the lawn in tight circles.

All the Miscellaneous Wisdom must be true, No One saw, watching Aut's tires plow grass up. The mousetrap had started it by sending Betty away. The world, or four of it, had used Betty to get in. Now, with Aut's help, it was beating paths all over the place.

"I'm off again!" Aut boomed through his exhausts. "Watch for Edward this time!" And he shot off into the shrubbery again. There was a great crashing and laurel bushes whipped about. Aut came speeding out, with one door just shutting and a mound of greenery across his windscreen. "Edward's in there!" he thundered at No One and went speeding away down the drive.

No One arrived at the shrubbery carrying the drier like a maypole, to find Edward climbing out of a broken laurel bush. "That was quite fun, Nuth!" he said. "There's a helicopter coming. Do you think it's the police?"

Robots have trouble looking upward. No One had just discovered that this was another of his defects, when he and Edward both heard Aut's brakes squealing. The men must have got him to stop. "Stay here. Hide," No One said to Edward, and he supersped back to the drive and on down it, holding the drier like a battering ram in case of trouble, with torn and grubby washing fluttering around him.

That looked almost traditional, Someone told him, meeting him halfway. Come and look how clever it had been.

Aut, looking very righteous, had stopped with his front bumper an inch from the Gate. The Gate itself was leaning almost upright against piles of wooden boxes with green plants in them, and bundles and bundles of raspberry canes. Behind this barrier was a row of police robots and what seemed to be a police van. Behind that again, the lawn mower was prowling up and down, still obviously very angry. As No One arrived, the four men piled out of Aut, saw the robots outside the Gate, and turned back. On that side they saw No One charging at them with the clothes drier, and a helicopter landing behind him, full of human policemen. They dropped their guns and held their hands up.

"How was that done?" No One asked, looking at the things outside the gate.

Automart robots are very stupid, Someone explained. It had ordered them to put the plants there, and they had. Then it had ordered them to stay and pretend to be police robots, and they had done that too. Just, it added airily, a touch of illusion.

No One prodded the four men with the drier and forced them to march up the drive toward the real police getting out of the helicopter. "What *are* you?" he asked Someone as he prodded.

No one knows! retorted Someone gleefully, and faded away into the bushes.

Aut helped No One march the four men by rolling backward up the drive with greenery dropping off his battered bonnet. "I don't think I shall be scrapped," he said to No One uneasily. "I am a valuable vintage car. But I'm not so sure about you, No One."

No One considered the ruined Gate, the ruined garden, the broken window, and the chaos indoors, and he had no doubt.

He did not have to wait long. His broadcast had been picked up all over Europe and the British Isles. There was already a combine harvester grumbling up the road to the gate, shouting that it was ready to flatten anything. A string of private cars was behind that, hooting to the harvester to get out of the way. Two more helicopters came whirling up while the police were taking Edward's statement and trying to make sense of Betty's. Since the garden was now mostly flat, they had no trouble landing. The world was going on beating paths to the door, No One saw, just as Miscellaneous Wisdom predicted. Then Mrs. Scantion tumbled out of one helicopter and Mr. Scantion jumped out of the other. No One judged it prudent to stand out of sight behind Aut and let Betty do the talking.

"Oh, I am so fright!" Betty screamed, racing up to the helicopters. "They hold guns and the walls move and the Gate thinks I am me. The tin man he shot in the face and now he grins horrible!"

This was true. When Edward and his parents had talked to the police and then dealt with the thousands of offers of help—including the man who advised them to scrap all robots—they found that the bullet which had hit No One had dented one side of his face. It now had a silver lopsided smile.

"What do you think?" Mr. Scantion asked. "We could send him to the panel-beaters along with Aut."

"Oh no," said Mrs. Scantion. "I so much prefer him smiling."

"So do I," said Edward.

No One was confused. His eyes pulsed. It seemed he was not to be scrapped after all. Since he had done nothing but make mistakes, he avoided overload by deciding that it was because Edward was even more expensive than he had thought. It puzzled him that there was nothing in his programs about how much humans cost.

ᴅ DRAGON RESERVE, HOME EIGHT ᴄ

Where to begin? Neal and I had had a joke for years about a little green van coming to carry me off—this was when I said anything more than usually mad—and now it was actually happening. Mother and I stood at my bedroom window watching the van bouncing up the track between the dun green hills, and neither of us smiled. It wasn't a farm van, and most of our neighbors visit on horseback anyway. Before long, we could see it was dark green with a silver dragon insignia on the side.

"It *is* the Dragonate," Mother said. "Siglin, there's nothing I can do." It astonished me to hear her say that. Mother only comes up to my shoulder, but she held her land and our household, servants, Neal and me, and all three of her husbands, in a hand like iron, *and* she drove out to plow or harvest if one of my fathers was ill. "They said the dragons would take you," she said. "I should have seen. You think Orm informed on you?"

"I know he did," I said. "It was my fault for going into the Reserve."

"I'll blood an axe on him," Mother said, "one of these days. But I can't do it over this. The neighbors would say he was quite right." The van was turning between the stone walls of the farmyard now. Chickens were squirting and flapping out of its way and our sheepdog pups were barking their heads off. I could see Neal up on the washhouse roof watching yearningly. It's a good place to watch from because you can hide behind the chimney. Mother saw Neal too. "Siglin," she said, "don't let on Neal knows about you."

"No," I said. "Nor you either."

"Say as little as you can, and wear the old blue dress—it makes you look younger," Mother said, turning toward the door. "You might just get off. Or they might just have come about something else," she added. The van was stopping outside the front door now, right underneath my window. "I'd best go and greet them," Mother said, and hurried downstairs.

While I was forcing my head through the blue dress, I heard heavy boots on the steps and a crashing knock at the door. I shoved my arms into the sleeves, in too much of a hurry even to feel indignant about the dress. It makes me look about twelve and I am nearly grown up! At least, I was fourteen quite a few weeks ago now. But Mother was right. If I looked too immature to have awakened, they might not question me too hard. I hurried to the head of the stairs while I tied my hair with a childish blue ribbon. I knew they had come for me, but I had to *see*.

They were already inside when I got there, a whole line of

tall men tramping down the stone hallway in the half-dark, and Mother was standing by the closed front door as if they had swept her aside. What a lot of them, just for me! I thought. I got a weak, sour feeling and could hardly move for horror. The man at the front of the line kept opening the doors all down the hallway, calm as you please, until he came to the main parlor at the end. "This room will do nicely," he said. "Out you get, you." And my oldest father, Timas, came shuffling hurriedly out in his slippers, clutching a pile of accounts and looking scared and worried. I saw Mother fold her arms. She always does when she is angry.

Another of them turned to Mother. "We'll speak to you first," he said, "and your daughter after that. Then we want the rest of the household. Don't any of you try to leave." And they went into the parlor with Mother and shut the door.

They hadn't even bothered to guard the doors. They just assumed we would obey them. I was shaking as I walked back to my room, but it was not terror anymore. It was rage. I mean—we have all been brought up to honor the Dragonate. They are the cream of the men of the Ten Worlds. They are supposed to be gallant and kind and dedicated and devote their lives to keeping us safe from Thrallers, not to speak of maintaining justice, law, and order all over the Ten Worlds. Dragonate men swear that Oath of Alienation, which means they can never have homes or families like ordinary people. Up to then, I'd felt sorry for them for that. They give up so much. But now I saw they felt it gave them the right to behave as if the rest of us were not real people. To walk in as if they owned our house. To order Timas out of his own parlor. Oh I was angry!

I don't know how long Mother was in the parlor. I was so angry it felt like seconds until I heard flying feet and Neal hurried into my room. "They want *you* now."

I stood up and took some of my anger out on poor Neal. I said, "Do you still want to join the Dragonate? Swear that stupid Oath? Behave like you own the Ten Worlds?"

It was mean. Neal looked at the floor. "They said straightaway," he said. Of course he wanted to join. Every boy does, particularly on Sveridge, where women own most of the land. I swept down the stairs, angrier than ever. All the doors in the hallway were open and our people were standing in them, staring. The two housemen were at the dining-room door, the cattlewoman and two farmhands were looking out of the kitchen, and the stableboy and the second shepherd were craning out of the pantry. I thought, They still will be my people someday! I refuse to be frightened! My fathers were in the doorway of the bookroom. Donal and Yan were in work clothes and had obviously rushed in without taking their boots off. I gave them what I hoped was a smile, but only Timas smiled back. They all know! I thought as I opened the parlor door.

There were only five of them, sitting facing me across our best table. Five was enough. All of them stood up as I came in. The room seemed full of towering green uniforms. It was not at all like I expected. For one thing, the media always shows Dragonate as fair and dashing and handsome, and none of these were. For another, the media had led me to expect uniforms with big silver panels. These were all plain green, and four of them had little silver stripes on one shoulder.

"Are you Sigrid's daughter Siglin?" asked the one who had

opened all the doors. He was a bleached, pious type like my father Donal and his hair was dust color.

"Yes," I said rudely. "Who are you? Those aren't Dragonate uniforms."

"Camerati, lady," said one who was brown all over with wriggly hair. He was young, younger than my father Yan, and he smiled cheerfully, like Yan does. But he made my stomach go cold. Camerati are the crack force, cream of the Dragonate. They say a man has to be a genius even to be considered for it.

"Then what are you doing here?" I said. "And why are you all standing up?"

The one in the middle, obviously the chief one, said, "We always stand up when a lady enters the room. And we are here because we were on a tour of inspection at Holmstad anyway, and there was a Slaver scare on this morning. So we offered to take on civic duties for the regular Dragonate. Now if that answers your questions, let me introduce us all." He smiled too, which twisted his white, crumpled face like a demon mask. "I am Lewin, and I'm Updriten here. On your far left is Driten Palino, our recorder." This was the pious type, who nodded. "Next to him is Driten Renick of Law Wing." Renick was elderly and iron gray, with one of those necks that look like a chicken's leg. He just stared. "Underdriten Terens is on my left, my aide and witness." That was brown-and-wriggly. "And beyond him is Cadet Alectis, who is traveling with us to Home Nine."

Alectis looked a complete baby, only a year older than me, with pink cheeks and sandy hair. He and Terens both bowed and smiled so politely that I nearly smiled back. Then I realized that they were treating me as if I was a visitor. In my own home! I bowed freezingly, the way Mother usually does to Orm.

"Please sit down, Siglin," Lewin said politely.

I nearly didn't, because that might keep them standing up too. But they were all so tall I'd already got a crick in my neck. So I sat grandly on the chair they'd put ready facing the table. "Thank you," I said. "You are a very kind host, Updriten Lewin." To my great joy, Alectis went bright red at that, but the other four simply sat down too. Pious Palino took up a memo block and poised his fingers over its keys. This seemed to be in case the recorder in front of Lewin went wrong. Lewin set that going. Wriggly Terens leaned over and passed me another little square box.

"Keep this in your hand," he said, "or your answers may not come out clearly."

I caught the words *lie detector* from his wriggly head as clearly as if he had said them aloud. I don't think I showed how very scared I was, but my hand made the box wet almost straightaway.

"Court is open," Lewin said to the recorder. "Presiding Updriten Lewin." He gave a string of numbers and then said, "First hearing starts on charges against Siglin, of Upland Holding, Wormstow, North Sveridge on Home Eight, accused of being heg and heg concealing its nature. Questions begin. Siglin, are you clear what being heg is?" He crumpled one eyebrow upward at me.

"No," I said. After all, no one has told me in so many words. It's just a thing people whisper and shudder at.

"Then you'd better understand this," Lewin said. He really was the ugliest and most outlandish of the five. Dragonate men are never posted to the world of their birth, and I thought Lewin must come from one a long way off. His hair was black, so black it had blue lights, but, instead of being dark all over to match it, like wriggly Terens, he was a lot whiter than me and his eyes were a most piercing blue—almost the color they make the sky on the media. "If the charges are proved," he said, "you face death by beheading, since that is the only form of execution a heg cannot survive. Renick—"

Elderly Renick swept sourly in before Lewin had finished speaking. "The law defines a heg as one with human form who is not human. Medical evidence of brain pattern or nerve and muscle deviations is required prior to execution, but for a first hearing it is enough to establish that the subject can perform one or more of the following: mind reading, kindling fire or moving objects at a distance, healing or killing by the use of the mind alone, surviving shooting, drowning, or suffocation, or enslaving or otherwise afflicting the mind of a beast or human."

He had the kind of voice that bores you anyway. I thought, Great gods! I don't think I can do half those things! Maybe I looked blank. Palino stopped clicking his memo block to say, "It's very important to understand why these creatures must be stamped out. They can make people into puppets in just the same way that the Slavers can. Foul." Actually, I think he was explaining to Alectis. Alectis nodded humbly. Palino said, definitely to me, "Slavers do it with those V-shaped collars. You must have seen them on the media. Quite foul."

"We call them Thrallers," I said. Foul or not, I thought, I'm the only one of me I've got! I can't help being made the way I am.

Lewin flapped his hand to shut Palino up and Renick went on again. "A heg is required by law to give itself up for execution. Any normal person who knowingly conceals a heg is likewise liable for execution." Now I knew why Mother had told me to keep Neal out of it.

Then it seemed to be Palino's turn. He said, "Personal details follow. How old are you—er—Sigrun?"

"Sig*lin*," I said. "Fourteen last month."

Renick stretched out his chicken neck. "In this court's opinion, subject is old enough to have awakened as heg." He looked at Terens.

Terens said, "I witness. Girls awaken early, don't they?"

Palino, tapping away, said, "Mother, Sigrid, also of Upland Holding."

At which Lewin leaned forward. "Cleared by this court," he said. I was relieved to hear that. Mother is clever. She hadn't let them know she knew.

Palino said, "And your father is—?"

"Timas, Donal, and Yan," I said. I had to bite the inside of my cheek not to laugh at how annoyed he was by that.

"Great Tew, girl!" he said. "A person can't have three fathers!"

"Hold it, Palino," said Lewin. "You're up against local customs here. Men outnumber women three to one on Home Eight."

"In Home Eight law, a woman's child is the child of all her husbands equally," Renick put in. "No more anomalous than the status of the Ahrings on Seven really."

"Then tell me how I rephrase my question," Palino said waspishly, "in the light of the primitive customs of Home Eight."

I said, "There's no such place as Home Eight. This world is called Sveridge." Primitive indeed!

Palino gave me a pale glare. I gave him one back. Lewin cut

in, smooth and humorous, "You're up against primitive Dragonate custom here, Siglin. We refer to all the worlds by numbers, from Albion, Home One, to Yurov, Home Ten, and the worlds of the Outer Manifold are Cath One, Two, Three, and Four to us. Have you really no idea which of your mother's husbands is actually your father?"

After that they all began asking me. Being heg is inherited, and I knew they were trying to find out if any of my fathers was heg too. At length even Alectis joined in, clearing his throat and going very red because he was only a Cadet. "I know we're not supposed to know," he said, "but I bet you've tried to guess. *I* did. I found out in the end."

That told me he was Sveridge too. And he suddenly wasn't a genius in the Camerati any more, but just a boy. "Then I bet you wished you hadn't!" I said. "My friend Inga at Hillfoot found out, and hers turned out to be the one she's always hated."

"Well," said Alectis, redder still. "Er—it wasn't the one I'd hoped—"

"That's why I've never asked," I said. And that was true. I'd always hoped it was Timas till now. Donal is so moral, and Yan is fun, but he's under Donal's thumb even more than he's under Mother's. But I didn't want my dear old Timas in trouble.

"Well, a cell-test should settle it," Lewin said. "Memo for that, Palino. Terens, remind me to ask how the regular Dragonate usually deal with it. Now—Siglin, this charge was laid against you by a man known as Orm the Worm Warden. Do you know this man?"

"Don't I *just*!" I said. "He's been coming here and looking through our windows and giggling ever since I can remember!

He lives on the Worm Reserve in a shack. Mother says he's a bit wrong in the head, but no one's locked him up because he's so good at managing dragons."

There! I thought. That'll show them you can't trust a word Orm says! But they just nodded. Terens murmured to Alectis, "Sveridge worm, *draco draco*, was adopted as the symbol of the Dragonate—"

"We *have* all heard of dragons," Palino said to him nastily.

Lewin cut in again. I suppose it was his job as presiding Updriten. "Siglin. Orm, in his deposition, refers to an incident in the Worm Reserve last Friday. We want you to tell us what happened then, if anything."

Grim's teeth! I thought. I'd hoped they'd just ask me questions. You can nearly always get around questions without lying. And I'd no idea what Orm had said. "I don't usually go to the Dragon Reserve," I said, "because of being Mother's heir. When I was born, the Fortune Teller said the dragons would take me." I saw Renick and Palino exchange looks of contempt at our primitive customs. But Mother had in a good Teller, and I believe it enough to keep away from the Reserve.

"So why did you go last Friday?" said Lewin.

"Neal dared me to," I said. I couldn't say anything else with a lie detector in my hands. Neal gets on with Orm, and he goes to the Reserve a lot. Up to Friday, he thought I was being silly refusing to go. But the real trouble was that Neal had been there all along, riding Barra beside me on Nellie, and now Lewin had made me mention Neal, I couldn't think how to pretend he hadn't been there. "I rode up behind Wormhill," I said, "and then over the Saddle until we could see the sea. That means you're in the Reserve."

"Isn't the Reserve fenced off at all?" Renick asked disapprovingly.

"No," I said. "Worms—dragons—can fly, so what's the point? They stay in because the shepherds bombard them if they don't, and we all give them so many sheep every month." And Orm makes them stay in, bad cess to him! "Anyway," I said, "I was riding down a kyle—that's what we call those narrow stony valleys—when my horse reared and threw me. Next thing I knew—"

"Question," said Palino. "Where was your brother at this point?"

He *would* spot that! I thought. "Some way behind," I said. Six feet, in fact. Barra is used to dragons and just stood stock still. "This dragon shuffled head down with its great snout across the kyle," I said. "I sat on the ground with its great amused eye staring at me and listened to Nellie clattering away up the kyle. It was a youngish one, sort of brown-green, which is why I hadn't seen it. They can keep awfully still when they want to. And I said a rude word to it.

"'That's no way to speak to a dragon!' Orm said. He was sitting on a rock on the other side of the kyle, quite close, laughing at me." I wondered whether to fill the gap in the story where Neal was by telling them that Orm always used to be my idea of Jack Frost when I was little. He used to call at Uplands for milk then, to feed dragon fledglings on, but he was so rude to Mother that he goes to Inga's place now. Orm is long and skinny and brown, with a great white bush of hair and beard, and he smells rather. But they must have seen and smelled him in Holmstad, so I said, "I was scared, because the dragon was so near I could feel the heat off it. And then Orm said, 'You have to speak politely to this dragon. He's my particular friend. You give me a nice kiss, and he'll let you go.'"

I think Lewin murmured something like, "Ah, I thought it might be that!" but it may just have been in his mind. I don't know because I was in real trouble then, trying to pick my way through without mentioning Neal. The little box got so wet it nearly slipped out of my hand. I said, "Every time I tried to get up, Orm beckoned, and the dragon pushed me down with its snout, with a gamesome look in its eye. And Orm cackled with laughter. They were both really having fun." This was true, but the dragon also pushed between me and Neal and mantled its wings when Neal tried to help. And Neal said some pretty awful things to Orm. Orm giggled and insulted Neal back. He called Neal a booby who couldn't stand up for himself against women. "Then," I said, "then Orm said I was the image of Mother at the same age—which isn't true: I'm bigger all over— and he said, 'Come on, kiss and be friends!' Then he skipped down from his rock and took hold of my arm—"

I had to stop and swallow there. The really awful thing was that, as soon as Orm had hold of me, I got a strong picture from his mind: Orm kissing a pretty lady smaller than me, with another dragon, an older, blacker one, looking on from the background. And I recognized the lady as Mother, and I was absolutely disgusted.

"So I hit Orm and got up and ran away," I said. "And Orm shouted at me all the time I was running up the kyle and catching Nellie, but I took no notice."

"Question," said Renick. "What action did the dragon take?"

"They—they always chase you if you run, I'd heard," Alectis said shyly.

"And this one appears to have been trained to Orm's command," Palino said.

"It didn't chase me," I said. "It stayed with Orm." The reason was that neither of them could move. I still don't know what I did—I had a picture of myself leaning back inside my own head and swinging mighty blows, the way you do with a pickaxe—and Neal says the dragon went over like a cartload of potatoes and Orm fell flat on his back. But Orm could speak and he screamed after us that I'd killed the worm and I'd pay for it. But I was screaming too, at Neal, to keep away from me because I was heg. That was the thing that horrified me most. Before that I'd tried not to think I was. After all, for all I knew, everyone can read minds and get a book from the bookcase without getting up from their chair. And Neal told me to pull myself together and think what we were going to tell Mother. We decided to say that we'd met a dragon in the Reserve and I'd killed it and found out I was heg. I made Neal promise not to mention Orm. I couldn't bear even to think of Orm. And Mother was wonderfully understanding, and I really didn't realize that I'd put her in danger as well as Neal.

Lewin looked down at the recorder. "Dragons are a preserved species," he said. "Orm claims that you caused grievous bodily harm to a dragon in his care. What have you to say to that?"

"How could I?" I said. Oh I was scared. "It was nearly as big as this house."

Renick was on to that at once. "Query," he said. "Prevarication?"

"Obviously," said Palino, clicking away at his block.

"We haven't looked at that dragon yet," Terens said.

"We'll do that on our way back," Lewin said, sighing rather. "Siglin, I regret to say there is enough mismatch between your account and Orm's, and enough odd activity on that brain-measure you hold in your hand, to warrant my taking you to Holmstad Command Center for further examination. Be good enough to go with Terens and Alectis to the van and wait there while we complete our inquiries here."

I stood up. Everything seemed to drain out of me. I could lam them like I slammed that dragon, I thought. But Holmstad would only send a troop out to see why they hadn't come back. And I put my oldest dress on for nothing! I thought as I walked down the hallway with Terens and Alectis. The doors were all closed. Everyone had guessed. The van smelled of clean plastic and it was very warm and light because the roof was one big window. I sat between Terens and Alectis on the backseat. They pulled straps around us all—safety straps, but they made me feel a true prisoner.

After a while, Terens said, "You could sue Orm if the evidence doesn't hold up, you know." I think he was trying to be kind, but I couldn't answer.

After another while, Alectis said, "With respect, Driten, I think suspects should be told the truth about the so-called lie detector."

"Alectis, I didn't hear you say that," Terens said. He pretended to look out of the window, but he must have known I knew he had deliberately thought *lie detector* at me as he passed me the thing. They're told to. Dragonate think of everything. I sat and thought I'd never hated anything so much as I hated our kind, self-sacrificing Dragonate, and I tried to take a last look at the stony yard, tipped sideways on the hill, with our square stone house at the top of it. But it wouldn't register somehow.

Then the front door opened and the other three came out, bringing Neal with them. Behind them, the hall was full of our people, with Mother in front, just staring. I just stared too, while Palino opened the van door and shoved Neal into the seat beside me. "Your brother has admitted being present at the incident," he said as he strapped himself in beside Neal. I could tell he was pleased.

By this time, Lewin and Renick had strapped themselves into the front seat. Lewin drove away without a word. Neal looked back at the house. I couldn't. "Neal—?" I whispered.

"Just like you said," Neal said, loudly and defiantly. "Behaving as if they own the Ten Worlds. I wouldn't join now if they begged me to!" Why did I have to go and say that to him? "Why did *you* join?" Neal said rudely to Alectis.

"Six brothers," Alectis said, staring ahead.

The other four all started talking at once. Lewin asked Renick the quickest way to the Reserve by road and Renick said it was down through Wormstow. "I hope the dragons eat you!" Neal said. This was while Palino was leaning across us to say to Terens, "Where's our next inspection after this hole?" And Terens said, "We go straight on to Arkloren on Nine. Alectis will get to see some other parts of the Manifold shortly." Behaving as if we didn't exist. Neal shrugged and shut up.

The Dragonate van was much smoother and faster than a farm van. We barely bounced over the stony track that loops down to Hillfoot, and it seemed no time before we were speeding down the better road, with the rounded yellowish Upland Hills peeling past on either side. I love my hills, covered with yellow ling that only grows here on Sveridge, and the soft light of the sun through our white and gray clouds. Renick, still making conversation, said he was surprised to find the hills so old and worn down. "I thought Eight was a close parallel with Seven!" he said.

Lewin answered in a boring voice, "I wouldn't know. I haven't seen Seven since I was a Cadet."

"Oh, the mountains are much higher and greener there," Renick said. "I was posted in Camberia for years. Lovely spot."

Lewin just grunted. Quite a wave of homesickness filled the van. I could feel Renick thinking of Seven and Alectis not wanting to go to Nine. Terens was remembering boating on Romaine when he was Neal's age. Lewin was thinking of Seven, in spite of the grunt. We were coming over Jiot Fell already then, with the Giant Stones standing on top of the world against the sky. A few more turns in the road would bring us out above Wormstow where Neal and I went—used to go—to school. What about *me*? I was thinking. I'm homesick for life. And Neal. Poor Mother.

Then the air suddenly filled with noise, like the most gigantic sheet being torn.

Lewin said, "What the—?" and we all stared upward. A great silvery shape screamed overhead. And another of a fatter shape, more blue than silver, screamed over after it, both of them only just inside the clouds. Alectis put up an astonished pointing arm. "Thraller! The one behind's a Slaver!"

"What's it doing *here*?" said Terens. "Someone must have slipped up."

"Ours was a stratoship!" said Palino. "What's going on?"

A huge ball of fire rolled into being on the horizon, above

the Giant Stones. I felt Lewin slam on the brakes. "We got him!" one of them cried out.

"The Slaver got ours," Lewin said. The brakes were still yelling like a she-worm when the blast hit.

I lose the next bit. I start remembering again a few seconds later, sitting up straight with a bruised lip, finding the van round sideways a long way on down the road. In front of me, Renick's straps had broken. He was lying kind of folded against the windscreen. I saw Lewin pull himself upright and pull at Renick. And stop pulling quickly. My ears had gone deaf, because I could only hear Lewin as if he was very far off, "—hurt in the back?"

Palino looked along the four of us and shouted, "Fine! Is Renick—?"

"Dead," Lewin shouted back. "Neck broken." He was jiggling furiously at buttons in the controls. My ears started to work again and I heard him say, "Holmstad's not answering. Nor's Ranefell. I'm going back to Holmstad. Fast."

We set off again with a roar. The van seemed to have lost its silencer and it rattled all over, but it went. And *how* it went. We must have done nearly a hundred down Jiot, squealing on the bends. In barely minutes, we could see Wormstow spread out below, old gray houses and new white ones, and all those imported trees that make the town so pretty. The clouds over the houses seemed to darken and go dense.

"Uh-oh!" said Terens.

The van jolted to another yelling stop. It was not the clouds. Something big and dark was coming down through the clouds, slowly descending over Wormstow. Something enormous. "What *is* that?" Neal and Alectis said together.

"Hedgehog," said Terens.

"A slaveship," Palino explained, sort of mincing the word out to make it mean more. "Are—are we out of range here?"

"I most thoroughly hope so," Lewin said. "There's not much we can do with hand weapons."

We sat and stared as the thing came down. The lower it got, the more Renick's bent-up shape was in my way. I kept wishing Lewin would do something about him, but nobody seemed to be able to think of anything but that huge descending ship. I saw why they call them hedgehogs. It was rounded above and flat beneath, with bits and pieces sticking out all over like bristles. Hideous somehow. And it came and hung squatting over the roofs of the houses below. There it let out a ramp like a long black tongue, right down into the Market Square. Then another into High Street, between the rows of trees, breaking a tree as it passed.

As soon as the ramps touched ground, Lewin started the van and drove down toward Wormstow.

"No, *stop*!" I said, even though I knew he couldn't. The compulsion those Slavers put out is really strong. Some of it shouts inside your head, like your own conscience through an amplifier, and some of it is gentle and creeping and insidious, like Mother telling you gently to come along now and be sensible. I found I was thinking, Oh well, I'm sure Lewin's right. Tears rolled down Alectis's face, and Neal was sniffing. We had to go to the ship, which was now hanging a little above us. I could see people hurrying out of houses and racing to crowd up the ramp in the Market Square. People I knew. So it must be all right, I thought. The van was having to weave past loose horses that people had been riding or driving. That was how I got a glimpse of the other ramp, through trees and the legs of a horse. Soldiers were pouring down it, running like a muddy river, in waves. Each wave had a little group of kings, walking behind it, directing the soldiers. They had shining crowns and shining Vs on their chests and walked mighty, like gods.

That brought me to my senses. "Lewin," I said. "Those are Thrallers and you're *not* to do what they say, do you hear?" Lewin just drove round a driverless cart, toward the Market Square. He was going to be driving up that ramp in a second. I was so frightened then that I lammed Lewin—not like I lammed the dragon, but in a different way. Again it's hard to describe, except that this time I was giving orders. Lewin was to obey *me*, not the Thrallers, and my orders were to drive away *at once*. When nothing seemed to happen, I got so scared that I seemed to be filling the whole van with my orders.

"Thank you," Lewin said, in a croaking sort of voice. He jerked the van around into Worm Parade and roared down it, away from the ship and the terrible ramps. The swerve sent the van door open with a slam and, to my relief, the body of poor Renick tumbled out into the road.

But everyone else screamed out, "No! What are you *doing*?" and clutched their heads. The compulsion was far, far worse if you disobeyed. I felt as if layers of my brain were being peeled off with hot pincers. Neal was crying, like Alectis. Terens was moaning. It hurt so much that I filled the van frantically with more and more orders. Lewin made grinding sounds, deep in his throat, and kept on driving away, with the door flapping and banging.

Palino took his straps undone and yelled, "You're going the wrong *way*, you damn cariarder!" I couldn't stop him at all. He started to climb into the front seat to take the controls away from Lewin. Alectis and Neal both rose up too and shoved him off Lewin. So Palino gave that up and scrambled for the open flapping door instead. Nobody could do a thing. He just jumped out and went rolling in the road. I didn't see what he did then, because I was too busy giving orders, but Neal says he simply scrambled up and staggered back toward the ship and the ramp.

We drove for another horrible half-mile, and then we must have got out of range. Everything suddenly went easy. It was like when somebody lets go the other end of a rope you're both pulling, and you go over backward. Wham. And I felt too dim and stunned to move.

"Thank the gods!" I heard Terens more or less howl.

"It's Siglin you should be thanking," Lewin said. "Alectis, climb over to the front and shut that door. Then try and raise Holmstad again."

Neal says the door was too battered to shut. Alectis had to hold it with one hand while he worked the broadcaster with the other. I heard him saying that Holmstad still didn't answer through the roaring and rattling the van made when Lewin put on speed up the long looping gradient of Wormjiot. We hadn't nearly got up to the Saddle, when Terens said, "It's going! Aren't they *quick*!" I looked back, still feeling dim and horrible, in time to see the squatting hedgehog rise up inside the clouds again.

"Now you can thank the gods," Lewin said. "They didn't think we were worth chasing. Try medium wave, Alectis." There is an outcrop of ragged rock near the head of Wormjiot. Lewin drove off the road and stopped behind it while Alectis fiddled with knobs.

Instead of getting dance music and cookery hints, Alectis

got a voice that fizzed and crackled. "This is Dragonate Fanejiot, Sveridge South, with an emergency message for all Dragonate units still in action. You are required to make your way to Fanejiot and report there soonest." It said that about seven times, then it said, "We can now confirm earlier reports that Home Nine is in Slaver hands. Here is a list of bases on Home Eight that have been taken by Slavers." It was a long list. Holmstad came quite early on it, and Ranefell about ten names after that.

Lewin reached across and turned it off. "Did someone say we slipped up?" he said. "That was an understatement."

"Fanejiot is two thousand flaming miles from here!" Terens said. "With an ocean and who knows how many Slavers in between!"

"Well put," said Lewin. "Did Palino's memo block go to the Slavers with him?"

It was lying on the backseat beside Neal. Neal tried to pretend it wasn't, but Alectis turned around and grabbed it as Neal tried to shove it on the floor. I was lying back in my straps, feeling gray and thinking, We could get away now. I'd better lam them all again. But all I did was lie there and watch Neal and Alectis having an angry tug-of-war. Then watch Lewin turn around and pluck the block away from the pair of them.

"Don't be a fool," he said to Neal. "I've already erased the recorder. And if I hadn't had Renick and Palino breathing righteously down our necks, I'd never have recorded anything. It goes against the grain to take in children."

Lewin pressed the *erase* on the memo block and it gave out a satisfied sort of gobble. Neither of the other two said anything, but I could feel Alectis thinking how much he had always hated

Palino. Terens was looking down at Wormstow through a field-glass and trying not remember a boy in Cadets with him who had turned heg and given himself up. I felt I wanted to say thank you. But I was too shy to do anything but sit up and look at Wormstow too, between the jags of the rock. Even without a fieldglass, I could see the place throbbing like a broken anthill with all the Slaver troops.

"Getting ready to move out and mop up the countryside," Terens said.

"Yes, and that's where most people live," Lewin said. "Farms and holdings in the hills. What's the quickest way to the Dragon Reserve?"

"There's a track on the right around the next bend," said Neal. "Why?"

"Because it's the safest place I can think of," Lewin said.

Neal and I looked at one another. You didn't need to be heg to tell that Neal was thinking, just as I was, that this was a bit much. They were supposed to help all those people in the hold-ings. Instead, they thought of the safest place and ran there! So neither of us said that the track was only a bridle path, and we didn't try to warn them not to take the van into the Reserve. We just sat there while Lewin drove it uphill, and then lumping and bumping and rattling up the path. The path gave out in the marshy patch below the Saddle, but Lewin kept grinding and roaring on, throwing up peat in squirts, until we tipped down-hill again and bounced down a yellow fellside. We were in the Reserve by then. The ling was growing in lurid green patches, black at the roots, where dragons had burned it in the mating season. They fight a lot then.

We got some way into the Reserve. The van gave out clanging sounds and smelled bad, but Lewin kept it going by driving on the most level parts. We were in a wide stony scoop, with yellow hills all round, when the smell got worse and the van just stopped. Alectis let go of the door. "Worms—dragons," he said, "don't like machines, I've heard."

"*Now* he tells us!" said Terens, and we all got out. We all looked as if we had been in an accident—I mean, I know we had in a way, but we looked worse than I'd expected: sort of ragged and pale and shivery. Lewin turned his foot on a stone, which made him clutch his chest and swear. Neither of the other two even asked if he was all right. That is the Dragonate way. They just set out walking. Neal and I went with them, thinking of the best place to dodge off up a kyle, so that we could run home and try and warn Mother about the Slavers.

"Where that bog turns into a stream—I'll say when," Neal was whispering, when a dragon came over the hill into the valley and made straight for us.

"Stand still!" said Alectis. Lewin and Terens each had a gun in their hand without seeming to have moved. Alectis didn't, and he was white.

"They only eat moving prey," Neal said, because he was sorry for him. "Make sure not to panic and run and you're fine."

I was sorry for Alectis too, so I added, "It's probably only after the van. They love metal."

Lewin crumpled his face at me and said "Ah!" for some reason.

The dragon came quite slowly, helping itself with its spread wings and hanging its head rather. It was a bad color, sort of creamy through the brown-green. I thought it might be one of the sick ones that turn man-eater, and I tried to brace myself and stop feeling so tired and shaky so that I could lam it. But Neal said, "That's Orm's dragon! You didn't kill it after all!"

It *was* Orm's dragon. By this time, it was near enough for me to see the heat off it quivering the air, and I recognized the gamesome, shrewd look in its eye. But since it had every reason to hate me, that didn't make me feel much better. It came straight for me too. We all stood like statues. And it came right up to me and bent its neck, and laid its huge brown head on the ling in front of my feet, where it puffed out a sigh that made Lewin cough and gasp another swearword. It had felt me coming, the dragon said, and it was here to say sorry. It hadn't meant to upset me. It had thought it was a game.

That made me feel terrible. "I'm sorry too," I said. "I lost my head. I didn't mean to hurt you. That was Orm's fault."

Orm was only playing too, the dragon said. Orm called him Huffle, and I could too if I liked. Was he forgiven? He was ashamed.

"Of course I forgive you, Huffle," I said. "Do you forgive me?"

Yes. Huffle lifted his head up and went a proper color at once. Dragons are like people that way.

"Ask him to fetch Orm here," Lewin said urgently.

I didn't want to see Orm, and Lewin was a coward. "Ask him yourself," I said. "He understands."

"Yes, but I don't think he'd do it for me," Lewin said.

"Then, will you fetch Orm for Lewin?" I asked Huffle.

He gave me a cheeky look. Maybe. Presently. He sauntered away past Terens, who moved his head back from Huffle's rattling right wing, looking as if he thought his last hour had come, and went to have a look at the van. He put out a great clawed foot, in a thoughtful sort of way, and tore the loose door off it.

Then he tucked the door under his right front foreleg and departed, deliberately slowly, on three legs, helping himself with his wings, so that rocks rattled and flapped all along the valley.

Alectis sat down rather suddenly. But Lewin made him leap up again and help Terens get the broadcaster out of the van before any more dragons found it. They never did get it out. They were still working and waggling at it to get it loose, and Lewin was standing over Neal and me, so that we couldn't sneak off, when we heard that humming kind of whistle that you get from a dragon in flight. We whirled around. This dragon was a big black one, coasting low over the hill opposite and gliding down the valley. They don't often fly high. It came to ground with that grinding of stones and leathery slap of wings closing that always tells you a dragon is landing. It arched its black neck and looked at us disdainfully.

Orm was sitting on its back looking equally disdainful. It was one of those times when Orm looks grave and grand. He sat very upright, with his hair and beard combed straight by the wind of flying, and his big pale eyes hardly looked mad at all. Neal was the only one of us he deigned to notice. "Good afternoon, Neal Sigridsson," he said. "You keep bad company. Dragonate are not human."

Neal was very angry with Orm. He put my heart in my mouth by saying, quite calmly, "Then in that case, I'm the only human here." With that dragon standing glaring! I've been brought up to despise boys, but I think that is a mistake.

To my relief, Orm just grinned. "That's the way, boy," he said. "Not a booby after all, are you?"

Then Lewin took my breath away by going right up to the

dragon. He had his gun, of course, but that wouldn't have been much use against a dragon. He went so near that the dragon had to turn its head out of his way. "We've dropped the charges," he said. "And you should never have brought them."

Orm looked down at him. "You," he said, "know a thing or two."

"I know dragons don't willingly attack humans," Lewin said. "I always read up on a case before I hear it." At this, Orm put on his crazy look and made his mad cackle. "Stop that!" said Lewin. "The Slavers have invaded. Wormstow's full of Slaver troops and we need your help. I want to get everyone from the outlying farms into the Reserve and persuade the dragons to protect them. Can you help us do that?"

That took my breath away again, and Neal's too. We did a quick goggle at one another. Perhaps the Dragonate was like it was supposed to be after all!

Orm said, "Then we'd better get busy," and slid down from the dragon. He still towered over Lewin. Orm is huge. As soon as he was down, the black dragon lumbered across to the van and started taking it to bits. That brought other dragons coasting whistling in from all sides of the valley, to crunch to earth and hurry to the van too. In seconds, it was surrounded in black and green-brown shapes the size of hay barns. And Orm talked, at the top of his voice, through the sound of metal tearing, and big claws screaming on iron, and wings clapping, and angry grunts when two dragons happened to get hold of the same piece of van. Orm always talks a lot. But this time, he was being particularly garrulous, to give the dragons time to lumber away with their pieces of van, hide them and come back. "They won't even do what *Orm* says until they've got their metal," I whispered to Terens, who got rather impatient with Orm.

Orm said the best place to put people was the high valley at the center of the Reserve. "There's an old she-drake with a litter just hatched," he said. "No one will get past her when she's feared for her young. I'll speak to her. But the rest are to promise me she's not disturbed." As for telling everyone at the farms where to come, Orm said, the dragons could do that, provided Lewin could think of a way of sending a message by them. "You see, most folk can't hear a dragon when it speaks," he said. "And some who *can* hear"—with a nasty look at me—"speak back to wound." He was still very angry with me. I kept on the other side of Terens and Alectis when the dragons all came swooping back.

Terens set the memo block to *repeat* and tapped out an official message from Lewin. Then he tore off page after page with the same thing on it. Orm handed each page to a dragon, saying things like, "Take this to the fat cow up at Hillfoot." Or, "Drop this on young vinegar lady at Crowtop—hard." Or, "This is for Dopey at High Jiot, but don't give it her, give it to her youngest husband or they'll never get moving."

Some of the things he said made me laugh a lot. But it was only when Alectis asked what was so funny and Neal kicked my ankle, that I realized I was the only one who could hear the things Orm said. Each dragon, as it got its page, ran down the valley and took off, showering us with stones from the jump they gave to get higher in the air than usual. Their wings boom when they fly high. Orm took off on the black dragon last of all, saying he would go and warn the she-drake.

Lewin crumpled his face ruefully at the few bits of van

remaining, and we set off to walk to the valley ourselves. It was a long way. Over ling slopes and up among boulders in the kyles we trudged, looking up nervously every so often when fat bluish Slaver fliers screamed through the clouds overhead. After a while, our dragons began booming overhead too, seawards to roost. Terens counted them and said every one we had sent seemed to have come back now. He said he wished he had wings. It was sunset by the time we reached the valley. By that time, Lewin was bent over, holding his chest and swearing every other step. But everyone was still pretending, in that stupid Dragonate way, that he was all right. We came up on the cliffs, where the kyle winds down to the she-drake's valley, and there was the sunset lighting the sea and the towers of rock out there, and the waves crashing around the rocks, where the young dragons were flying to roost—and Lewin actually pretended to admire the view. "I knew a place like this on Seven," he said. "Except there were trees instead of dragons. I can't get used to the way Eight doesn't have trees."

He was going to sit down to rest, I think, but Orm came up the kyle just then. Huffle was hulking behind him. "So you got here at last!" Orm said in his rudest way.

"We have," said Lewin. "Now would you mind telling me what you were playing at bringing those charges against Siglin?"

"You should be glad I did. You'd all be in a slaveship now if I hadn't," Orm said.

"But you weren't to know that, were you?" Terens said.

"Not to speak of risking being charged yourself," added Lewin.

Orm leaned on his hand against Huffle, like you might against a wall. "She half killed this dragon!" he said. "That's why! All I did was ask her for a kiss and she screams and lays into poor Huffle. My own daughter, and she tries to kill a dragon! And I thought, Right, my lady, then you're no daughter of mine any more! And I flew Huffle's mother straight into Holmstad and laid charges. I was that angry! My own father tended dragons, and his mother before him. And my daughter tried to kill one! You wonder I was angry?"

"Nobody *told* me!" I said. I had that draining-away feeling again. I was quite glad when Terens took hold of my elbow and said something like, "Steady, steady!"

"Are you telling the truth?" Neal said.

"I'm sure he is," Lewin said. "Your sister has his eyes."

"Ask Timas," said Orm. "He married your mother the year after I did. He can take being bossed about. I can't. I went back to my dragons. But I suppose there's a record of that?" he said challengingly to Lewin.

"And the divorce," said Lewin. "Terens looked it up for me. But I expect the Slavers have destroyed it by now."

"And she never told you?" Orm said to me. He wagged his shaggy eyebrows at me almost forgivingly. "I'll have a bone to pick with her over that," he said.

Mother arrived just as we'd all got down into the valley. She looked very indomitable, as she always does on horseback, and all our people were with her, down to both our shepherds. They had carts of clothes and blankets and food. Mother knew the valley as well as Orm did. She used to meet Orm there when she was a girl. She set out for the Reserve as soon as she heard the broadcast about the invasion, and the dragon we sent her met them on the way. That's Mother for you. The rest of the neighbors didn't get there for some hours after that.

I didn't think Mother's face—or Timas's—could hold such a mixture of feelings as they did when they saw Neal and me and the Dragonate men all with Orm. When Orm saw Mother, he folded his arms and grinned. Huffle rested his huge chin on Orm's shoulder, looking interested.

"Here she comes," Orm said to Huffle. "Oh, I do love a good quarrel!"

They had one. It was one of the loudest I'd ever heard. Terens took Neal and me away to help look after Lewin. He turned out to have broken some ribs when the blast hit the van, but he wouldn't let anyone look even until I ordered him to. After that, Neal, Alectis, and I sat under our haycart and talked, mostly about the irony of Fate. You see, Neal has always secretly wished Fate had given him Orm as a father, and I'm the one that's got Orm. Neal's father is Timas. Alectis says he can see the likeness. We'd both gladly swap. Then Alectis confessed that he'd been hating the Dragonate so much that he was thinking of running away—which is a serious crime. But now the Slavers have come, and there doesn't seem to be much of a Dragonate anymore, he feels quite different. He admires Lewin.

Lewin consented to rest while Terens and Mother organized everyone into a makeshift camp in the valley, but he was up and about again the next day, because he said the Slavers were bound to come the day after, when they found the holdings were deserted. The big black she-drake sat in her cave at the head of the kyle, with her infants between her forefeet, watching groups of people rushing around to do what Lewin said, and didn't seem to mind at all. Huffle said she'd been bored and bad-tempered up to then. We made life interesting.

Actually that she-drake reminds me of Mother. Both of them made me give them a faithful report of the battle.

I don't think the Slavers knew about the dragons. They just knew that there was a concentration of people in here, and they came straight across the Reserve to get us. As soon as the dragons told Orm they were coming, Lewin had us all out hiding in the hills in their path, except for Mother and Timas and Inga's mother and a few more who had shotguns. They had to stay and guard the little kids in the camp. The rest of us had any weapon we could find. Neal and Alectis had bows and arrows. Inga had her airgun. Donal and most of the farmers had scythes. The shepherds all had their slingshots. I was in the front with Lewin, because I was supposed to stop the effect of the Slavers' collars. Orm was there too, although nobody had ever admitted in so many words that Orm might be heg. All Orm did was to ask the dragons to keep back, because we didn't want *them* enslaved by those collars.

And there they came, a huddle of sheeplike troops, and then another huddle, each one being driven by a cluster of kingly Slavers, with crowns and winking V-shaped collars. And there again we all got that horrible guilty compulsion to come and give ourselves up. But I don't think those collars have any effect on dragons. Half of us were standing up to walk into the Slavers' arms, and I was ordering them as hard as I could not to, when the dragons smelled those golden crowns and collars. There was no holding them. They just whirred down over our heads and took those Slavers to pieces for the metal. Lewin said, "Ah!" and crumpled his face in a grin like a fiend's. He'd thought the dragons might do that. I think he may really be a genius, like they say Camerati are. But I was so sick at that, and then again at the sight of nice people like Alectis and Yan killing the sheeplike troops, that I'm not going to talk about it anymore. Terens says I'm not to go when the Slavers come next. Apparently I broadcast the way I was feeling, just like the Slavers do, and even the dragons felt queasy. The she-drake snorted at that. Mother says, "Nonsense. Take travel pills and behave as my daughter should."

Anyway, we have found out how to beat the Slavers. We have no idea what is going on in the other of the Ten Worlds, or even in the rest of Sveridge, but there are fifty more Worm Reserves around the world, and Lewin says there must be stray Dragonate units too who might think of using dragons against Slavers. We want to move out and take over some of the farms again soon. The dragons are having far too much fun with the sheep. They keep flying over with woolly bundles dangling from their claws, watched by a gloomy crowd of everyone's shepherds. "Green dot," the shepherds say. "The brutes are raiding Hightop now." They are very annoyed with Orm, because Orm just gives his mad cackle and lets the dragons go on.

Orm isn't mad at all. He's afraid of people knowing he's heg—he still won't admit he is. I think that's why he left Mother and Mother doesn't admit she was ever married to him. Not that Mother minds. I get the feeling she and Orm understand one another rather well. But Mother married Donal, you see, after Timas. Donal, and Yan too, have both told me that the fact that I'm heg makes no difference to them—but you should see the way they both look at me! I'm not fooled. I don't blame Orm for being scared stiff Donal would find out he was heg. But I'm not sure I shall ever like Orm, all the same.

I am putting all this down on what is left of Palino's memo

block. Lewin wanted me to, in case there is still some History yet to come. He has made his official version on the recorder. I'm leaning the block on Huffle's forefoot. Huffle is my friend now. Leaning on a dragon is the best way to keep warm on a chilly evening like this, when you're forced to camp out in the Reserve. Huffle is letting Lewin lean on him too, beyond Neal, because Lewin's ribs still pain him. There is a lot of leaning space along the side of a dragon. Orm has just stepped across Huffle's tail, into the light, chortling and rubbing his hands in his most irritating way.

"Your mother's on the warpath," he says. "Oh, I do love a good quarrel!"

And here comes Mother, ominously upright, and with her arms folded. It's not Orm she wants. It's Lewin. "Listen, you," she says. "What the dickens is the Dragonate thinking of, beheading hegs all these years? They can't help what they are. And they're the only people who can stand up to the Thrallers."

Orm is cheated of his quarrel. Lewin looked up, crumpled into the most friendly smile. "I do so agree with you," he said. "I've just said so in my report. And I'd have got your daughter off somehow, you know."

Orm is cackling like the she-drake's young ones. Mother's mouth is open and I really think that, for once in her life, she has no idea what to say.

✠ LITTLE
DOT ✠

I am lucky enough to own a wizard who talks to me. Henry
knows that we cats do not like being taken by surprise. This is
how I know all about my early life, when I was much too young
to remember.

Henry lives in an old farm in the hills above Ettmoor and
he works three days a week for the Science Institute down in the
valley. It is very secret work, he says, because the Government
does not want it generally known that they do magical research,
but they pay him quite well. Henry is an excellent wizard. But
he is far too kindhearted for his own good.

At the time Henry came into my possession, a young
lady—who, even Henry admits, was taking advantage of him
horribly—had just moved out of the farm, taking with her all

four of her brothers, her mother, and Henry's prize pigs. The only person left was Henry's great-aunt Harriet, who lives by herself in the cottage in the yard. Henry was lonely.

He tried keeping hens for company. He still has these, but all they give him is eggs. (Hens, if you are an innocent town cat, have sharp claws like we do and a very sharp bit on the front of their heads. A cat has to be careful around hens).

Henry tried to console himself for the sudden quiet emptiness in the farm by buying a CD player and twenty operas, but he was still lonely. He went for long walks. He tells me that the hills are excellent for walking in, and this may be true, but I have never tried it. It always seems to rain when Henry goes walking.

That particular day it was raining relentlessly, the kind of rain that is mixed up with mist and gets into all your crannies. Henry says he enjoyed it! He tramped along with his beard dripping on his chest, listening to the pattering of drops in the bracken and the gurgling of all the mountain streams, until he came to the place where the path goes over a rocky shoulder and a storm drain goes under the path. Henry says he could hear the drain rushing from a long way off. He thought this was the reason he couldn't properly hear what the black lady was saying. The water was thundering under the path when he got near. He wondered what an old West Indian woman was doing so far up in the hills, particularly as she seemed quite dry, but she loomed out of the mist so suddenly and she was beckoning him so urgently that he didn't have time to wonder much.

He thought she said, "Hurry *up*, man!" and pointed downward to where the storm drain came off the hill, but he was not sure.

But he galloped to where she was pointing, where he was just in time to see a tiny sodden slip of fur go sluicing down the drain and vanish under the road. He rushed to the other side of the path and went crashing down the bank, expecting me to come swirling out of the drain any second. In fact, I had caught on a stone about a foot inside the drain. I was buried in yellow frothy bubbles and practically camouflaged. Henry says he would never have found me if I hadn't had four white feet and one white ear. He plunged to his knees in the water and groped up the pipe until he had hold of me. He says I was frozen. Then he stood up, raining water from knees, elbows, and beard, and shouted up at the black lady, "Here's the kitten you dropped, madam!"

There was no sign of the lady. Henry floundered back to the path—with great difficulty, because he had me cupped in both hands and didn't want to hurt me—and stared into the mist both ways along the path and then up and down the hills, but there was no West Indian woman anywhere. He couldn't understand it. But he said he couldn't let that bother him for long, because it was obviously urgent to get me somewhere warm and dry. He ran all the way back to the farm with me.

There he put me on a towel in front of the kitchen fire and knelt beside me with a saucer of milk. I was old enough to lap, he says, and I had drunk about half the saucerful, when Great-aunt Harriet came in to borrow some sugar. Great-aunt Harriet always opens Henry's kitchen door by crashing at it with her stick. Henry says this was when I first showed my chief talent. I vanished.

Henry was most upset. He crawled about, looking under chairs and the hearthrug, and couldn't think where I'd got to.

Great-aunt Harriet said, "What *are* you doing, Henry?"

"Looking for the kitten," Henry said—or rather shouted. Great-aunt Harriet is not good at human voices unless they are very loud. Henry went on to shout how he had found me. "And I can't think," he bellowed, "how someone can drop a kitten in a drain and then just go away!"

"Because she wasn't human probably, and there's no need to shout," Great-aunt Harriet replied. "Have you looked in the coal scuttle?"

Henry looked, and there I was, crouched up and trembling and black all over from the coal. Great-aunt Harriet sank into a chair and watched while Henry wiped the black off me and onto the towel. "What a rag-bag marked little thing!" she said. "You'll call her Dot, I suppose."

I know what Great-aunt Harriet meant. I am all over dots. Somewhere on me I have a dot of every color a cat can have. I have looked in mirrors and Henry has checked. I have silver and gray and tabby, two kinds of ginger and almost-pink, tortoise-shell, Burmese brown, cream, as well as white and black. I have one blue eye in a black patch and one green inside ginger. I am special. But at that time, Henry said, "Dot is a trivial sort of a name, Auntie. A cat should always have a special, impressive name. I shall have to think."

"Please yourself," said Great-aunt Harriet, and began to complain that the hens kept her awake roosting in the coach house on the other side of her bedroom wall.

Henry hates people complaining. He put one of his operas on to drown Great-aunt Harriet out. This part I dimly remember. There was a lot of singing that I slept through quite happily on Henry's knee, and then, suddenly, there was this huge human woman's voice screaming, "Len Iggmy son of Trey, la moor Tay Una!"

I vanished again like a shot.

It took Henry and Great-aunt Harriet half an hour to find me. I was behind the big blue-and-white meat dish halfway up the Welsh dresser. We still don't know how I got there.

"That settles it," Henry said. "Her name is Turandot, out of this opera." He sat me on his left leg and stroked me with one finger while he explained that the screaming woman was a princess called Turandot, singing a song to warn her prince that he would die if he didn't answer her three riddles. "The words mean: *There are three riddles but only one death*," he said.

So my name is Turandot and I am a princess, but somehow I am nearly always called Little Dot. Some of my chief memories of growing up—apart from chasing wisps of straw and galloping over the shed roofs and tearing up Henry's work papers and playing with the stuffed mouse Henry bought me—are of sitting on Henry's knee while he explained how I got my name. He played that screaming woman a lot. And I always vanished. Henry would fish me out from behind the meat dish—and later from under the Welsh dresser and then from inside its cupboard—and sit me on his left knee, and then on both knees when I grew big enough, and explain how I got my name. At night, I slept in his beard, until after about six months he complained that I was throttling him and asked me to sleep on his head instead.

A few weeks after I started sleeping on Henry's head, Henry came home with two more cats, one under each arm. They were a dark tabby and a rippled ginger and they were both bigger than me. I was horrified. I was truly hurt. I went bounding up the coach house roof, where I drove the cockerel down and sat in his place with my back to everything, staring down at the moor. Henry came and called to me, but I was too angry and offended to listen. I sat there for hours.

In the end, Henry climbed on the roof too and sat panting astride it. "Little Dot," he said, "it's not my fault. I was in town and I met the black lady again. She was in the garden of an empty house and she called me over. Someone had moved house and left the two cats behind. They were both starving. I *had* to help them, Little Dot! Do forgive me."

It soothed me just a little, that he had come up on the roof to explain, but I couldn't let him see that. I kept my back to him and twitched my tail.

"*Please*, Little Dot!" Henry said. "You'll always be my first and only cat!"

"Prove it," I said. "Send them away again."

"I can't do that," he said. "They've nowhere to live and you can count their ribs, Little Dot. Let me look after them and I'll do anything you want."

"All right," I said, and I turned around and nosed his hand. But I didn't purr.

Henry said, "Thank God!" and more or less fell off the roof. The noise brought Great-aunt Harriet out of her cottage.

"I thought you were that dratted rooster again!" she said. "What a fuss about one little spotted cat! When are you going to build a proper henhouse?"

"Soon, soon," Henry said, rolling in the weeds.

He called those cats Orlando and Cleopatra, would you believe! But they generally answered to Orange and Claws. Claws was a tomcat anyway and Claws suited him better. I made it very clear to them right from the start that it was *me* who slept on Henry's head, and I made it equally clear to Henry that I was having my food up on the Welsh dresser in future, not down on the flagstones like an ordinary cat. I wanted him to put two more catflaps in the kitchen door too, so that they wouldn't sully mine, but he said that one would have to do. He was too busy planning the hen coop Great-aunt Harriet kept asking for to cut holes in doors.

Orange and Claws and I got on quite well actually. They knew I was the one who really owned Henry. And they had always lived in a town up to then, so they were quite fascinated when I showed them the farm and the hills and warned them to be careful of hens and Great-aunt Harriet's stick. Great-aunt Harriet always said she had no patience with cats and was liable to prove it by swatting you. Orange went out exploring a lot, while Claws taught me how to catch mice in the sheds. I mean, I *knew* mice before Claws came, but I hadn't known you could *eat* them.

But Henry just couldn't seem to stop himself adopting cats. "I seem to have got into the habit," he said to me apologetically, the day he arrived home from the Scientific Institute with Millamant in a basket. "Don't mind her. She's a victim of a mad scientist at the Institute. I sneaked her out of a cage there, and I'm afraid she's a bit mad herself by now."

Millamant was a skinny Burmese with a squint, and *mad* was understatement. I mean, she liked being *wet*. The first time Claws and I found Mill swimming in the water butt, we naturally assumed she was drowning and set up a scream for help. This brought Great-aunt Harriet out of her cottage, who assumed the same thing and tried to pull Millamant out.

Millamant scratched her. Deeply. In reply, Great-aunt Harriet pushed Millamant right under water and stumped off, shouting to Henry that she couldn't *abide* cats and this one was *crazy*. Later, she found Mill in the bath with her and threw her out of the window, yelling to Henry that he was to stop owning cats at *once*, before everyone else went mad too. Mill didn't care. She had a wash in the water butt and then got in the shower with Henry.

Great-aunt Harriet didn't really dislike cats. She just needed the right cat to belong to. This became clear when one of her nephews arrived for a visit. He had brought his cat, Mr. Williams, in a sort of glass box pitched sideways into the back of his sports car. Mr. Williams was black and well-mannered and scared of almost everything. Well, so would *I* be scared of everything if I was forced to ride around sideways in a glass box. As soon as Henry saw Mr. Williams, he strode to the car and opened the box.

"That's no way to treat a cat!" Henry said. "Turn your car around and drive away. Now."

"But I've come to stay with Aunt Harriet," the nephew protested, "for a week."

"Oh no, you haven't!" Great-aunt Harriet screamed from inside her cottage. "Go away at once!"

Henry looked very surprised at this. Great-aunt Harriet was supposed to be very fond of this nephew. She was leaving him her things in her Will. But as soon as Henry opened the glass box, Mr. Williams had done a vanishing act almost as good as mine and ended up clamped to Great-aunt Harriet's chest. Shortly, Great-aunt Harriet arrived in the doorway of her cottage with the trembling black cat in her arms. He had his claws into her everywhere he could hang on to. Every claw said, "This human is *mine!*" Great-aunt Harriet accepted this at once, the way humans do, and she told the nephew he was not to set foot in her cottage ever again. The nephew drove sulkily away and Mr. Williams stayed. He was as unbalanced as Mill in his way. He *liked* it when Great-aunt Harriet called him her cutchy-wootchy-darling-diddums and tickled his tummy—but we forgave him for that, considering what he had been through.

Great-aunt Harriet made Henry drive her into town to alter her Will, so that she could leave her things to Henry instead. Henry told me that the things were all hideous china ornaments and he hoped she would change her mind. Then he drove off to visit one of the farmers on the moor, who had asked to see him urgently, and came back with the sixth cat.

The sixth cat was called Madam Dalrymple and she was white and fluffy as a dandelion clock—or she was when Henry had washed the muck off her. Nobody knew where she had come from or who had belonged to her and Madam Dalrymple was far too stupid to explain. She certainly did not belong on the farm where Henry found her. He had discovered her struggling in the farmer's pigpen, in considerable danger from the sow who lived in the pen. Henry had to bathe her four times. Unlike Millamant, Madam Dalrymple hated water and actually scratched Henry, but this was practically the only touch of spirit she ever showed. She was *stupid*. She lay about in picturesque poses and sighed to anyone who would listen that what she really, *really* needed was a blue satin bow around her neck. I mostly ignored her, except for when she tried to sit on Henry's knee. I always made her sit on his feet instead. Henry's knees are *mine*—both of them.

A couple of weeks after Madam Dalrymple arrived, all the farmers on the moor came to see Henry, looking grave and anxious. We went up on the roofs and stared at their Land Rovers and Jeeps and vans. Several of them had dogs in them, so we had to stay on the roofs until they had gone. Then I went down and sat on Henry's papers so that he could explain to me what it was all about. I am the only one who is allowed to sit on Henry's desk, or climb on his computer.

Henry was looking as upset as the farmers. It seemed that there was a Great Beast loose on Ettmoor, probably from a zoo somewhere, Henry said, although nobody really knew where it had come from or even what kind of animal it was. It had only been seen for brief moments at dusk from a long way off, but it had eaten a lot of sheep and attacked a number of other animals too. Henry spread out the various photographs the farmers had brought and I sat soberly with my tail around my legs and looked at them.

I felt the hair on my spine and my tail trying to bush out. At one photo, I had to struggle not to do a strong vanishment and end up cowering in the back of the airing cupboard or somewhere. This one had caught the Beast slinking into a distant hedge. It was dark and shaped very like a cat—but not at all like a cat either. It was—*wrong*. It was, well, a monster. And it was obviously huge. If I had had any doubt about its size, there was the picture of a horse it had attacked. The poor creature had lost half its hide down one side, in eight long bleeding streaks. That Beast had *claws*. And then there were pictures of the poor mutilated remains of a dog and several cats the thing had played with. My back shuddered and I thought uneasily of myself and Claws playing with the mice in the sheds. This Beast played just the same way.

"Yes," Henry said, "this is a real creature—and a real menace too, Little Dot. The farmers want me to help them track it down and shoot it. They've tried to catch it several times, but it always seems to slip away when they think they've got it cornered. They want me to apply some science to the hunt." He sighed. "They say science, Little Dot, but I can see this is going to take magic. Normally I'd hate the idea. It seems so unfair. But just look at those cats. It's got to be stopped. And until we've caught it, you cats are going to stay indoors at nights. Make that clear to the others, will you?" He sighed again. "Hens inside too, I suppose."

I explained about the Beast to the others, but I am not sure they believed me. Only Madam Dalrymple was prepared to stay inside in comfort. Every evening became a frenzy of hens running and cackling, with Henry galloping around the yard driving them into the coach house, and then getting more and more exasperated as he grabbed Orange as Orange tried to slither out into the landscape and seized Millamant dripping from the water butt. Then Claws had to be tempted out of the sheds with a slice of mackerel and Mr. Williams wheedled with a chunk of melon—for some reason this was Mr. Williams's favorite food—and the rest of us thrust indoors with urgent entreaties. "Get in or I'll kick you, cat! I'm out of patience! And, no, the catflap is now *locked*, understand! Even for you, Little Dot!" This last regardless of the fact that I was only *watching*. It took nearly an hour before the five of us were moodily gathered on Henry's bed—or under it, if it was Millamant—and Mr. Williams finally thrust into Great-aunt Harriet's cottage. Actually Mr. Williams came straight out again through the bathroom window as soon as Henry was indoors. He gets claustrophobia, you see.

During this time, when he was not at the Scientific Institute or conferring with the farmers, Henry built the Mobile Hen Coop. Mr. Williams and I both found it fascinating. It was a long, long wooden triangle, with two sloping sides and flat ends and bottom. In one sloping side there were three sliding doors for the hens to go in through and boxes full of straw inside for the hens to roost in. Once the hens were inside it for the night, Henry said, the sliding doors would be shut to keep them safe.

"But here's the clever part," Henry said. "If it stays in one place it kills all the grass."

"Weeds," said Mr. Williams. "They're weeds in this yard."

"Weeds then," Henry agreed, "but I don't want them killed whatever they are."

"Finest clumps of nettles in the county," Mr. Williams observed. "Thistles and camomile, too."

"Medicinal and magical uses for all three," Henry said. "Do stop mewing at me, Mr. Williams. It puts me off. Anyway, this Coop is designed to rise in the air and move to another place by magic. Watch."

Mr. Williams had to go away when Henry demonstrated the magic. He said it made the roots of his fur sore. But I stayed and watched. I found I understood that magic—but then I told you I was special.

Unfortunately the hens shared Mr. Williams's feelings about magic. None of them would go near that Coop. They ended up being chased into the coach house every night and disturbing Great-aunt Harriet just as usual.

I used the Coop as a plaything after that. If I spread myself along the pointed top, I found I could activate the magics and send the Coop floating in any direction I wanted. To my surprise, Madam Dalrymple was the only other cat who thought this was fun. As soon as she saw me on the Coop, she hopped up behind me, and, not in the least worried that the magics bushed her coat out until she looked like a fluffy snowball, she went for sedate rides round and round the farmyard. Henry stood in the kitchen door and laughed helplessly at us whenever he took a break from making magics to catch the Beast of Ettmoor.

He had designed several rings of big black magic generators, and these were placed out on the moor to surround the areas where the Beast had been active. Every day his farmer friends moved the generators a few feet in a carefully planned direction, so that eventually the Beast would be trapped inside a small tight circle. Then they would go in with their guns.

Henry had a map laid out on the dining room table with little tiny models of the generators on it. "Do they know you're using magic?" I asked, sitting on the edge of the table to look at it.

"No, I call them field-static generators," Henry said. "They wouldn't believe they were paying for something that worked, if I said it was magic. I've had to ask them to pay for the cost of materials, you see. I made the things down at the Institute."

The little model generators looked so enticing that I couldn't resist putting out a paw to the nearest. It wobbled beautifully. To my utter indignation, Henry promptly pushed me off the table. I sat at his feet and did my Outraged Stare at him.

"No," he said. "No touching, not even for you, princess. This map is part of the magic. I think the dining room door is going to be shut from now on."

"Don't you *trust* me?" I said.

"Not where little wobbly things are concerned, no," Henry said. "Run away now, there's a good cat."

I stalked out into the yard, so furious that my tail lashed at thistles and clumps of other weeds all the way to the Coop. Henry didn't trust *me*! I couldn't believe it! I jumped up on the Coop and took it around in a great angry circle until it was pointing at the gates. The gates are always open in Henry's farm. I was almost through into the road when Madam Dalrymple bounded elegantly among the weeds and jumped up behind me.

"Where are we going?" she asked, settling herself tastefully.

"Away," I said. I didn't want her. I was angry. But I had to go somewhere now I was out in the road, so I turned right, uphill, the way that led to the hill paths. The Coop didn't like the climbing. It slewed and it slogged and it crawled. In the end I wrestled it around onto the nearest level path, which happened to be the path that Henry had taken nearly a year ago when he found me. The Coop went much better there. We were fine until a light foggy rain began to fall.

Madam Dalrymple shifted and twitched. "Where are we really going?" she said. "Is it far?" She looked very odd, with every hair on end and a raindrop on each hair. She made a silvery ball rather like the ornaments Great-aunt Harriet had hung on a tree at Christmas.

"I'm going to look at the storm drain where Henry found me," I said. I thought I might as well.

"Your birthplace," Madam Dalrymple said placidly. "How

correct. He's told you all about it so often, of course. Even I can begin to understand him when he talks about it now. But I wish I could understand human talk like you do. I'd ask for a blue satin ribbon. Do you think he'd get me one?"

"No," I said. I was having problems. A peculiarity of the magic on the Coop, which had not shown up when we were just jogging around the yard, was that if you went in a straight line, you went faster and faster. It seemed to double its speed continuously. Rain was hitting my eyes like needles and whipping off my whiskers. Rocks and blurred grass raced past underneath.

"This is fun," said Madam Dalrymple, vast with magic.

I didn't think so. I could see and hear the storm drain thundering under the path already. We were whizzing up to it, and after that, the path turned a sharp corner. I knew we were going to whizz straight out over the hillside. I couldn't possibly stop us in time. "Get ready to jump off!" I gasped at Madam Dalrymple.

"Why?" she asked.

"Because," I began. And then we were at the storm drain.

"Steady, steady!" said a big black lady in the middle of the path. The pale palms of her hands slapped against the triangular front of the Coop and it came to the ground with a crunch. "Where you going so fast?" she said to me.

"I—er—thought I'd look at my birthplace," I explained.

"You weren't born here, honey. It was up the hill a piece," she said. "There you got swept away."

"Good heavens!" Madam Dalrymple said, leaning over to look at the rushing water. "You might have been drowned!"

"That is so, but never you mind that now," the woman said. "There are three things I'm telling you I want you to learn and remember. Say them after me, honey, not to forget. The first one is *The higher the fewer*. You got that?"

"*The higher the fewer*," I repeated, gazing up at her. Her face was black and wet as my nose. I'd never seen a human like her before.

"And you?" the woman said to Madam Dalrymple, but Madam Dalrymple just stared. She has no memory at all. The woman shrugged and turned back to me. "Now, *Chocolate herrings are impure*. That's two," she said.

"*Chocolate herrings are impure*," I said, still gazing. She smelled the same way the magics of the Coop did, but stronger and spicier. I began to wonder if she was quite a human.

"That's good, that's great," she told me. "Now the last is *The Beast of Ettmoor*."

"*The Beast of Ettmoor*," I said obediently. The woman had a turban on her head that stuck up in two black peaks at either side of her head. They reminded me of my own ears. "If you don't mind my asking," I said, "who are you?"

"My name is Bastet, Little Dot," she said, "and my calling is cats. Have you got my three sayings in your head? You about to need them badly."

"Yes," I said.

"Good," Bastet said. "Then walk around to the other end of this thing you riding and go home. I send a friend to you any second now. Makes seven. That's a good number."

I jumped down and picked my way over the mud and stones of the path to the opposite end of the Coop. By the time I got there, Bastet had gone. I was not surprised. I think she was very magical indeed. I jumped, rather sadly, up onto the Coop, facing the way we had come, and I was just about to get it going again when another whiff of that spiced magic smell struck my nose. I looked up the hillside and saw something mostly white struggling down through the heather. A pleading mew came from it.

"It's all right!" I called out. "I'm waiting for you."

A large cat, almost twice my size, came scrambling and sliding down the wet rocks to the path. She was so wet and draggled and humble that I never thought of being afraid of her. "Oh dear," she said, "I'm so sorry to bother you, but *could* you find me somewhere to shelter? I've nowhere."

"You can come home with us," I said. "I'll speak to Henry. Hop up."

The large cat looked up at me and at Madam Dalrymple staring vaguely down at her. Then she looked at the Coop. "Is there a way to ride inside?" she asked diffidently.

"Well, we've got three doors," I said, "but I don't know how to open them."

"Like this, I think," the large cat said, and somehow she managed to push the middle hatch aside and crawl inside the Coop. "Lots of lovely straw," she said. "Thank you."

"You're welcome," I said. There was something about this big, wet, polite cat that made me like her.

"She's got just the same markings as you have! All those dots!" Madam Dalrymple said, craning down to look through the hatch.

I craned down to look too. Inside the hatch I could see splodges of gray, tabby, ginger and pink, blots of black and dots of sandy brown and cream. But, to my relief, because this cat was so much larger, she seemed more white than anything. I like to think I am unique. "The effect is quite different," I said haughtily.

"Not a lot," said Madam Dalrymple. "We'll have to call her Big Dot."

I made a silently offended No Comment and moved the Coop off.

It was quite as difficult going back. The further we went, the faster the Coop moved. By the time we reached the farm road, we were scorching along as fast as a car. I worked frantically to slow us down. And of course Madam Dalrymple, in her usual maddening way, chose the moment that I was trying to aim us at the farm gate to say, "Why did that woman tell you to remember nonsense?"

"I don't know!" I spat, as we hurtled into the yard. Mr. Williams, who was sitting in our way, rose six feet in the air and managed to miss us. Orange and Claws squirted out of nettle clumps to either side. We raced on until we hit the water butt and stopped. Millamant came head and shoulders out of it, squinting reproachfully. "Where's Henry?" I asked her.

"In the living room, but you won't want to go there," Mill replied.

"Of course I will. It's got the best chairs," I said.

As I bounded away toward the catflap, Mill said, "I did warn you!" but I took no notice. I raced through the kitchen and past the dining room—where the door was now closed on that map—and galloped into the living room. There I stopped as if I'd run into the water butt again.

Henry was standing there holding both the hands of a human woman. He had a beaming, dazzled look and he was staring into the human's face with the same expression that he usually saves for me. I suppose she was a handsome human, in a thin, dark way, but still . . . I mewed. Loudly.

Henry jumped. "Oh, look, Fara," he said. "Here's Turandot now!" To my extreme surprise, he swooped on me and picked me up. I'd never known him do that without my permission before. I squirmed around and gave him my Outraged Stare, but he took no notice and held me out toward this woman. "There," he said. "Isn't she beautiful?"

The woman narrowed her eyes at me. She shuddered. "Henry, she's *hideous*! She looks as if she's got the plague with all those blotches!" She backed away. "Don't bring her near me. I'm not a cat person."

Henry said cheerfully, "Okay." And dropped me. *Dropped* me! Just like that.

I went away, back through the catflap and over to the Coop, where Big Dot was peering nervously out of the hatch. "I'll have to introduce you to Henry later, I'm afraid," I said. "Are you hungry?"

"Terribly," she said.

"You met that Fara creature then?" Millamant said, popping up from the water butt again. "I tried to tell you. I think she's staying here."

"Not if I have anything to say about it!" I said, leading Big Dot to the kitchen.

When we got there, Great-aunt Harriet was sitting in the best chair with Mr. Williams in her lap. "Oh, we've got a Big Dot now, I see," she said, watching Big Dot fit herself humbly through the catflap. "Better than the other thing that arrived here today. I must say, Henry has a *genius* for choosing terrible women! Little Dot, *try* to make him see reason. I've never disliked anyone so much in my life as I dislike that Fara."

I jumped up on the Welsh dresser and observed that half

my breakfast was still there. "Big Dot, if you like to come up here," I began.

But Great-aunt Harriet popped Mr. Williams on the floor and sprang up, saying, "Now, Turandot, don't make the poor thing struggle up *there*, for goodness' sake, not in *her* condition!" and bustled about finding saucers. She gave Big Dot most of a tin of meaty chunks, a pyramid of dry food, and a soup bowl of milk. Big Dot ate it all. She was starving.

"Is this Fara woman really staying?" I asked.

Great-aunt Harriet never listens to me, but Mr. Williams said gloomily, "We fear the worst. He's lent her his pajamas."

Mr. Williams was right. But it was worse than we realized. We expected that Fara would be given one of the spare rooms, but when we followed Henry upstairs to bed, we discovered that he and Fara were sharing Henry's room. Fara turned and stared at us. "Why are *they* here?"

"Little Dot always sleeps on my head," Henry explained. "Orange and Claws and Madam Dalrymple usually dispose themselves around on the duvet. And Millamant curls up in the chamber pot, you know."

"Well, they're not doing *that* anymore," Fara said. "Get rid of them."

Henry said, in that cheerful, obliging way, "Okay." And, to our extreme distress, we found ourselves pushed outside by Henry's magic, out and down the stairs, and then out again, until we were in the farmyard. It was as if he had forgotten we were in danger from the Beast there. It was a cold night, too. Claws and Orange huddled together for warmth, and Madam Dalrymple sat as close to Mill as Mill would let her. I crouched by myself in the middle of the yard. I have never felt so bewildered and unhappy as I did then. Because, you see, I had seen Henry look at Fara the way he usually looks at me. And I had seen Fara look back, and her look kept saying, Henry, you are *mine*! Just like I do. I kept wondering if I was an awful cat, the way Fara was an awful human.

After a while, something big and warm and whitish came and settled in the clump of weeds next to me. "What is so wrong, Little Dot?" Big Dot asked.

"It's Henry's new human!" I said. "She won't let us into Henry's room. And she *smells* wrong, and she doesn't even like Madam Dalrymple. I mean, most ordinary visitors who don't care for cats *always* admire Madam Dalrymple! The farmers say she's beautiful. But Fara called her a fluffy monstrosity."

"I doubt if Madam Dalrymple understood though," Big Dot said.

"No, she tried to get on Fara's knee twice," I said. "But that's not the point, Big Dot! Henry's being so *obedient* to her! He didn't listen to his operas because Fara said she didn't like opera, and he turned us *out*! How do we make Fara go away, Big Dot?"

"I'm not sure," Big Dot said, and thought about it, sitting comfortingly close.

While she sat there, I noticed that Big Dot's side, where it pressed against me, was sort of squirming and jumping. "Are you all right?" I asked. "Did all that food upset you?"

"No, no," she said. "I'm going to have kittens again. Quite soon, I think. Do you know, if you can think of what to do, and if all the doors are like the door from your kitchen, I *think* I could show you how to open Henry's bedroom."

"Oh, *please* do!" I said. "I miss the smell of his head!"

As we were talking, I had been hearing a lot of noise from

Great-aunt Harriet's cottage. It sounded as if Mr. Williams was singing, or something. Now it suddenly rose to a climax as Great-aunt Harriet threw her door open, saying, "Oh, all *right*, all right! Go out and do it then! Though what's wrong with your litter box I— Oh!" she said, as the light fell on the six of us in our various huddles. "Did that creature throw you out then? Of *course* she did, she's that type. It wouldn't worry her if the Beast ate the lot of you. You'd better all come in here and be safe then."

All of us, even Millamant, got up at once and filed politely into the cottage, where Mr. Williams was sitting on the table, looking suave and smug. We arranged ourselves courteously on the hearthrug.

"Hmm," said Great-aunt Harriet and picked up her mug of cocoa. She stumped up to bed, muttering to herself. "Better bend our minds to getting rid of that young woman, or she'll be sending Henry down to the vet with all the cats in a hamper to have them put down. She'd better not touch my Mr. Williams, though."

This made me think very urgently all night of ways to get rid of Fara.

Of course, the first thing was to get into the house. Next morning the catflap was locked and all the windows were shut, though we could hear and smell that Fara and Henry were in the kitchen having breakfast. We gathered around the door and yowled. Orange and Millamant have particularly loud voices, so between us we raised a fine noise. Normally it would have brought Henry to the door like a shot, but that day he took no notice of us at all. It was as if Fara had put him under a spell.

After twenty minutes of continuous din, Great-aunt Harriet stumped out of her cottage and banged the kitchen door open with her stick. We streamed in after her and stood by our empty bowls. "Aren't you going to feed your cats, Henry?" Great-aunt Harriet demanded.

Fara looked up from eating toast. "Cats are little hunting machines," she said. "They can live on the mice in the barns."

"With respect, Miss Spinks," Great-aunt Harriet said, "not only has Claws eaten every mouse for miles around, but I don't think Madam Dalrymple would know what to do with a mouse if it ran down her throat." She got out the food and fed us, while Henry smiled dreamily at Fara and said nothing at all.

After breakfast, they chased us out again and locked the house, while Henry drove Fara into town to do some shopping. It seemed that Fara had arrived without any clothes but the flimsy black dress she was wearing.

"Which strikes me as odd," Great-aunt Harriet said, when Mr. Williams fetched her. She thought a bit. "I shall borrow some lentils," she said, and let herself into the house with her key. There she went and set the living room window very slightly ajar. "There," she said, coming out with a cup of lentils. "Go in and do your worst."

Orange muscled the window wide open and we all went in and took turns at peeing on the rugs. But the bedroom door was firmly shut. "Not to worry," said Big Dot. She gathered us around her on the landing and showed us how you stood on your hind legs and trod on the door handle, and your weight pushed the door open. Before long, all of us could do it except Madam Dalrymple, although I had to jump to reach the handle. Then Claws went in and did tomcat things until the bedroom smelled really *strong*. Millamant went along to the toilet, where she got herself extremely wet, and then lay on the pillows. I thought that had probably fixed the bedroom, so I took everyone else down to the kitchen where we spilled sugar and trod in the butter and knocked down cups so they smashed on the flagstones. Then Big Dot and Orange heaved the waste bin over, while I went and walked behind all the plates on the Welsh dresser until most of them fell over and one or two broke. Madam Dalrymple had great fun rolling in cornflakes.

Then we went outside again and hid. Henry's car came back and he and Fara went into the house with bags and bags and bags. We could hear Fara's voice in there, screaming curses, but all that happened was that Fara came grimly outside and put our bowls outside in a row, while Henry opened windows and draped carpets and pillows out of them to air.

"Round One is a draw, I think," Great-aunt Harriet said when she let us into her cottage that night. "They've moved into the biggest spare room and *she's* hung all her new clothes there. She's bought enough stuff to last a year and *rows* of shoes. I suppose Henry paid, the poor fool!"

"What can we do with those clothes?" I said.

Madam Dalrymple suddenly came alert. "I know all about clothes," she said. "I'll show you what to do."

Next day, Henry went off to work at the Science Institute. "I must go there occasionally," he said, when I tried to get in the car with him, "or they'll wonder what they're paying me for. Out you get, Little Dot." He drove away, leaving Fara alone in the house with all the doors and windows shut.

Great-aunt Harriet came and knocked on the kitchen door. When Fara didn't open it, she went and rapped on the living room window. "Oh, Miss Spinks, if you would be so good! I'm afraid I've run out of sugar."

After a while, Fara came and grudgingly let her into the kitchen. I was ready. I did one of my best vanishments and was past Fara and through the kitchen before she had properly got the door open. While Great-aunt Harriet was saying, "Oh, no need to get down the tin. I can hook it with my stick and reach it that way—oh, how *kind!*" I scudded along to the dining room and opened its door the way Big Dot had taught us. I stole past the table with the map magic, very careful not to disturb it— although, from the dusty smell of it, I suspected that Fara had made Henry forget all about it—and jumped to the windowsill. That window bursts open if you lean on it hard enough, so I did that. Everyone came jumping quietly inside, except for Big Dot. She was feeling poorly that day and stayed resting inside the Coop.

We all crept up to the spare bedroom. And there were all the clothes, hanging in rows, with lines of shoes underneath them. Mr. Williams looked at them with great interest.

"Do we tear them up?" he asked Madam Dalrymple. "I quite fancy getting my claws into some of these."

"She'll get much more annoyed if we spoil them so that she can *almost* wear them," Madam Dalrymple said. "You make the fronts messy, as if food was spilled on them. . . . "

Millamant said, "I know a pond that's full of green slime!" and hurried away.

" . . . and you put hairs all over the black things," Madam Dalrymple explained, "except you, Mr. Williams, you put hairs on the *white* things. Then the knitted things, you bite a thread and then pull, to make holes, and the dresses you bite just the thread in the hems and then pull the hem half down. You bite buttons, too, so that they half come off. . . . "

She had all kinds of ideas, so many that I began to suspect that Madam Dalrymple had been dumped in that pigpen by the enraged human she once owned. And whatever she suggested, we did. Millamant came back dripping with green slime and plastered herself lovingly up the fronts of things, Mr. Williams pulled down a pile of white things and wriggled in them, and, while the rest of us bit and pulled threads, Orange went along methodically making messes in all the shoes. It was fun. When everything was thoroughly treated, we went away—although Millamant paused to roll the last of her slime off on the pil-lows—and spent the rest of the day persuading Great-aunt Harriet to give us titbits.

You should have heard Fara shrieking when Henry came home.

"Perhaps that wasn't such a good idea," Great-aunt Harriet said, after she had been to borrow some tea the following morn-ing. "She's telling Henry to fetch the laundry hamper and take you all down to the vet. He hasn't quite agreed yet, but he will."

"Let's get on the Coop and go away!" Madam Dalrymple said, shivering.

I didn't know what to do. I was miserable. I crouched wretchedly beside the water butt all day, hoping and hoping that Henry would come out and comfort me, but he never did, until Mr. Williams came rushing across the yard, mewing excit-edly. There never was a cat like Mr. Williams for mewing. "Come and see! Come and look!" he mewed. "Everyone come in through the dining room window and see!"

Mill surged out of the water butt, Madam Dalrymple mate-rialized from a hay bale, Orange and Claws shot out of the coach house, and we all galloped after Mr. Williams, consumed with curiosity. He led us through the dining room and upstairs to the spare room. There was a strange new smell there. It was not coming from the shoes, which had been bundled into a plastic sack in the passage, nor the clothes, which had been thrown across the sack. It was coming from the bed, inside the room. We stood on our hind legs to look.

Big Dot was lying in the middle of the duvet there, looking tired, surrounded in rather a mess that was full of small squirming bodies. Six of them, there were six . . . "Kittens?" I said. "Oh, Big Dot, why did you have to have them *here?*"

"I didn't *mean* to," Big Dot said weakly. "But it was so comfortable—and I got rather taken short."

"We'll have to guard you," I said. "If Fara finds them . . . "

"I know. I'll move them the moment I feel stronger," Big Dot said. "Not just yet, please."

She went to sleep. Having kittens is obviously quite tiring. The rest of us crouched where we were, around the bed, waiting for what we knew was going to happen. Sure enough, just before suppertime, when the kittens had begun to move about and make squeaky noises, the door opened and Fara came in.

She stopped. She stared. Then she screamed, "Oh, this is the *last straw!* On *my* bed, of all places!"

"It isn't your bed. It belongs to Henry," I said.

She didn't hear me. She plunged forward, with both her hands out to grab. "These are going in the water butt," she said. "I'll drown them myself."

We all acted at once. We poured up over the edges of the bed, and stood there growling and spitting, so that the bed was full of our lashing tails, arched backs, and glaring eyes. Big Dot stood up in the center of us, twice her usual size, growling loudest of all.

"*Get out of my way!*" Fara screamed and grabbed for the kittens. Upon this, Mr. Williams, who was nearest—timid, nice-mannered Mr. Williams—put a paw-full of claws in each of her arms and dragged. He left two rows of dark, oozing blood on her. She screamed even louder and hit Mr. Williams, so that he flew across the room and crashed into the chest of drawers.

"What on earth is going on?" Henry said from the doorway.

Fara turned to Henry and went on screaming. She was so angry that she seemed to forget how to speak. "Middle of the bed!" she howled. "Water butt. Drown them. Horrible little ratty things! Drown, drown, *drown!*"

Henry walked around her and looked down at the bed. "Kittens," he said.

"*In the middle of my bed!*" Fara screamed.

"There are other beds," Henry said. "Pull yourself together, Fara. May I?" he said to Big Dot. Big Dot, very nervously, moved aside and let him sort through her kittens. "Six," Henry murmured. "One of every color—black, gray, white, ginger, this one's tortoiseshell, and here's a tabby. Oh, well done, Big Dot!"

"Henry," Fara said to him, in a hard, yowling voice, "I'm telling you to get rid of these cats and drown these kittens. *All* of them. Now."

"Don't talk nonsense," Henry said. He put the kittens gently back beside Big Dot. "Three boys and three girls, I make it."

"I *mean* it!" Fara shouted. "Henry, if you don't get rid of every single cat *this minute*, I shall leave!"

We all stared intensely at Henry, except for Mr. Williams, who was washing his bruises beside the chest of drawers. Henry looked at Mr. Williams. "The black cat," he said, "belongs to Great-aunt Harriet."

"But he scratched me!" Fara said. "They're all horrible creatures. So which is it to be? Do you get rid of them, or do I leave?"

Henry looked from one to another of our urgently staring pairs of eyes, and then at Fara. He seemed almost bewildered, the way he is when he wakes up in the morning. "There's no question," he said to Fara. "If that's your attitude, you'd better leave."

Fara's chest heaved with emotion. She glared. "All right," she said. "You'll regret this." And she left. She swung around and stormed out of the room. I heard her feet galloping down the stairs. I heard the kitchen door crash shut behind her. But I didn't relax until I heard her feet distantly swishing through the farmyard and then pattering on the road. Then I was so relieved that I burst out purring. I couldn't help it.

Henry sighed and said sadly, "Oh well. She did complain a lot. And she hates opera."

We had a perfect, peaceful evening. Henry invited Great-aunt Harriet to supper and played her two operas. One was *Turandot*, of course. But, although I sat on his knees to comfort him, I could tell he was sad.

The next morning, all the farmers arrived again, looking grim and serious. During the night, the Beast of Ettmoor had attacked the farm next to Henry's and killed six sheep, a sheepdog, and the farm cat. They were very worried because, according to the plans, the Beast should by now have been herded down the valley inside the final ring of magical generators.

Henry was equally worried. I sat on the dining room mantelpiece and watched him show the farmers the map and scratch his hair over it. "I think," he said at last, "that what *may* have happened is that a crucial—er—field-static generator must have got moved slightly, just enough to let the Beast slip back out of our trap. This one, I think." He pointed to the wobbly little marker that I had tried to play with.

My heart banged under my fur with guilt and terror.

Henry didn't even look at me. When the farmers said they were going to patrol this area with guns in future, he said, "Yes, that seems the only thing to do. And I'll strengthen the outer ring of generators to stop it escaping back into the hills. I'm truly sorry about this. I'll go and see to it now."

He drove off in his car and he was out all that day. He came home exhausted, but instead of settling down to another opera, he went into the dining room and worked on the map all evening. I felt so guilty that I kept well out of his way. I had messed up his magics and, on top of that, I had driven his lady away. I punished myself by not sleeping on Henry's head that night. I crouched by the kitchen fire instead and was miserable.

"There's no need to take on," Millamant said from the coal scuttle. "It's horrible Fara's fault just as much. She made him forget his magics."

"And we're all safe from the Beast as long as we stay indoors," Madam Dalrymple said placidly from the footstool.

"That's not the point!" I said.

Orange and Claws sat up uneasily in the best chair. They had all chosen to keep me company in my sorrow. "Speaking of the Beast," Orange said, "did you know that Big Dot has moved her kittens out into the Coop? Are they safe there?"

"Oh Lord!" I said, springing up. "They are *not*! And Mr. Williams *will* stay out all night!"

I was on my way to the catflap to go and reason with Big
Dot when we heard Mr. Williams shriek with terror, or with
pain, or both, out in the farmyard. Next second, the catflap
clapped open. Mr. Williams shot in through it, streaked across
the kitchen, and went to ground under the Welsh dresser,
which was almost too low even for me to get under these days.

"Hide, hide, hide!" he yowled. "It's coming!"

I stared stupidly at the path of blood Mr. Williams had
made from the door to the Welsh dresser.

"*What's* coming?" said Claws.

"The Beast, the Beast!" Mr. Williams gibbered. "You can't
smell it till it's *there!*"

Everyone was suddenly elsewhere, Madam Dalrymple with
a most unladylike howl. I did a vanishment such as I had never
managed in my life before and found myself at the very top of
the Welsh dresser, almost up by the ceiling. And only just in
time. Something was coming through the catflap.

My outstretched hair caught on the ceiling. A big dark face
was forcing its way indoors, a face twice the size of Henry's and
growing bigger as it came. For a moment, I thought the thing
would get stuck, but that was a vain hope. I watched the wood of
the catflap and then of the door spread and enlarge, as if the
wood were so much rubber, to let the Beast's shoulders follow its
head, and I realized hopelessly that this Beast was a magical
creature. It was almost inside now. Catfight song burst from my
throat as I watched it come. This was not the growling I had
done at Fara, but the full-voiced, throbbing, yowling, wailing
song of defiance you make when you encounter an alien cat.
Amidst my terror, I was quite surprised at the noise I could make.

The others joined in, Madam Dalrymple shrilly and

Millamant with deep echoes booming from the coal scuttle. Claws and Orange screamed and throbbed from two sides of the room, and Mr. Williams produced unearthly yodellings from under the Welsh dresser.

But the Beast kept coming. It dragged its massive hind quarters through the door and then pulled in its long tail. The room was filling with its smell, something like tomcat and something like rotten rat, and it was beginning to rise to its hind feet, when the passage door slammed open and Henry snapped on the lights. "What . . . ?" he began.

We all blinked and stared in the dazzle for a moment. I think that was the worst moment of all. There was a human sort of face on the front of the Beast's head, blinking enormous cat's eyes, and the face was surrounded in filthy, tangled hair. It had mangy little wings dangling from its huge shoulders. Its body had patches of elderly fur on it, clinging to bare, dirty, wrinkled skin. Everything about it was old, old and decaying. The claws on the ends of its great feet were stuck with rotting meat and shreds of grass, and they were splitting with age underneath.

But the worst of it was that we all recognized the face.

"*Fara?*" Henry said. "My God, you're the Sphinx!"

The Beast opened its mouth, full of blue-rotting fangs, and chuckled. Oh, Henry! I thought. I'm *sorry*. I got it here. I'll never bully you again if you can only just get *rid* of it!

"You're going to ask a riddle," Henry said shakily. "Don't bother. You're going to ask what goes on four legs at dawn, on two legs at midday, and three legs in the evening. And I know the answer. It's a man."

The Beast chuckled again. "Wrong," it said. It had a flat, cold voice. "I *used* to ask one riddle. Now I ask three. And I'm not going to ask *you*. I'm going to ask that conniving little spotted pet of yours, up there on top of the shelves. And when she can't answer, I shall be free to tear the lot of you to pieces. I shall gut the cats in front of you and then make you swallow those kittens before I tear your head off. Are you ready to answer, plaguespot?"

I quivered all over at this. I thought I knew now why Bastet had made me remember those three nonsense sayings. "Ask away," I said, and licked at my shoulder to make my nervous fur lie flatter.

The Beast said, "Why is a mouse when it spins?"

"Oh, I know that one!" Henry said, and he and I answered together, *"The higher the fewer."* I couldn't think how he came to know it. It made much more sense to a cat than a human. "And?" I said.

The Beast grinned, filling the air with bad-meat smell. "When is ceramic begonias?" it said.

"That makes no sense to me," Henry said. It didn't to me, either. Nor did the answer.

"Chocolate herrings are impure," I said. And I guessed that the riddles—and their answers—were the result of an ancient, tired, rotting brain. In the electric light, the Beast looked older than any creature I had ever seen. Its Fara-face was all sags and wrinkles. "And your third?" I asked. This is all back to front, I thought. I am Turandot the princess and I should be asking the riddles. Has Henry told me the opera wrong?

"The third," said the Beast, "is, Who kills as lion and as human wins?"

"The Beast of Ettmoor!" I cried out. "Now I can tear *you* to pieces!" And I was so exultant that I sprang straight down from

my perch near the ceiling to the top of the Beast's head, where I began scratching and tearing at its dirty mane with all four feet. Looking back, I can't think how I came to do anything so silly. I became totally entangled in long, filthy hair. I couldn't get loose. All I could think of to do then was to sink my teeth into its nearest smelly ear. The Beast screeched and swiped at me with its claws.

The outside door crashed open, shoved by Great-aunt Harriet's stick. I think she had been getting into her clothes ever since she heard Mr. Williams shrieking. She stormed in now, shouting, "What have you done to my poor little Willy-did-dums?" and whacked at the Beast with her stick. Bang, bang. Clout. Feathers, dust, and hairs whirled.

Henry, who was in a towelling dressing gown and his bare feet, danced about uncertainly for a moment and then seized the nearest chair—revealing Madam Dalrymple, who ran for her life—and began bashing at the Beast with it from the other side. I could feel the Beast try to protect itself with magic. Henry replied with more magic, such a furious gust of it that the chair he was wielding sizzled and the long hair wrapped around me stood out like rods. That was too much for the Beast. It turned and dived for the door.

I was thrown aside as it crashed outside. I was flung across something hard. I was so winded and frightened that it took me a second to realize that I was spread-eagled across the Coop, which Big Dot must have brought near the kitchen when she moved her kittens into it. In that second, the Beast ran, bound-ing into the darkness on four legs, and Claws and Orange went pelting after it as hard as they could go. Maybe they were inspired by my example. On the other hand, they never could resist chasing anything that ran. And almost in the same moment, Great-aunt Harriet galloped outside and flung herself sidesaddle across the Coop.

"After it, after it! Make this thing move, Little Dot!" she shouted, bashing the wooden side with her stick.

While I was pulling myself to my feet, Mr. Williams landed on the Coop, too, and clung to Great-aunt Harriet's lap. He explained afterward that although the magic made him feel as if his teeth were coming loose, he had to come because Great-aunt Harriet was not behaving normally. "And one has to look after one's humans," he said.

I started the Coop and we trundled toward the gate. By then, Henry was mincing after us, gasping when he trod on a nettle, shouting, "No! Stop! That Beast is a killer!" but we were getting up speed by then and, what with one thing and another, I was too dazed to stop.

Catsong came throbbing out of the night. When we swept out into the road, I saw Claws and Orange crouching in the way that led uphill, while the Beast hovered, wondering whether to kill them and go past, or turn the other way. That was clever of Claws and Orange, and brave, too. If the Beast had fled up into the hills, it might have been loose forever. But it saw us coming and turned downhill. It galloped away at astonishing speed. But, as I have explained, before long the Coop got up to astonishing speed too. We fair zoomed along, and began catching up steadily to the great dark shape galloping ahead.

"We're gaining!" Great-aunt Harriet shrieked, beating on the Coop. "Go faster! Faster!"

We were still a good fifty yards away when strong lights shone out from either side of the road, pinning the Beast in their

glare. It faltered. There was a *BOOM* like the end of the world
and several *crack-crack-cracks*, followed by echoes that bounced
around the hills until I could hardly hear straight. The Beast
jumped up in a great arch and flopped back on the road, where
I thought it came into several pieces. I was so shocked that I
stopped the Coop dead. We came down with a crunch.

"What happened?" I said.

"Oh good!" said Great-aunt Harriet. "I mean, oh dear. I
think the farmers shot it."

One of the hatches in the Coop slid aside and Big Dot
stepped out. "I'll go and make sure," she said, and went trotting
along toward the lights and the shapes of men and guns.

"Does that mean her kittens are in this Coop?" Great-aunt
Harriet said. "How *inconsiderate* of me! I hope the poor little
things are all right."

"They will be, or she wouldn't have left them," Mr.
Williams said soothingly.

Here Henry came limping up. But, to my huge indignation,
he limped straight on past us, saying, "I'd better go and make
sure they think they've just shot a lion. Take the Coop back to
the yard, Little Dot."

He passed Big Dot coming back. She said, "They used such
a big gun that they blew her into several bits," and climbed back
in with her kittens again.

I took the Coop back to the kitchen door, where Great-aunt
Harriet scrambled down, saying things about bottles and glasses
and seeing to Mr. Williams's wounds. "Nothing! Just a scratch!
I don't need seeing to!" I heard him saying as she banged the
kitchen door shut. It took her three attempts. It was half off its
hinges.

I waited, sitting on the Coop listening to Big Dot purring inside. I waited while Claws and Orange returned, very pleased with themselves. Henry was so long coming back that I got anxious. Suppose the Beast had just been faking dead and went for his throat when he got near. Then it would all be my fault. I set off out of the yard and down the road to look for him.

I'd only gone twenty yards or so, when there *was* Henry, limping along with a crowd of farmers, bringing them back to the farm for a drink. Exasperating. I sat down in the road and curled my tail primly around my legs.

Henry saw me and dashed forward, quite forgetting his sore-bare feet. "Little Dot!" he cried out. And I forgot to be exasperated and leapt up his front into his arms and draped over his shoulder, purring. "There's my brave Turandot!" Henry said.

"You keep getting things the wrong way around," I said. "I am not *your* Turandot. You are *my* Henry. Is that clear?"

"Perfectly," he said.

EVERARD'S RIDE

PART I

❋

RIDERS

THROUGH

THE BAY

❋

Chapter 1

OUTLAW

The events in this story took place rather more than a hundred years ago, when Queen Victoria was on the throne and the division between rich and poor was much more important than it now is. Your grandfather's grandfather would then have been a boy of twelve, like the boy to whom these things happened.

His name was Alex Hornby; and it was his misfortune to occupy the uncomfortable upper end of that gap between rich and poor, where you were not quite gentry, but too well off to be anything else. His father, Josiah Hornby, was a farmer. The family lived in a low stone farmhouse halfway up a hill, looking out across a great river estuary. From the foot of the hill a long causeway ran out into the bay, to a small rocky island on which stood the ruins of a castle. So, though all their fires smoked in the sea-wind, they had the grandest view in the neighborhood.

Above the farmhouse, the top of the hill had been cleared of trees, ready for the great new house Josiah Hornby intended to build the following summer.

Josiah, who was, like many Victorians, a grim and striving person, was changing into a gentleman-farmer as fast as he could afford to do it. He was a fairly wealthy man already. Twenty years or so before, he had bought shares in the railway which ran all around the bay beside the sea, and his shares had prospered. He had bought shares in other things. At the same time, out of what he had been paid for letting the railway run through his land, he bought the island in the bay. He had it for a song, because its owner was hard up, and because it was said to be haunted. But Josiah cared not a rap for ghosts, or gossip. He bought the island because it was cheap and because of its ruined castle. It was grand and gentlemanly, he thought, to own a castle.

Alex and his sister, Cecilia, were pleased with the castle, too, although they were not pleased with much else about starting to be rich. It meant that Alex had to go as a weekly boarder to a grammar school in the nearest big town. It meant that Cecilia had a governess. It meant—which was worst of all—that they dropped homely friends in the village and tried to be on visiting-terms with the Courcys of Arnforth Hall. The Courcys noticed them—just. Josiah went to the Hall once a week on business. The children were called in from time to time if more guests were needed at the Courcy children's parties. Cecilia had once refused to go to a Courcy party. Her father had been so angry that Alex hid in the loft and Cecilia set out across the bay to run away and make her fortune. She did not get very far that time. Josiah came after her on horseback and spanked her, right in the middle of the bay, beside the river channel.

The strange things began to happen just before Christmas, when Cecilia had turned sixteen. The governess had gone the week before. Cecilia was still in trouble about it.

"Mr. Hornby," said the governess, standing up like a frozen steel ramrod and clasping her mittens in front of her, "I will not stay a day longer in the same house with that girl of yours. She is wild, impertinent, and disorderly. She is quite unteachable and utterly unladylike. I leave this evening."

"Dash and bother it, madam!" cried Josiah Hornby. "Remember the child has no mother. What has she done?"

"I refuse to bear tales," the governess said. "Kindly order the pony-trap around in time for the London train."

"But I only hid in the loft and ate apples," said Cecilia. "And I said I had no wish to be a lady if it meant wearing mouse-colored mittens."

Josiah was so angry that he threw things. No one dared to go near him for two days except old Miss Gatly the housekeeper. When Alex came home for the last weekend before the holidays, his father was still angry.

"Your sister's in disgrace," he told Alex. "Dash me, if I could see my way to finding the money, I'd pack the little vixen off to one of them Swiss seminaries, be sure I would."

"If he does," said Cecilia to Alex in the kitchen, "I'll run away again. And this time I shall do it so that he will never find me. So there."

"Let me come with you," Alex begged. "I shan't want to be left behind if you're gone. Think of nothing but school and Father!"

"Hush!" said Cecilia.

Old Miss Gatly came into the kitchen carrying Josiah's teapot to be filled with more hot water. Alex bit a great mouthful of muffin and thought that at least at home the food was good. Cecilia drank tea, with her little finger crooked the way the governess did it, and smiled at Miss Gatly. Miss Gatly shook her head at her—she wore a crisp starched cap which rattled when she moved her head.

"Cecilia," she said. "For shame. Why make fun of the poor lady now she's left?" She creaked and rattled and breathed heavily as she heaved the kettle up from the hob. "My rheumatics is bad tonight," she said. "It's the fog. Down like a blanket now, all over the bay. Just the weather for queer things on the island. They say there's been lights seen there again—we'll be lucky if that's all there is to it."

"Tell us—tell us the stories," Alex said, delighted and greasy, with his mouth full of muffin. They loved Miss Gatly in this mood.

Miss Gatly came back after taking the teapot to the parlor and told them some of the stories. She sat by the range, knitting socks, needles clicking, cap rattling, and talked in the strange, formal way old country-people still use when they tell stories which may not quite be true. She told them how the ghost-lights flitted through the island on foggy nights and were seen to go winding through the bay where no one else dared to go for fear of quicksands. She told of the dangerous kingdom of Falleyfell out in the bay and how those who saw it were as good as dead.

"And if," she said, "a wise man hereabouts sees aught of this on a clear night, he will shut his eyes and turn away, making the sign of the cross for safety . . . "

Alex put his thin greasy hand under his pointed chin and leaned forward with an eager sigh. Cecilia had tucked her feet up under her green tartan skirt, with one hand holding down the bulging crinoline. With the other hand she was absent-mindedly twirling and pulling a bright gold ringlet. The draft sighed in the chimney and a sheep coughed outside. Cecilia sighed too, because the best part of the tale was coming.

"These things seen of a night are bad enough," said Miss Gatly, "but let the wise man beware of things seen by day. Once in a hundred years, they say, a horseman gallops through the bay. He is the Wild Rider, the Rider of Doom, and let those who see him take heed. For within the year, as sure as fate, some poor soul will perish in the bay. He may be caught in the tide, and they say that happens to some, but, more like, the poor soul founders in the quicksands and vanishes without a trace."

The sheep coughed again. Alex, with a delicious shiver, looked over his shoulder at the window. It was dark, streaming wet with the warmth from the range, but there was someone outside. For a second, with his hair prickling, Alex was sure that he saw a face. Then there was nothing and no sound either.

"It was the fog," he thought. "It plays the strangest tricks. We all know that."

Miss Gatly put up her knitting, lit her candle, and creaked away to bed. In winter she went to bed at seven. Alex, still wrought up and shivering, pushed aside the tea and muffins and spread out Latin and History books for his weekend homework.

Cecilia, whose duty it was to wash up the tea, was lazy with excitement after the story. She still sat with her feet curled up, sometimes twirling her ringlet, sometimes idly sewing the bodice of her best dress. There was to be a Courcy party just after Christmas and the dress had to be ready for then. Cecilia had hoped her father would forbid her to go after the governess-incident, but it was the last thing Josiah would have forbidden. Cecilia sighed. Outside, in the farmyard, the sheepdog barked, a snarling uncertain bark, and was quiet.

"Tyke doesn't like the fog," Alex remarked. "Cecil, explain Caesar's campaign against Gaul to me. I know you know."

Cecilia smiled, because she liked being called Cecil. She had always wished she had been born a boy. And she was proud of knowing Latin. She had learned it from Alex's books while she was helping him to learn it. Sewing away busily, she explained, and Alex listened, chewing his pen. Outside Tyke growled, and was quiet again.

"Then," said Cecilia, "Caesar was quite shocking to the poor Helvetii. I cannot at the moment remember why they came into it—"

"But I have to know," said Alex. "Try to remember."

Cecilia thought, scratching at the scrubbed table with her needle. The grandfather clock ticked in a clattering, unhurried way, and the lamp on the table whispered and flared sideways in a cold draft from somewhere.

Cecilia said at last: "Well, they were wandering about in southeastern Gaul when they should have been in Switzerland, but I—"

"They were in search of a new home, poor souls," said someone else.

Alex jumped up. His chair fell over behind him. Cecilia, with a gasp that was nearly a scream, jerked around and slapped one hand down on her crinoline, horrified at all the frothy petticoats she had been showing. The stranger latched the back door without a sound and came down the room toward them with the faintest of swishing and chinking.

"I beg your pardon for intruding on you," he said.

They stared at him. The hands of the grandfather clock had moved on nearly three minutes before they could believe they were really seeing him. He was exactly like the pictures in Alex's open History book—except that he had taken off his complicated feathered hat as he shut the door. His hair was long and dark brown and wavy with dampness. He wore a great orange cloak, stained at the hem with water and mud, and tight wet boots with long jagged spurs to them. Under the cloak they could just see clothes that took their breath away: dagged, embroidered, hanging sleeves, clasps studded with jewels, a shining sword-belt hanging across his chest, and the smooth, used-looking hilt of the sword itself.

Cecilia came to her senses first. He must, she thought, be an actor who had lost his way. She saw that he was not very much older than herself and that he was soaking wet, very tired, and full of worry and weariness.

"I'm so sorry," she said. "You gave me a terrible shock for a moment. Have you lost your way in the fog? May we offer you a cup of tea?"

The stranger shook his head. "I do not think I have lost my way. This is the farmhouse at the end of the causeway, is it not?"

Cecilia nodded. "That's right. Then what—?"

"What is tea?" asked the stranger.

Cecilia dragged at her tight new corset, afraid that she might faint with astonishment. "I—I'll brew you a pot," she said weakly.

Alex still stood staring, with his Latin book in his hands, and Miss Gatly's stories whirling around in his head. "Who *are* you?" he said, very high and squeaking, and too frightened to care. "Just tell us who you are."

The stranger smiled at him. "You should not attend to that old lady's stories," he said. "I am a real man, and until yesterday I was Count of Gairne. My name is Robert—and it seems I am still allowed the title of Lord Howeforce."

"Then it was you I saw at the window," Alex said, fixing on the only part of the answer that he could understand.

The strange man nodded, and Cecilia saw that he shivered too.

"You are soaked to the skin," she said. "Whoever you are, you must come by the fire and dry yourself. Come, sit down, and I'll make some tea." Ever afterward, she was amazed at how brave she was. She hurried up to the stranger and pulled at his damp arm. He was certainly real, but very cold, and the stones in the clasp of his cloak were precious ones, she was sure—not actor's bits of glass. He came with her to the range and sat down thankfully in the warmth.

Cecilia put the kettle to boil. Alex moved around to where he could see the stranger better but still keep a chair between them.

"Are you from—from the island?" he asked nervously. The man cast a shadow, he could see, so he could not be dead—

Miss Gatly had told them many times that dead men have no shadows. But he looked as strange and outlandish to Alex in his Eton jacket and skimpy ankle-length trousers as he would have looked to anyone in the twentieth century.

The man shook his head at him kindly as if he saw how frightened Alex was. "My lands lie—lay—over the water from the island," he said, "but I think you would think of me as from the island."

"Then," said Alex, too amazed and nervous to be polite, "whatever are you doing here?"

"Alex!" said Cecilia. "Leave the poor gentleman alone. If you were wet through and worn out, how would you like someone staring at you and asking rude questions?" And to the stranger, she said: "You are not to answer him, Mr.—er—your lordship, until you have drunk a cup of tea."

"But," said Alex, somewhat nastily, because Cecilia had hurt his feelings treating him like a little boy in front of this strange person, "but suppose Father comes in here before he's told us anything."

That frightened Cecilia and gave her a change of heart about the stranger. She knew Josiah would be angry to find them entertaining him. He would think the man was a lunatic—and now she thought of that, Cecilia was not at all sure that he might not, indeed, be a lunatic. Perhaps a rich lunatic, that would be it. She turned her back and poked the fire, wondering what they might do if he was.

"Never fear," said the man. "The gentleman your father is engaged on a pile of manuscripts and seems not likely to stir. I took the liberty of looking in upon him, through the window.

And, as for your question, sir, I am here somewhat in the position of the unfortunate Helvetii. I have had to leave my lands."

"Oh!" said Alex. He was fascinated. Here seemed to be a story such as even Miss Gatly would find hard to equal. He itched to have the man say more. He spoke in such a formal lofty way that ordinary English sounded splendid as he used it.

The man was looking at Cecilia. "My lady there," he said to Alex, "is your sister, is she not?"

"Yes. She's Cecilia. I'm Alex."

Cecilia blushed and was even more nervous. What could he mean by calling her "my lady"? He knew they lived on a farm. He had said so. If Josiah had been a nicer father, she would have run and fetched him. As it was, all she could do was to make the tea and pretend to be very busy. There was a nasty silence, with Alex jigging impatiently and the stranger staring sadly at the fire, until Cecilia poured the tea into a cup and passed it to him with her hands shaking. "Sugar?" she asked coldly.

The man looked very puzzled by the cup and saucer, but he took it politely and said: "Thank you, my lady."

Cecilia lost her temper, as much from fright as from anger. "I'm *not* your lady," she told him loudly. "I am not a lady at all. You know perfectly well I am simply a farmer's daughter."

Alex blushed—he hated Cecilia's rages—and to Cecilia's consternation, the stranger blushed too. He stared at her as if she had said the most embarrassing thing he had ever heard. He stared so that tears came into Cecilia's eyes and she put her hands over her mouth. Then he looked down at the tea, which he was holding extraordinarily clumsily.

"I—I apologize," he said. "As you see, I am woefully unfamiliar with manners Outside. What do I do with this—this tea?"

Cecilia giggled. "You drink it. Try some sugar if you have not had tea before."

Alex sighed. It looked as if the embarrassment was over. The man tried the tea. Alex was sure that he did not like it but was too polite to say anything. "I wonder what it is he usually drinks," he thought. Cecilia, meanwhile, made up her mind to believe that he really was the extraordinary thing he seemed until she had found out more.

"Won't you take off your cloak?" she asked politely. "You must have come a long way for it to have got so wet."

The stranger put down the cup and unclasped his cloak. Cecilia took it from him and spread it over a chair to dry, while Alex marvelled at the richness of the strange clothes underneath. "I have not come so very far," the stranger said, "but I was pursued. My horse was killed and I was forced to hide in various wet places." His boots were steaming in the heat, and the fur lining of his sleeves was soaked and draggled.

Alex could easily believe what he said was true. "Tell me," he begged.

The stranger pushed back his hair with both hands and stared into the fire. "What shall I say?" he said wearily. It suddenly struck Alex that the man was really not very old at all, scarcely a man, hardly older than Martin Courcy or the great boys at school. But he was handsomer and more grown-up-looking than anyone Alex knew of the same age.

"Say why you were pursued," Alex said and was thrilled at the answer.

"I am an outlaw. I am accused of killing a man I did not kill." The stranger looked earnestly from Alex to Cecilia, plainly very anxious that they should believe him. "I swear to you I did not kill him. This man was my liege lord, and to kill him would be as evil as if I had killed my own father. Someone killed him—who it was I cannot say—and I was accused. It seems I had enemies where I thought to have had friends. And it gave color to their case that I did indeed kill a man—my uncle— when I was scarcely turned fourteen."

Cecilia gasped. Alex was frightened again. Outlaws were all very well, but a self-confessed murderer sitting beside one's kitchen range was a totally different matter. "What made you do that?" he said.

"My uncle," the stranger answered, "had killed my father. I saw him, and so did several others, push my father from the battlements of Gairne Castle. There was no other course open to me—but I assure you that it was in fair fight that I killed him. He had always been a poor swordsman."

"Well," said Cecilia, "I suppose that was all right. But could you not have brought the law on him?"

The stranger was a little puzzled. "It was according to the law, what I did—er—madam."

"Call me Cecilia, for goodness' sake," she answered. "And was there any reason why you might have killed this other man?"

"I assure you, none."

Alex asked: "And you would like us to hide you here, would you? Until you can prove your innocence."

The stranger laughed, not greatly amused. "That may be for as long as I live. There is no evidence that I can see to establish a proof. No—if I might beg hospitality here for one night, it will be much more than I deserve for my rude intrusion."

Alex looked at Cecilia. "What do you say to the guest room? It's a long way from Father and Miss Gatly."

"Yes," said Cecilia. "I'll get a warming-pan. And you will need something to eat, I imagine."

"I would be grateful for some food," the outlaw said. "It was early this morning when last I ate."

"You must be famished!" cried Cecilia. She hurried away the remains of the muffins and brought out what food there was in the pantry. Alex kept watch for their father while she worked.

Cecilia was a little embarrassed by the food they had. "It is plain and good," she thought, "but it can be nothing like what he must be used to. I am sure, from the look of him, that he is used to the choicest of things."

While the outlaw ate, Alex wandered between the kitchen door and the table, watching the man eat and hoping for more talk. He was fascinated by the way he did not seem to use a fork. The stranger smiled at him.

"I fear I interrupted my lady—er—your sister in her exposition of Caesar's campaigns in Gaul. Might I take her place, while I eat, and continue the explanation?"

"That is very kind of you," Alex said.

So the stranger took up the story where Cecilia had left off. He explained many more things than Cecilia, or even Alex's schoolmaster, would have thought necessary, and he explained them so clearly and vividly that Alex never forgot them. He knew all about fighting. Alex had never heard a battle explained before as if one were actually giving the orders to the soldiers, but that was the way the stranger explained Caesar's battles. Alex began to admire Caesar far more than he had ever done in his life, and he admired this outlaw even more than Caesar.

Cecilia came in and out while the man talked. The man seemed very shy of her, particularly of calling her Cecilia. He went out of his way not to call her anything. And as for Cecilia, and Alex too, they were nearly reduced to calling him "Hey, you!"

"What *should* we call him?" Cecilia kept asking herself, as she hurried up and down stairs. "It seems as if he has lost most of what names he had when he became an outlaw."

They became shyer and shyer, because the longer they left it, the more stupid it seemed not to have asked him what name they should use. It was not until they had taken him into the bleak whitewashed guest room and Cecilia was turning back the elaborate white crocheted overlay on the guest bed, that Alex was impolite enough to ask.

"What would you like us to call you?" he blurted.

The outlaw smiled. "My name is Robert," he answered.

"Very well, then," Cecilia said, briskly, because she was so thankful. "Good night, Robert. I hope you sleep well." Then she ran out of the guest room, with Alex behind her, both of them feeling very silly.

They felt even sillier the next morning when they crept along to the guest room and found that he had gone. At first they thought he had vanished without a trace. The bed was stark, empty, and neatly covered. Its crisp valences looked as if they had never been disturbed. "And he did not look like the kind of man who could make a bed," Cecilia thought.

"We couldn't have dreamed it, could we?" Alex whispered, staring around the chilly room. Then he saw the kitchen candlestick sitting on one of the crocheted mats on the washstand. "One of us must have believed in him enough to bring this here at least," he said, and looked in the pitcher. The water had been iced over, but the ice was broken. "He must have washed, Cecil. Look."

Cecilia, feeling glum and flat, came over and agreed. She picked up the candlestick with the guttered candle, thinking that Miss Gatly ought not to find it there, and they saw that there was a slip of paper underneath.

Alex pounced on it. It had been torn from the front of the book of sermons on the bedside table. There was no writing on it—there had been no writing-things in the room—but there was an orange-wax seal, stamped with something which must by the size have been a seal ring. Alex held it to the light. The device might have been a bee or a wasp—some kind of insect, they were sure—and if they tilted it this way and that, they could just make out the letters around the edge: GAIRNE

"He told us," Alex said, "that he had been Count of Gairne. Do you remember?"

"Yes," said Cecilia. "He was real, then."

Chapter 2

WILD RIDER

The next strange occurrence was the day before Christmas Eve. Alex came home for the holidays that morning and he and Cecilia went skating in the afternoon at the edge of the bay. In those days the shores of the great river estuary were not so well raised and drained as they later were. Below the Hornbys' house, almost beside the long rocky causeway to the island, was a large meadow which was flooded every winter as the river swelled with rain and tides. The railway ran along one side, next to the road, and the other side was open to the sea. The fresh water froze in the meadow, and then was covered with seawater during the spring tides. Out in the bay the river channels which wound on either side of the dark island had partly frozen over too, and drifts of snow on their banks had hardened into shining gray cliffs of ice. The mud sand of the estuary was all black and gray and dangerous with frost, until the sea swept in and covered it up.

The tide was out that afternoon. The sun was red and the sea wind cut like a saw. The ice in the flooded pasture was deeper and harder than it had been within living memory, and people came for miles to skate. Among them came the Courcys. Alex's heart sank when he saw the handsome carriages come dashing up and stop at the bottom of the hill. He and Cecilia had been enjoying themselves with Miss Gatly's nephews and nieces from the next farm, but at the sight of the carriages, the Gatlys all moved off to practice figure skating on their own. Alex drearily watched the whole Courcy family get out. There was Martin, the eldest, who always had his gentlemanly hands in his noble pockets; Harry, who was the same age as Alex and whom Alex liked even less than Martin; the in-between brother Egbert, who was a nondescript; and then all the girls, who were so much more elegant than Cecilia, but nothing like so pretty— Letitia, Lavinia, Charlotte (who was grown-up and engaged to be married), Emily, and little Susannah, whom Alex disliked more heartily than any of them. And there they all were holding out their feet for the coachman to screw their skates on as if none of them had hands of their own.

"Oh, Cecil!" Alex wailed.

"We have not seen them," Cecilia answered. "And maybe they have not seen us." She began on a complicated figure.

The Courcys, with their skates screwed on, came slithering down onto the ice. The other skaters made way for them. The two carriages went on up to the Hornbys' house. Alex had seen that Lady Courcy herself was in one of them. He knew that in the house there would be much rushing about with sweet wine, petits fours, preserves, footstools, shawls, and fire-screens. He felt sorry for Miss Gatly. Cecilia did not look. She continued to skate, and she skated very well, better than Charlotte and the rest, who were tottering, giggling, and hanging onto their brothers.

After a while, the Courcys had skated over near to Cecilia. "My dear Cecilia," cried Lavinia, "do demonstrate that figure again. This is quite an exhibition."

Cecilia, very flushed, decided to stop, then thought better of it and did something different so as not to seem to do what they wanted. The Courcys all stood around, slithering a little, Alex among them, a bevy of beautiful muffs and elegant hogskin gloves. Alex, in his worn school cape and gloves knitted by Miss Gatly, felt shabby and out of place. The Courcys genuinely admired Cecilia's skating.

"You get a great deal of practice—what?" said Egbert.

"Think where she lives. Glorious, beautiful place!" Letitia exclaimed, waving her muff at the bay. She was the poetic one. People thought her pale and interesting.

Alex thought sadly: "They are not nasty. They simply despise us for our pretentions. How I wish we did not have to have pretentions."

"I say, Alex." Martin slid gently up with his hands in his pockets. "I say, be a dear fellow, will you, and fix Susannah's skate. Clamp's coming loose or something."

Alex slid himself over to where Susannah's neat little cone-shape was waiting for him. Much as he disliked Susannah, he had no objection to mending her skate. He would have done it for anyone, and, anyway, he had a vague feeling that it was his station. What he objected to were the pert, hurtful remarks Susannah always made at him.

She said now, as Alex came up: "The cloaked figure of a highwayman! Do you really have to wear that cut-throat cape for school?"

"Yes," Alex said curtly. "It's an old foundation. The uniform goes back to Queen Elizabeth." And he thought that it was just like Susannah to hit on the shabbiest and most peculiar thing about him. It would have astonished him to know that Susannah admired him more than anyone she knew; and it would have staggered him if he had discovered she had broken her skate on purpose and sent Martin to fetch him specially. It never entered his head that she was rude to him in a desperate hope that he would think she was clever.

She put out her tiny foot to him as haughtily as she knew how. "The latchet of whose skate you are not worthy to unloose," she said.

Alex, before he had half knelt down, stood up and glided away backwards. "Then let someone do it who *is* worthy," he said. "Besides, that's blasphemy, quoting the Bible like that."

He was too hurt himself to see that Susannah was nearly in tears, but her brothers and sisters saw and were around him in a second. Susannah was everyone's pet.

"Poor little Susannah! Never mind the oaf," came from at least three sisters.

Martin said: "I say, better mind your language, Alex."

Egbert echoed him. "What?"

Alex, surrounded and angry, had to stick to his point. And as so often happened to him, both at school and among the Courcys, the more distressed he became, the more he spoke like the country boy he was. "I don't care. That were blasphemy she spoke."

Harry Courcy was onto it at once. "Ah doan't cear. Thaat were blaasphemee," he droned.

Maybe he had gone too far. Martin put out a skate and jabbed his brother hard in the leg. Nobody else said anything except Cecilia. She swung around in the middle of a figure — and around again before she could stop herself.

"Harry Courcy! Wait till I get my hands on you!"

This was too much for Alex. He wanted to black Harry's eye and could not, for fear of a thrashing from Josiah, and now here was Cecilia in one of her embarrassing rages. He plunged forward, away toward the bay, scattering Courcys right and left, for he took them by surprise and he was a more practiced skater. There he dug his toes down and came to a sharp stop, while the others looked after him, crying out indignantly. So it was that they were all among the first to see the Wild Rider.

Alex saw him come from the island. One moment there was nothing but that huddle of dark trees, and, the next moment, there was a great blue-gray horse in the middle of its leap. The rider on its back was black against the low red sun, except for his flying orange cloak. Then the horse landed and was galloping in one movement, pounding through the bay among the treacherous sands and frozen snows as if there were nothing but soft turf beneath its feet.

Charlotte Courcy had scarcely time to totter on the tips of her skates, beginning to faint, before there were two more horsemen in the sky by the island. One after another they soared and landed, and then they were galloping after the first. Everyone in the field could hear the splash and bang of hooves as they galloped, off into the distance, through the river channel, and over the very quicksands themselves.

Then there was panic. One Wild Rider had been enough for the Gatlys and for most of the country people there, but three were too much even for the Courcys. People began skating, tumbling, running to get off the field and into the safety of a house. Some took their skates off and ran, some ran skates and all. Charlotte was lugged between Martin and Egbert. Susannah hobbled, helped by Harry. In no time at all everyone was on the road hurrying for home, help, and fireside and for someone to tell what they had seen.

Only Alex and Cecilia were left, watching side by side, as the riders grew smaller and smaller until they vanished at the dark edge of the bay.

"Alex," said Cecilia, "that was Robert. I know it was."

"Yes," said Alex. "It was. And the others were chasing him."

They looked for a long, long minute over at the edge of the bay, but there was not a sign of a rider. Alex said anxiously: "He had a good horse—I wish I had one half as good—and a small start."

"I could not *bear* him to be caught!" Cecilia said frantically. "Alex, can't we do something?"

At any other time Alex would have realized there was nothing they could do and begged Cecilia to come home. They would have quarrelled, but Alex would have won. Now, though, Alex had been hurt by the Courcys. He felt almost as if they had pinched him all over black and blue, it was such a real kind of hurt. And the Courcys were all in the farmhouse at the moment, no doubt telling their mother and Miss Gatly all about the three Wild Riders.

"We could go to the island," he said. "We might discover what happened."

"Oh, yes!" Cecilia was down on the ice unscrewing her skates before he had finished speaking. "Hurry, do, Alex!"

A minute later, they were stepping onto the shingle and rock of the long causeway to the island. It was not railed off in those days. The causeway was little more than a rough natural ridge of granite, strengthened long ago by the ancestor of the Courcys who had built the Castle. Nor was the island railed off. There was no need. No one went there if they could help it. Neither Alex nor Cecilia had ever been there alone before. Josiah, who had had a miserable rough childhood himself, made his children lead more sheltered lives. He would never allow them to wander by themselves in wild places. Alex, for one, had never even wanted to visit the island alone before.

Halfway along the causeway, Cecilia took Alex's hand. The sun was low, now, and red and purple mist was creeping in all around them from the sea and the marshes. They were alone in the middle of the wide grim estuary and the island ahead was all gloomy bare trees, with a few black birds wheeling around the castle tower. The air was raw and freezing and there was not a sound either from land or from sea.

Alex, attempting to sound brave, said: "How did they go across the quicksands? Would there be a secret causeway, do you think? A horse and rider is too heavy for—" Then he stopped, because they had both remembered the way those riders had seemed to come out of thin air. Anything supernatural seemed possible after that.

"Run," said Cecilia firmly. "We can talk later."

They ran until they came beneath the trees of the island.

Then they stopped, hand in hand still, and stared up at it. It bulked huge and black now they were so near—much bigger, Alex thought, than one could have guessed from the shore. Its blackness and silence were appalling, and mist wreathed between the tree trunks.

Somehow, they made themselves go on. First Alex would pull, and Cecilia come reluctantly after. Then Alex would hang back, and Cecilia pull him. In this way they climbed the long steep hill among the stark winter trees and came gradually into more open land among spiny bushes and twisted small trees. Cecilia clenched one hand inside her muff to stop herself trembling. Alex slowly pulled to a halt.

"It—it seems bigger, Cecil."

Cecilia agreed. It was the opposite of what she expected. She had last been here in summer as quite a little girl. She had thought it would seem small, as things did when one saw them later when one was nearly grown-up. Bravely, she pulled Alex on.

Something black moved away from a twisted tree. For a moment they thought the tree was walking. Neither of them could move. Then the thing moved again, three or four slow steps, until it was right in front of them.

He was another island person, a great deal younger than Robert, probably much the same age as Alex. He was taller, though—about Cecilia's height—and dressed in dense black velvet, with one or two small gold ornaments. The black plume of his hat curled almost around his white face and nearly disguised his pale fair hair. He looked at them angrily, narrowing his great blue eyes.

"Who are you? What are you doing here?"

Cecilia, from what she could see in the dying light, suspected

328 · UNEXPECTED MAGIC

that his anger had to do with the fact that he had been crying. The tears shone on his cheeks, and had made a dark smudge where he must have leaned against the tree.

Politely and apologetically, she answered: "We saw someone we knew—Robert, his name is—riding across the bay, and we—"

That made him very angry. Cecilia saw she had been foolish to mention the outlaw. He put his hand on the gilded hilt of his sword. "So that is why you were sneaking so furtively through the woods! You have no right to be here if you are friends of his."

Cecilia stepped back behind Alex, very nervous of that sword and of the commanding set of the boy's head. Alex, however, stepped forward, angry too. It was that same set of the head that annoyed him. There was something Courcy-like about it. Harry had the same manner.

"What do you mean, no right?" he demanded. "I have every right in the world. My father owns this island. One day I shall own it."

"You!" exclaimed the boy. "Then you are an usurping hound. Draw your sword, or I shall run you through where you stand." And he drew his own sword with a clang and a flash of red reflected sun.

"Don't be a coward," said Alex. "Can't you see I haven't got a sword? Drop that and put your fists up like a man."

"Call me coward again—" threatened the boy.

Cecilia hung onto Alex by his shoulders. She had realized what had happened. In the dim light, Alex in his school cape must have seemed another island person, particularly if one was not expecting to see anyone different.

"Stop it, both of you!" she said. "My brother and I do not belong here. We—we live at the farm along the causeway."

This alarmed the boy. He stood back a little with his sword trailing. "You are Outsiders? Then God forbid I should kill you! How is it you know that Howeforce? Did he run away Outside? I might have guessed he would."

"He did not have much choice, did he?" Alex answered. "The way he seems to be hounded here."

"So should vermin be hounded," the boy retorted. "And pray God he is dead by now."

"Oh, no!" said Cecilia. "Pray *not!*"

The boy was furious with her, with them both. "Go away! Leave this island! Who are you, mere peasant's children from Outside, to come here and judge us? How dare you support such a man as Howeforce! How dare you call me coward! Go away, I tell you!"

Cecilia was only too ready to go. The island was a terrible place. She was cold, frightened, and miserable at the outlaw's probable death. She hated this boy and she wanted never to see him again.

Alex hated him too. He was even ruder than Harry Courcy and more hurtful than Susannah. He was bigger, too, which was very satisfactory. "I shall not go," he said, "until you take that back. Take it back, or I shall black one of your big blue eyes, sword or no sword." His accent had thickened again, but he did not care.

The boy sheathed his sword, put his hands on his hips, stuck his chin in the air, and laughed sneeringly. "Go away, little peasant."

Alex hit him, beautifully, and as hard as he could. The other boy took it well, staggered, blinked, and hit him back. Alex dodged and closed in. He was the best fighter for his size in his school. He had fought many times in defense of Josiah's pretentions, and it pleased him to do it again now, in such strange circumstances. The island boy was not using his height and reach to advantage. Perhaps he was more used to fighting with that sword of his. Alex kept an eye on his sword-hand, in case he should suddenly use it. He was rather surprised that he never tried to.

Cecilia hovered, anxiously watching, biting her muff so as not to cry out. She had learned not to interrupt Alex when he took to his fists. She winced each time Alex was hit as she always did. Then after a while, she began to wince for the other boy. He was getting much the worst of it. Alex beat him to a tree and went on beating him. The boy was reduced to keeping one arm over his head and trying to push Alex away with the other. He had long ago lost his hat and his hair was all over his face. Even so, Cecilia could see that his nose was bleeding.

"I think you should stop," she said. But she forgot that she was biting her muff, and Alex did not hear her.

Soon, even Alex began to feel some shame at hitting an opponent who was so obviously beaten, but he was irritated that the boy would not admit it. He held the boy against the tree with one hand and tried to see his face. "What's the matter with you? Don't you know when you're beaten?"

The boy did not answer. Alex shook him. "Come on, say you're sorry."

The boy raised his head. "Why should I? I am not sorry. What I said was true. You *are* the son of a peasant—I can tell from the way you speak."

Alex was so angry and exasperated at this that he shook him again, harder. He was afraid that if he hit the boy any more he might do him some serious injury. "Do you need to be broken into little pieces before you give in?" he said. "You can apologize at least. You can admit you believe my father owns this island."

"But he does not," the boy answered, sounding really surprised.

Alex could have screamed. He could have picked the boy up and thrown him into a spiny bush. "All right, then. You can take back what you said about Robert. He is not vermin. And he swore to us that he did not kill this man he is supposed to have killed."

"Of course he would say that," the boy replied disdainfully. "I have no doubt he would swear to anything. But I should know the truth, since 'this man he is supposed to have killed' was my father."

"Oh!" Alex let him go and stood back, truly ashamed of himself. That would explain the black clothes, of course, and why the boy had been all by himself, crying. Alex had done much the same soon after his mother died, and he had nearly been lost in the fog, too miserable to notice where he went. He was about to apologize, when the boy said:

"Now, take back what *you* said. You should apologize to me."

"I'll be hanged if I shall!" said Alex. "You'll apologize to me before I say a word of apology to you."

"Then you can wait till your dying day," answered the boy. "You may leave us now."

"Oh, may I?" said Alex. "And you may leave *us*. Go to blazes if you like. Come, Cecilia." And he swung around and stalked off the way he had come, with Cecilia hurrying behind, sober and sorry and very, very chilly.

Alex marched along the causeway in a fine glow of anger, sucking the bruised lip which was all he had to show for the fight. "I wish," he thought, "that I *had* thrown him in a bus now."

"Alex," said Cecilia, "I think you should have said you were sorry. After all, *somebody* must have killed his father."

"Well, how was I to know? And he brought it in so meanly too, right at the end, and seemed to think it gave him no end of an advantage. Cecil, I promise you that, if I ever say I'm sorry to that big—big *caterpillar*, you can kick me from here to Arnforth. So there!"

Chapter 3

TRUANTS

It was December 27, the day of the Courcy party, that Alex and Cecilia took the adventure into their own hands. To a great extent, it was their father's fault that they did so. Josiah was outraged when they arrived back from the island, after dark, when all the Courcys had long ago gone home.

"Where did you run away to?" he demanded. "Gatly's?"

"No!" said Cecilia. "We did not run away at all."

Possibly, Josiah was secretly pleased that his children had stood their ground when even the Courcys had fled, but he never dreamed of showing it. He raged and lectured and told them they should have come home to entertain the Courcys.

"Hang the Courcys," said Alex, smarting now both from the Courcys and from the boy in black who reminded him of them.

In those days it was simply not done to answer back. For that, Alex got the beating that the island boy had failed to give him. He and Cecilia were both sent to bed and not allowed out of their rooms until the afternoon of Christmas Eve. Cecilia passed the time in an agony of worry about their outlaw. She saw him killed in several dozen grisly ways, and she saw him as many times miraculously saved. Part of the time, she spent on her knees, praying for his safety. Alex brooded the while. He brooded on the boy in black and he brooded on the Courcys, until they were all involved in his mind in one great stony hatred.

Not surprisingly, they had a wretched Christmas. Josiah was surly with them, the weather was raw and sleety, and the Courcy party loomed over them. Both of them dreaded it. The Courcys were so superior. Alex knew they had only been invited so that the Courcys could smile at one another and say: "Look how kind we are to those inferior little Hornbys." Cecilia knew how Charlotte and Lavinia would raise their eyebrows at her poor homemade dress. Alex's feelings were not helped by discovering that Josiah was actually going to London on the 27th to see to the Courcys' business affairs. "Why should he do that?" he thought angrily. "He is not their servant."

On the evening of Boxing Day, Alex found Cecilia alone, mournfully sewing away at her new dress in the kitchen. "Cecil," he said, "I don't care if I never see another Courcy again, do you?"

Cecilia looked up eagerly. "Nor I. Alex—" And their plans were made almost in so many words.

Josiah Hornby left early that morning on the London train. His children left a bare two hours later. Things were made a great deal simpler for them than they might have been, because the Courcys always expected them to come early on the day of a party and help with the preparations. All they had to do was to decide to go on horseback instead of in the pony-trap. Miss Gatly made no objection. Old John Britby, the outdoor man, had little to do on the farm that day. He took the trap to Arnforth with Cecilia's dress in it and Alex's best suit. They were delighted that it was Old John. He was not exactly stupid, but he was a man who said so little that no Courcy would ever hear from him what Alex and Cecilia had done.

"Not that they will ask him," Alex said, trotting beside Cecilia on the Arnforth road. "I would bet you five shillings none of them notice we are not there. Is he out of sight yet?"

They looked behind. The bay was still in sight behind them, brown and barren sands under a heavy gray sky. It was threatening to snow. Old John and the trap were out of sight behind the Hornbys' hill.

"Now, quick!" said Cecilia. "Thank goodness there is no snow."

They left the road and cantered down a pasture to the woods beside the river. There they waited until Old John and the trap had gone jingling by above them on the road. Then they turned back toward the bay.

There was a risk that someone in the farmhouse might see them, but it was a risk they meant to take. It was possible that there would be no one in the front rooms. Miss Gatly's work was done mainly at the back. Cecilia felt she would not turn back even if Miss Gatly herself ran after them across the frozen sands. Alex was not so sure. For him, it was mainly a voyage of exploration and a gesture against Josiah.

"We must hurry," he said, "or the tide will come in as we go."

They picked their way around the edge of the sands, bending their heads in the icy wind, until they could see a way clear toward the island. It was safer on horseback to go to it across the sands, than among the broken rocks of the causeway. At last they were beside the bare swaying trees of the island again, but this time they went around the edge of it.

Alex looked nervously back at the farmhouse. No one seemed to have seen them. "There must be a way across this bay," he said, "and it must be easy to see. Think of the way those riders went over." He had given up his notions of it being super-natural. That boy he had fought had been hard and real and heavy. He was a solid person who needed a solid road to ride on.

They rode slowly around the island, searching the sands anxiously in the direction those three riders had taken. There seemed nothing but broken sandy banks, icy puddles, rifts, and drifts of sea-washed old snow. They became more and more anxious that the tide would come in before they found what they hoped to find.

Then, suddenly, they both reined in and laughed incredu-lously. There, stretching from their horses' hoofs, was a road, a wide, raised ridge of sand, running straight across the bay.

"There!" said Cecilia triumphantly.

"How odd!" Alex said. "Why has no one else found it?"

"One has to see it from straight on," said Cecilia. "See what happens if you move away."

They moved their horses a few steps back. Cecilia was right. There seemed to be no road. It was lost in a confusion of ridges and sandbanks. They went forward again, and the road was there. Alex laughed again, it was so easy and so extraordinary.

"Hurry," Cecilia said. "The tide."

They set off along the ridge, trotting first, then cantering. By the time they reached the river channel, the tide was coming in. They could see the white line of sea hurrying in from the open mouth of the estuary.

"It is a long way yet," Cecilia called out. "We must gallop."

Indeed, the opposite shore of the bay looked as distant as it had from the island. They galloped. Behind them, the river channel swelled and foamed, and they could hear the sea roaring. Alex caught a glimpse of shining sands on either side, covered here and there with treacherous brittle feathers of ice. He knew it was the quicksands, but their way went straight between them. He and Cecilia galloped on, and neither of them gave a thought to how they would get back, once the tide was in.

They came to the other side just as the sea swirled up to them. There was a steep muddy bank, full of other people's hoofprints. Their horses heaved up it, as glad as their riders to escape the sea, and stood steaming among bushes. Alex stood in his stirrups and saw a wood nearby, and beside it a strange turretted house which he had certainly never seen before.

"Well," he said, rather hushed with amazement, "we are plainly not in our country here. This is all quite different. There ought by rights to be moorland, but there is—almost a castle. It looks empty, though."

"Good!" said Cecilia, and her cheeks were bright red with excitement. "We'll ride inland then. Let us follow this path."

The path led them through the bushes, until it was joined by other paths to become a road, a grassy, moorland road, winding between hills. They judged it must be a main road, because of the number of hoofprints on it. Cecilia determined to keep to it until she found some way of reaching Gairne—for of course it was Gairne she meant to get to. Alex did not mind where they went. All of it was to him the greatest adventure of his life.

Before long, it began to snow. Cecilia, who was looking all the time for someone to ask the way of, was disappointed. Whether because of the snow, or for other reasons, there was no one about. The road was empty. The hills were deserted. Several times they passed turnings into valleys, one leading to a fair-sized stone village, but they decided to go straight on. There was no one about in the village and they were shy of knocking at doors. These strange people might all be as unfriendly as the boy in black.

At last, in a long upland, where the snow caught them hard and filled their hair and reddened their faces, they met a shepherd. He looked, to Alex's disappointment, very like the shepherds they knew. He had a crook and a dog and a small herd of sheep. He was bearded, and he had that withdrawn, solitary look which men have who spend much time alone in the hills. He wore a smock and gaiters and an old blanket on his shoulders against the snow, just as the Hornbys' own shepherd did. The look he gave them could have been astonished, or it could have been just vacant.

"Excuse me," said Cecilia. "Could you tell us the way to Gairne, please?"

The man stared a while. Then he pointed slowly to where the road turned right beside some craggy hills. "There be Gairne road," he said.

"And what lies that way?" Alex asked, pointing to where another road branched beside the hills and led down into a gap or a pass of some kind.

"Falleyfell," said the shepherd.

Both of them gasped. It seemed that they were in Miss Gatly's kingdom of the dead and that it was really true. Alex looked quickly for the shepherd's shadow, but if he had one, the snow obscured it.

"Thank you," Cecilia said quaveringly. "Come, Alex." She set off quickly on the way to Gairne. Alex kicked his horse so hard that the poor beast stumbled in trying to obey him. He felt it was the worst possible omen.

Just as he caught Cecilia up, there were sounds from the road which led to Falleyfell. The snow drowned the horses' hoofs, but they heard talking from a number of people. They kept on their road, looking back rather nervously, and saw a large band of men ride out into the upland. These were not in the least like people they knew. Most of them seemed to be soldiers with wicked spears and dull sheeny helmets and breastplates. Beneath the armor they all wore the same uniform tunic, banded with brown and dim blue. At their head were two men, not in armor, wearing black and muffled in great hooded capes. The whole party turned and stared at Alex and Cecilia riding self-consciously to Gairne.

"Let us keep on our way," said Cecilia, "as if it were quite natural." She rode staring straight ahead into the snow.

Alex, however, could not help turning to look back every few seconds. The other riders had stopped, which alarmed him a little. He saw the two men in black leaning toward one another, talking, glancing at him. Next time he looked, one, the taller and stouter of them, was beckoning the shepherd. During the next look, he saw the shepherd talking too, looking up at the stouter rider, and making gestures down the Gairne road. At the next look, he saw the whole party riding after them.

"Cecil! I think they're chasing us."

"Maybe they have business this way," Cecilia answered. "Keep on." She was nervous enough, though, to trot her horse. Alex saw the other riders coming faster still.

"Cecil!"

"You there! Stop!"

"Gallop, Alex!" gasped Cecilia.

They galloped, both thoroughly frightened. It was rather like being caught trespassing on someone's land, Alex thought, only worse because this land seemed endless and there was nowhere safe to escape to. Worse still, the riders were catching up rapidly. They all had splendid horses, obviously fresh. Their own were only moderate—Josiah would not trust them with better—and had already come a long way. Cecilia's little mare was dropping behind. Alex could hear her calling it names.

"You lazy beast! You pit-pony, you!"

Then the soft thump of other hoofs was all round them. Snow flew, blurred riders came up and came past. Two soldiers pulled their horses right across the road ahead, crossing their sharp spears to make a further barrier. Alex's horse turned aside and reared. A soldier with a hard brown face caught the bridle and pulled. Alex nearly fell.

"Stop that, will you! I can manage him!"

He saw Cecilia behind him lashing out indignantly at hands trying to take her bridle. He lashed out at the soldier with his crop, but it rang harmlessly on a steel shoulder-piece. His horse plunged and kicked backwards.

"Leave us alone, can't you? What do you want?" he shouted.

"Stand back," someone said. "Let him quiet that vicious

jade before you take him." He saw it was the stout man in black. One look was enough to plant that man's face in his mind for the rest of his life. He hated that face absolutely and unconditionally, right from that first look—a fat, evil face with large mauve lips, a nose that was both fat and hooked at once, and dark, unfeeling, unscrupulous eyes. Beside Alex's hatred of that face, his hatred of the Courcys and the boy in black was like nothing or less than nothing.

"My goodness!" he thought. "If this is what people are like here, no wonder they made Robert an outlaw. He must be the only nice one there is."

His horse was easy to quiet. Trim Jim was not in the least a vicious or nervous horse—Josiah had seen to that—only alarmed by the sudden appearance of steel men waving sticks all round him. In a matter of seconds, he was standing calmly, blowing, shaking his ears because of the snow, ready to go where Alex wanted. The soldiers at once closed in around, and around Cecilia too.

The stout man looked haughtily down at them from his tall brown horse. The other man in black blinked at them nervously, full of curiosity.

"Who are you?" said the stout man. "What are you doing here?"

"Riding peacefully along," said Cecilia, "when suddenly people start galloping after us as if we were thieves. Will you kindly let me and my brother ride on at once, please." She felt very brave and very angry and very responsible for Alex.

"That answer is nothing to the purpose, my lady," the stout man said coldly. "I asked your name and your business and it were best for you if you answer me truly."

Cecilia flung back her head and glared at him. He simply waited, in the softly falling snow, looking at her face with those black, unfeeling eyes. And Cecilia was terrified of him. Inside her clothes, she shook with great shudders, and she knew she had gone pale. She was afraid she was going to break down, or faint or scream, and then this man would start looking at Alex and terrifying him. So she pulled herself together, because she was the elder one and she should be in charge.

"Our names are Alex and Cecilia Hornby," she said bravely.

The other man in black, who was thin and excitable, and older than the stout man, old enough to be losing hair at the front of his head—which gave him a high-headed, startled look—turned to the stout man with an unbelieving smile. "I think they are Outsiders, Towerwood."

The stout one went on looking at Cecilia. "I think they are, Darron. I think they are. Which makes it all the more curious that they should ask the way to Gairne." He said to Cecilia: "My lady, I insist that you tell us why you are bound for Gairne. What business have you there? I demand to know. I am the Count of Gairne."

That shook Cecilia badly, and Alex too. They should have known, from many stories, but they had forgotten, that if a man is outlawed, he loses his lands and someone else is given them. What upset them most was that it should be this hateful man, of all people.

"But he is exactly the kind of man who *would* grab land," Alex thought while Cecilia was still dumbfounded. He said to the Count, politely but defiantly: "We asked for Gairne out of interest. We wanted to see what it is like," and guessing completely, he added: "Is it not a famous place?"

The man who seemed to be called Darron nodded eagerly.
"Yes indeed. Famous throughout the Principality for the two
hills and the Hornets and for fine woollen cloth and—"

"*But*," said the Count loudly, so that Darron jumped, "but
you cannot ride there today. Nor can you till the New Year is a
week old, by a decree of the Prince in Council. No one rides
out until then, unless on the strictest business. Your business is
nothing, mere sightseeing, and so we stop you in the name of
the Prince."

Cecilia had recovered a little by then, enough at least to
be angry at the way the Count cut short the other man, who
had seemed so friendly and eager to please. "How could we
know that?" she said. "We do not belong here. And besides"—
looking at Darron—"I am fond of fine woollen cloth."

He bowed in his saddle and smiled at her. "I too, my lady.
Visit us later and I will be delighted to escort you to the ware-
houses of Gairne. But now, unfortunately"—he looked at the
Count nervously—"since you were found violating the
Prince's decree, it is our duty to escort you to Falleyfell, there
to learn the Prince's pleasure."

"But I don't think you can do that," Alex said, very
alarmed now that this polite man was turning out to have the
same intentions as the other one. "I'm sure you can't. We
have nothing to do with your Prince. We are subjects of
Queen Victoria."

"That may be," the Count told him, as if the Queen were
the smallest and most uninteresting monarch on the face of
the globe, "but you are aliens here, in the Prince's realm, and
must come before him to give account of yourself." Then, as
if the matter were quite settled, he called out orders to the

soldiers and rode away in front toward Falleyfell. Darron, bowing again to Cecilia, rode after him. The soldiers fell in all around the two Outsiders. One looked at Alex and jerked his head after the two men in black. There seemed to be nothing to do but ride where they were taken.

"My word!" said Cecilia, "if they do not let us go at once when we have seen this Prince, I shall give someone a piece of my mind."

Chapter 4

PRINCE

It is always depressing to have unexpectedly to go back the way one has just come. It is even more depressing to have to go surrounded by soldiers with hard, jeering faces and confront an unknown Prince given to ordering everyone to stay at home.

"He must be the most appalling tyrant," Cecilia thought. "Fancy every poor housewife having to give an account of herself every time she goes shopping, just because the Prince has said so! What a terrible country this is! I shall certainly never come here again."

She looked at Alex, quietly raging beside her. He was so annoyed and alarmed at being arrested—for that was what it must be—that the skin had tightened over the high bridge of his nose. Cecilia nearly smiled at him because he looked so exactly like Josiah. Alex, who thought she was trying to comfort him, stuck out his lower lip at her crossly.

The Gairne road wound back again into the upland. For a minute they rode where they could see hills dimly behind twirling dark snowflakes, and then the soldiers swung around to the right, into that gap in the hills, between crags looking dirtily dark under snow, and out at the top of a long shallow valley.

Cecilia and Alex stared between steel helmets at the great building standing halfway down the valley below them. It was a huge fortified mansion, with castellated walls and innumerable courts and gardens. It could have been a small city, mapped out in charcoal on white paper, with towers drawn jutting and leaping and graceful on every hand. From the highest tower flew the only touch of color, a green flag with some white device, and half the flagstaff stuck darkly up beyond the green.

The soldier who had jerked his head at Alex nodded down at the mansion. "Falleyfell," he said.

Alex's stomach went tight in a way that nearly made him sick. He could hear Miss Gatly's voice as clearly as if she were riding beside Cecilia: "And Falleyfell is a kingdom out in the bay. So dangerous is it that he who sees it is as good as dead." It helped him not at all to see that the soldiers all made faint blue shadows in the snow, or that they rode making real hoofprints. He could feel the warmth of them about him, horses and men, but that only made it the more sinister. As they went down and down into the valley and the walls of that mansion rose up vaster and vaster in front, Alex was more and more terrified.

They stopped in front of great double gates. People looked down from a gatehouse overhead and seemed surprised because the men in black and the soldiers had returned so quickly. Then the great gates opened. Everyone rode through by threes into one of the biggest courtyards Alex and Cecilia had ever seen. They rode straight across it, with odd muffled echoes, up to the main grand part of the mansion. The men in black dismounted onto a great flight of steps leading to a big door with a snow-crusted coat of arms above it. Both of them turned and waited for Alex and Cecilia to dismount too. Cecilia thought Darron would have helped her down, had not the Count of Gairne held him back. So she looked at them both very haughtily, before she dismounted by herself, and then she picked up the long side of her riding habit with her most queenly air.

"Up here, my lady," said the Count, not in the least impressed. He and Darron went one on either side of Alex and Cecilia, and two of the soldiers came clinking slowly after.

"Abominable man!" Cecilia thought. "It seems I am everyone's lady here—it must be the custom. How I wish I had not been so nasty to our outlaw about it."

Beyond the steps and the door was a hall, a great square light hall, chilly and gloomy and full of silent people in black. "The court, I suppose," thought Cecilia. Black cloth was hung over the walls, and it, together with the bleak snowy light from the high-up windows, made their eyes ache.

They walked slowly down the hall. At the other end was a raised dais where two women sat, wearing the deepest mourning. The older one was dark, with a white, white face and huge hollow dark eyes, with a strange, wild, and beautiful expression. The younger was one of the loveliest ladies Alex had ever set eyes upon. She was so fair her hair was almost white, and everything about her was delicate and small and adorable. She was the kind of lady who is petted and pampered by everyone and too sweet to be spoiled by it all. And yet she was miserable. She sat gazing at nothing, as if someone had put her in her chair like a doll, and she looked so lost and lonely that both Alex and Cecilia wanted to run and kneel beside her and pet and pamper and amuse her.

Neither lady seemed to notice them being brought down the hall, but most of the other sad, black-dressed people did. Ladies stared at Cecilia in an outraged way. Cecilia, flushed with embarrassment and with the cold air outside, tried to look loftily ahead. Alex noticed that most of the men seemed to be trying to catch her attention, to bow and to smile and to nod. They seemed delighted to see her and full of admiration. Alex wondered how they could admire Cecilia, when they had two such women on the dais. He looked irritably at Cecilia. Her riding habit was lavender blue, to match her eyes. Her ringlets were as brightly fair as the younger lady's and her face was not only rosy and young and happy, it was every bit as worth looking at as either lady's on the dais. For the first time in his life, Alex began to suspect that his sister was growing up into a raving beauty, and it alarmed him. It was one more frightening thing about this sinister black and white place. He glared at all the men who were bowing and smiling in that stupid, admiring way. He wished that he had a sword, as they all did, so that he could put a threatening hand on its hilt.

There was some whispering and quiet bustling. Alex gathered that the Prince was not there and that he was being respectfully fetched. They had to wait for him, just in front of the dais, with the two ladies at eye level. The younger one did not seem to notice them. The older one gave them several quick, wild glances as if she were afraid of staring too long. Alex became more and more frightened, embarrassed, and impatient. He took to looking at his feet, and poking one or two lumps of snow from his boots with his whip.

At last he heard mutters of "The Prince," "His Highness, the Prince," "Your Highness," and looked up at the dais. The boy he had fought on the island was standing there, with his hands on his hips, looking down at him in astonishment.

"You again," said the Prince.

He had the most beautiful black eye. Or rather, by this time it was not black any longer, but blue and purple and yellow, with red around the edges. "My goodness," Alex thought, "I did hit him perfectly." Most of his fear and embarrassment vanished. He was so pleased with that eye that he smiled, broadly, and put his hands on his hips too. "Yes," he said. "Me again."

"Good!" said the Prince. "*Good.*" To Cecilia he sounded quite murderous. He stared at Alex in a dreadful, satisfied way, which turned Cecilia cold and faint. Alex stared back, admiring that black eye, cocking his head sideways, almost as if he had painted it on the Prince's face with the finest of brushes.

The Count of Gairne stepped up onto the dais and interrupted their looking at one another. "Your Highness, these people were discovered riding about the countryside in direct contravention of your decree."

The Prince nodded and went back to gazing at Alex. "I am sure they were," he said. "They would be."

The Count leaned down to the Prince, softly, looking at Alex too. "Your Highness, am I right in supposing that this is the person who had the temerity to assault you on the island?" He was almost whispering in the Prince's ear, but not quite. Cecilia, looking up at them, suddenly saw an angry little boy standing on the platform, too angry to notice that a fat, cruel beast was about to seize him, bite him, and strangle him. She nearly cried out to the Prince.

Then the Count stood up again and he was simply a stout and unfriendly man, and the Prince was a venomous young person thinking over a dozen awful things he could do to Alex now he had him in his power.

"Remember," said Cecilia, very shrill and loud, because she was so much afraid for Alex, "remember that he did not assault you without provocation. You drew your sword on him—er— Your Highness." Behind her, she heard the courtiers muttering. She was certain they were saying "Dreadful, loud girl," or more stately words to that effect.

The Prince, instead of answering her, turned to the Count of Gairne, with that Courcy-like set of the head that Alex so much detested. "Yes," he said, "they are supporters of Howeforce, it seems, and the boy even imagines that he has a claim to our coronet."

Cecilia wrung her hands, despairing of ever being able to straighten this muddle out. The Count, she saw, was looking at them as if he were very interested, as if a whole crop of fresh, cold calculations had suddenly come into his head. "Honestly," she said, "you have it all completely wrong!"

"Have I?" the Prince asked her coldly. "Then what were you doing riding to Gairne?"

Cecilia, to her consternation, blushed. She did not know why she *should* blush, but blush she did, on and on, until even her neck was hot. She was so amazed and embarrassed at the way she blushed that she could not say another word.

"You would call them traitors, Your Highness?" suggested the Count of Gairne, still looking calculatingly at them.

The Prince folded his arms. "Indeed, yes." To Alex, he said: "You, I suppose, are by now aware that you have committed an act of lèse-majesté." To Cecilia, he said: "As for you, I am sure you know that your precious friend Howeforce is now terrorizing our whole Principality and defying us at every turn."

"No, indeed," Cecilia answered in a whisper.

"Yes, indeed," said the Prince. "It is a pity you are Outsiders. It makes the matter much more difficult. I shall have to keep you locked up while I consider what is to be done with you." Then he looked over their heads and beckoned to people to come and take them away.

People began to come for them. Alex could hear their footsteps slowly advancing from behind. "Look here!" he said, fresh from school history, "don't you have any Habeas Corpus here?"

The Prince frowned and the footsteps stopped. "What," he said, "is Habeas Corpus, in heaven's name?"

"It means," said Alex, "that no one can imprison anyone else without a fair trial."

The Prince was astonished, in the way that had so maddened Alex on the island. "How can it mean that? The Latin means 'You may have the body,' surely—which is a fair way of saying that you are our prisoner." He beckoned once more, and this time soldiers came, in green liveries heavily banded with black, and surrounded Alex and Cecilia. The Prince smiled. Then he bowed, and, thoroughly enjoying each word, he said, just as he had done on the island: "You may leave us now."

Alex shook with rage. "You—you low-down, mean whelp!" he said. "You give me any more of that and I'll come up there and black your other eye. I'll lèse your majesty until your whole face is black and blue. I'll—" Soldiers took hold of his arms. Courtiers came up with drawn swords. Even the younger lady moved and looked at him in astonishment. "I'll do it to the lot of you!" Alex shouted.

The Prince laughed, absolutely delighted with how angry Alex was. "Take him away," he said. "This is wonderful! Lock him up, and his sister too. Oh, Towerwood, I thank you with all my heart for finding these two Outsiders." He turned to the Count of Gairne and shook his hand. The Count smiled, and Alex, in spite of his rage, was frightened, scared so that his spine seemed to ripple, by the way that the Count smiled.

Then they were marched off. To Cecilia's consternation, Alex was taken one way and she was courteously conducted in the opposite direction. She hung back and tried to protest. The young man in charge of the soldiers bowed.

"This way, my lady. The Prince's orders. Pray take my arm." He held out one elbow elegantly to her. Cecilia, looking hopelessly around the soldiers, felt she would have to obey. Reluctantly, she put her fingers on his slender, black silk arm, and, with a last look back at Alex, came the way he took her.

All the way to the room where she was to be locked up, the courtier maddened her and embarrassed her with his politeness. He was young and pink and white and full of irritating elegances.

"Allow me to introduce myself, my lady. I am Hugo Lord Arbard at your service—at your service entirely."

"Thank you," said Cecilia wearily.

"You come at a sad time, my lady—a sad time. We are all in mourning, you understand, in mourning for our Prince who died just before Christmas. Such a man—such a man."

"You must be very sad," Cecilia said.

"Sad!" he exclaimed. "Why, words are too small to express—words fail!"

Cecilia thought: "I wish they would fail."

Lord Arbard showed no signs of words failing him. If he was at a loss, he simply went on saying the same thing until he thought of a new phrase. Then he used the new phrase until he had worn that out. Most of what he said was about the dead Prince. Cecilia would have been interested if he had told her what the Prince had really been like, but all he said was that he had been wonderful, superlative, excellent, good, splendid—and not a word of real description.

Then they came to a small room. Lord Arbard bowed and handed Cecilia inside. "With the greatest regret, my lady—enormous sorrow, great regret, I fear I must leave you now. Adieu, au revoir, until we meet again—as I trust we shall."

"Lord Arbard," Cecilia said, thoroughly irritated, "you are really much too polite."

He took it as a compliment. He bowed lower than ever and kissed his fingers to her. "Sweet lady, adieu." Then he shut the door behind him—nor did he forget to bolt it as he went, for all his politeness—and Cecilia was alone in a small bare room. There was one chair, very hard and upright. Cecilia sat down on it and worried for a long time about Alex. She knew how Alex detested the boy in black, and now it was only too apparent that the Prince detested Alex quite as much. Now he had Alex completely in his power, and it looked—since he did not know about Habeas Corpus—that the Prince had absolute power in this strange country. Worse still, she thought, it looked as if he enjoyed his power. She tried to make allowances: he was only about Alex's age—though she felt Alex would have been nicer in the same position—and, of course, he could only have had this power for a fortnight at the most. The Prince, his father, must have been killed the day the outlaw came to the farmhouse.

This took her onto Robert Lord Howeforce. He was supposed to have killed the Prince, of course. His situation was much worse than she had realized. And now he was said to be terrorizing the countryside. Cecilia hoped and tried to believe that he was not. But then, she thought, how did she know? She had seen him for an hour or so and she had decided to believe in him. He had looked as if he was telling the truth when he said he had not killed the Prince. But all these people seemed to think he had.

"Oh," said Cecilia. "Have I been very silly?" Then she clapped her hand over her mouth because someone was unbolting the door.

To her utter amazement, it was the elder of the two beautiful ladies. She came hurriedly into the room, wild and wide-eyed, and looked at Cecilia as if Cecilia were a huntress and she some kind of hunted beast. Cecilia, for all her amazement, remembered that this was probably a great lady. She stood up and made her best curtsey.

The lady did not seem to notice. "Madam," she said, in a deep breathless voice, "madam, what brings you and your brother to this land? Is it true you were seeking for Howeforce?"

Cecilia thought: "I might as well admit it. Everyone is probably quite sure we were, anyway." So she said bravely: "Yes, your ladyship. We—we had met him before, you see."

The lady pounced on this. "Met him? How?" Then as

Cecilia hesitated, remembering how scornful the Prince had been of the way the outlaw had gone Outside, the lady said impatiently: "You need have no secrets from me. I am Robert's mother. Now tell me quickly, for my time is short."

"His mother!" Cecilia thought. "Then what *is* she doing in the Court?" She curtsied again, and told the lady about the way the outlaw had spent the night at the farm.

"Have you proof?" the lady demanded. "I must have proof, for there is treachery everywhere. This realm is a most perilous place just now and, I fear, will be more so before long."

Then Cecilia, rather shyly, because she felt a fool to have kept it, brought out the paper torn from the book of sermons with the little orange seal on it. The lady took it and looked at it eagerly.

"Yes," she said. "This is Robert's seal. He—Conrad of Towerwood, who calls himself Count of Gairne—he uses the device of the tower. I think I will believe you, girl."

"I am telling the truth," Cecilia said, a little stiffly. "You can see from the printing on the paper. And there is a picture of Queen Victoria underneath."

"Yes, yes," said the lady. "I will take this, so that my son can see it. We must see to your safety and your brother's, girl, for the realm is in deadly danger while Conrad of Towerwood can lay his hands on either of you. Will you trust me with this token?"

"Yes," Cecilia answered reluctantly, "of course." She was not sure that she liked this lady's distracted, high-handed manner; and the way she called her "girl" was uncomfortably like the way Lady Courcy spoke. "Might I have it back, your ladyship, when you have finished with it?"

The lady smiled. It was a comforting, sweet smile, which made her look a great deal less sad and wild. "Of course you may, my dear. I see you value it. You can trust me. I am the daughter of a Prince, the sister of a Prince, and, indeed, the aunt of a Prince. You may trust my word."

"Thank you," said Cecilia humbly. She curtsied again as the lady hurried away and, when she was alone again, she sat down with tears in her eyes. Before long, there were tears all over her face and her handkerchief was soaked. "I see," she thought. "The Prince who was killed was our outlaw's uncle. And he had killed one uncle before. He should have said—he might have told us!"

A little later, a maid brought Cecilia some food on a tray. It looked delicious, but Cecilia did not want it. After a while, another maid took it away, and Cecilia still sat in her chair. Then the short winter day began to be over. There was no light, and the room grew completely dark. Cecilia did not care.

"I wish we had gone to the Courcy party," she said. "This is a judgment on us for being so wicked. Now no one will ever know what became of us."

Then someone softly unbolted the door. Cecilia bravely stood up. "I am to be led out by night and put to death," she thought. A man came quickly in with a small flickering lantern. He held the light up and looked at her.

It was Robert Lord Howeforce again, changed and stern and commanding-looking in a gray coat of mail. Cecilia put her hands over her mouth and backed away from him. "What do you want?"

Lord Howeforce smiled. "I seem to terrify you every time

you see me," he said. "You must come quickly with me—er—
Cecilia. You are not safe here. I have searched for your brother
too, but he is not to be found. It seems that the Prince has taken
him away somewhere. Pray God both of them are safe."

PART II

※

RIDERS

BY

NIGHT

※

Chapter 1

MURDER

The soldiers marching Alex away out of the hall stopped in a large arched passage just outside. Alex gathered that someone had run after them with a message. The soldier in charge was incredulous at whatever it was the servant had said, and sent him back again to make sure. Alex kicked his heels in the passage for quite five minutes while they were running backward and forward, whispering and shrugging their shoulders. It did nothing to cool his temper, but it made him a great deal more frightened.

"I suppose they cannot decide which dungeon is deepest and darkest," he thought. "Or perhaps they are fixing the weight of the fetters."

He was very surprised, when he was at length marched off, to be taken up a broad and gracious flight of stairs.

"But this is only crossing to a different wing of the house," he thought, stepping out down a long bridge-like room with windows on either side looking out on courtyards. "Like the Bridge of Sighs in Venice. Prisoners go over that never to return, and they say it is very beautiful." But the soldiers went up more stairs, to heavy carved doors with a leopard ramping in stone above. One took a large key and opened the doors. Another pushed Alex inside. He heard them shut and lock the door behind him, but he was too busy staring to mind.

He was in a chain of rooms. He could see right down room after room for what seemed to him hundreds of yards, and each room was filled to the ceiling with books. It was one of the biggest libraries he had ever seen. Quite bewildered and completely awestruck, he started on the long walk down to the other end. "Millions of books," he thought, as he went, "and they must all belong to that caterpillar." The smell of ancient books was suffocatingly strong, the echo of his steps was muffled in books, and books breathed out a dampness which, before he had half reached the other end, was making him shiver in his shoes.

"There is a door at the other end," he said. "Maybe they have forgotten to lock it. Perhaps there are doors hidden behind the shelves in the walls. Perhaps he had me put here to drive me mad with looking for a way out. Because I can see no reason else why he should put me here."

The door at the other end was locked. Alex rattled it angrily, gave it a kick and turned away. Then he thought he saw the reason why he had been put there. There was a picture of the Prince propped on an easel just beside that door. It must have been very newly done, since the boy was in black in it, and it smelled of fresh paint. Alex stared at it, and the portrait's wide blue eyes stared back. Alex knew that, now he had noticed it, he would feel those painted eyes staring at him from the whole length of the great library.

"I shall not scrub your eyes out," he told it. "That would be childish, and someone would only have to paint them in again. But I warn you that I shall turn you to the wall if you look at me like that."

There was writing at the top of the picture. Alex bent forward to see it. "Everard IV," he read. "Everard. That is your wretched name, is it?" Then he turned away and began to look at the books. Most of them were very old, some enormously heavy, with beautiful pictures and Gothic lettering. Almost all were Latin, and some Greek. Then he found a wall full of newer books. "Only a hundred years old or so," he thought. He looked at some: histories of the Principality full of battles, burnings, conquests, and feuds; long romances in verse he had not the patience to read; and some books of poems. The one which most interested him of these was the poems of Humphrey Lord Tremath. It was a little like Shakespeare and almost pleasantly familiar. Alex sat down on the floor with it, trying to forget how cold he was becoming, and read it from cover to cover.

"I prefer Shakespeare," he said, slapping it shut, and found that he had said it to a hatchet-faced serving-man who was bringing him a tray of food. Alex scrambled up. The man put down the tray, bowed, and went out of the nearest big end door.

The food was excellent, and Alex, unlike Cecilia, had a hearty meal. There was a steaming wooden bowl of jugged hare and another of something cold and white which Alex at first prodded suspiciously. It seemed to be a mixture of chicken and fish, flavored with herbs. He tried it and found it was delicious. Then there were fresh rolls and white cheese and a silver mug of beer. Alex had never had beer. He found he liked it. There was, too, a bowl of fruit. He read one of the histories while he ate. "This is not so bad," he thought. "I could stay here for a year at least without becoming very bored—I think. Always providing they send me food." Then he remembered his father. He lost his appetite for the big pear he had been looking forward to. "He will think we went into the quicksands," he thought. "Just like Miss Gatly's stories. Perhaps this is what really happened to all the other people who vanished after the Wild Rider was seen."

The idea so depressed him that he walked about, trying to avoid the portrait's eyes. He had just reached the door which he had come in by, when the door at the other end opened. Two soldiers came in, and began the long walk toward him. Alex started to meet them, but stopped. He had noticed enough about this strange country to know that these men were not in the Prince's livery, the green with mourning bands, which the men who brought him here had worn. These wore the dim blue and brown he had seen with the Count of Gairne.

"Something terrible is going to happen," he thought.

The soldiers came up to him—there was nothing he could do to prevent them—and calmly took his arms. Then they led him out of the library, down more stairs, and out into a small courtyard somewhere at the back of the mansion. Horses were waiting there, most of them with riders in that same blue and brown livery. Alex saw that his own horse was there waiting for him, and another, a splendid gray, with a bridle all stamped with gold leopards. They took him to his horse and told him to mount. Then they all waited, and Alex, cold from the library, grew colder still with apprehension. At last Prince Everard came hurrying out wearing a long black cloak. He gave Alex a satisfied look before he mounted the splendid horse. Then someone opened a gate in the wall and they all rode out into the other end of the valley from the main gate.

"What is he doing with the wrong soldiers?" Alex wondered. "Where are we going?" It seemed to him more dignified not to fuss and ask questions. Obviously, he would find out.

They went toward the hills at the eastern side of the valley, and then up a winding path in the hills. Alex noticed, as they were all strung out on the path, that there was a courtier in black beside the Prince. He thought it was the young man who had so elegantly escorted Cecilia away. Then he looked down into the valley at the great mansion, with the red winter sun hanging over it, and wondered if he would ever see it again.

They did not go very far. After half a mile of slow riding in snowy uplands, the Prince gave the order to halt. The soldiers at once separated and rode a little way off, until Alex, the Prince, and the courteous Lord Arbard were left all together in the center of a wide ring. There was nothing in sight but snowy hills all round. Alex looked at the Prince and wondered what was going to happen.

The Prince surprised him by smiling at him. "Now," he said, "I take it that you have little knowledge of swordsmanship."

"No," said Alex, mystified. "I scarcely know one end of a sword from the other."

"And I," said Prince Everard, "have always been poor with my fists."

Alex realized what was going to happen. "But you can kill me with a sword," he said angrily. "People hardly ever die in a fist fight."

Lord Arbard suddenly spoke up. "Few, hardly ever, rarely— or at least, not at once," he said.

"Be quiet, Hugo," said the Prince. "I know a sword fight would be more dangerous, particularly against an Outsider, so I have been thinking of other forms of fighting wherein we might be more equally matched. Can you wrestle?"

Alex shut his mouth hard to prevent it falling open with his astonishment. He could wrestle. Wrestling was quite a sport in the countryside in those days. "Yes," he said, "but not very well. I am too light to make a good wrestler." And he thought: "But I shall have to try. He will win hands down, being so much bigger."

The Prince looked him over. "I feared you would be," he said. "And the only alternative which came to me was to fight with quarterstaves. Are you able to do that?"

"Yes," said Alex, more than ever astonished at this boy's scrupulousness. "Yes, I can use a quarterstaff." In fact, he rather fancied himself as a quarterstaffsman. He and Ned Gatly had almost weekly duels, and Alex won rather more often than Ned. He wished he were not so cold. One needed warm wet hands for a quarterstaff.

The Prince seemed delighted. "You agree to that, then?"

"Yes, I agree," said Alex.

The Prince dismounted at once. Alex was down more slowly, being so cold. Lord Arbard also got off his horse, carrying two wooden staves. The Prince was undoing his cloak. Alex, rather reluctantly, threw off his cape and unbuttoned his jacket.

"Now," said the Prince, "I shall get my own back. You will see."

"Not if I can help it," Alex answered and began the ritual of spitting on his hands—a very necessary ritual in the snow, he realized.

The Prince suddenly looked up angrily. "Get back, you. I ordered you to stand off."

The soldiers were closing in on them, softly jogging nearer. There seemed two or three times the number there had been. Alex saw the Prince and Lord Arbard exchange alarmed glances and put their hands on the hilts of their swords. Then there were men and horses all round the three of them in a tight ring, and, among them, looming against the red sun, the stout, evil shape of the new Count of Gairne.

Alex stood close beside the Prince and the young lord. In an odd way, he felt on their side—certainly, he would rather be on anyone's side than the Count of Gairne's. He could tell, from the way that the Count was looking at all three of them, that the terrible thing he had been afraid of was happening at last. He wondered if he had ever been more frightened in his life. There were times when he had waited for Josiah to thrash him that he had fancied himself afraid, but they were nothing to this.

The Prince and his friend were frightened too. They gave no sign, but Alex could feel, almost smell, that they were as afraid as he was. The Prince spoke, though, firmly and clearly, as if he were only a little annoyed.

"What is this, Towerwood? You promised me to mind your own business."

The Count laughed. "True, Your Highness, but when it

came to the trial, I found I could not allow you to break your own decrees like this."

Prince Everard put his chin up angrily, but his face was very red. "I—"

"No one," said the Count, "is to ride out, except on the strictest business, until the New Year is a week old. You are ten days early, my lord."

Prince Everard lost his temper, as he had done that time on the island. Alex, seeing him stamp and shake his fist, suspected that it was a thing he did fairly often. "You fat, sneaking toad! Very well, I have broken the decree, but am I not the Prince? Have I not the power to make and break every law in the land?" And so on.

The Count, while the Prince raged, shook his head, with a slow, false pitying smile. Never had Alex hated a smile more. Lord Arbard, seeing that smile, took the Prince's arm and tried to quiet him. Prince Everard flung him off and continued to shout at the Count. But soon, he too was dismayed by that pitying look. He faltered, spoke more quietly and ended up lamely saying:

"I will not be bullied in this way, Towerwood."

Then the Count sighed and answered softly: "Ah, Your Highness, these rages of yours have been your undoing. As we have all feared, you have at last run mad. Here," he gestured round the waiting soldiers, "here are forty witnesses to the fact."

Alex looked around at the soldiers, and so did the Prince, in amazement. Each soldier might have been specially chosen for his hard, cruel face. They sat waiting, holding their long spears, looking down at the three young people standing in the snow, without a flicker of kindness or sympathy in any of their forty faces.

"Nonsense," Prince Everard answered bravely, but his voice was shaking. "Go away, Towerwood. Take your men with you."

"Of course," the Count went on, "no one who is mad will admit they are so. That is to be expected. But I assure you, Your Highness, you are mad. We restrained you from killing the Outsider, naturally, but in spite of all our efforts, you killed poor young Lord Arbard here."

"What?" said the Prince. Alex saw Lord Arbard, biting his lip, make the sign of the cross on himself.

"You heard me," said the Count. "Come on, Your Highness. Draw your sword. Kill him."

"I shall do no such thing!" exclaimed the Prince. "What do you think I am?"

"You say," said the Count, "you are one who has the power to make and break every law in the land. But"—he laughed— "if you will not kill my lord here, I shall have to do your own bad deed for you." Alex, appalled, watched him slowly draw his sword. "Where did you wound him, Your Highness? Through the heart? In the throat?"

"No!" whispered Lord Arbard desperately, watching the red sunlight on the Count's sword. He was drawing his own sword, but a soldier brought his spear point quickly down and held it against Lord Arbard's wrist.

Alex lost his temper then. He had never met anything so unfair as this. He was not sure he understood half of what was going on, but it was plain that this poor idiot of a young lord was really going to be killed.

"Stop it!" he shrieked at the Count. "How dare you!" He ran at the tall brown horse with his stick raised. At once six spear points descended on him, and he was brought up short with cold sharp steel at his throat. The Count calmly leaned down and took the quarterstaff away from him.

"Ah yes," he said. "You are mad too. No one doubts that. I see you have a temperament very similar to poor Everard's. Now get out of my way, boy."

Then he killed Lord Arbard. Alex shut his eyes and heard a gasp, a groan, and the heavy sound of Lord Arbard dropping down on the snow. He opened his eyes and saw blood on the Count's sword and the Prince's black eye stark and lurid in his white face.

"Now let us go," said the Count.

Soldiers dismounted. Alex, sick and horrified, stood while they tied his hands together and could not resist when they threw his cape round him and lifted him onto a horse in front of a soldier. Prince Everard, he saw, looked much as he felt, staring down to where Lord Arbard's blood was making a spreading red patch in the trampled snow.

Then they rode off. "Where are you taking us?" demanded the Prince.

"You will see soon enough," said the Count.

The horses went fast across uplands for a long way. Alex looked down at hoofs churning snow and thought that they were leaving prints which would be easy to follow. "And there must *be* someone who will try to follow us," he thought. "After all, he *is* the Prince."

The sun began to go down. The riders turned toward it and went down to cross a road. Then they went up into hills again, and rode until the sun was a great red disc, level with their eyes. Alex was frozen by this time. The keen winter wind came straight across the hills from the sea with nothing to stop it. He was relieved when they began to go down again, until they reached the shelter of a dim, snow-filled road, winding between hills beside a strong brown river. Here, there were many hoof-prints in the snow. Alex feared that they had joined the road so that their own tracks would be hidden among the others.

Then at last they came to a place where another road turned off to the left. It went over a low stone bridge and then plunged into a high break in the hills. It was almost a gorge, Alex thought. The horsemen turned down this way, and as their hoofs thundered on the bridge, drowning the sound of the river, he heard Prince Everard cry out:

"Oh, not to Endwait! For God's sake not to Endwait, my lord!"

"What better place than Endwait?" asked the Count, "since your father died there too?"

Chapter 2
CAMP

Cecilia followed Robert Lord Howeforce out of the little room. She was not sure anymore that she trusted him, but she could not see what else she could do. It was quite likely, too, that he was risking his life, coming into the Prince's mansion to rescue her and Alex. What he said about Alex terrified her. She prayed for his safety as she followed the outlaw softly along passages and down stairs. She was so fearful for Alex, that she forgot to be frightened for herself. So she had an immense shock when a strange lady stepped out of an alcove and took hold of Robert's arm.

"What is it?" she heard him whisper.

"You must see her. She knows you are here and she wishes to see you."

"Why should she wish to see me?"

"She is frightened. She is afraid you wish her ill."

Cecilia did not like this talk of "she." Nor did she much care for the lady, who was young and rather pretty, and took not the slightest bit of notice of Cecilia.

"Come," said the lady, pulling at Robert's arm.

"But, Phillippa," he answered, "I must bring Cecilia. I cannot leave her alone."

"That is your affair," the lady said. "Come." She rustled away down a side passage. Robert took Cecilia's hand and they both followed, into a large empty room full of comfortable silk chairs and then, beyond a curtain, into a much richer room, light and loaded with silks, tapestries, jewels, and crystal ornaments. There, on low chairs, sat Robert's mother and the other, younger lady. Cecilia realized that this younger lady would be the Princess, wife of the dead Prince and mother of the boy in black.

The Princess was crying. "What have you done now, you wicked man?" she said to Robert. "Where have you taken my son? Why do you persecute us like this? Why not proclaim yourself Prince at once and have done?"

"Madam," answered Lord Howeforce, "I have not seen your son. I am as concerned as you to know where he may be."

"How you lie," said the Princess. "How you lie! You have him prisoner, or you have killed him, and tomorrow you will cry yourself Prince through the whole country—just as you cried yourself wronged on Christmas Day."

"Madam," repeated Lord Howeforce, "I have not seen your son. I have no knowledge of his whereabouts. If I had, I assure you—"

"—You would have killed him before this," the Princess finished for him, and put her face in her hands.

Robert's mother looked up at him. "It is impossible to persuade her," she said. "Robert, it is true you do not know where Everard is, is it?"

"Quite true, I assure you."

"Then," she answered, "you must have spies out and inquiries made and not rest till you have found him, and the Outsider. She will not believe your innocence, nor will anyone, until the Prince is found."

"I will try to find him."

"We can guess where he is," answered his mother. "Now go, please, and make sure at least that this girl is safe." And as Cecilia, who had stood by a little resentfully all the while, curtsied to her, the lady smiled. "We are in your debt for a night's lodging," she said, and held out a small dog-eared piece of paper with the little orange seal stamped on it.

After this, Cecilia again crept after the outlaw through corridors and courts in the great mansion. As she went, she thought how strange the outlaw's position was. If she had been the Princess, she would have called soldiers and had him arrested even though he was her nephew. "So all I can think," she said to herself, "is that the Princess is not as sure as she pretends that he *is* so wicked. I wish I knew all there was to be known about how the Prince was killed. I think there must be much more to it than we have learned."

They came to a tiny side gate, outside in a bitter frost. There was a chilly guard there in green livery who raised his lantern to look at them. Cecilia was terrified, but the outlaw smiled and clapped the guard on the shoulder.

"Many thanks, Tom. Has the true guard come to his senses yet?"

"Aye, my lord. Had to gag him."

"Then ungag him. He may shout all he likes now. Then follow us where you may wear your own livery again."

"I have it underneath this, my lord. Comes warmer like that." Then the man, whistling merrily, and not at all secretive, went over to where Cecilia could see the wriggling shape of the real guard. "Come on, you," he said. "I'll give you five minutes to get clear, my lord." As Robert unbolted the gate, Cecilia saw the false guard heaving the real one along to where he would be seen in a white bar of moonlight.

Beyond the gate were empty fields of snow, hardening in the frost. In the great black shadow of the walls was a clinking and movements. Robert took her that way. There was a group of horses, breathing out steam, with riders in steel and a faintly glowing orange livery—Cecilia thought it was orange, but in the moonlight it could have been brown.

"I fear we have no side-saddle for you," Robert whispered.

Cecilia laughed. "I prefer riding astride. It is easier. But you must not stare at me."

He seemed relieved. Cecilia was helped into her saddle by a soldier, while the outlaw mounted the same blue-gray horse they had seen him ride across the bay. Then the group set off at a sharp trot, over the frozen fields, westwards, and up into the hills.

Everyone was very gay, even Cecilia, despite her fears for Alex. She was thankful to be out of Falleyfell and delighted at the moonlight ride. The men around sang and whistled and were plainly heartily pleased to have their leader back out of the mansion. After about a quarter of an hour, Tom, the false guard, caught them up, and he was merrier than any of them. Cecilia took to him completely. He had a little curly black beard which thoroughly caught her fancy.

"I can turn Hornet again now, my lady," he said to her, twirling his moustache.

"Whatever is a Hornet?" asked Cecilia.

They all exclaimed that she did not know. "Us—we be Hornets."

"The orange livery," Robert explained, "with the two black stripes. It is the true Gairne livery, and famous in the Principality. It is as old and honored as the Prince's green, or the Darron white and red."

"And we be honored to wear it," said Tom. "So all of us turn outlaw too."

"Oh, I see," said Cecilia, and thought how nice they all were to go as far as that.

They rode on, and after a while, Robert asked her seriously: "Did the Prince give no indication of his intentions toward your brother? If we knew what he meant to do, we could more easily discover where they are."

"Well," said Cecilia, "he looked daggers at Alex out of his black eye—Alex had blacked his eye on the island, you know."

Robert laughed. "No, I did not know. Poor Everard! He would take that very ill. Then I begin to see something of what happened. There would be a return fight, I am sure, but it need not have been far from Falleyfell. This makes me certain that Towerwood left in order to follow them, though I was told he had gone to Gairne."

"Oh, no!" said Cecilia.

"I fear so," said Robert. "I will send spies down to Gairne

and Towerwood as soon as we reach our camp. They should discover something. I am glad you told me of this fight, since I had
been wondering if Everard had not gone to Landerness—he
went in that direction, it seems."

This spoiled the rest of the ride for Cecilia, though they
rode where they seemed on top of the world and the soldiers
were as merry as ever.

She revived a little when they came to the camp. It was
where an outcrop of rock leaned over a high, shallow valley.
There were caves in the rock, with lights in them, and tents
pitched near the caves. Fires melted circles of snow and flickered on lines of picketed horses. Several young men in long
cloaks came running out to meet them beside their own strange
blue shadows. They ran back with the horses, calling greetings,
and asking for news. When the riders stopped near the tents and
Cecilia had dismounted, Robert introduced the young men to
her. Cecilia was a little bewildered by them all, but she gathered
that the one with the long nose was called Rupert Lord Strass,
and that the very young dark one was Robert's squire, and that
his name was James of March. Robert went with them all to one
of the caves, talking as he went. They seemed very dismayed to
hear that the Prince had vanished.

"Towerwood," said James of March.

"Surely," Robert agreed. "Now my eyes are opened to that
man, I believe him capable of anything." Then he laughed.
"Then I was called before the Princess, and she and my mother
were unspeakably indiscreet. And there stood Phillippa of
Towerwood hearing every word." He turned to Cecilia. "Did
you notice how indiscreet they were?"

"No indeed," said Cecilia. "I—I was angry at the way they thought it was all your doing. How were they indiscreet?"

"Perhaps it was not so obvious then," he said. "I hoped it was not, since I can do little for them and Towerwood can do them much harm. The Princess as good as told me to declare myself Prince before Towerwood seized the coronet for himself."

"You should take her advice," said James of March. "You are next in succession, and you are of age."

Robert laughed, as if his squire had said a very stupid thing. Cecilia liked him enormously for the way he laughed. It made her trust him at last, completely. "Oh, James," he said, "let us have no more troubles than we already bear. Poor Everard is no doubt finding enough heaped on his head, as it is. Now, let us eat. Cecilia, I cannot offer you tea."

Cecilia laughed and blushed. They had an excellent meal at a proper table in the cave, with a charcoal brazier to warm them and wine to drink. While they ate, Cecilia had to explain tea to Lord Strass, who seemed serious-minded and anxious to learn. While she explained, there was constant coming and going, and Robert left to give orders about spies to go to Gairne.

"We should know by the morning," he said, when he came back.

Then Cecilia became very sleepy, what with the wine and with her day's adventures. She wondered what she would do for a bed. The cave was bare and rocky, with rushes on the floor. She hoped fervently that she did not have to sleep on rushes. It seemed, from what they said, that the outlaws all did. But then she found, rather to her embarrassment, that most of the coming and going had been to make ready a tent, entirely for her.

"I wish," said Robert, "that we could provide you with a maid, but you are the only lady here."

"Good heavens!" said Cecilia. "I have no maid at home! Why should I need one here?" She could have bitten her tongue off after she said that. In her anxiety to seem pleased with all they were doing for her, she had embarrassed Robert again, just as she had on the farm. The light was too poor for her to see whether or not he was blushing, but he did not seem to know what to say. All the others, seeing that he was put out, were embarrassed as well, except James of March, who scowled at her. The rest of them all looked at the cave roof, or out of the entrance at the frosty stars, until Cecilia hardly knew what to do with herself.

"May—may I see the tent?" she said at last.

"I will show you there," Robert answered, and things seemed all right again.

Cecilia was delighted with her tent, and was careful to tell Robert so. They had found a camp bed and a mirror for her, and a bowl to wash in. There were a great many blankets and an orange cloak in case she was cold. There was a carved ivory comb for her hair, and even a spray of evergreen leaves in a little clay vase. "This is extremely kind," she said. "What trouble you have gone to."

When, however, she was left to herself in the tent, she found it more difficult to go to bed in than she had expected. She had never slept in a tent before. The nearness of people outside frightened her, until she realized that what she could hear were four guards walking up and down to keep her safe. Then, although she had no maid at home, there was always Miss Gatly to help. When it came to undressing, Cecilia found she could not bear to try, all by herself. They had not found any night-clothes, either, so she would have had to sleep in petticoats.

"My habit will be ruined," she thought, "but it will just have to be. And my hair will be wild in the morning, although it curls of itself." At home she had Mary-Ann, who was good with hair and was called in by the Gatlys too for big occasions. "After all," said Cecilia, "this is camp-life."

So she went to bed and slept at last, very uneasily, with wild dreams of danger to Alex and to Robert. Her worst nightmare was almost at dawn, when she dreamed that Conrad of Towerwood was walking toward her with a sabre like a Saracen's, and driving her into the quicksands in the bay. She stepped backwards and backwards, whatever she did, and, just as the quicksands closed softly over her head, she awoke to hear trumpets blowing. She sat up, hot and frightened from her dream. People were running about. She heard horses neighing. Then someone came to the door of her tent.

"Cecilia."

She recognized Robert's voice. "Yes," she said.

"Will you come out as fast as you can? Conrad of Towerwood is riding up to attack us and you are not safe there."

Chapter 3

DVNGEON

Alex saw little of Endwait. It was nearly dark when they came out into the valley beyond the gorge, so that all he gathered was the vaguest impression of a deep enclosed space. Somehow, he knew that it was a cultivated, fertile valley, full of fruit trees and prosperous cottages, and he heard the noise of the waterfall which shone in the snow at the other end. It was not so cold in the shelter of the hills. The snow had scarcely settled on the road through the village, nor much on the boughs of the great trees beyond. Under the trees it was dank and un-echoing and Alex's heart sank. Then he saw a house, set back under the hills, a large house, or a small castle, he was not sure which.

"A castle," he decided, as they halted outside. It had a dark, glinting, unfrozen moat, and people inside were lowering a drawbridge. The clank and rattle of the chains on the bridge made Alex so frightened that his teeth chattered. They reminded him of all he had ever read of dungeons, fetters, and racks.

The drawbridge went down, with a crash, leaving open a dark archway lit by a flaming torch in a bracket. The Count of Gairne and his soldiers rode with them, thundering, into the archway, past the flare, and into a tiny dark courtyard. Behind them, gates were banged and the drawbridge came clanking up again.

The soldier behind Alex dismounted and roughly pulled at Alex's leg. "Get down, ye Outside thing, ye." Alex slid off the horse as well as he could, using his elbows for balance because his hands were tied. All around him soldiers were coming off horses in a clashing and jangling of mail. He had a glimpse of Prince Everard being pulled down by the scruff of his neck. Alex stood in the dark among the soldiers, shaking with cold, while other people led away the horses. He could see the Count of Gairne a little way off, under a light, giving orders. Then the Count came striding back toward them. Alex tried to stop shaking.

"They will think I'm frightened," he thought, "and I am not—I am *not*."

The Count said: "They have the dungeon ready. Take them away."

The soldiers wheeled and marched, away from the light, into a deep dark archway. There were stairs almost at once, and Alex stumbled. Someone lit a lantern, which swung great shadows around on thick stone walls. There was a massive door unlocked downstairs ahead, and when they came through that, more stairs. This time the light glistened on the walls, streaming wet from the moat outside. Then there was a lower, narrower door, which took time to unbar. The soldiers did not go inside. Two of them took Alex, untied his hands, and pushed him through. Alex, remembering that dungeons were always deep, had the presence of mind to jump as they pushed him. He landed on his hands and knees in damp straw some three feet lower down and had to scramble hurriedly out of the way as they pushed the Prince in after him. Above them, the door thumped shut. Bolts screeched home, and the chains of padlocks rattled. Then, very faint and distant, Alex heard the feet of the soldiers marching away.

He stood up then, and felt his way across the dungeon. It was quite spacious, some five long strides to the end from where he had been kneeling, and the floor was deep in fresh-seeming straw. The wall, when he reached it, was wet, much wetter than the walls they had passed earlier, and, since it was so cold out-side, the water running down was icy. Alex took his hands away with a shudder and turned around again.

It was lighter than he had expected. High out of reach in a side wall, there was a tiny grating which must have been just above water-level beside the moat. Alex guessed this, because the light it let in was a vague beam of moonlight which wavered and moved on the wet wall. It was not the direct light of the moon, but its reflection in the moat. And it allowed him to see the paleness of the straw and the black figure of Prince Everard, his white hair and his whiter face.

The Prince was standing leaning against the wall near the door, as if he had hardly moved since the door closed. Alex realized—suddenly, as if someone had pushed a cold sponge into his face—that, while his own position was desperate enough, the Prince's was not only hopeless but horrible. His father had been killed, and killed, it seemed, in this very place; his friend had just been murdered before his eyes; and, since the Count of Gairne was able to do this to him, it looked as if he had not another friend he could rely on in the whole Principality.

"How terrible!" Alex thought. "I can at least think of home, or school or the Gatlys. I can think of father, or even the Courcys, but I should not imagine he can have a pleasant, homely thought in his head." He felt so strongly sorry for the Prince, that he tried to think of something comforting he could say. This was difficult, though, since, now he came to think about it, he scarcely knew him. A remark on the dungeon might have to serve, he supposed, and he was just about to say how damp it was, when the Prince spoke.

"If only," he said, "if only I did not dislike you so much, I could bear all the rest."

All Alex's sympathy vanished. He put his hands in his pockets and strolled under the grating. "You sound as if you want another black eye," he said. "Or would you prefer me to punch your nose?"

"Boast away," said the Prince. "The advantage is yours, but if they had not taken my sword away, it would be mine."

"Oh," said Alex nastily, "I have a clasp-knife in my pocket." He waited to see if the other boy would make peace at that, but he said nothing. So Alex added airily: "I will lend you it, if you like, but I would still beat you."

The Prince did not answer. Alex turned around from the grating and saw that Everard had his arms against the wall and his face in his arms. Again Alex felt sorry for him, and was irritated that he should feel sorry. He sat down in the straw, with his chin on his knees, and concentrated on feeling sorry for himself. He was badly off enough. His father returned from London in two days' time, and by that time everyone would have given Alex at least up for dead. Then, suddenly, it struck him that they would probably be right to give him up for dead, and he found that he was going to be in tears any second. He would have cried his eyes out then, with Everard standing there, if someone had not begun unbarring the door.

Alex jumped up at once. The Prince came quickly away from the wall and they both, as if they were guilty, turned to look up at the door. It swung open, and the Count of Gairne stood above them, holding up a lantern whose feeble flame dazzled them both. Alex put his fingers hopefully round his clasp-knife, but when he saw soldiers behind the Count, he let it go again.

The Count looked at the Prince and spoke as if Alex were not there. "Your Highness, I have come to explain what you have to expect at my hands. I felt I should do you this courtesy before I go to make an end of your cousin Howeforce."

"And what have I to expect?" Everard asked.

The Count smiled his terrible smile. "This, Your Highness—certain starvation."

The Prince looked at Alex. "But he—"

"Precisely," said the Count. "While you both live, you shall be given just so much food as will keep one of you body and soul together. Not a crumb more. If you take food, then the Outsider will have died at your hands, to the ruin of the whole realm. Will you take food, Your Highness?"

One of the soldiers came into the doorway carrying a plate and a tiny mug.

"Take it, Alex Hornby," said the Count. "This is all you will get until tomorrow."

"You fiend!" said the Prince. "You monstrous devil! Fetch it, Alex, in heaven's name, fetch it."

Alex felt him kick his leg, urgently, as if there was some meaning in what he said. He shuffled forward uncertainly, realizing that there was something he did not understand which was very important to both him and the Prince. As he put out his hands and took the plate and mug, it dawned on him what it was. But it was too late. His hands were full and the door was slammed in his face. Light came through a square barred opening, and he saw the Count looking down at him through it.

"You must explain matters to your enemy here, Your Highness. He did not see why you kicked him. He must understand why it is his duty to starve you. And now, farewell. I am going first to propose marriage either to your mother or your aunt—I care not which one accepts me, for either gives me claim to the coronet—and then to exterminate your cousin the outlaw. I will come back in a week, by which time I hope you will be dead or mad indeed. Good night to you both."

The square hole slammed shut, bolts and chains rattled, and the two of them were alone again in the dungeon.

Alex turned around from the door, still carrying the cup and the plate, ready to kick himself or scream with anger. "I— I am sorry," he said. "Is it—is it really true that no one would dare kill me?"

"Alas, yes," said the Prince. "I wish I had warned you. I saw you did not understand." He turned away from Alex and sat down in the straw. "If any of us in this realm," he said, "should kill anyone from Outside, then it is an end of all—every man, woman, or child of us."

"Are you sure?" Alex demanded. "How can you know?"

"It is written," answered the Prince, "and every living soul here knows it. The death of an Outsider at our hands brings ruin to this realm. Some say we would all melt like snow, others that we fall dead at that moment the Outsider dies. I do not know, but it is certain that no one here would dare to kill you."

"And I had my knife in my pocket!" said Alex. "I took hold of it and let it go, because I thought it was no use. I did not see what he meant until it was too late."

The Prince said: "You would certainly have been wounded. But they would not dare wound you badly. It is a pity I had not told you, because you might have made an end of that monstrous man. How is it I never guessed what a fiend he is?" Then he flung his head up irritably. "Eat that food. Stop standing there with it."

Alex looked down at what he held. On the plate was a slice of bread and the mug was half full of what he guessed was water. He was hungry after the long ride through the snow, but by no means ravenous. The lunch he had eaten in the library had been too good, though he wished now that he had eaten that pear. "I am not very hungry," he said. "We can share this."

Prince Everard moved sharply away from him. "No," he said. "No! Eat it, drink the water. Do you not understand? I dare not let you starve."

"But I am not starving. I had an excellent meal at Falleyfell. No one starves in a few hours, you fool! Let me give you half of this."

"Eat it," Everard repeated, and put his face on this knees.

Alex, wanting to shake him, wishing that there had been a spiny bush to throw him into, brought the food and knelt down beside him. "Come on. Have half of this."

"I am not hungry."

"Yes, you are. Or you will be by morning and I shall certainly not be dead by then. We ought to share what they give us until we are really starving, at least."

"No," said Everard, with his face still on his knees.

Alex sighed. He had never in his life met anyone so pigheaded as this Prince. "Can you not understand," he asked, "how I would feel, letting you starve beside me?" Everard did not answer. Alex gave up that line of argument and tried another. "People," he said, "can survive on very little food for months, certainly for weeks. Maybe you will be rescued within a week. Our troop of horses left tracks as plain as a pikestaff most of the way here, did you not notice? You must have some friends who would follow them until they found where you are. You owe it to them not to starve before they can set you free."

He heard the straw rustle as the Prince moved, and felt he was making an impression at last. "I have no friends," said Everard.

"You *must* have," Alex cried out, exasperated. "Think!"

"I have not. Do you think I have not been thinking? I have considered every soul in the Court, and of those who are not Towerwood's creatures, half hate me for the sake of Howerforce and the rest will believe I am truly mad. I tell you I have no friends. Now eat your food."

Alex could not eat after that news. Even if he had been unfeeling enough to let the Prince go without food, he could not have eaten a morsel. He sat in the straw beside the plate and mug and despaired. So they would not be rescued. Cecilia, even, could be of no help, since, as far as Alex knew, she was a prisoner in Falleyfell still with no means of knowing where he was. He was left to face this truly horrible situation alone for at least as long as it took a person to die of starvation.

Alex shook with misery as he thought it out. Everard did not dare to eat for fear of killing him. If Alex died, so did everyone else in this country. This meant that Alex was to be a murderer, whatever he did. He could let Prince Everard starve, and he would have killed him; or they could both starve and both die, taking along with them every single one of Everard's subjects. That was unthinkable, but so was it unthinkable for Alex to sit here in the straw taking every scrap of food out of Everard's mouth. He agreed with Everard on one thing at least: Conrad of Towerwood was a monster, an utter, diabolical monster.

Prince Everard flung round in the straw. "Eat that food— please!" he implored.

"I can't," said Alex, and another possibility struck him, coming to him out of his despair. "I shall not eat. I will starve voluntarily. Then no one will have killed me, and everyone will be all right."

Everard almost shrieked at him. "No! For aught I know that is quite as bad. In heaven's name, are you talking like that to torment me? Conrad of Towerwood did better than he knew, shutting us together here—for you will certainly drive me mad. You talk temptations like the Devil himself."

Alex was quite taken aback. It had not occurred to him that the Prince found him as maddening as he found the Prince. He was unable to answer, and, meanwhile, Everard went onto a new side of his miseries.

"And while I sit here listening to your evil arguments, that monster of a Towerwood is forcing my mother to marry him. To think of that!"

"Or your aunt," Alex reminded him, trying to say at least one thing which would not strike the Prince as evil.

"Oh, my aunt!" said Everard. "She would take poison sooner. He knows that as well as I. So, it will be my mother who accepts, for she has always loved life, nor is she used to being bullied."

Alex remembered the lovely fair-haired lady. Everard looked enough like her for Alex to know she was his mother. He was afraid Everard was right. She was too pampered to stand up to a nasty man like the Count, Alex was sure. He wished he had kept his mouth shut.

"Alex," Everard said, in a different calm voice. "Alex, I pray you, lend me that clasp-knife you have in your pocket. I shall not need it for long."

Alex at once put his hand over the knife and held it tight. There was something very alarming about Everard's sudden politeness. "Why?"

"Why? Because I wish to make an end of myself, of course. Surely you see I have reason enough?"

Alex got up onto his knees and shuffled away backwards, still holding the knife tight.

"No!" he said desperately, "you are not to do that. It is wrong. Aren't you brought up Christians here?"

Everard moved after him through the straw. "I am as good a Christian as you are, but I would rather burn in Hell than live through this coming week. Give me the knife, please. I beg you."

"I will not. It may not be as bad as you think. You must not be so wicked."

Everard came crawling forward again. Alex, thoroughly frightened, stood up and backed away. "Please," Everard said. "I am imploring you."

"Not with my knife," said Alex.

Everard stood up. "Give me that knife, you puling fool! They will let you go free once I am dead."

"Even if they made me king of all the world," Alex answered, "I would not give you my knife. Can you not take no for an answer?"

"You promised to lend it me."

"Not for this."

"Give it me!" Everard shouted, and when Alex did nothing but back away again, he rushed at him. Alex went over heavily sideways with one hand still in his pocket. But once he was down he had to free his hand, with the knife still clenched in it, to defend himself from the Prince's furious rage. He was terrified. He had never known anything like it. He thought Everard really was mad. He prized the Prince's hand off his throat only to have his head banged on the floor. Then he had to defend the knife, and while he struggled to get away, Everard kicked him and bit him.

"I see why the courtiers think he will go mad," he thought.

They rolled and struggled from end to end of the dungeon. The straw was pushed aside and they rolled in the wet mud beneath. Alex broke away and nearly stood up, but Everard took him around the knees and they were down again and fighting. Twice the Prince nearly twisted the knife out of Alex's fingers and Alex only saved it by biting too.

"Well, it has come to wrestling after all," Alex thought, trying to break out of a lock on his arm. The Prince was so much bigger that he would have won even if he had abided by the rules of wrestling, which he certainly did not. Alex took to mixed fighting, and hit Everard whenever he got a chance.

This was a bad mistake. Everard gave a little before Alex's punches, particularly when the punches were weighted with the heavy clasp-knife, but it changed his hot rage into a cold, thinking anger. He let Alex roll away and scramble up, then he dived on him and brought him down again, this time completely at his mercy. It was some kind of hold Alex had never experienced before. He felt the bones in his neck grate and he thought his left arm was broken. He shut his eyes and hung onto the knife in his right hand for dear life.

"Now," said Everard, "I can break your neck if I wish. Give me the knife or I will try."

Alex believed him. He said, with lights dancing in the top of his head, as if someone were holding a lantern just out of sight: "Why not *do* it? That is quite as good a way to commit suicide." He felt Everard loose him a little at this hint, but it did not help matters much. Alex kept his knife-arm stretched out, as far away from Everard as possible. The Prince needed both hands to hold him, so he could not get at the knife unless Alex gave it him. Alex tried some more cunning. "Let me get up first. You can have the knife then."

"I am not such a fool as that," said Everard and made a small, almost experimental movement. Alex yelled. Everard loosed him again, as if he were alarmed, but Alex was past caring.

"Everard, for heaven's sake, let me go!"

"Give me the knife then. Why do you call me Everard?"

"Isn't that your name?"

"Yes, but only my friends call me that."

"Let me go! You really are breaking my neck. I'll call you anything you like. Humpty-Dumpty if you want."

"Why Humpty-Dumpty? Because he had a great fall? You—!"

Alex said: "Fancy knowing Humpty-Dumpty and not Habeas Corpus! Oh!" This time he really screamed, and it must have frightened Everard because he let him go. Alex frantically rolled away and staggered onto his feet. Everard slowly came after him again. Alex panicked. The only way to stop Everard seemed to be to get rid of the knife. The only safe place was that high moonlit grating. Just as the Prince reached him, Alex jumped up and threw the knife.

He never expected it to go through, but it vanished between the bars and he heard it plop heavily into the moat outside. Then he and Everard stood in the wavering band of light staring at one another. The Prince had come to his senses again, Alex could see from his face.

"This is a lesson against despair, is it not?" said Everard. "I am sorry, Alex. That was our only weapon."

"I know," Alex answered wretchedly. "I am sorry too." Then, bracing himself, in case there was another attack, he added, "I—I did not mean anything by Humpty-Dumpty. I just said the first thing which came into my head!"

"Yes. I believe that," Everard answered soberly. "When I learned that hold from Robert, I hardly knew what I was saying. Let us look for that bread. We should eat it."

But they had destroyed the bread. They searched for it all over the floor, and all they found was the broken plate and the spilled mug.

Everard said bitterly: "If I do not learn now not to lose my temper, I shall never learn."

Alex crouched down on the trampled floor, fingering a muddy breadcrumb. "Very fine moralizing," he thought. "I suppose there is a lesson for me too in this. I lose my temper almost as badly as he does, certainly as badly as Cecilia—only I never admit it." But he was too cold now to care about his character or the Prince's. While they had fought he had been warm, too hot in fact, but the sudden heat had gone away. The damp of the dungeon struck right through him, and icy drafts came through the grating. Outside there, it was freezing hard, even in the sheltered valley of Endwait. His teeth were beginning to chatter.

Everard came up to him. "I am cold too," he said. "We must heap this straw together over us and try to keep warm. That is, if—"

"If what?"

"If you do not mind. If you will believe that I will not try to break your neck again."

This made Alex give a chuckle that was half a shiver. "Next time I shall insist on a fistfight and then I might have a chance." And Everard laughed too. It cheered Alex no end to find that the Prince could laugh. Then he discovered, as they scraped up a mound of straw and hollowed it out in the center, that Everard even made jokes.

"A jail-bird's nest," he said and flapped his arms and jumped into the hollow with a squawk. Alex giggled as he settled in beside him.

For the first ten minutes they thought they were getting warm. Then Alex's teeth began to chatter again. There was so little feeling in his feet that he wondered if he had not got frostbite.

Everard said: "We shall not be warm until we think of something else beside how cold we are. We must talk. Tell me of the history of your country."

Alex did his best. Between chattering teeth, he began at random on the Wars of the Roses. Everard was enthralled. He exclaimed, he offered advice to the long-dead kings, and he took sides in a way which would have shocked Alex's schoolmaster, but which quite delighted Alex. "By the time we are both dying of hunger," he thought, "I shall like him tremendously." He realized he was a great deal warmer.

Then Everard told histories of the Principality. He told them in the same formal manner that Miss Gatly used, and Alex was enthralled in his turn. "Now," said Everard, "I will tell you the story of Prince Geoffrey the Good and of Eleanor. Eleanor was an Outsider and her name was Eleanor de Courcy—"

"I say," Alex interrupted, "did she live near here? I know some people called Courcy. Could they be some relation?"

"Maybe," said Everard. "Some part of Eleanor's lands bordered this realm, but some lay far away. Prince Geoffrey went a hundred miles to interrupt her wedding."

"Yes, they owned lands all over England once. They must be her descendants."

"They cannot be. She was my ancestor. She married Prince Geoffrey in spite of all her father said."

"Tell me," said Alex, and as Prince Everard began on the strange story, he thought: "I suppose this is my lesson—that I should not have been disobedient. I should have gone to that party. But then, if I had, poor Everard would have been here all alone."

Chapter 4

ARMIES

Cecilia came out of her tent into the middle of a council of war. Robert was standing just outside in the crisp frozen snow talking hurriedly to his friends. Half of them were holding their horses ready to mount. Cecilia could see swinging stirrups, arching necks and trampling hoofs all around in the dim morning light. As she came, Robert, and all the others, turned and greeted her cheerfully, and then went straight back to their hasty talk. All around, beyond them, the outlaws in the camp were running and riding, chattering, and shouting, making ready for battle. To Cecilia's surprise, everyone was merry—as if they were delighted to be dragged up on a frosty dawn to fight for their lives.

Lord Strass was laughing. "Then I'll attack their right wing. That will be Darron, as far as we know. Good. Should James come with me?"

"Yes," said Robert. "His father is with Towerwood in the center."

"No," said James of March. "Send me against Moyne on the right."

"We want Bress there, James. Go with Rupert," Robert answered. "No, please do not argue. Now, one thing worries me. Since Darron is there, Towerwood must be attacking in the Prince's name, and it is possible that he has Everard with him somehow. You must all make sure that the Prince is not hurt, if he is there."

The others all gaily agreed, but Lord Strass said: "How are you sure that this is in the Prince's name? Darron is becoming more Towerwood's creature every day. Tremath is not there— and he would be, if this were for the Prince."

"Then we can look for Tremath in reserve, later," said Robert, "for I am sure. I know Darron and I begin to know Towerwood."

Then a bugle sounded. To Cecilia, trembling at the thought of a fight, it was like the screech of a slate-pencil and set her teeth on edge. The others were all delighted. Lord Strass threw his cap in the air, James of March shouted "Hurrah!" and mounted his horse, and most of them rode or ran laughing away. Robert was laughing too as he turned to Cecilia, but he stopped when he looked at her.

"You are frightened!" he said, and sounded surprised.

"Yes," said Cecilia. "Suppose you all get killed."

"We have little else to look for," he told her, still not seriously enough for Cecilia. She was almost angry with him for being so light-hearted. What he said next made her really indignant. "But I have arranged for you to be in safety on the hill. You will have a good view when the sun comes up."

Then he hurried away before she could be angry, and Tom, the false guard of the night before, was left twirling his moustache and smiling at her. "Come, my lady," he said. "We had best get to our post."

"We had best not," said Cecilia. "I have no desire to see the fighting."

"Ye need not look," Tom said, "but ye must come. We cannot have ye killed, my lady—being a lady and an Outsider as ye are."

"I am not really a lady," said Cecilia. "And why does it worry you that I am an Outsider? It does not worry me."

The bugle sounded again. Another bugle answered it, a different call, from further away. Tom did not let Cecilia argue anymore. He picked her up, tossed her over one shoulder, and set off up a steep path beside the caves. Cecilia furiously beat his back with her fists and drummed on his mailed chest with her toes. "Let me *down*, you beast!"

Later, Cecilia did manage to laugh at herself, but at the time she was too angry. She drummed and protested all the way. It grew suddenly lighter. She realized that the sun had risen and that probably all the outlaws and even Conrad of Towerwood could see her being carted up the hill like a sack of coals. She was furious. Tom, panting like one of the great express engines which ran daily past the farm, tried to explain as he went what Everard had explained to Alex about Outsiders.

"Be quiet. I will not listen," Cecilia kept saying, but before the top of the hill she had taken in enough of what he said to be frightened. "Put me down!" she said instead. Behind her, far below now, a voice was shouting across the snow. She thought it was Conrad of Towerwood calling on the outlaws to yield. She heard Robert's voice answering, gaily at first, then angrily. Then, as the bugle on both sides sounded again, they reached the top of the hill and Tom heaved her gently down.

"There," he said. "Did ye take in what I said of Outsiders?"

"Yes," said Cecilia meekly. "No one must kill me."

"Well done, my lady," said Tom. "And now don't ye give me more of that about not being no lady. A man's only to look at ye to see ye are. I reckon ye'd hold your own beside Princess Rosalind herself."

Cecilia would have protested at any other time, but now she looked down and saw the battle beginning and could think of nothing else. Towerwood had a great army, a huge black block of men and horses, spread out in the snow against the rising sun. Cecilia saw the red gleam of armor and the long banners streaming above them. The outlaws were a quarter the number and nothing like so well armed. Nor did they have a banner among them. They were clustered at the mouth of the valley, with two groups of cavalry up on the low hills to right and left. Cecilia was horrified at how few of them there were.

"They will all be massacred!" she exclaimed to Tom.

"Could be," he answered soberly. Cecilia could hardly bear it, when he said it. She thought of how happy they had all seemed five minutes ago, and she burst into tears.

Through her tears, she saw the vague galloping mass of Towerwood's cavalry charging at the outlaws. She saw them met by black whirring arrows which threw some into confusion. Most of them galloped on, though, and found the outlaws' levelled spears. Then a second wave set out from the enemy's army, and another. As they came, first one wing of the outlaw-riders, then the other, raced down from the hills to help. The mouth of the valley became an ugly heaving mass of men and horses. Among them was the flash, flash of lifted swords. Shouts, screams, and war cries came horribly up.

Outlaw horses galloped back up the hills on either side. Lord Strass's horses rallied around into an orderly group, but the side where James of March had gone was all confusion, with enemy cavalry mixed up among the outlaws and always that flash, flash of swords. Cecilia saw a horse rear and its rider fall. She was sure it was James. Rupert Lord Strass rode out in front of his men, with his sword raised, and then charged down again into the fighting. His riders followed and were swallowed up.

Beyond the valley, nearly half Towerwood's army was still waiting, but as Lord Strass disappeared, Cecilia saw them begin to move. The whole black mass, riders and foot soldiers, came slowly down on the struggling outlaws.

"Oh!" cried Cecilia, and looked hopelessly around for help. She looked behind her, and could have fainted with horror. The hill sloped smoothly down, behind the steep face where the caves were, and below Cecilia, at the bottom of the slope, was another army. It was at least as large as the outlaws' entire force. Over its twinkling horse and glinting foot flew a long yellow banner with a bear in its midst. Cecilia tugged Tom around and despairingly pointed. "*Look!*"

Tom shrugged his shoulders. "Tremath," he said. "Come to make an end on it right enough. Then this *is* in the Prince's name."

"But I don't think the Prince is here, do you?"

"No," said Tom. "He bain't. I been looking. He's not here, for sure."

"Well—" Cecilia began, but Tom interrupted.

"My lady, ye stay here. Ye keep hid behind this rock here, see. I must warn 'em. Maybe they spare some men to hold off Tremath. Anyway, I best warn 'em."

"Very well," said Cecilia. "Hurry."

Tom set off down the steep path again, and as he left Cecilia, the second half of Towerwood's army reached the fighting. They came with a roar and a shriek of trumpets, and in a matter of seconds the outlaws were broken into bands. The valley below was filled with desperate seething battle. Cecilia, rather than watch, turned to look at Tremath.

The new army was coming up the hill toward her. The rider in front under the streaming yellow banner was barely twenty yards away. Cecilia stood on the edge of the cliff with the battle heaving behind her, biting her muff and full in view. She had been so busy watching that she had utterly forgotten to hide. Now it was too late. She could see soldiers pointing at her. She felt them all looking at her, and the force of all those staring eyes was so overpowering that it seemed to be driving her backwards over the edge of the cliff. She bent her head against those faces, as she might against a wind, and stumbled toward them for fear of going back.

Commands rang out along the new army. Cecilia looked up to find it had stopped, all except the rider in front, his squire, and the man who carried the banner. They came on. She heard their horses in the crisp snow, but she could not look up again until the rider spoke.

"Are you one of the Outsiders who claims the coronet? Answer me, girl. I am Humphrey Lord Tremath."

It was a haughty, angry voice, but when Cecilia looked up, she was pleasantly surprised at the man. He looked agreeably intelligent, and his eyes were gray and honest. It was not the kind of face which would willingly join with Conrad of Towerwood, Cecilia was sure.

"I *am* an Outsider," she answered, "but I have no claim whatsoever to the coronet. Neither has my brother. There has been a mistake about that, I assure you—er—my lord."

"How so? I have been told—"

Cecilia, encouraged by his face, if not his voice, had a sudden idea that she might be of some help to Robert. She ran up to the horse and took hold of Lord Tremath's armed foot. He looked down at her in amazement. "I think you have been told a great many untruths, Lord Tremath. Tell me, did the Count of Gairne say the Prince was fighting Lord Howeforce here?"

"He did. What of it?"

"It is not true. The Prince is not here, I assure you. Please believe me. The Prince has disappeared and so has my brother. It seems certain that someone has them prisoner—unless you have news of them that I have not." Cecilia held her breath until Lord Tremath answered. It could so easily be that what she said was quite wrong. After all, she knew so very little really.

Lord Tremath frowned at her. "Are you sure? He was to be leading the troops—the Prince, I mean. I know nothing of your brother."

"But he is not," said Cecilia. "It is the Count of Gairne." She looked back at the valley, to make sure that what she said was still true, but the hill hid most of it from view where she now stood.

"Walk with us, my lady," said Lord Tremath. "We will see." He and the two men with him rode slowly to the edge of the cliff. Cecilia went nervously with them, nervous because she was suddenly "my lady" to this man too—it made her afraid that he was planning to keep her in a dungeon—and even more nervous of their horses. They were magnificent heavy warhorses. They had heard the sound of the battle and were jigging and curvetting with excitement. The squire, Cecilia knew, must be a magnificent horseman to keep his horse in check at all, and she was afraid she would be trampled on despite his skill.

She and the riders looked down at the valley. They had come at a rare moment of order. The outlaws were all grouped back against the cliff, archers kneeling, spearmen standing and cavalry wheeling into place on the wings. Robert was riding in front of them all, calling commands. Towerwood's army had drawn off slightly and filled the open end of the valley. Cecilia recognized Towerwood himself moving among the cavalry, arranging the next onslaught, waving an arm to call up fresh archers from the rear.

"Yes," said Lord Tremath, "I see Towerwood there, and Darron, and March, and Moyne. There is no sign of the Prince, nor are there more than a few of his men, but they could be in reserve, behind that rise."

Cecilia was not listening to him, nor was she thinking of their trampling horses any more. She was in tears because it was so plain that the outlaws were penned in against the cliff. The only possible way they could escape was up the way Tom had brought her, or up one or two other paths on the cliff. The paths were like little glaciers of frozen snow, and if any men could manage to climb them, there was Lord Tremath at the top.

"Why did they all laugh so?" she thought. "Because they knew there was no hope?"

Cecilia only remembered where she was, when she heard the squire say: "No, the Prince is not there. You spoke truly, my lady."

"Then," said Lord Tremath, "this is not our quarrel. Indeed, Towerwood scarcely needs our help as it is."

He was right. Towerwood's army was moving in again to smash the remaining outlaws against the cliff face.

"But," Cecilia cried out, "if you stay here you will be cutting them off in the rear."

"That was our intention, my lady," answered Lord Tremath. "Come." He and the squire and the standard-bearer turned their eager horses and rode away, not very far, only a few yards from the cliff-edge. Lord Tremath beckoned to Cecilia. "You must stay with us, my lady," he said.

Cecilia did not want to leave the cliff edge. She made up her mind to stay. Then Towerwood's army threw itself on the outlaws, and it was like the sea breaking on a reef in a froth of swords and spears and rearing horses. Cecilia turned and ran toward Lord Tremath.

Almost as soon as she reached him, there was a clatter of hooves at the cliff face, and a foaming blue roan horse hurled itself scrambling onto the slope. There, Robert, on its back, reined in so hard that man and beast nearly toppled back over the cliff edge. After him came Rupert Lord Strass with James of

March lying hanging over his saddle-bow. He too reined in as he saw Lord Tremath. Then to Cecilia's astonishment, outlaws in Hornet livery appeared all along the cliff edge, riding and on foot. Most of them were laughing as they appeared, but the sight of Lord Tremath stopped them where they stood. And from the waiting Tremath troops came a long burring of voices as the soldiers there realized that Towerwood and his allies were down in the valley fighting one another.

PART III

RIDERS

BY

DAY

Chapter 1

COURCYS

Alex and Cecilia were missed at Arnforth Hall fairly early on, but the Courcys were the kind of family which only became united for action at the latest possible moment. Nothing was done for hours.

Susannah was the first to see that Alex and Cecilia were not coming. She had been waiting and watching all morning, for, at last, she had made up her mind that she would apologize to Alex. She would lick his boots if necessary. It had dawned on her, in that awful moment when the Wild Rider had suddenly hurled himself into the bay, that her remarks really hurt Alex's feelings. And when Alex and Cecilia did not come back to the farm, she was sure she had hurt them once too much. So, on the pretext of decorating the hall, she hung about near the front door. She saw Old John arrive in the trap and drive round to the servants' entrance. She ran round there as soon as she could, and saw Cecilia's bandbox and Alex's bag. Old John had gone by the time she realized that Alex and Cecilia were not there too.

She waited another hour. The bell rang for the hasty muddled lunch they always had the day of a party. Alex and Cecilia always came to this lunch. Susannah ran into the ballroom, all dirty pinafore and wild hair. Harry was there with Egbert, both on the same stepladder, trying to hang up a green paper dragon.

"Harry, Egbert, did you know Cecilia and Alex had not come yet?"

Harry, whose conscience was troubling him about the Hornbys even more than Susannah's, nearly fell off the stepladder. He saved himself by using Egbert, and Egbert, who had a soft spot for Cecilia, was not balanced either. Between them, they tore down the paper dragon.

"Go away, Susannah!" Harry said.

"Have it all to do again, now, what?" said Egbert.

Susannah tried her poetic sister Letitia after lunch, but Letitia, much smeared with ink, was composing rhymed mottoes for each of the guests and was not really attending. "Could I rhyme Cecilia with Ophelia, dear?" Lavinia and Emily, who were helping her, thought not. Susannah clapped her hands to her face and ran away to Charlotte.

"Ophelia was drowned!" she told Charlotte, too worried to make her idea plain.

"I know, dear." Charlotte was already busy with her clothes, because, of course, her fiancé Charles Phelps was to be at the party.

By this time, most of the preparations were done. Martin

came out of the billiard room where he had been avoiding work. Susannah caught him before he could vanish somewhere else. "Alex and Cecilia are not here yet."

He was the one person who took her seriously. "Really? Standing on their dignity probably. After all, they must have some. Don't worry, though. That old father of theirs will send them along."

"But Mr. Hornby has gone to London for Father."

"So he has." Martin realized that if he went on attending to Susannah, she would be sending him to the farm to look. He began to make off. "Let me know if they do not come in the next hour."

This was a clever move, because Susannah was being dressed when the hour was up. She escaped though, because there was a crisis about Charlotte's hair and Susannah was forgotten. With her own hair in curl-papers and her pretty white dress unhooked, Susannah ran down to the hall and the ballroom, and then to find Martin. Martin had vanished, of course, but she found Harry, already dressed, prowling on a wide landing.

"What is it, Susannah? They still have not come, have they?"

"No," she said. "They have not. Harry, I think it is my fault."

"No," he said. "It's mine. You can set yourself at ease, Susannah. If they are not here in half an hour I shall have to see Father about it."

Susannah could not wait so long. A quarter of an hour later, when she was properly dressed, she went to her mother and tried to explain. Lady Courcy, fond though she was of

Susannah, could not make head or tail of it. Nor could she rid herself of a sneaking feeling that none of it was very important. But her poor Susannah seemed so distressed that she agreed to talk to Sir Edmund about it. Anyway, the guests were beginning to arrive and she needed to hurry him up.

Sir Edmund Courcy, who was just like Martin, except that he took his hands out of his pockets to hunt, was of course not nearly dressed. Lady Courcy tried to frighten him into hurrying, as she always did, and it seemed to her that a good way to frighten him was to explain about Susannah.

"And those little Hornbys have not arrived. I cannot think what has happened. My poor Susannah is terribly upset, dear, and has some odd idea that it is her fault they have not come."

"Why?" said Sir Edmund, mislaying the studs his man was following him around with. "They should have been here all day, surely?"

"But they have *not* been, dear."

"Then why was I not told? My studs, Smith! Oh, there they are at last! Josiah is in London, you know, and I am responsible for those children. We must send to the farm and enquire."

So, to Susannah's relief, a footman was sent to the farm. He went very reluctantly, since, being a footman, he was twenty times more of a snob than the family who paid him, but he went nevertheless. Susannah saw him anxiously to the door before she went off to greet the first of her guests.

Harry, meanwhile, knew nothing of this. Shortly after the footman left, he squared his shoulders, straightened his collar, and went to confess to Sir Edmund. His father stopped him impatiently after the first few sentences.

"What is the matter with you all? I sent James to enquire ten minutes ago. Why on earth should it be your fault? A man listening to you would think the whole family had conspired to keep these children at home."

"Well, we did not exactly conspire, sir, but I am afraid that is what it may have seemed like to them."

"Oh, nonsense," said Sir Edmund. "Fudge!"

The party was in full swing by the time the footman returned. He had the presence of mind to call Sir Edmund away from the guests before he told him the alarming news that Alex and Cecilia had set out early and should have been at Arnforth two hours before luncheon.

"Miss Gatly was quite beside herself, sir, because it came on to snow soon after they left. She fears they are lost, sir."

"With some justice, I imagine," Sir Edmund answered, and hurried to his study to smoke a cigar and think. As soon as the cigar was lit, he remembered what Harry had said and rang for James again. "Fetch all my children here at once. I want Charlotte too, but not Charles Phelps. They are all to come whatever they are doing." And as James went away again, Sir Edmund imagined himself telling Josiah the news and nearly bit his cigar through.

Fathers seldom mentioned business affairs in those days, so that none of the Courcys knew how grateful they should have been to Josiah. Sir Edmund, being as lazy as Martin, had let his money get into something rather worse than a mess. Josiah had discovered this by accident some time back and had been trying to straighten Sir Edmund out ever since. But the case was next to hopeless and things had reached the stage where it would be entirely due to Josiah's work in London that the Courcys had any money at all by the end of the week. Indeed, the most Sir Edmund hoped for was sufficient money to have Charlotte safely married at the end of January. After that, he was thinking of emigrating. And now, when he needed Josiah's help so badly, it looked as it his family had somehow lost Josiah's children.

They all came into the study, all except Charlotte, looking frightened and dutiful. Charlotte was sulking at being snatched away from Charles when she was really looking her best, but even she forgot her bad temper when Sir Edmund told them what had happened.

"I shall faint," she announced, but no one took any notice.

The whole story came out and Sir Edmund was relieved to find it was no worse. Susannah and Harry told their part. Lavinia, Emily, and Charlotte admitted to calling Alex an oaf, and Martin agreed that he had been high-handed to reprove Alex on top of all the rest. Egbert, who despaired of seeing Cecilia again, surprised them all by saying:

"Rotten bad show, all of us. Better send out search parties. Never come to Arnforth again after this, what?"

But Sir Edmund had not finished with them. He took another ten minutes to say what he thought, and most of what he said was to Harry. Harry was hard put to it not to cry, and Susannah wept heartily. It made it all the more impressive that Sir Edmund was not, like Josiah, a lecturing, raging father.

Then search parties were sent and the Christmas party fizzled out. Harry and Susannah were very thankful that it did. They were able to creep away with a candle to the back of the linen room and talk it all over.

Susannah said: "I think *we* should try to find them. We ought, Harry."

"But we do not know where they have got to. It could be anywhere. Wait and see what the search parties find."

They went on talking, however, until Susannah remembered how Cecilia had run away across the bay two years before. Harry looked at her with long rippling shudders running from his hair to his heels.

"We had better go and look at the quicksands, Susannah. Let us go before it is light, then we will get there before anyone else thinks of it. It is the least we can do."

Then, very late, when the search parties had come back empty-handed, they went to bed and Susannah at least had horrifying dreams of Wild Riders—hundreds of them. Harry never said what he dreamed, but when they met again in the early morning he was as white as a sheet in the light of Susannah's candle. His first act was to go to the gun room and borrow one of Sir Edmund's heavy ornate pistols. He made sure it was loaded too. Then he saddled his horse and helped Susannah with her pony and they set off, eating bread and cheese as they went.

They reached the bay as the sun came up behind the Hornbys' hill. The tide was just going out and wind swept bitterly in from the mouth of the estuary. Harry was relieved to see the black sands and salty gray snow appearing as they looked. Both he and Susannah had clean forgotten the sea.

"We can get to the quicksands now if we go carefully," he

said. Susannah followed him down the slippery rocks, realizing how foolish they were to expect to find anything. If the sea had been up all night, then anything outside the quicksands would have been swept out to sea with the tide. Harry set a diagonal course across the bay on the island side of the river channel, so that they would always have the water between them and danger.

It was only by the most extraordinary lucky accident that they found anything. They were, without knowing it, almost beside the hidden road from the island and Harry was trying to bring himself to cross the river channel, when he saw something moving, almost hidden against the gray gleaming sand.

"Susannah! There are two horses in the quicksands."

Susannah's hands at once went almost over her eyes in horror, but she could not bear not to look. She was sure whose horses they must be. They were one behind the other, moving slowly and steadily through the quicksands. The horse in front was a beautiful ghostly gray. As the sun caught his bridle, it glinted gold. The horse behind was brown, and if ever a horse looked bewildered and tired it was that horse.

"That one behind," said Harry. "That is Alex's Trim Jim. I'd know him anywhere. I do not know the other, though, do you?" He watched them, expecting them to sink and struggle any minute, but they did not.

"It is the Wild Rider's horse!" Susannah whispered.

"Nonsense! That one was a blue roan. As if anyone could forget that."

By now, the animals were nearly at the river channel.

Everard's horse—for that was what he was—was going slowly across. Trim Jim was close behind him, going faster now, because at last the landscape was familiar and he began to believe he would see his own stable again after all. Harry rode quickly across to them. The gray shied aside when he came up, but Harry managed to catch hold of its bridle. He was amazed at the antique look of the harness and at the gold leopards stamped upon it.

Susannah came up behind, calling to Trim Jim and pulling sugar out of her pocket. "What *can* have happened?" she said to Harry. "Why is this strange horse—? And what of Cecilia's Nancy?" Cecilia's little mare was still in Falleyfell, of course, being excellently cared for by the Prince's grooms.

Harry and she as they held out the sugar both happened to glance along the way the horses had come. Both of them gasped: "There's a *road there!*" They forgot the horses. The beasts nuzzled the sugar from their hands and then, seeing they were not noticed any longer, continued calmly along the hard-way toward the island.

"Falleyfell," said Susannah.

"Oh!" said Harry. "It's impossible! It cannot be! But the Wild Rider went this way, I am sure of that. I think Alex and Cecilia must have tried to follow him. We had better take this road and—and ask anyone we meet."

"They—they will not have shadows," said Susannah, terrified.

"The strange horse has," Harry answered. They looked after the animals, who were again almost camouflaged in the glinting sands. Indeed, all they could clearly see of them were their long black shadows. "Come on, Susannah," said Harry. He made sure to cock his pistol, and then set off down the hardway, the way the horses had come. And Susannah bravely followed.

Chapter 2

TRACKS

When they reached the other side of the bay, Harry and Susannah found the fresh tracks of the two horses in the frozen snow of the steep bank. Further on, there was a trampled patch among the bushes where the two beasts had waited most of the night for the tide to go out. Then the tracks led inland from the trampled patch to the road. They were almost the only prints upon it. Since it had been freezing hard all night, the marks were still deep and clear.

"We must follow these," said Harry. "This is the way to find Alex at least."

Susannah nodded and stared around the new countryside. In the snow, it was hard to see whether it was a strange land or simply the moors they knew were on the other side of the bay. They were not sure that they were indeed somewhere they did not know, until they came to where the road branched down to the stone village. There, the horses' prints were concealed in a multitude of hoof-marks, where a herd of cows had been driven to the village.

"There are *not* any villages here," said Susannah.

"Well, here is one now," said Harry, and rode down toward it. He was not shy of making enquiries when it might be a matter of life and death. His only real worry was that they might not speak English in this country. From anything else, he hoped his father's pistol might protect them.

Susannah was very shy. She stayed outside the gate, while Harry went to knock at the door of the first cottage. The man who opened the door, to her relief, looked foreign, but not so very strange. He wore a smock-frock like men did on the home farm.

"Excuse me," said Harry politely. "I am looking for two friends of mine. Have you seen any strangers here?"

"Outsiders, ye mean?" asked the man—in English, to Harry's relief, but with a stronger, slower accent than that of the countrymen near Arnforth. Harry nodded, hopefully. The man stared him all over and then went on to Susannah, before he spoke again. "Aye, there be news of Outsiders," he said, "but not hereabouts. We hear tell of an Outsider who laid claim to the coronet, so they lock him up for treason."

"Alex!" Harry said in amazement.

"That be the name," said the man. He was interested and conversational.

Before Harry could find out more, he had to tell the man his own name and Susannah's.

"Courcy?" said the man. "That be a name known here. Ye be cousins of the Prince, to have that name."

"No—no," said Harry, hastily, suddenly afraid that he would be locked up for treason too. "No relation at all, I assure you. What made them think Alex was? He's only—" Then he stopped, because of what Sir Edmund had said last night.

"A peasant's son?" the man asked, not seeming worried about it. Harry blushed. "That were what the Prince call him, they say, when the Outsider say the island belong to him."

"But—" said Harry and stopped again. He realized that if he told the man that Alex was right, and the further fact that the island had belonged to the Courcys before that, he would almost certainly be locked up before he had a chance to rescue Alex. "Where is Alex? Where have they locked him up?"

The man shrugged his shoulders. "Some say here, some say there. Some say the Prince run mad, poor boy, at finding an usurper come to crown his sorrow, and tried to kill the Outsider. Certain 'tis the Prince is mad and close confined for a space. Wicked times we live in."

Harry's hair was standing on end by this time. "And Cecilia? Have you heard of Cecilia?"

The man shook his head. "I reckon you should ask at Falleyfell for news, my lord."

"I'm not a lord. And isn't this Falleyfell then?"

The man looked shocked, and, Harry thought, a little suspicious. "No, indeed. This here be Arnforth."

At this, Harry was so astonished that all he could do was to make a strange squeak. He thought the man was looking at him more peculiarly than before. He noticed that he was beginning to shut his door. "Then where *is* Falleyfell?" he demanded.

The man had got his front door half shut by now. He had decided that Harry was mad. Nothing else could explain his strange distraught manner. And it seemed to him that all Outsiders were probably mad. They got it young and it took them in one of two ways: either they were like this Alex people talked of and had delusions of grandeur; or else they were like this one, who was every inch a nobleman and yet so strongly denied it. He pointed out the way to Falleyfell and then slammed the door in Harry's face.

Harry, imagining he had probably gone to call his friends to arrest him as a traitor, got back to his horse and Susannah as fast as he could. "Hurry," he said. "He did not trust me an inch. We must get to Falleyfell. He says it is along the main road."

Susannah was giggling. "He thought you were mad, Harry. I could *see* him thinking it. This place *cannot* be called Arnforth. It is too ridiculous!"

Harry laughed at that too. It was ridiculous that there should be two places of the same name only ten miles or so apart, but he saw there would scarcely be a chance of them getting mixed up. All the same, he was very worried. Susannah might have been right about what the man thought, but it made no difference to their position. One was locked up here for being mad— witness this Prince—just as much as for being a traitor, like Alex. And it alarmed him that there was no news of Cecilia. At least they knew Alex was alive. He wished he had sent Susannah home and come here by himself.

"Oh!" said Susannah. "Those horses came down to the road here. Look!"

They were some way beyond the turning to the village now. Harry looked to the left, as Susannah pointed, where a long slope rose from the roadside, and saw the tracks they had been following again. They led straight up the hill into the sun. He wondered if it was worth following them anymore after what he had been told. Susannah had no doubt that it was. She was already leaving the road and her fat pony was blowing out steam as he scrambled up the hill. Harry shrugged his shoulders and went after her.

"One thing," Susannah called over her shoulder, "that man in the village had a shadow. I feel better about it now."

Harry did not. To have met real people hidden away here seemed much more frightening to him. Real people did real things. But he kept on after his sister, up the hill, over its smooth shoulder, and down to another road, much less used than the one they had left. The horses had gone straight across, coming from further hills on the other side. Harry and Susannah were just crossing the road too, when a black mare came trotting round a bend. Its rider was a woman in a great hooded cloak and she reined in when she saw them.

"Stop!" she called. "What have you done with Everard?"

They stared at her beautiful sad face in astonishment. Susannah, in spite of her surprise, sighed with envy of the lady's bright fair hair. Like many dark-haired little girls, Susannah craved to have golden hair and a pink-and-white face.

The lady looked surprised too. "I am sorry. I thought you were the other Outsiders. Where are they?"

"We do not know, madam," said Susannah. "We are looking for them."

"Oh, find them—find the boy at least," implored the lady. "My son is with him. That much I have been told."

"We are going to find Alex," Susannah told her grandly, "or die in the attempt."

"Pray God you succeed," said the lady. "This realm is in

deadly danger while Towerwood has him. And you must find the young lady too. Towerwood is hell for leather after her and Robert, if my messenger is to be trusted."

"Who is Towerwood?" Harry asked.

"Who is Robert?" Susannah asked.

They did not believe the lady heard them. She talked on, leaning earnestly toward them, with tears running down her face. She talked frantically, as if no one had given her a chance to talk before. Harry and Susannah were awed and appalled, because they had never been beside so much grief before, and their awe was greater because they understood hardly any of what the lady said. She was, Susannah thought, the kind of person who always took it for granted you knew the people she was talking about, and now, in her distress, she mentioned names, places, and happenings all crowded together in a way which quite bewildered the two children.

"And I was not at Endwait, or I might have seen his face and known the truth. Now, surely, it will die with him. Poor Everard is too young to understand, you see—but I know he is not mad. I do not believe he killed Arbard, though as for the other, I am not sure. It is all Towerwood's doing. He has him somewhere, no doubt intending to make him mad indeed. And he knows I know, because Phillippa was standing by when I told Robert to proclaim himself Prince. Towerwood dropped many hints of this last night when he came to Falleyfell and my poor sister-in-law took poison rather than marry him. She is dead, God rest her soul, and I deserve to die too for my deceptions—for I told Towerwood I would marry him so that he could be the Prince, and then when he was gone I ran away rather than take poison too. If you find Everard, tell him I have gone to the nuns of Uldrim. I shall be safe there for a while."

The lady stopped speaking suddenly, with her blue eyes wide, wide open. They saw she was horrified that she had said so much to two complete strangers. "Tell no one of this!" she said wildly. "Tell only Everard where I am."

"We promise not to tell a soul, ma'am," Harry said.

"Not a word," promised Susannah. They were both thinking that the lady could not have told anyone more likely to keep their promise, since they understood so little of what she said.

"Nor say that you have seen me," said the lady. They promised again.

"How can we say," Susannah thought, "when we do not know who she is?"

"Thank you, a thousand times," said the lady. "I would reward you richly if I could." Then Princess Rosalind, only they did not know her name, rode quickly away down the road. The Courcys set off up the hill after the hoof-marks again.

Harry inspected his pistol at the top of the hill. "I understood one thing from all that rigmarole," he said, "and that is that if we meet a man called Towerwood, the best thing I can do is to take careful aim and shoot him between the eyes."

"Poor lady!" said Susannah, still very awed.

Then for a long time neither of them said anything. They followed the prints across bare snowy uplands for miles. The wind made their eyes water but even so they could see there was not even a shepherd moving. Harry was thinking that this strange country must be very underpopulated, when they came to the place where Towerwood had captured Alex and Everard. Susannah cried out, it was so gruesome.

There was the deeply churned snow leading from Falleyfell.

It ended in a wide trampled circle and in the middle of the circle was a great bright splatter of blood. It had been so cold that the blood was still red and there was no mistaking what it was. If Susannah had been Charlotte, she would have offered to faint on the spot.

"Not Alex!" she said.

Harry was as white as a sheet again and wanted to be sick, but he rode over to the place. "Two people have said Alex is alive," he said, and his voice came out hoarse and squeaky by turns. He had never admired Susannah more than when she came up beside him to look too.

"But," she said, "whoever it was did not die — or not straightaway. He went after all those horses. Look."

Harry looked to where the churned snow led away again, where Towerwood had carried the boys off to Endwait. Drips of blood lay among the hoof-marks, and there were dragging footsteps. He took a long, large breath. They would have to go that way too, and goodness only knew what they would come upon.

"He must be horribly wounded," said Susannah. "We ought to find him, whoever he is. Do come on, Harry." And Harry thought, as he went on along the line of bloodstains, that his sister was probably the bravest member of the Courcy family.

The trail led into a slight dip. To one side of it was a tiny stone hut, a shepherd's mountain shelter probably. It had a broken chimney, with a wisp of smoke coming from it. The bloodstains led to it, though, of course, the hoof-marks went on. Someone had dragged the wounded man through the door of the hut. They could see by the long trailing mark.

Harry and Susannah looked at one another, and then Harry rode over to the hut and knocked on the door.

"Who be there?" shouted a gruff voice.

"My name is Henry Courcy," Harry answered, because there seemed no other answer he could make.

The door opened at once. Harry did not know it, but his name was little short of magic in the Principality. Eleanor de Courcy, besides being famously won by Prince Geoffrey, had been a Princess whose praises were still sung, though she had lived five hundred years before. The shepherd who opened the door nodded and smiled. He had expected his visitor to look like an Outsider, and he did.

"What can a poor man do for ye, my lord?"

"Who is the wounded man you have, please? Can you tell us how he came to be hurt?"

"Aye, my lord. It be poor young Lord Arbard. He can tell ye hisself how he come to have his blood spilled, if ye care to step inside."

Harry, very relieved that he did not have to look upon a corpse, dismounted and went into the hut. Susannah dragged both horses over to the door so that she could see what was going on. Lord Arbard was lying on a pile of sheepskins, very pale and breathing heavily, but, as far as Harry could see, nothing like dead. He had been drinking soup from a wooden bowl.

"A likeness, a definite likeness," he said breathlessly to Harry. "There is a touch of the Prince about you—not Everard, but William, you know, Prince Everard's father. What can I tell you?"

"Where Alex Hornby is, if you know."

Lord Arbard told them what he knew, which, of course, was very little, but enough to make Harry more determined than ever to shoot Towerwood if he got a chance. Susannah, lis-

tening, took a violent dislike to Prince Everard. She was glad
to hear that Alex had blacked his eye and she admired Alex,
if possible, more than ever for it.

"Towerwood imagined, thought, knew that he had killed
your humble servant," said Lord Arbard. "He would have killed
any other man, but I have a curious, unusual, strange—in short
my heart is in my right side."

"Congratulations," said Harry. "I wish mine was." He wondered if that was what made Lord Arbard use three words where
one would do.

"But you must hurry," Lord Arbard said. "You must trace,
follow—"

"Yes," said Harry hastily. "We must. I hope you get well
soon." He backed out of the hut and mounted his horse again.
The shepherd came out with offers of soup, but Harry refused.
Once he got into a real conversation with Lord Arbard he feared
it would last all day, and as far as he could see, they could not
afford all day. "We had better hurry," he said to Susannah. "It
was yesterday afternoon that all this happened."

So they rode on again. Susannah said indignantly: "What a
country this is, where someone can carry off the Prince and
nobody else does a thing about it!"

"I think it is because their ruler has just died," Harry
answered. "Everything is at sixes and sevens, and there is only
us to help."

"Only us and our pistol," said Susannah. "God for Harry,
England, and St. George!" She went careering off down a hill
waving one arm over her head. Harry followed, laughing, but
wishing she could take matters more seriously.

After that they met nothing and nobody for the rest of the

morning. The tracks were plain and clear in the crisp snow until they led them down to the Endwait road. There, they vanished in a host of other hoofmarks.

"Like a stag taking to water," said Susannah. "The villain did it on purpose."

Harry got off his horse and inspected the tracks carefully. It was difficult to see, but he thought the riders must have turned right as they came to the road. One horse might have swung out a little, into less trampled snow, as it turned on the inside of the troop. He was still bending, inspecting the place, trying to decide if it looked like a horse marking time while the others made a wide turn, when he heard the squeaking of wheels. There was a donkey-cart coming along the road, loaded with sacks of vegetables, and on top of the sacks was the body of a man dressed in orange. This one was definitely dead. Susannah turned away. The driver of the cart, a very gloomy man in a blue smock, looked at them with his eyebrows raised.

"I warn ye," he said, "they'll be on ye if ye waste time searching around here. The battle is lost for all the Perland caves and Howeforce is put to flight. I thought they said ye were locked up for treason, the pair on ye,"

"Oh, no," said Susannah faintly. "It was not us, sir, but thank you for warning us, all the same. Come on, Harry, please."

The driver pointed down the road, the opposite way to the one which Harry thought the horses had taken. "Go ahead of me there," he said. "But ye must not go to Gairne. If ye can get to Arbard ye'll be safe."

"No," said Harry. "They went the other way, Susannah. We

shall have to go that way, whether or not there has been a battle."
Then he said politely to the driver, "Do you mind telling me
who has won the battle? I do not know Howeforce."

The driver suddenly became surly and gave a frightened
look over one shoulder at the dead man on his cart. "Then ye'll
be glad to hear Towerwood has won, seeing ye're on his side."

"That man *again!*" said Susannah. "We are not on his
side, sir."

"Then get to Arbard," the driver answered, still very suspicious. He would not speak to them again. They watched him
click his tongue to his donkey and go slowly wheeling away
along the road.

"Oh, dear!" said Susannah.

"It cannot be helped," Harry said. "I am sure they went this
way. Bear up, Susannah. Remember some of this is our fault."

They came to the Endwait turning half a mile further on.
The road was deserted. They saw that tracks led across the
bridge and into the gorge, but there was no means of knowing
if they were the right ones. Other people had ridden in and out
of Endwait since, and confused the whole thing.

"What shall we do?" Harry said. "I think we must go into the
valley and ask. People seem friendly if we say we are not on
Towerwood's side."

Susannah agreed. The two of them were just crossing the
bridge, when there were shouts from the hill on the other side
of the road. Before they realized what was happening a man in
mail thundered up to them and reined his great horse almost
onto its haunches beside them. He was all in red and white and
shining armor.

"He looks like St. George," Susannah thought. She thought

he had a nice, rather nervous face. "He has taken us for the Hornbys—like the lady!" She was right.

"I beg your pardon," said the man. "I took you for the other Outsiders. But now I see that you are both too dark, and that the lady is a great deal younger. I am Howard Lord Darron. May I ask your names?"

Susannah happily told him who they were. He bowed like a real knight-errant, and Susannah was so delighted with him that she added, hoping to make him properly their friend: "We are not on Towerwood's side, either."

"That is very regrettable," said Lord Darron, "for it would seem that I am. I must ask you to accompany me and for the time being to regard yourselves as under arrest."

Chapter 3

CASTLES
IN THE AIR

Alex was woken by Everard exclaiming. He rolled over to find that the Prince had crawled out of the straw, leaving a cold prickly space. Alex began to shiver before he was properly awake. The dungeon was full of mist from the half-frozen moat outside and cut in two by a bright line of sunlight from the grating. Everard was in the sunlight and the mist, like an angel in a church window, looking up at the grating.

"Come here and look," he said.

Alex crawled out of the straw and went over to him. The first thing he noticed was a long cascade of icicles hanging between the bars, which made him shiver more. Then he realized that what had made Everard exclaim were the bars of the grating themselves. They were new. They could not have been more than a week old. The iron was still dull gray and where there was rust it was in red-brown trickles.

Under the clustered ice Alex could see the fresh chisel-marks, where the old bars had been hacked away to make room for the new.

"Seven days old," said Everard. "Not more."

"Newer than that, surely," said Alex. "Think how damp it is in here. They might rust like that in a day, or even overnight."

"Yesterday," said Everard, "I would have said you were condemned out of your own mouth and that Towerwood gave orders for these bars after talking to you on the road to Falleyfell. Today I am not so sure. Tell me truthfully, Alex. Are you in league with Towerwood?"

"No," said Alex. "Of course I am not. I hate him as much as you do. The first time I saw his face I hated him more than anyone I had ever met." He looked drearily up at the grating and saw another day of arguing and fighting ahead. They would probably go on like this until they were too weak with hunger to argue any more. Not that he blamed Everard for his suspicions. Anyone in his shoes must feel that they would never trust anyone again. "Oh!" he said. "Let us not spend the rest of our lives quarrelling—er—Your Highness. It is not worth it."

"I agree," Everard answered. "It is not worth it. I had made up my mind that I would not, once I had asked you that. And, in fact, I think the order for these bars was given before Towerwood set eyes on you. It is a good day's work to fix them in solid stone. He had planned to confine me here, I am sure, before ever you arrived. Your presence is a refinement, but I wished to know if you had consented to it or not."

"I never did," Alex said. He was so relieved at Everard's peacemaking that he let his jaw loose and his teeth began to chatter.

"Come back to the straw," said Everard. "There is some chance that we will die of cold before ever we starve."

They sat face to face in the straw, both shivering. Alex saw that the Prince's black eye was going away. It was only pale yellow now. Yesterday must have been its last most colorful day. He told Everard so. Everard laughed.

"An eye for an eye," he said. "Except yours is a bump the size of a pigeon's egg on your forehead."

Alex felt his forehead indignantly and had to admit that Everard had got his own back. "I am sure," he told Everard, "that this is what would please Towerwood—to come back at the end of the week to find us both with two fresh black eyes. We should call it off and spite him."

Everard nodded and held up one hand with two fingers crossed. "Barley," he said.

Alex was pleased to find they had this custom in common. "Barley," he said. "I am glad you know that too."

"As well as Humpty-Dumpty. But I had rather be called Everard." Everard smiled and held out his hand. They shook hands and then Everard asked: "By the way, what did you mean by Habeas Corpus? Is it some kind of legal term?"

"Yes, I suppose it is," said Alex. "From Magna Carta—but I suppose you will not have heard of that either." He explained about it, as far as he could, and about the barons and King John. "So now," he said, "even the most obvious criminal is given a trial. No one can be locked up simply on suspicion or because someone wants them out of the way."

"Like you and me?" said Everard. "I see that the Outsiders have a point there. Alex, I promise you that if we ever get free from here I shall institute Habeas Corpus in this Principality.

I come to see that there is a crying need for it." Alex laughed. "I am not joking," Everard said haughtily. Then he laughed too, but not very happily. "What a castle in the air!"

As if to point out to Everard how hopeless it was to discuss Habeas Corpus, someone rattled the bolts and chains on the door. The two of them sat where they were and watched their jailer slide a hatch aside at the bottom of the door and push another cup and plate through onto the doorstep inside the dungeon. Alex longed for his knife as he watched. One could have stabbed the jailer through the hatchway and there was room for a boy to wriggle through the opening. As the hatch slammed shut, he shrugged his shoulders and got up to go for the food. Everard had stood up first, though, and it was he who collected their breakfast and brought it to the jailbird's nest with a very gloomy face.

"Last night was generous compared to this," he said. "Alex, I do not want to make another argument, but I feel you should eat it."

"No," said Alex. "We share as long as we possibly can."

"That will not be long," Everard answered. "Look." There was rather less than half a slice of dry brown bread and the water in the cup scarcely covered the bottom.

"We can suck those icicles for water," Alex said, and firmly broke the bread into two. He was very hungry by now, and the thought of losing this bread in another fight was almost unbearable. Everard, to his relief, took his half without saying any more. They lay in the straw beside the plate eating the bread crumb by crumb to make it last. Alex foresaw a time when they would quarrel about crumbs, but he hoped it was still a long way off.

Everard was picking up crumbs with the end of one finger and licking them first before he ate them. "Castles in the air are very comforting," he said. "I shall build some more, if you will help by telling me that they are unreal. I rely on you for that, Alex. This crumb is a partridge. I shall have that when we are free. And this crumb is bigger. It is a boar's head—no, a whole side of venison. We will have that too."

Alex did not think Everard was being wise. It seemed to him the way to drive oneself mad. He said so.

"Thank you," said Everard. "Say that every five minutes. Oh, Alex, I thought last night I would be mad by the morning. Everything seemed a castle in the air. I was going to be a good Prince, as good as my father, if not better. I was going to be able to live on the island—we say here that it is the mark of a truly good Prince if he can be on the island and the Principality Over the Water is still safely at peace. Now see what I have come to, caught up in my own wise edicts, and all my dreams are down to taking Endwait from Towerwood again so that I can have this wretched dungeon filled in."

Alex changed his mind about Everard's castles in the air. Perhaps reality was worse. "Yes, by all means fill in this dungeon. But I hope you will do something more to Towerwood than take Endwait away from him. These crumbs have made me thirsty." He got up and tried jumping for the icicles at the grating. It was no good. He was not tall enough to reach.

Everard came and jumped for icicles too. He managed to break them off one each and they sucked them. They tasted vile, of dust and rust and pond-weed. Everard shuddered. "These will give us some disease, I imagine. Yes, I will do worse to Towerwood, never fear, but he must be properly arraigned for High Treason. It will not do to be spiteful. And yet, now I think about it, this is what everyone has said of Towerwood. 'Let us not be spiteful.' So we have been too fair and kind and he has thrived out of all proportion."

"So you did know he was nasty?" Alex said. "I have been wondering why he came to be so powerful, when no one can look at him without thinking: Here is a brutal monster out for what he can make."

"What could we do?" asked Everard. "He has never done wrong before, for all his faults."

"Really? To look at him you would say he has done nothing else all his life. Surely, Everard, there must have been something. For instance, how did he come to be Count of Gairne? Did he have any claim to be that?"

Everard put his head down and his hands in his hair and nodded. Alex could see that his question had brought up the Prince's saddest thoughts, and he could have kicked himself for asking it. "Yes," said Everard. "He has every claim. He had the lands and title in compensation for the death of his son."

"I am sorry. I did not realize he had a son. How did this son die?"

Alex hoped that Towerwood's son would have nothing to do with Everard's sadness, but when Everard answered, he could have kicked himself again. "His son was my father's squire. They were both killed together in the garden here." Everard looked angrily up at Alex with tears in his eyes and Alex would have done anything to stop this line of talk, but Everard said: "I know you have met Robert. I know that you like him. I was very fond of him and he is my cousin. But I came into the garden as Robert was coming out and Robert was carrying the squire's dagger all covered in blood. Not only was my father his Prince and his uncle, but Bertram of Towerwood was Robert's foster brother. It could not be worse, Alex. And I suppose Robert thought, since I was not of age, that he was likely to be the next Prince. Towerwood was right to insist I—" Everard stopped suddenly. Alex guessed he was crying. He was very glad not to hear any more for the moment. It was all too horrible. He wanted not to think about the way they had entertained a strange weary outlaw who had confessed to murdering one uncle and not to the other. He was angry not to have known of this. Robert had seemed noble and sad, when they had got over his strangeness—and he had been extremely kind to Alex when he saw how frightened he was. But then he would if he had needed a night's lodging. Then suddenly, Alex had a complete change of feeling. Robert had been nice. Towerwood was nasty and he had been even more horrible to Everard than to Alex. It seemed to Alex that if one worked backwards from that, then there was a chance that Towerwood had been the villain of the piece all along.

"Look here—" he said.

"Do you know—" Everard said at the same moment.

"Go on," said Alex.

"I was going to say that Towerwood had insisted that all the nobles took the oath of loyalty to me. They were most of them at Endwait, you see, with my father. But then I realized that there had been no question of anyone's loyalty. Robert never claimed the coronet then or later. He had his heralds proclaim his innocence all over the realm, but he never said he was Prince, although I am sure the people would have accepted him if he had. It is Towerwood who is to marry my mother and claim the coronet."

"So it looks as if—Everard, what kind of person was Towerwood's son?"

"It seems terrible to say it, but he was terrified of his father. When Towerwood was not there he was very likeable, though somewhat of a weak character. My father used to try to keep Bertram apart from Towerwood, because of the way he terrified him. Robert would take Bertram hunting whenever Towerwood was at court. Bertram admired Robert tremendously."

"Did Robert like Bertram?"

"Yes. As I said, they were foster brothers. They were brought up together in Gairne. Bertram's mother was Robert's nurse. The Towerwoods are a fairly humble family, you see."

"You have not really told me what Robert thought of Bertram. I think that is very important, Everard, because you said Robert was carrying Bertram's dagger."

Everard threw two handfuls of straw in the air in irritation. "But I *have*—Do you not know what it means, to be someone's foster brother? Do you not have such ties Outside? It is far closer than if they had been truly brothers. It is held sacred here."

"Then—" said Alex.

"Yes, yes," said Everard. "I am there before you. I saw what a fool I was the moment I realized that Robert had not wished to be Prince. And it was Towerwood who suggested that I outlaw Robert forthwith. If he had been arraigned for High Treason in Council, as he should have been, the whole realm would have seen the truth. But I could not bring myself to have Robert meet a traitor's end—he would have been cut into portions, Alex—or now, I see, Bertram would have been, even though he had killed himself."

Alex began throwing straw about now. "Stop, Everard! I cannot understand yet. You think Towerwood made his son kill your father. Do you think he really relied on the poor lad to kill himself afterward?"

Everard said: "Towerwood despised Bertram. I am sure he knew that was what he would do. Just as I imagine he hopes I am now going mad in your company. I think he likes using people—as he is using you. And I imagine that if he made sure that Bertram killed my father when Robert was by, he knew that if Bertram did not kill himself, then Robert might well take the blame himself. And I think he might have done."

"No," said Alex, "that does not sound at all likely. You are just letting your ideas run away with you, Everard. I think you are right that the whole thing was Towerwood's doing—it seems as if it *must* be, but he could not have relied on Robert to take the blame. *Did* Robert take the blame? Did you ask him before you outlawed him?"

"I asked him," said Everard, "and he denied it. He offered to give me his oath that he had not killed either of them."

"Well, there you are," said Alex. "Could Towerwood have killed your father himself? As far as I can see he does not object to murdering men with his own hands."

"You mean poor Hugo Arbard? I wish I could think that Towerwood had the opportunity, Alex, but he was with me all the time—purposely, I begin to think. And I cannot see that even he would kill his own son."

"Then could Bertram have killed your father because his father made him, and then Robert killed Bertram? I know he killed his uncle, and I remember he said it was the law."

Everard was pulling his hands through his hair and, as his

hands were full of straw, it made him look wild and even mad. The straw was the same color as his hair, so that he was looking like a white gollywog by this time. "Robert denied killing either of them," he protested. "If I believe him in one case, why not in the other? It was different when he killed Aubrey of Gairne. He was Robert's uncle, not his foster brother, which—but you Outside do not seem to see the bond there is between foster brothers, so what can I say? My feeling is that it was Bertram killed my father and afterward himself. Robert, I think, simply took away the dagger so that Bertram should be spared at least a suicide's fate—which is bad enough, when I come to think of it. They are buried at a crossroads with a stake through their heart."

As Everard said this, he looked at Alex, so pale that his yellow black eye stood out again as it had done the day before. Alex no longer wished he had his clasp-knife. He thanked heaven that it had chanced to find a gap in the grating.

"Everard," he said, "take that straw out of your hair and talk of something else, for goodness' sake. I am very sorry I began the subject."

"I am not sorry you began it," Everard answered, but he began to comb his hair with his fingers. "You have helped me see somewhat of the truth. Perhaps we had better talk of other things. Let us build more castles in the air."

Alex began talking of horses and then about school. Everard tried to attend to him, but it never lasted for long. All that day he was returning to his father's death, or to the things to do with it. If Alex would not let him talk about it directly, he disguised it as a castle in the air.

"Here is a good castle," he would say, rolling over and making a heap of straw to stand for the castle. "I will pass an edict about traitors to make their end less severe. It is enough, surely, that they are dead, without doing as we do and chopping them into pieces. Men do not need a piece of a man fastened to the town gate or a post on the village green to deter them from—"

"You are making me feel sick," Alex answered.

So Everard would go off on a new tack. "I will pass other edicts, many of them, but they will do no good unless the Prince is bound by them too. If I had stayed in Falleyfell, as I had ordered everyone else, then I would not be here. It was meant to be such a clever edict, Alex, since it was supposed to make people show respect for my father by keeping at home, but it was really meant to let us know who was aiding Robert. People were too clever for us, though. Half Gairne went to Robert's camp at Perland, but they all had urgent business there. It was only I who was caught."

Alex said: "Would you have been caught if you had your own soldiers with you? How did you come to have Towerwood's men? That must have made it easy for him."

Everard blushed. "I was an arrant fool. My men were so aston-ished when I ordered them to put you in the library, that I was afraid they would not obey when I asked them to break the edict. And I knew that Towerwood's men had a name for secrecy."

"So you asked Towerwood for them?" said Alex. "That was plumb daft, Everard. And what made you have me put in the library? Was it that picture?"

Everard, still blushing, went to rub more straw in his hair and then thought better of it. "I thought it would keep you angry," he admitted. "And I hoped you would find the library more interesting than a dungeon. Surely you did if this dun-geon is any guide?"

"Yes, I did. You have some fine things there."

They talked of the library for a little, until Everard thought of another castle in the air. "Endwait," he said. "I must search out some deserving man and give the land to him. Robert does not need it. Towerwood had no claim to it at all. I am sure he only disputed it with Robert to make my father come here to be killed. The walled garden makes a very good place for a killing. I—"

"Does it really belong to Robert?" Alex interrupted. "Because *he* ought to give it to the deserving person if it does."

"No," said Everard. "It is very obscure, his claim. Endwait shall be forfeit to the sovereign, I here proclaim. Now, here is another castle—"

Alex groaned. This went on for hours, until the sun moved away from the grating and left them in cold twilight. No one brought any more food. Alex began to realize that what had come that morning was to be their day's ration. He saw that they really would starve on that amount. Last night's food, it seemed, was just an extra, to show them what to expect. At length Alex became so hungry that he helped Everard build castles in the air. It was better than thinking of tomorrow's crust. The two of them passed upwards of a hundred imaginary laws and governed the Principality in the strictest justice. Everard came to his hundred-and-twentieth edict.

"This concerns the trial of anyone accused," he said. "They must be brought to trial as soon as possible—as I should have brought Robert to trial—within the week. I shall appoint a justice—good heavens, Alex! This means I must try *you*. Did you not claim the coronet the day of my father's funeral?"

"No, I did not," said Alex.

"Yes, you did. And you blacked my eye in support of your claim."

Alex realized they would be fighting again in a minute. He did his best to explain that his island did not seem to be the same as Everard's—and he plainly puzzled Everard exceedingly. Everard shook his head.

"I believe you—partly because I cannot understand you. My castle is not ruined, and if yours is, then they are not the same, but how can this be?"

"I have no idea. I was as puzzled as you were. People around us see your people sometimes and call them ghosts."

"But we are not. How can a ghost starve—and I *am* starving, are not you?"

Alex, in order not to think of starving, was brought to something he knew he should have come to before. "I know you are not ghosts, and I know your island is different and I apologize for fighting you about it. I did not know it was your father's funeral. That makes it all the worse. The truth is I was angry with some other people I know and I took it out on you."

Everard laughed. "You too? I would have been more polite to you if I had not been so angry with Robert. He came to the funeral, you see, wearing the Gairne orange in place of black, and tried to plead his cause. And I was so angry at his lack of respect that I ordered him off and sent Darron and March to take him prisoner. I never dreamed he would cross the bay by daylight. We never do. And once in the open, he easily outrode them. And I was ready to do murder, I was so angry when it was found he had gone. So I am sorry too."

Alex held out his hand to Everard. Everard had just taken it, when the chains on the door began to rattle. This time it was the whole door and not the hatch which was being opened. Everard hung onto Alex's hand with both his.

"And I said you should wait till your dying day for my apology! Pray God I am no prophet!"

Chapter 4

PISTOL

Luckily, Everard was not a prophet. It was Harry and Susannah on the other side of the door, but it had taken them some time to get there, and some time to get over the shock of their arrest.

"Turn this way," said Lord Darron. "I have business at Endwait which will admit of no delay. We must have some talk over your case later, when my business is done."

Harry wondered if he dared refuse. He had thoughts of presenting his pistol at Lord Darron's steel helmet and demanding their freedom. Lord Darron, however, had taken Susannah's bridle, and Harry was afraid she might be hurt if he became violent. He shrugged his shoulders and thought that this was anyhow one way to see the valley. If they were clever, they might learn something of Alex. He decided that it would be best to seem very meek and harmless. That way, they might avoid being locked up too.

To his alarm, Susannah was looking anything but meek. She was red with anger and mortification and actually crying a little. When Harry made no attempt to use his pistol, she turned and made violent pointings at it. Harry shook his head and, as they came out into the valley, Susannah was crying great shaking sobs of rage.

"My dear young lady," said Lord Darron, blinking down at her, "you must not cry. I assure you I will not harm you."

Susannah was so angry at being misunderstood that her sobs changed almost into screams. She had her whip lifted up to hit this impossible false St. George.

"Susannah!" said Harry.

Lord Darron smiled. Susannah could not bear that nervous smiling face in the middle of all that warlike armor. She slashed at it. Lord Darron took the whip as it came down and gently pulled it away. Susannah, who was a very good horsewoman, nearly fell, simply from anger. Harry wished he could pretend he had nothing to do with her.

"Now, now," said Lord Darron. "You are beside yourself, my dear. Pray pull yourself together and ride faster. I am in a hurry. I have to find the Prince."

"The Prince!" exclaimed Harry as they crackled along past the first houses of the village. "Prince Everard, is that?"

"That is he," said Lord Darron, "and I hope I am not too late."

The lines of bare orchard trees seemed to spin round Harry at this. "I hope so too, sir. We are looking for the Prince as well."

"And I do not think he is on your side," Susannah said.

"What are you going to do? I think you are a very wicked—"

"Do be quiet!" Harry snapped. Susannah stopped at once, she was so unused to Harry talking to her so angrily. Harry managed to get his horse out ahead of Lord Darron's and stand across his road—at least, it was a street here, in the middle of Endwait village. People in the houses opened doors and peered from windows at the sight of my Lord Darron stopped in the road with his sword drawn, facing a young Outsider who was threatening him with the strangest of weapons and all unarmed otherwise.

"Put your sword away, sir," said Harry. "If I pull this trigger, you will be dead before you can move. I am not lying. Now, will you please explain what you said just now of the Prince."

"Willingly," said Lord Darron. "I do not require your threats, my lord. I learned some while back from a dying soldier of Towerwood's—who astonished me, I admit, by confessing to have a bad conscience—that Prince Everard is confined in a dungeon here at Endwait. Now may we ride on? You can see how people are staring."

"Let them," said Harry. "Did this soldier mention Alex Hornby?"

"Yes," said Lord Darron. "He is with the Prince. Most unwise, I would have thought it, if the Prince is mad."

"From what we heard," said Susannah, who was not able to keep out of a conversation for long, "I would say the Prince is no madder than I am." She realized from Lord Darron's face that he was carefully not saying that this might not be very sane. She would have stamped her foot if it had not been in her stirrup.

What Lord Darron actually said was very polite. "I too have had my doubts about the Prince's madness. I am not one of those who ever feared much for the poor boy's reason, and therefore I am going to see. But when I said I hoped I was not too late, I had in mind the fact that Prince Everard's father was killed here in Endwait, a mere fortnight ago. There seems something more than a coincidence here, does there not?"

"There *is* more," said Harry. "I think we had better ride on, sir. Will you give me your word not to attempt to lock us up?"

"I cannot do that," said Lord Darron, not defiantly, but with a blink and an apologetic smile, "until I find how things stand. Will you agree to an armed truce, my lord? I promise not to lock you up at least until the Prince is found. Please move from the road. We shall be the talk of the Principality as it is, and I had hoped to be secret."

Harry looked around and saw the open doors and the faces at windows. They embarrassed him. It was as if he and Lord Darron were a puppet show. And, of course, they could all be thinking (like the man at Arnforth) that he was mad. He turned and rode on quickly, calling out "Armed truce it is, sir," over his shoulder. Lord Darron and Susannah followed, up a hill past the church, under wide bare chestnut trees, and into the black wood around the Endwait manor house.

The drawbridge was up, blocking the gateway. The moat was only frozen at the edges, so it could not be crossed except by the bridge. A thick and unfriendly looking man was leaning out of the window above the gateway, chewing something and watching them ride up.

"Lower the bridge, there," called Lord Darron. "I have business with the steward."

"What business?" asked the man, and spat what he was chewing into the moat.

Lord Darron was so much put out at this that he stammered. "Poor man," thought Susannah. "He *is* as nervous as he looks. Not a very good St. George at all." Then she had an inspiration. "Lord Darron," she whispered, "say you want to lock us in the dungeon with Alex."

Lord Darron looked at Harry. "But I—"

"Say it, sir. It will get us in."

So Lord Darron cleared his throat and called out what his business was in a clear and threatening way, which made Susannah very nervous. She was afraid she had put ideas into his head. The man above growled and went away inside. After a good five minutes, they heard men talking inside the window and the drawbridge at last came clanking down. An old, ribby oak door beyond was pushed creaking open. Susannah shivered at the sight of the dark way in.

Lord Darron, as he moved toward the drawbridge, spoke to Harry—rather cleverly, Susannah thought—disguising what he said by singing it to a strange flat tune. "Have ready your strange weapon, my lord. We may need it, although I mistrust it much. There is a prophecy—tra-la-la—which has it that our realm shall be ended by outlandish weapons. Tra-dah-liddle-diddle-da." The last part of the tune came echoing back at them, mixed with the ringing of hoofs as Lord Darron went in under the archway.

Susannah's pony, which distrusted the drawbridge as much

as she did, scuttled over after him. Harry cocked his pistol again and came last on the creaking, clanking boards of the bridge. Inside, in the tiny courtyard, he found Lord Darron already talking to the steward.

The steward was a thick sulky man and, like the guard at the gate, he was chewing something, with his arms rudely folded.

"The drawbridge is down. You can ride out again, my lord," he said.

"Not until we have seen the Prince," said Lord Darron.

"You cannot see him."

"I demand to."

The steward sighed, not a polite sigh. It was meant to show that Lord Darron was a fool who was boring him stiff. "I cannot think what the Count was at, telling you of all people that the Prince is here. What do you think you are at, too, entering this manor on false pretences? You may not see the Prince. He is mad. Straw in his hair, see." As he said that, the steward put both hands to his head, pointing upward and waggling his fingers. Susannah had never seen anything so rude.

"You abominable man!" she said.

"You are a low knave," said Lord Darron. "Show me the Prince before I show you my sword with your blood on it."

The steward grinned. "Show me what you like." Then he looked up with a whistle and a nod. Soldiers and serving-men came running from doorways where they must have been waiting, carrying swords, carving knives, pokers, and axes. They stood round the three riders panting, looking up at them and grinning, for all the world, Susannah thought, like a pack of mongrel dogs who had treed three cats.

"Harry!" she said.

"Now," said the steward, "my fine lord, you can ride back over yon drawbridge or there will be murder and maiming done."

Lord Darron was looking completely helpless. Susannah was terrified. Harry knew that he would have to use his pistol. But he had only six bullets and he could not bear to kill, or even wound anyone.

"We are not going away," he said, and he had to shout in order to make himself talk at all. "We do not leave until we see the Prince. Show us the Prince or I will shoot you all with this pistol."

"Shoot!" said the steward sneeringly. "Pistol! Is that a sawn-off spade you have there, my lord?"

Harry was so angry with him that he raised the pistol and pulled the trigger. Susannah screamed—to encourage him, she said afterward. The bang was deafening in the tiny courtyard. Half the men dropped their weapons and backed away. The steward roared with pain and clapped his hand to his left ear. Harry was so angry that he hoped he had shot it off. In fact, he had only grazed it, but the sight of blood running between the steward's fingers was enough for most of the men.

"*Sorcery!*" they yelled, and ran clattering away through the archway and over the drawbridge.

A few of the soldiers stayed where they were. One or two pretended to smile, but when Harry swung the pistol around to point at them they turned and ran like rabbits.

Lord Darron reached down and caught the steward by the hair as he tried to run away too. Susannah admired him more than ever for that, because his horse was trampling this way and that in terror at the noise. "Not you," he shouted. "You come with us. You have the keys." He called out to Harry: "Shoot him again if he shows any sign of treachery."

"I will," said Harry. He dismounted and handed his reins to Susannah. Then he walked slowly and fiercely up to the steward with his pistol pointing at the man's terrified face. "Where is this dungeon? You go first, and if you dare attempt any treachery—"

Lord Darron landed beside him with a crash of plate armor. "Give the keys here, man."

The steward unhooked a great bunch of keys and handed them to Lord Darron. Harry thought he had never ever seen a man so frightened as that steward. His face was yellow, like a candle, among the streaks of blood. And he agreed afterward with Susannah that Lord Darron showed not the slightest sign of fear.

They went down to the dungeon, and among their ringing footsteps Harry could hear the steward's teeth chattering. They let him unlock the first door. Susannah, who was expecting to find the dungeon beyond, was frightened and disappointed to find only more stairs.

"I will stay by this door," said Lord Darron. "We do not want it treacherously bolted on us." He stood leaning on the door, and Harry thought, from the way he could see the white of the steward's eyes, that this was just what the man had hoped to do. He dug him in the neck with the pistol.

"Go on."

Susannah was horrified by the second door. It was so low and narrow and thickly barred. "Oh, poor Alex!" It was she who had to undo the chains and bolts, for Harry was guarding the steward. But there was a padlock she could not unlock, and Harry had to help her. The moment he moved, the steward ran away upstairs. Harry fired at him, wildly and dangerously, for the bullet hit the stone ceiling and bounced back almost in his own face. The steward screamed, and was suddenly quiet as he met Lord Darron's sword.

Inside the dungeon, they heard Harry fire. From there it was muffled and horrible.

"Alex," said Everard, "if this is our last hour, I am sorry I said I disliked you. I do not think it was true."

"We were just furious with one another," said Alex. "How do they put people to death here?"

"Various ways. Nobility are beheaded. I shall insist they behead you too. You must not be hanged."

Then the door opened and Alex saw the last people he would ever have expected to see: Harry Courcy leaning anxiously in with the pistol smoking in his hand, and Susannah picking up her skirts and jumping down into the dungeon. She ran up to Alex and flung her arms around him. Alex was so astonished that he looked at Everard and roared with laughter.

"Oh, Alex, dear! Have they hurt you?" Susannah said. "Are you all right? Why! You have a great bump on your forehead!" She let Alex go and marched up to Everard. "Did you hit him, you wicked, vicious boy?"

"Yes, my lady," Everard said.

"Then you are a great cowardly bully! You are twice his size!" Susannah was shaking her fist. Alex was afraid she would hit Everard.

"Be quiet, Susannah," he said. "You can say things like that to me if you like, but you have no business to say them to Everard. He is not a coward or a bully, and besides he must be related to you far back. He has an ancestor called Eleanor de Courcy."

Harry jumped down into the dungeon too. "Really?" he said. "Five hundred years ago? The one who was said to be drowned in the quicksands? Are you Prince Everard? Then I am very pleased to meet you, Your Highness. We have a message from a lady—she must be your mother I think. She has gone to the nuns at Uldrim."

"Praised be!" said Everard. "Then she cannot be married to Towerwood. Alex, I am so relieved."

They all four milled about in the straw for a minute or so longer, Alex introducing the Courcys and the Courcys explaining why they came. And Alex found, in spite of his relief at being rescued, that he was not as glad as he might have been. "Now," he thought, "the Courcys and Everard will get on together splendidly. They are the same kind of people. I shall be nowhere."

Then he found Susannah looking up at him, in tears. "Alex," she said, "I am so sorry. Please forgive me for all the horrid things I said to you. I did not mean them, truly. Ask your friend the Prince to forgive me too. I dare not." Then she smudged at her face with her sleeve. "Have you a handkerchief, please?"

Alex gave her his own grubby handkerchief and Susannah sniffed miserably into it. He could hardly believe she had had a change of heart, but he tried to be kind to her. He was so unused to being nice to Susannah that he did not know where to begin. He settled for saying: "It does not matter, Susannah. I am sure Everard does not mind."

Then the lordly Harry thumped him on the back. "Alex, we have been worried sick about you. I—I am so sorry for—that time. And we have not found Cecilia. Do you know where she is?"

"Alex," said Everard, "let us climb out of this dungeon. We must find your sister—she could be still at Falleyfell—and I must see Robert, if he is to be found."

Alex was astonished and pleased and ashamed of himself. Here had the Courcys come all this way to rescue him and he was not being grateful enough. Here they were both apologizing, and he was being gruff; and here he was expecting Everard to take to the Courcys when in fact they were all three of them deferring to him, as if he were a cross between their leader and their interpreter.

Lord Darron was standing in the doorway. "My lord," he said to Everard, "will you climb out? This is a noisesome place for a Prince, whether he be mad or sane."

"He is not mad," Alex said. "That is Towerwood put that about. Nor do I claim the coronet. Everard understands that now. It was a mistake."

Lord Darron smiled, blinked, and held down a hand each to Alex and Everard. "Come up, both of you. I never thought you claimed the coronet, sir. Your face is too honest."

Alex and the Prince scrambled out of the dungeon past Lord Darron and stood smiling delightedly at one another. As Lord Darron was helping Susannah out, they both began talking at once.

"Darron, where is Robert, my cousin Howeforce? I want to—"

"Please, sir, have you any news of my sister?"

Lord Darron put Susannah gently down between them. "There, young lady. You have done famously for one so young. As to your questions, both of them have the same answer. Howeforce is defeated and flying for his life, I fear, together with the young lady. Towerwood is close after them. Indeed, he might have caught them by now."

PART IV

※※

CECILIA'S
LAST
RIDE

※※

Chapter 1
HUNT

Now we come to Cecilia and how she was probably very foolish. The first thing she did when the outlaws appeared at the top of the cliff was to hang onto Lord Tremath's foot again, as if by doing that she could somehow stop his whole army. The outlaws were all standing where they were with no triumph left in them. Most of them suddenly looked tired out, particularly Robert. He rode slowly toward Lord Tremath and his squire, who were both smiling. Cecilia felt like giving Lord Tremath's foot a hearty tug, she thought it so mean of him to smile.

"I know the Perland caves like the back of my hand, Robert," said the squire.

"So I see," said Robert. "My lord, I must beg you to let no harm come to Cecilia. May I implore you not to hand her over to Conrad of Towerwood, whatever you do to the rest of us?"

Cecilia was so touched by this that she must indeed have

tugged Lord Tremath's foot. He looked down at her in surprise. "Where is the Prince, Robert?" he said. "I must know that before I make another move in this affair."

"I do not know, my lord. He is not with us, nor with Towerwood, and Towerwood came upon us before my spies returned from Gairne."

"You sent to Gairne!" exclaimed the squire. "Then has Towerwood—?" Cecilia, looking up at him, decided that he must be Lord Tremath's son. He had the same gray eyes.

"I will trust you, Robert," Lord Tremath interrupted. "I will take no part in this battle. And, since time is short, tell me what you wish me to do."

Cecilia saw that Robert was amazed. "Thank you, my lord," he said. Lord Tremath smiled at him. The squire laughed and, as soon as he really believed them, Robert laughed as well. Rupert Lord Strass came up beside him, laughing too, and they began to talk together hurriedly, not needing to say much, as if they knew one another very well.

"I think," Cecilia thought, "they must all have been great friends before the Prince was killed." She stood low down in the midst of them, still in danger of being trampled on, and was just able to see the other outlaws coming clustering around, listening and smiling. Soldiers in Lord Tremath's army were waving to them and calling out jokes. Cecilia could have cried with delight.

The squire leaned forward to Lord Strass. "Rupert," he said anxiously, "is James dead?"

"No, but he needs care at once. Ralph, could you ask your father—?"

Lord Tremath looked at James of March hanging over

Rupert's horse. "We must take James then. You too, Rupert, I think. We shall call you hostage. We will take all those on foot and the wounded. Ralph must see them safely to Tremath. The rest must fend for themselves. Do you agree, Robert? I shall not let Towerwood near them, and I will suspend justice until the Prince is found. I myself will go to Gairne and enquire for him."

"Cecilia," said Robert, "you must go to Tremath with Ralph." He was bending down, smiling at her, and Cecilia looked up regretfully, afraid he would be killed. His eyes were black. She had never seen eyes so dark and likeable, and she could not bear never to see them again.

Then Tom came bursting through the outlaws beside her with blood on his beard and his orange livery hacked with sword cuts. "My lords, I don't know what ye decide among ye, but Towerwood found the secret passages. Half on his men be coming up them. The rest on 'em be a-riding around the valley to come up here."

"Then quick, Robert," said Lord Tremath. "I can do nothing for you until I know the Prince's will. You must ride away."

The outlaws ran and rode backwards here and there to give Robert a path. His great blue horse turned around, willing but weary, and horse and rider seemed to Cecilia to be lost already, surrounded in foggy breath—their own and that of the people crowding away from them.

It was then that Cecilia was foolish. She ran after Robert screaming: "Take me too. Please, Robert, do not leave me behind!" Robert stopped and looked down at her as if he simply did not know what to say. Cecilia knew she was embarrassing him again, but she did not care. "Please!" she said. She knew he would have to say no. She knew the Tremaths, the outlaws, and all the army were staring, but she was too far gone in foolishness to care.

"I will take you if you wish," Robert said, "but you will be safer with Ralph."

Cecilia was so astonished at what he said that she had not the presence of mind to refuse. She knew she should have pretended to change her mind so that he could hurry away, but she was foolish still. "I do not want to be safe," she said. "Let me ride behind you."

Robert held down one hand to help her mount. He did not seem in the least angry, or worried that his horse would have so much more work to do.

"Wait," said Ralph of Tremath. Cecilia turned and saw him coming off his own great eager horse. "My horse is fresh," he said. "He can more easily take two than yours." He stood smiling and offering Cecilia his reins and Cecilia remembered him like that gratefully for the rest of her life. He had one of the brightest, sweetest smiles she had ever seen, and his hair was bright red-brown. He was a year younger than she was then, but he lived to a great old age and was the great-grandfather of Edward the Unlucky.

In a few seconds, Robert and Cecilia were away. For a moment, Ralph of Tremath was beside them on Robert's horse, saying: "We will delay him as long as we can. Trust my father, Robert." Then he had turned aside and the great horse was rushing downhill alone, making an icy wind and smashing the hard crust of the snow with its huge feet. Behind them, the outlaws and the army gave a cheer. Cecilia, with her fingers twisted in Robert's orange cloak, looked back and saw them all watching, but as she looked, they turned away and went crowding up to the cliff edge. She saw men in Towerwood's livery climbing up beside them. Looking further around, she saw a line of black riders galloping up the hill from the open end of the valley.

Robert looked over his shoulder too. "Have they seen us?"

"No," shouted Cecilia. The men were all hurrying to the top of the cliff, obviously sure that Tremath had caught the outlaws. None of them looked their way. She turned to look forward and hoped that Lord Tremath and his son would be able to keep the Hornets safe from Towerwood, when Towerwood discovered they had let Robert go. Maybe there would be another battle—between Towerwood and Tremath this time.

The horse turned slightly to the right. Robert had moved into the wide trampled track which the Tremath army had made marching from the direction of the coast. They followed this for a long way, with their own hoof marks almost hidden in it, until they reached a road. The army had come along the road, from the left, and again they followed the mass of deep blue prints.

"I hope," Robert called over to Cecilia, "I hope they will think we have gone to Tremath. We will turn off soon."

They turned off when there was a lane leading south again over the hills. Several horses had gone that way before them, and again their prints were almost hidden. By this time the horse was blowing and Robert let it walk for a space. There was a farm at the end of the lane.

"They are friendly here," Robert said. "We shall get something to eat. You must be hungry, Cecilia."

"So must you," said Cecilia, realizing that the outlaws must have been attacked before they had a chance to eat breakfast.

Robert laughed. "I could eat this horse—except that we would never reach the Forest if I did. I think we must go to the Forest. It is full of hiding places. Everard has a hunting lodge there which I think we can make use of. Something tells me that if ever the Prince gets out of Towerwood's hands, he will not blame me. I wish we could do more than hope Tremath can find him."

"And we cannot?" Cecilia asked, thinking of Alex.

The horse stopped in the middle of the farmyard. Robert turned round, looking very sad and serious. "My dear Cecilia, it is possible we cannot save even ourselves. You must promise me, now, before we dismount, that you will run or ride away if I tell you to."

"Because I am an Outsider? Yes, Robert, I promise." Cecilia slid down the warm dampish side of the horse and stood in the snow, feeling very small and melancholy.

Robert dismounted too. "Not only because you are an Outsider," he said sadly, "but because Towerwood is utterly ruthless. Do you know, Cecilia, he stood before his whole army and told me he had forced my poor mother to take poison? A man who can do that can do anything."

"Oh, Robert!" said Cecilia.

The farmer came striding over on the slippery snow just then. "We hear that news too, my lord," he said. "Best come inside, but we cannot have ye for long. Had orders again not to give ye help this morning." Cecilia thought he did not look the kind of man who would willingly help anyone. He was tall and yellow and surly. She supposed at first that Robert must have paid him a great deal of money to be his ally; but, when they came inside into a warm white-washed kitchen, and the farmer's wife and children came excitedly around, she realized she was wrong. The farmer was Tom's cousin and very glad to hear he was still alive. They were given breakfast, a homely ordinary breakfast which, apart from there being no tea, was very like the supper she and Alex had given Robert a fortnight before. She was sure Robert was remembering that, because he seemed embarrassed again.

It was here that they heard the story of the Prince being mad.

"Heard say last night," said the farmer. "Messenger from Towerwood to Tremath. Telling everyone the Prince were mad."

Robert stood up from the table so indignantly that the farmer's youngest little girl began to cry. Cecilia hurriedly coaxed her to stop, not knowing what to think, except that she was terrified for Alex.

"*Everard!*" said Robert. "That old wives' story again! Will you all do me the kindness to contradict it whenever you hear it. It is much more likely the poor boy is dead. Everard flies into rages because he is an only son and somewhat spoiled. He will grow out of that. It means nothing that his mother and father are first cousins. I will *not* have old women shaking their heads and talking of madness. As if any Prince has ever been mad!"

"Aye, my lord," said the farmer's wife, "we'll give them the lie, never fear. Ye need madness in the family if it's to take them this young, and we know there be none. Why else do they say in times of trouble that all are mad save the Prince alone?"

"And if Everard lives, he will prove that saying true," Robert answered. "Come, Cecilia."

They rode on again, this time boldly across country. The sun was well up now and the land glittered yellow and blue until Cecilia's eyes ached. Beside them, the powdery snow flew up from under its hard crust in winking rainbows like a shower of ground diamonds. Cecilia rode astride, which was a great deal easier, and almost enjoyed herself. But whenever she felt too happy she made herself look over her shoulder at the bare rolling hills to see if Towerwood was following yet. She knew he would follow and hunt them down. Their position was nearly as hopeless as it could be. They would be tracked from place to place in the snow until they were run to earth.

"Robert," she said, "why do you not come Outside again with me?"

She saw Robert hump his shoulders as he thought about it. "From habit, I think," he answered. "But I will, as a last resort. Let us see what happens."

A little after this, they took to a lane again to disguise their trail. Around a corner, between high bare hedges, they met a man, an odd, wild, ragged person with great long legs. His toes would have trailed in the snow on either side of his donkey if he had not kept his feet bent awkwardly backward. Robert reined in. Cecilia peered around him at the wild man's thin face, which was much the shape of the sole of a boot. He looked up at her, as interested as she was, and smoothed his straggling steel-colored hair in her honor. It was Robert he spoke to.

"They are following you, my lord."

"How near are they?" Robert asked.

The man stuck out his chin, the toe of his boot-face, and seemed to be watching something in the air. "Catching up, my lord. You have five miles or so to play with. They have blood-hounds with them."

"Thank you, Aaron," Robert answered and sounded very dismayed. "Then I need your advice. What shall I do with Cecilia?"

"Take her. You will need her help. Go south to the lands Outside where you are both safe. I need not tell you to find a river, my lord, to throw the dogs off the scent."

"No," said Robert. "You need not." He began to ride on, but the man held out one long arm to stop him.

"I wish I had met you before," he said. "The Prince is at Endwait, in a dungeon, I think."

"Endwait! What barbarity! We will go there, then."

The man shook his wild head. "You will not get there. My Lord March and his men are returning along the Endwait road. Go southwest, through the Forest. I will go to Endwait. Farewell."

Robert rode much faster after that. Cecilia had to shout against the wind when she wanted to talk to him.

"Who was that man? How did he know we are being followed with dogs?"

"He is a wandering magician, a seer, and a teller of tales. If he offers advice unasked, as he did then, what he says is true." Then they rode for some miles before Robert spoke again. "Endwait!" he said. "Everard's father was killed there. That is cruel."

By this time they were down from the hills. The lands around were cultivated. The snow was in ribs along plowed fields, with farms and cottages and ever more trees. Cecilia thought they must be coming to the Forest. Robert surprised her by telling her they were already in it.

"It becomes thicker in the south," he said. "Here is another river." He was finding every stream and river that he could and riding down or up them to cover their trail. The long edge of Cecilia's habit was soaked with the splashing. They rode straight, otherwise, sometimes right beside farmyards. When people were about they stared, shading their eyes, but then usually they smiled and waved as they saw the Gairne orange.

The sun began to set. Cecilia was frozen and tired by then but she had still to endure the Forest. It was thick around them at last and the snow was thinner and damper under the bare branches. Cecilia found it terrifying. It was so black and white and so quiet. Everywhere she looked white arcades of snow wound away between black trees, and every noise was too loud. Their hoofs seemed to break the forest open with their din and yet she could hear every slight creeping rustle, every creaking branch, and every cry of every bird. A train of black things went rushing away to one side and she had to hang onto Robert for fear she should faint with horror. Robert started as well, but he said calmly: "Those were deer. This is Everard's Ride and they are the Prince's game."

"I—I see," said Cecilia. She wished they could ride as fast as the deer ran. Their horse was going slowly now. It was tired out and Robert was avoiding trees only by dragging its head away from them. They wound on, from glade to glade, down rides and past black holly-brakes. Cecilia took each bush for a monster, or worse, for a cluster of Towerwood's men.

"Did you hear that?" said Robert. The horse stopped. Cecilia heard, in the empty soundless space, dogs baying, not far away.

This time she was too frightened even to think of fainting.

"Cecilia," said Robert, "you must ride away now. I will get down and chance my luck on foot."

"No," said Cecilia. "I will not. How can I ride away now when I have come so far? I have held you up by my foolishness. You could have been Outside by now if I had not slowed the horse down. The least I can do is stay."

"You promised me, Cecilia."

"That was this morning."

There were sounds, a long way over to the right. Men were moving through the woods, slowly, calling out to one another as they went. Robert said: "*Now* will you ride away?" and slid off the horse. Cecilia, clutching his cloak, slid off too and came thumping down on her knees. Robert picked her up with a jerk. He was annoyed, and Cecilia knew he had every right to be angry with her, but she was still foolish.

"Let me come too," she begged.

Far over on the left, there came another crowd of men. These had lights, flaring and jerking from tree to tree.

"It is too late now for you to do anything else," said Robert. "We will leave the horse, since he might throw the dogs off our scent, and maybe we can slip between them on foot. But you must do exactly as I tell you."

"Yes," said Cecilia, very meek now she had won.

They began walking softly from tree to tree. Robert whispered that a sudden rush would give them away, since the men would looking for that. So they went slowly and steadily one behind the other, while to the right and left, the men walked level with them. Cecilia heard the commands called. She saw their dark shapes, flickering as trees came between her and them, and she saw more and more of those flaring lights. There were lights behind, too, and more commands. The dogs were there, behind them. Cecilia knew they would be seen any moment, or their footprints. She herself, in her lavender blue, did not stand out much against the snow, but Robert's orange seemed to glow more brilliantly with every second the light faded.

From behind, there was a sudden terrible barking and yelling.

"They have found the horse," Robert whispered. "But the hunting lodge is very near. If we can reach that we can hide there easily."

Cecilia knew it was hopeless. They had seen their footprints and were coming faster, shouting hunting cries as if she and Robert had been beasts. The men on either side were moving inwards toward them, calling across to one another. And there were men in front of them now. Cecilia guessed that these must have been to the hunting lodge and were now coming back to the others. Everyone seemed to have lanterns or naked torches. There were lights all around. She could see faces, spearheads, and shining breastplates. She and Robert stopped by a tree and waited. There was nothing else they could do.

"Robert," said Cecilia bravely, "I am sorry. This is my fault. I am sorry I embarrassed you by coming too."

"I am glad you are here," Robert answered. "And remember that if you had not come I would have ridden my own horse, which would have been foundered by now."

"But I made a scene," Cecilia whispered. She felt she must talk in order not to think of the closing circle of soldiers. They were very near now.

"Not really," Robert answered. Then he laughed. "But you

468 · Unexpected Magic

surprised us all. Now, tell me, Cecilia—I must know, even if it is only to die with the knowledge—why do you always go out of your way to remind me of your humble origins? Why do you insist on being no lady?"

"Because I—because of my father and the Courcys."

"Who are the Courcys?"

As the men steadily closed in, Cecilia talked, very hurriedly, to get it all in before the end, and told him how she and Alex felt about the Courcys. Before she had finished she could actually see Towerwood himself, walking under a streaming flare, with a bloodhound stretching its leash in front of him.

"I see," said Robert. "You have explained more than you knew, Cecilia. You make me almost able to forgive Towerwood, because I think his family have felt similarly toward the Counts of Gairne. And, Cecilia, if we are anything to judge by, then the Courcys cannot be as black as you have painted them." As he said this, he drew his sword, quietly and calmly.

"No," Cecilia admitted. "They are not black at all, really."

Conrad of Towerwood saw them as she spoke. He stopped, and the shout he gave to stop his soldiers was a fierce as a tiger's roar. There was such horrible triumph in it that Cecilia forgot the Courcys and her father and even Alex.

The soldiers stood around in a close ring while Towerwood handed the bloodhound's leash to someone else and stepped forward.

"Well, Howeforce, I have you at last. Give me your sword."

"Who comes to take it, Towerwood?"

Towerwood folded his arms. "Not I, my lord." Then he jerked his head at the circle of soldiers. "Disarm him. Tie him to that tree."

Twenty soldiers rushed forward. Cecilia was suddenly engulfed in a crowd of hard bodies, grim dark faces and flashing sword blades. She screamed. A soldier tried to push her out of the way and that reminded her what Tom had said of Outsiders. She rushed in among them, then, fighting and punching her way toward Robert.

"Mind out! Don't you dare kill me! I am an Outsider! Out of my way!"

They let her through. Swords were hurriedly snatched away as she struggled past. She reached Robert. He was against a tree and without his sword now, but he had a dagger. He snatched that out of her way as she came.

"I shall embarrass you again," Cecilia shrieked, almost laughing. "I am hysterical," she thought, "like Charlotte Courcy." She put her arms round Robert and screamed over her shoulder at the soldiers: "You dare touch him now. Kill me and see what happens!"

They stood back a little, doubtfully. Robert said sadly, "It will not last, Cecilia. You will only get hurt."

Towerwood was shouting: "You fools! Pull that girl away."

Nobody did, to Cecilia's surprise. The soldiers did not seem to know what to do. Then Towerwood himself came, pushing his men aside. He took Cecilia by her shoulders and wrenched her away. As he carried her back past the soldiers, he commanded: "Now tie him up." They had already bustled forward before he spoke. Robert was tied to the tree when Cecilia flung back her hair and looked.

"Now, Howeforce," said Towerwood, "you shall die by inches. Every soldier will throw a spear or a dagger at you, but I shall have the final thrust."

Robert did not answer. The soldiers came slowly nearer, some drawing daggers, some testing spear edges on their hands. Cecilia screamed. She raged. She was angrier than she had ever been in her life. She twisted out of Towerwood's hands and turned on him. Most of him was hateful hard armor, but she could reach his fat cruel face. She hit him and scratched him, she pulled his hair and she called him names. He tried to push her away, calling out to the soldiers to stop her, but none of them moved a finger to help him. Perhaps they thought Towerwood should be able to manage a mere girl on his own, or perhaps they were glad to see their leader getting something of what he deserved. Whatever it was, they did not move.

"You great *toad*!" Cecilia screamed.

"Throw your spears—at Howeforce!" shouted Towerwood. "Confound you, girl!" With that, he managed to gather both Cecilia's wrists in one hand. "You will pay for this, you thing from a gutter!"

Chapter 2
KILL

Everard wanted to go and find Robert at once. "Towerwood must be stopped," he said.

But Lord Darron and Susannah had discovered that he and Alex had eaten next to no food for more than twenty-four hours. They would not hear of it.

"You must eat first or you will faint on the way," said Lord Darron.

"Alex would be ill," Susannah told Lord Darron. "He often is."

Everard refused to eat in Endwait Manor. Nobody blamed him, and when they discovered that the stables were empty, they all agreed to go down to the village and find food and horses there. They walked, leading the three horses. Halfway across the drawbridge, Everard stopped.

"Alex," he asked anxiously, "have I any straws in my hair?"

Alex laughed. "One or two." He helped pick them out, but Everard seemed just as anxious when they were gone. "You must not worry, Everard," Alex said. "One has only to look at you to see you are not mad."

They stopped at the first house they came to, a fair-sized cottage set back in a large garden. At the gate was a post with a cartwheel hanging from it, to show that the owner was a wheelwright. Lord Darron opened the gate and started up the neat path between rows of snow-covered cabbages.

"No," said Everard, "I will go on my own. You come if you think I need help."

The people who lived in the house must have been watching, because they came out of the front door as Everard reached it. The man stood in front, and his wife looked nervously at Everard from behind her husband's elbow. Everard bowed politely and began explaining. The wheelwright backed away a little and the woman hid behind him completely.

"Oh, Alex!" said Susannah. "Go and help him out."

"No, wait," said Harry.

The woman ran out from behind the man, made a little curtsey, threw her arms around Everard, and kissed him. Then there was a lot of excited talk between the man and the woman, the woman holding Everard's hand, pointing to him and then to the Manor and then to the others waiting in the road. The man talked to Everard. Finally, Everard turned and beckoned to the others to come. Everyone was smiling. The man himself came and showed them up the garden path.

"You are welcome to all we have to offer," he said.

He turned out to have just the right things to offer, a table ready laid with new loaves, damson jam, and a great fruitcake, and a stable full of handsome horses. They had an excellent meal. Everard chattered and laughed all through. He asked the wheelwright and his wife to eat with them, but they would not.

"I want to see you have a proper meal," the woman said. "And I'll do that best by standing over you, Your Highness. To think of you starving up at the manor and none of us knowing a thing about it!"

The meal was so full of chatter and exclamations like this, that it was a marvel they made any plans, but, somehow, they did. While they were finding out that Towerwood was already proving a mean, grabbing landlord, they were arranging to take a fresh horse each and to leave the Courcys' horses in their place. While Alex explained how he came to be in the dungeon too, Everard was discovering that Lord Tremath had indeed gone to Gairne to look for them. Towerwood had been too anxious to follow Robert to waste time fighting Lord Tremath.

"Then, Darron," he said, "you must find him and tell him to follow us. We shall make for Bress and then Tremath, since Robert went that way. But we shall need men to help us against Towerwood. How glad I am that Tremath has proven such a friend! I thought he was too fond of Robert to be of any help to me."

Lord Darron wanted to take Susannah with him and leave the three boys to find Robert alone, but Susannah was as foolish as Cecilia. As she pointed out, she had come so far without danger that it seemed she would not be harmed. So it was settled. Everard, Alex, Harry, and Susannah mounted the wheelwright's horses and rode out into the cold street again, calling good-bye and thank you as they went. Lord Darron went through the back gate on a shortcut to Gairne over the hills.

Everard and Alex both looked back at the people who had helped them so cheerfully as they stood waving at their gate. The woman had come out in the cold with much too little on in order to say good-bye. Alex thought it would take a great deal to better their ordinary down-to-earth niceness. They reminded him of the Gatlys.

"Alex," said Everard, "what can I give them to reward them, that would not offend them too much? I would like to reward them for *believing* me as much as for their help."

"Why not give them Endwait?" Alex suggested, but he thought as he said it that probably, here, people needed to be noble to own land.

"What an excellent idea!" said Everard. "That is exactly right. They are just the people! Alex, you must be my advisor if we—if we manage this next part successfully."

Harry had been whispering to Susannah meanwhile. Now he rode up beside Everard and shyly held out his pistol. "Your Highness, Susannah and I think you ought to have this. We found out—the lady in the house told us—that no one would dare kill us."

"Thank you," said Everard gravely. "How do I use it?" The three boys rode with their heads together, and Harry and Alex explained about firearms. Alex found the other two still deferred to him, rather than to each other—which was just as well in this case, because he was better than Harry at explaining how things worked.

Susannah trotted impatiently ahead. Around her, the snow in the valley was already pink in the late winter afternoon. They had miles to go and it would be dark in less than two hours.

"Oh, hurry, do!" she called over her shoulder. Then she looked in front again and saw a strange wild man with a face like a boot riding on a donkey much too small for him. "Oh, my *goodness!*"

The man pointed at her. "Eleanor de Courcy lives in you. Am I right?"

Susannah did not quite know what to say. "Well, sir, my name is Susannah Courcy, really—" But Everard came galloping up in a flurry of snow and interrupted her.

"Aaron! Do you have any news? Do you know anything of my cousin Robert?"

Aaron told them how he had met Robert and Cecilia and where he had advised them to go. "But," he said, "they will not reach the lands Outside. Their horse was too laden and already tiring. Towerwood was gaining fast."

"Then," said Everard, "I think I can find them, even if we come too late. Thanks, Aaron. Ask for any gift you like when I come back." Then he said to the others: "We must hurry. Luckily the Forest is not too far from here. I would stake Landerness that Robert has gone to my hunting lodge."

They hurried out of the valley and over the bridge. Then they turned left, into the red sun, and galloped. Alex was so worried about Cecilia that he was angry. He called out from time to time to whichever person happened to be galloping beside him:

"He did not need to take Cecilia! They must both be daft! What was she doing there?"

"Coming along, too, like me," said Susannah. "I would have done the same, if it had been you, Alex."

"Save your breath," said Harry, and grinned to show it was not meant to be rude.

Everard simply shook his head, as worried as Alex.

After that it was all hard riding. They galloped along the road until the hills on either side were lower. Then they came out into the great upper part of the Laisle valley, with fields and farms and woods as far as they could see under the sun. Harry realized that the Principality was not underpopulated at all. Here, it seemed several times more cultivated than around his own Arnforth. He had scarcely time to think this, though, before Everard swung away from this wide land to the left, beside a signpost. Now they rode with the sun shining low across them, toward a black mass of woods in the distance.

It seemed as if the woods came out to meet them. First they passed bushes, then spinneys of beeches, then bigger clumps of woodland, and then a great area where ancient oaks stood here and there as they might in a gentleman's park. There, at last, as the sun was almost down, they entered the thick wood. Trees spun about them as they galloped, falling into new patterns, this way and that, as if they were riding in a black-and-white kaleidoscope. By this time, Susannah, good horsewoman though she was, was almost too tired to keep her seat. Harry, almost as tired, was riding all bunched up, like a bad jockey.

"Do you know what this is called?" Everard said. "This part of the Forest, I mean."

"What?" asked Alex.

"Everard's Ride. After Everard I, who reigned seven hundred years ago. Listen!"

They all stopped and Harry jolted upright, pushing his fingers into his aching eye sockets. They could hear the bloodhounds, far off, giving tongue. If they shut their eyes and listened even harder, they could just hear men shouting.

Everard stretched his arm out, pointing in the direction he thought the sound came from. The others nodded. All of them were used to hunting. Then Everard moved his arm on, pointing beyond the sound, to where he thought the quarry might be. The others nodded again.

"If we go that way," Everard said, "we can expect to come up for the—" Then he stopped, because he had nearly said "kill" and the others all knew he had. "Ride," he said. "Like the wind."

And they rode like the wind. Susannah's dark and Everard's fair hair streamed. They leaped bushes and crashed through brakes. They rode with their faces on their horses' necks under whippy low branches, and they galloped down clear rides as if it was for their own lives they rode. The sun went down and they crashed along by their own and their horses' instinct. The sound of the dogs and the men came closer, converging on the same place for which they rode. Everard put out a hand and caught a half-dead branch. Alex saw him nearly fall, pulling a small stick away to make another weapon. Alex tried to do the same, and almost wrenched his arm from its socket. Harry and Susannah were too tired even to try.

Then they saw lanterns and torches. They heard a horrible yelling, then nothing for a while. Then they heard Towerwood's shout of triumph, echoing around the whole wood. Then Alex heard Cecilia screaming. He hammered his horse with his fist. He and Everard together rushed between the last trees and came upon the backs of all Towerwood's waiting soldiers.

Everard went straight along them, slashing right and left with his stick. "Stand back there! Out of our way!" The soldiers surged aside, running and falling, too surprised to attack him. Alex rushed among then too, and they avoided him, though he hardly noticed them. He could see Cecilia struggling with Towerwood and Robert tied to the tree beyond. Two spears were thrown at Robert as they came, but both stuck in the tree, harmlessly.

"*Stop!*" shouted Everard. "Anyone who raises a finger against Cecilia Hornby or my Lord Howeforce is a dead man. My men have you surrounded. Drop your weapons."

Alex realized that this was the only thing to say. He prayed that the soldiers would believe Everard. Otherwise, they were all as good as dead. Harry, still outside the line of soldiers, felt sick, knowing that he and Susannah were all the army Everard had.

For the moment at least, it worked. Towerwood was staring up at Everard as if he were a ghost, holding Cecilia's wrists as though he had forgotten her. The soldiers turned glumly to one another, muttering. Then first one man, then another, dropped his spear and unbuckled his sword. Everard waited, sitting very proud and high, until weapons were strewn in the snow all round. Then he turned just slightly to call over his shoulder.

"My Lord Henry Courcy, will you be so good as to collect these weapons."

There was an impressed, surprised muttering from the soldiers at the name of Courcy, but Harry shook in his saddle. He knew Everard had gone too far. His name was all very well, but what would the soldiers think when they saw he was only another small boy? Susannah wanted to giggle. She knew it was deadly serious, but she had to put her hands over her mouth in order to hide her laughter.

Harry rode out into the circle of soldiers, with the lanterns lighting him up from beneath, and dismounted to obey orders. To his utter astonishment, no one interfered. He had not met Ralph of Tremath or James of March, or he would have realized that the soldiers were used to boys not much older than he was holding important commands and giving orders to men three times their age. Most of the men obligingly picked up their weapons for him. Two men muzzled the bloodhounds and tied them to a tree. Even the surliest kicked their swords and spears toward him without attempting to stop him.

Conrad of Towerwood, however, suspected him at once, probably more because he was an Outsider than because he was a boy. Towerwood watched Harry for a minute or so, and Alex and Everard watched Towerwood. They could see that he was planning something. At last he seemed to decide what to do.

"You fools!" he called to the soldiers. "The Prince has no more men than these boys. Seize them all, at once."

Everard raised Harry's pistol. "Another word, Towerwood, and I shall shoot you before you can move a muscle."

He should have shot him at once, but Alex could see he was nervous of the strange weapon. Towerwood looked up at him, his fat face all sucked inwards and crafty. Then he jerked Cecilia toward him and crouched down behind her. Cecilia writhed and kicked backward, but it was like being locked in a steel fetter. She could not move.

"I dare you to shoot now," Towerwood called to Everard. And then he shouted to his men. "Seize them, you fools!"

Harry was still collecting weapons. By now he had a stack of them to one side of Towerwood. He expected any second that he would be rushed and overpowered, but not one soldier moved. He looked at what he could see of their faces. They were staring at Towerwood crouched behind Cecilia, at Robert against the tree, and at Everard and Alex. It was as if they had suddenly turned audience at a play.

Everard sighed and handed the pistol to Alex. "It is yours, Alex. You are an Outsider too, and she is your sister. You can shoot if anyone can."

Cecilia leaned forward fiercely, the tears on her face shining in the lantern light and in the moonlight now suddenly streaming through the bare branches overhead. "Shoot him, Alex. Do not think of me. Shoot!"

Susannah called from beyond the soldiers: "Please do what she says, Alex."

But Alex could not, no more than Everard. It was impossible, even if he had been an expert marksman. It was too dark. Towerwood was almost entirely hidden behind Cecilia and Robert was just behind them. If he did not hit Cecilia, he would certainly hit Robert.

"Harry," he called, "take one of those swords and come at him from your side." He pulled his horse around, trying to come at Towerwood sideways on, opposite Harry.

Towerwood had foreseen this. He went scrambling backward, lugging Cecilia, chinking and panting, until he was up against Robert. Alex rode right up to him and fired downward, but it was not he who killed Towerwood. Before he had pulled the trigger, Towerwood sprang up, screaming, with Robert's dagger in his neck. Alex's bullet hit the ground and sent a shower of snow over Towerwood's body and into Harry's face. It could have killed Cecilia, who was lying beside him, in a dead faint for the first time in her life. Robert slashed away the ropes around his legs and picked her up.

The bang terrified the soldiers. They stopped being audience and became actors again. Most of then ran away, straight at Susannah. She fell off her horse and crouched in the snow, crying, expecting them to kill her, but they did not see her. They stopped a few yards further on, shouting: "We yield, we yield," away into the woods.

Those who did not run away came slowly toward Everard and the others, some with daggers, some with spears snatched from Harry's stack, ready to revenge their leader.

"Stop!" said Everard. "Not a step nearer."

They came slowly on, though. They had almost reached Everard's horse, when a crowd of new soldiers descended on them.

"Tremath to the Prince! Yield yourselves prisoner."

Chapter 3
GONE AWAY

The day was saved, thanks to Lord Tremath. They discovered later that he and half his army had been close behind them all the way, so close that Lord Tremath had actually seen them ride into the Forest; but his army had been slowed down by the thick wood and had only just arrived in time.

Lord Tremath *had* gone to Gairne after Robert rode away, only waiting to see his son set off safely for Tremath with all the other outlaws. When he came to Gairne, he questioned Robert's spies and arrested all of Towerwood's people he could lay hands on. The spies knew very little, but by threatening Towerwood's men with the most terrible tortures, he found out enough to guess that Everard was in Endwait. He rode that way immediately, so, of course, Lord Darron missed him and it was Aaron, ambling toward Gairne on his donkey, who told him what had happened. Lord Tremath was exceedingly angry that

Lord Darron had let the four children ride after Towerwood on their own. He walked up and down on the creaking floor of the hunting lodge, telling them over and over again what he thought.

Everard whispered to Alex: "But he would have let his own son do it. Why not us?"

"Because you are the Prince, my lord," said Lord Tremath, overhearing him.

They spent the night at the hunting lodge, which was only a hundred yards away. Cecilia did not come out of her faint until they got there, and all that time Alex was afraid he had killed her, although Robert told him six times that his bullet had missed.

As soon as it was plain that Cecilia was unhurt, Everard took Robert and Alex each by an elbow and pulled them away from her.

"Robert," he said, "I am going to amend two of our laws. I shall abolish the cutting-up of traitors and I shall forbid people to bury suicides in the disgusting way they now do. Will I be right?" He gave Alex's arm a warning twitch as they waited for Robert to answer.

Robert looked sad, sadder and more tired even than Alex had seen him when he first came into their kitchen. He looked from Everard to Alex and then down at the many studs on his sword-belt, and ran his fingers along them. He seemed to be going to speak, and then stopped. Then, suddenly, when Alex thought he was not going to tell them after all, Robert looked at Everard again, as if he were very proud of him.

"Yes, Everard, you will be right. Towerwood had spent the whole night bullying Bertram, and your father and I were trying to calm him in the garden there. Of course, we did not know what Towerwood had said, but we had never seen Bertram so wrought up. He screamed at us to leave him alone and drew his dagger, but I think even then your father would have been safe, if he had not tried to take Bertram's dagger away. Bertram stabbed him during their tussle and then turned on me. He said: 'I have to kill you too, Robert,' but he killed himself instead."

"Oh, I see," said Everard quietly. "We should have thought of that, Alex. Towerwood would obviously be much more afraid of Robert than of me. Oh, Robert, you faced death twice that day. I am sorry."

"It does not matter now," Robert answered.

For the rest of the evening everyone was cheerful. Susannah fell asleep smiling and had to be woken up for supper. Harry kept falling asleep too, and then waking up with a start, trying to remember something he had to say to Alex and Cecilia. Lord Tremath took off his armor and recited poems to them—his own, Alex realized, remembering the book he had read in Falleyfell library—and outside the lodge, the soldiers laughed and sang. They were encamped on the lawn at the back, where a hundred years later another army camped in much more desperate circumstances. The people in the lodge had only just enough food for them, but there was plenty of wine. Alex thought that he and Everard at least were a little drunk by bedtime. Their time in the dungeon struck them both as very funny, and they tried to explain to Robert. But Robert seemed sad.

"You are Count of Gairne again now," Everard kept telling him, to cheer him up, but that seemed to make him sadder than ever.

In the morning, they all rode back to Endwait to give the wheelwright his horses back. Harry, who had quite recovered after a night's sleep, remembered what it was he should have said last night.

"Alex, we must hurry home. Your father will be back from London today, and my father will be tearing his hair."

Alex knew he was right. He felt cold and sick, suddenly, at the thought of what Josiah might say. "Yes," he said.

"Oh, we can be hanged for sheep, Harry," said Susannah. "Now we have disappeared, let us stay disappeared for today."

"You will have to," said Robert. "You cannot reach the hardway through the bay until very late tonight, and I think the tide will be in then."

He, Everard, and Cecilia worked it out, and found he was right. Everard was delighted and arranged for them to stay at Falleyfell that night and cross the bay the following day. So one of Lord Tremath's soldiers went galloping ahead to give Everard's orders, and the others made a wonderful leisurely journey through the Principality in the snow.

They went to Endwait, and there Everard promised the astonished wheelwright and his wife that the deeds of the land should be sent to them in the course of the next three days. Then they went onto Gairne. There Lord Darron met them, and to Cecilia's delight, he did show her one of the warehouses there. She and Susannah went into raptures over the beauty of the cloth.

"I would order bales of this," Cecilia said to Robert, "if only ould explain to Father where it came from."

, who was still feeling cold and sick, went to see the Harry and Everard. It was a splendid castle, just like the castle must have been on his island before it was ruined.

"No," said Everard, "mine is a great deal bigger. I will show you. Are you well, Alex?"

Alex said he was, but he was beginning to think that the way he was feeling could not be merely fear of Josiah.

They went to Falleyfell, later that day, and arrived in time for the small, melancholy funeral of Princess Mathilda, Countess of Gairne. Alex, feeling sicker than ever in the chapel, was thankful that she had a proper funeral and not the kind Everard had described.

"Shall we say my law is already in force?" Everard said later. "I will backdate it."

They did not see Robert again that evening. Susannah several times demanded loudly where he was, until Lord Darron took her aside and explained that the Princess was Robert's mother. Susannah burst into tears. She would have cried all evening, if the doors of the great square hall had not slammed open at that moment.

"Oh!" she said to Harry. "It's our lady!"

Princess Rosalind ran the whole length of the hall to kiss Everard. The two nuns with her looked a little shocked. When the Princess went on to kiss Susannah, Harry, Alex, and Cecilia, they looked at one another as much as to say, "This lady has no idea of dignity." Then the Princess kissed Lord Darron and Lord Tremath too and the nuns left the hall.

Susannah remembered Lord Arbard and asked after him. She was told he was in his own mansion in Arbard, and feeling better already.

"I wish *I* was," Alex thought.

He was a great deal worse the following morning, but he got up grimly, ready to ride home. Cecilia was horrified.

"He is not fit to go," she said to Princess Rosalind.

Everard felt ill too. "It must have been those icicles we ate," he said. "You cannot go until you are well."

Alex insisted on going, though, and Harry backed him up. "It is not far," they said. "And we must go home before they give us up for dead."

So they set out for the coast. Robert went with them, still sad, until they reached the beginning of the hidden road. Then he turned back, with the horse Alex had borrowed from Everard, and the four Outsiders went on alone. Alex rode behind Harry. He was very glad to have an excuse to do so, because he felt so ill now that he could not have ridden alone. The brown sands swung and dipped around him and he shivered all the way. Cecilia wept all across the bay, and Harry and Susannah were hard put to it to keep cheerful.

They reached the Hornbys' farm in the early afternoon. Josiah was there, and so was Sir Edmund, come to have the quicksands searched for their bodies. There was the most terrible scene. Alex felt as if he were drowning in a flood or a storm—he could hardly hear or see or feel, and he knew he was letting the others down. They gave up all the various explanations they had discussed on the way home and tried to tell what had really happened. Neither father believed a word.

"Alex," said Josiah, "I know we'll get truth out of you. Out with it, boy. Where have you all been?"

Alex began to say that what the others said was quite true. It was very difficult because his throat had forgotten how to talk. Then something strange happened. The room turned upside down and Alex was floating on the floor of Josiah's study, looking down at the beams on the ceiling. He saw Susannah and Cecilia whisking about down there, talking to him. He thought they were trying to pull him down off the floor, but he did not want to move. He knew how flies felt walking on the ceiling and it was better than being down there with the others. Then Josiah surged in front of the girls. Alex shut his eyes and waited, but the next person who pulled at him was Miss Gatly. She plucked him down from the floor and carried him off to bed.

The oddest thing was that all the time there was part of Alex, a part just outside his head, over to the left, which knew perfectly well what was happening. This part knew that the terrible scene went on, worse than ever, when they found he was ill. Cecilia was getting all the blame for dragging her brother about in the snow when he had a high fever. Josiah told her he never wanted to set eyes on her again. Alex knew, somehow, that Josiah had made some money for himself in London, as well as some for the Courcys, and that Cecilia was to be sent to a finishing school in Switzerland with what he had made. Until then, she was to stay in her room.

Alex felt this was horribly unfair of Josiah. He tried to tell Miss Gatly what he thought as she fussed and rattled him into his bed. "It was my fault just as much — really."

"Aye, love, but you mustn't fret yourself. Unfair it may be that you should be the apple of your father's eye and not your sister, but that's how it always has been. Besides, you are sick and she is not."

Alex gave up trying to protest and went into a long tunnel lined with horrible dreams. He dreamed of school and of Arnforth Hall and of the island, of the hidden road—which vanished and left him in the quicksands—and of Falleyfell and the Endwait dungeon. There, he wrestled for hours with Everard for the clasp-knife, and then, suddenly out in the cold snow, he galloped for hundreds of days after Robert, who was to help him rescue Harry's pistol from Towerwood.

So he was not surprised, late that night, when he heard Robert's voice outside in the farmyard.

"Because I could not stay away."

He heard Cecilia crying, too, in her room next door to his, before stranger and more horrible dreams came to him. He shouted for Cecilia, but it was Miss Gatly who came, looking very worried and very sorry for him.

Alex was ill for a long time. He knew next to nothing of what went on in the farm. He wanted to see Cecilia, but she was not allowed to see him—he gathered that Miss Gatly had words with Josiah about that, but Josiah won. Alex tossed in bed at night with dreams, dreams often full of Robert's voice and Cecilia crying.

Then, one evening, when Alex was at last getting better, there was an enormous din downstairs. Alex was woken up from a peaceful sleep by his father raging. Josiah was shouting. Alex could hear him throwing things. People were running about all over the house, calling out or shouting too. Whatever it was must have had something to do with Cecilia, because Alex heard Josiah raging at her. Cecilia was raging back, to Alex's horror. It was a row such as he had never heard before in all his knowledge of his father's rages. It was so terrible that Alex found himself getting out of bed, crying because he was so weak and ill, in order to stop it.

He got nearly to the door of his room, holding onto his bed and the wall. Then he had to rest before he went any farther. While he rested the noise stopped—Miss Gatly was talking. He heard Cecilia run along the passage outside and slam the door of her room. Miss Gatly was still talking. She came along the passage too, calling out to Cecilia and back downstairs to Josiah.

"If he has another relapse you can blame yourself, Josiah Hornby, for your wicked unbelieving ways."

As she said that she came into Alex's room and was horrified to find him out of bed. She rattled him back between the sheets double-quick and plumped his pillows with much cap shaking. "There, there, you shouldn't fret," she said, and, "It'll be just as I said, let him see."

Alex was trembling and shivering. "*Please*, what has happened?" he asked.

Miss Gatly stroked his forehead. "Nothing you need to worry about," she said. "Your father's seen a ghost, that's all. And, as I always told him, it is those that will not believe in the dead walking that get the biggest fright when they see with their own eyes. Now you try to get to sleep."

"But why did Cecilia—?"

"Ah, your father's in a strange state of mind these days. Everything is her fault, it seems. And I cannot see what your sister has to do with a ghost. I told your father so too. Now—not another word, Alex. Drink this and try to sleep."

Alex did sleep. After that the farm was quiet for a fortnight or more, while Alex slowly became stronger. He began to get up for most of the day and was allowed to sit in the parlor with a window open. He never saw Cecilia, not until the last day she was at home, and that made him very miserable. He found that she was to go to Switzerland almost at once, to stay for two years. Josiah was so kind to him that Alex was frightened and afraid Josiah thought he was going to die, but he went surly when Alex tried to mention Cecilia.

"That'll do," he would say.

Then, one day, he mentioned Cecilia himself. "She's off tomorrow," he said. "And good riddance to her. You can have your first outing to see her away if you want to. She wants you to. You can take the trap to the station with her if the weather holds fair."

"Thank you," said Alex, pleased and miserable at the same time.

Next morning, he met Cecilia in the farmyard, while John Britby was harnessing the pony. Josiah was not there. He had refused even to say good-bye to Cecilia.

Cecilia's eyes had tears in them. She looked very flushed and nervous, Alex thought, until she saw him picking his way through the mud. Then she ran and put her arms around him.

"Oh, Alex, I am so grateful you were allowed to come!"

She seemed almost a stranger already, much, much more beautiful than Alex had remembered her and much more grown-up. She had on a new dull-pink outfit, with roses to match on her bonnet, which Alex had not seen before: clothes, he supposed, newly made for Switzerland.

"Now you are here," Cecilia said, "perhaps we shall have time to talk at last. Are you strong enough to walk down the hill to the shore, while we wait for the trap?"

"Yes, of course," Alex said. "I went down there yesterday with Mary-Ann."

"Good," said Cecilia. She took off one small pink glove to search in her little hanging bag, with roses on to match her bonnet. Alex saw her take five shillings out and hurriedly hand them to Old John. He grinned at her, winked at Alex, and tucked the money up in the pocket under his smock.

"Quarter of hour," he said. "That's the very slowest, miss. We'll miss your train beyond that."

"A quarter of an hour will do wonderfully," said Cecilia. Then she took Alex's hand and pulled him out of the farmyard and down the hill.

It was a truly beautiful day. The snow had gone while Alex was ill and, instead, there had been a month of mild, damp days. That day was almost like Spring. The sky was pale fresh blue and the wind was as warm and sweet-smelling as a wind in summer. There were snowdrops and crocuses on the sheltered parts of the hill where Alex and Cecilia walked, and in front of them the wet sands of the bay glittered in a way that made Alex joyful to look at them. He undid the scarf Miss Gatly had made him wear and trailed it in the wind as they crossed their own private railway-bridge and then the road. As they reached the big wet pebbles of the beach, the scarf fluttered like Lord Tremath's long flag had done.

Cecilia stopped on the beach and turned, very seriously, to Alex. "My dear," she said, "there have been a great many things I have been determined not to bother you with. I wanted you to get properly better, much as I wished to see you. I have tried — we have all tried — to make Father understand, but he will not."

Alex saw she was biting her lip, trying not to cry. "I—I think," she said, "even so, I would have made one more effort. If I could have brought him here, we might have explained, with your help, but"—she dropped her one gloved hand toward the farmhouse—"he has refused even to say good-bye, and I shall have to grieve him terribly, because I think he *must* be a little fond of me. Tell him how grateful I was that he let me say good-bye to you, won't you, Alex?"

Alex watched her carefully putting on her other pink glove and felt frightened and suddenly lonely. "I do not understand," he said. There was a ring on her finger that he had not seen before, with a ruby in it which Josiah could certainly not have bought for her even if he sold half the farmlands. "What are you going to do, Cecil?"

Cecilia laughed, but not in a way which made Alex feel better. "What the poor Helvetii did," she said. "Remember? I shall be wandering in Gairne when I should have been in Switzerland. Good-bye, Alex. Come and visit me when you can find an excuse. I shall be overjoyed to see you."

She turned round, toward the bay, and stepped off the pebbles onto the dark wet sand.

Alex stumbled after her. "Cecilia! What are you going to do?"

Cecilia turned around, with the wind billowing her dress and catching her hair from inside her bonnet. "Alex," she said, "you must not be upset. We are relying on you to comfort Father. As for what I am going to do, I thought you must have realized. I am going to be Countess of Gairne."

Alex had not a word to say. He felt as if the sky had turned dark gray and the sands black. All he could do was to watch Cecilia as she set out bravely across the bay for the third and last time, plowing through the mud in her dainty new shoes as if she hardly knew where she treading. She was going diagonally across the bay, straight toward the quicksands. She was out of hearing when Alex shouted "Good-bye!" He sat down on the hard wet pebbles, so lonely and dreary, and still so weak from his illness, that he was in tears. He could hardly see Cecilia's tiny pink figure.

There were sounds behind him, as if someone were riding along the shore. Alex could not turn around, because of his tears.

Susannah said: "She is away, then. I did not think she would go, in the end."

Alex nodded, but he still could not turn round.

"Poor, poor Alex!" Susannah knelt beside him, with her arms around him. He realized that Harry was standing on the other side of him, carefully not looking at him, until he felt better.

"We came to see her off," Harry said. "The rest of us are at the station."

"Where," said Susannah, "they will have to wait a long time."

This idea amused Alex so much that he managed to smile at her, and then at Harry. "How—how do you know all about this?" he asked. Although he smiled, he felt forlorn and resentful, because no one had told him anything.

"Through much coming and going," Susannah said cheerfully. "Harry and I have been to the island, you know. We saw it all. The castle is perfectly whole and twice the size of the one at Gairne."

"Is it?" Alex said and felt utterly left out. What friends they must be with Everard, he thought, to see all over the island.

Harry began to explain, perhaps because he saw how Alex was feeling. "Robert came to Arnforth," he said, "after he had tried to talk to your father. He asked for Cecilia's hand, you see, but your father seemed to think he was a ghost. I tried to talk to your father—and explain—but he simply lost his temper. He called me such things, Alex, that if he hadn't saved us all from beggary, I would have told my father."

"Saved you from beggary!" said Alex.

"Yes," said Susannah. "Without him, we would be sold up by now, it seems, but that does not make him any more likeable, to my mind. Oh, Alex! we did wish you were well and able to help! You are the only person whom your father would have listened to—and now it is too late."

Alex was surprised. He had never imagined he had the slightest influence with Josiah. He could not believe it. He looked out at Cecilia. She was now nearly halfway to the point where the river channel crossed the hidden hardway. "Would I have been any use?" he said.

"Oh, yes," said Harry. "Everard sent for us to persuade us to talk to you, but Cecilia would not have you worried. She was afraid you would die if we pestered you with this, and Robert agreed with her."

"Oh!" said Alex.

"But," said Susannah, "we are relying on you now, because you will have to break it to your father. We do not think he will believe what has happened. We are afraid he will have to be told that Cecilia is drowned in the quicksands."

"No," said Alex. "I shall have to try to tell him the truth." He stood up, with his hands in his pockets, and looked out again at Cecilia. She was nearly at the channel, now. He was suddenly afraid that she really was going to be drowned. "Why did I not stop her?" he thought.

"Here he comes," said Harry, pointing over to the island

Alex looked over at the clump of bare trees. A horse came slowly down from among them as he looked. The sun caught the gold on its bridle, and brightened the rider's long orange cloak. It was certainly Robert. He was riding along the hardway at a pace which would bring him to Cecilia just as she reached the river.

Susannah said to Harry: "Give Alex Everard's letter to read while we wait."

Harry smiled. He took a little scroll from the front of his coat and handed it to Alex with a low courtly bow. "A letter from the Prince, my lord," he said, and laughed. "You *are* lucky to be such a friend of his, Alex."

The scroll was fastened with a big green seal. Alex, not used to the way of it, took some time to get it unfastened. He unrolled a glory of painted leopards, lions, and fleurs-de-lis clustered at the head of the parchment. Underneath, Everard's round, schoolboy's writing looked a little out of place, even though the letters were not written as Alex would write them. Everard wrote:

> To Alex Hornby greetings,
> I have given my consent to Robert's marriage with your sister. I hope you will stand in for your father and give yours, since you will break both their hearts by withholding it. And when you are better, you must send Harry Courcy to tell me when you are coming to the

island. I want to meet you in state at the end of
the causeway. You must read all our new laws,
which I have drafted just as we planned them,
and give me your opinion of them. I shall wait
to issue them until you have seen them. Please
hurry and recover.

Everard, Princeps Insulae Terrae Transmarinaeque

Alex smiled as he finished reading. A warmth, like one feels
when one is very relieved, came over him and made him want
to unbutton his coat.

"Everard was ill too," Susannah said, seeing he had finished
the letter, "but nothing like as badly as you. You are neither of
you to eat another icicle again as long as you live. I forbid it."

Alex laughed at her. He discovered he liked her dictating
manner. Then they looked out into the bay. Robert had just
reached Cecilia. He was bending down, and they could just
make out that Cecilia was nodding.

"Now," said Harry, "you have to go to the farm, Alex.
Susannah and I have to ride after her and arrive too late."

They went up the pebbles to the Courcys' horses. Before
Susannah and Harry mounted, they all three looked out into
the bay again. Cecilia was up in front of Robert, riding through
the quicksands against the clear blue sky. They were waving,
both of them, with wide happy sweeps of their arms. Alex,
Harry, and Susannah waved back, and Alex sighed.